Moon Marked Trilogy

Moon Marked

Aimee Easterling

Published by Wetknee Books, 2019.

MOON MARKED TRILOGY

First edition. December 1, 2019.

Copyright © 2019 Aimee Easterling.

ISBN: 978-1686816598

Written by Aimee Easterling.

This box set contains the complete Moon Marked Trilogy, including *Wolf's Bane, Shadow Wolf,* and *Fox Blood.*

Wolf's Bane

Chapter 1

The first time my mother spoke to me from beyond the grave, my little sister was defying gravity.

"The nail that sticks out gets hammered down," the disembodied voice of my dead mother noted inside my head just as a very real Kira called out: "Look, Mai! I'm flying!"

Jolting at Mama's unexpected intrusion, I swiveled to take in my sister's long legs scampering atop the six-foot high-wall at the edge of the cemetery. I usually didn't pay much attention to Kira's affinity for gymnastics in high places. But it wasn't every day a long-dead Japanese woman tapped on the inside of my skull and demanded that I take notice.

So—"Careful!" I called just as Kira's right foot touched down on a section of wall where the weight of the hillside had pushed the cinder blocks out at an angle, ivy and dirt promising to send the unwary tumbling off her stride.

"I know what I'm doing!" my sister replied, tossing her head and rolling her eyes just like she'd done yesterday and the day before and the day before that while walking home from school. All the while human feet pranced through the debris with the agility of a fox, proving that she was right and I was wrong. My concern—and the warning from our dead mother—had been for nothing.

Or so it seemed until my sister raised her chin toward the surprisingly bright March sunshine, closed her eyes to better soak up the warmth...and ran smack dab into the largest male body I'd seen in my life.

A moment earlier, I could have sworn that the cemetery—or at least what I could see of it from the recessed sidewalk—was entirely devoid of life. But now my little sister's shoulders were caught in the grip of hands that could oh-so-easily slide upward to settle around her unprotected neck.

Veins stood out from the assailant's rippling muscles. And I didn't need to lift my nose to the breeze to understand what had taken place.

Kira had been waylaid by our worst possible enemy—an alpha male werewolf.

FOR HALF A SECOND, they wobbled there together atop tilting chunks of concrete. One girl who hid a secret punishable by death. And one predator who was willing and able to perform said execution.

Beneath them, I clenched my fist around the strobing ball of light shielded by the fabric of my pants pocket while at the same time assessing possible approaches. The trouble was, while I *could* jump directly onto the wall from my current location, doing so would be royally stupid within view of an alpha werewolf. But ascending in a human manner would mean running halfway down the block to the gateway Kira had so agilely leapt across...while leaving my sister unprotected in the interim.

So I stood for one endless second mimicking a stranded fish, mouth gaping and metaphorical fins flapping while I tried to decide which approach was least likely to get my sister killed. Meanwhile, beneath my clothes, the incorporeal light that held half my soul oozed out of my pocket, slid around my hip, and slowed at last in the empty scabbard strapped to my back. There the ice-cold tendrils of my star ball lengthened and solidified into my favorite weapon—a rapier-thin sword, just waiting to be drawn and wielded against the unwary.

The entire magical manipulation—plus associated brain freeze—had taken only a second, one blink of the eye during which my sister's assailant didn't appear to notice he had any audience other than one twelve-year-old child. His slender fingers had neither loosened nor tightened, and he spoke now in a voice so deep it was dangerous. "Someone's hunting innocents in this city. You shouldn't be out here alone."

Half of my brain occupied itself assessing that assertion. Was this werewolf—the most hazardous being we could possibly run up against—honestly warning my kid sister to steer clear of other predators?

Or was that a threat half hidden beneath the throaty timbre of his overtly protective words?

But most of my attention remained focused on planning out my subsequent actions. I couldn't toss the sword to Kira and risk her being cut on an edged weapon, not when the twelve-year-old still used training blades in the school gymnasium where I taught. And was it even a good idea to provide a weapon in the first place when anything I threw upwards could just as easily end up in the lightning-quick hands of an overpowering alpha?

While other possibilities flicked through my brain with the force of strobe lights, Kira answered back as airily as if she and this werewolf were chance-met friends chatting during a stroll through the park. "Oh, I'm not alone," she said blithely. "I've got Mai."

"Your what?"

"No, not 'my.' *Mai.*"

Which is when I decided that running up the three-inch-wide staircase created by the cracking wall was *almost* easy enough to appear human. After all, the werewolf's fingers remained poised inches away from my sister's jugular. Didn't Kira realize that a being so powerful inevitably thought anything he could hold onto was his to keep?

So, relinquishing all concern about appearing human, I took the first two steps up the side of the wall in one lunging leap. Then I froze as the male's chin tilted down toward me.

His eyes were windows I was unprepared to gaze into. Piercing and assessing and, at the same time, as deep and full of mystery as the bottom of a well. He quirked arching eyebrows, the faintest hints of crows' feet appearing at his temples...only to fade as he took in the rapier I'd unconsciously extended to prod against his jeans-clad calf.

"Ah, I see," the male answered. "You *are* quite admirably protected. My mistake."

Then, without so much as nudging the sharpened steel away from his flesh, the werewolf released my sister's shoulders and offered me a perfunctory half-bow. He was as lithe as a swordsman, his body as perfectly proportioned as a statue hailing from ancient Greece.

"It's a pleasure to meet you, Mai." And to my sister—"Mind your balance, child." With that parting shot, the werewolf slid back out of my sight line, disappearing into the cemetery as quickly as he'd materialized in the first place.

And me? I was left with a hint of sweetness on my lips that reminded me of near-forgotten teenage kisses. Swiping one hand across my mouth to remove the tell-tale flavor, I jerked my chin at my sister. "We need to get you home."

After all, my second job was calling. Cage fights wait for no woman.

Chapter 2

I wouldn't dream of heading into battle without my black leather jacket and knee-high boots, but there was more to this gig than fighting. So I showed up at the Arena an hour later in a baby-pink blouse, ruffled neckline drooping low enough to show off my nearly nonexistent boobs. I tied up my hair in two above-the-ear pigtails. And I splashed enough smoky blue and silver eye shadow on either side of my nose to accentuate the slant of my half-Japanese eyes.

The effect wasn't me...but I'd do a lot to put food on the table for my sister. In this case, unfortunately, a lot wasn't quite enough.

"...did you hear about the hooker they found dead down by the river last week..."

"...new bar with two-for-one appetizers..."

"...wouldn't bet against Mai if you paid me to..."

The news of the day swirled around me in a cloud of horrors, excitement, and—unfortunately—overwhelming appreciation for my prowess. As if to prove the last point, a meaty hand came down on my shoulder as a random audience member congratulated me on my most recent win. "Nice job against those bozos," he boomed.

The male in question was a head and shoulders taller than my five-feet-zero frame, and he likely could have lifted me off the ground with one arm tied behind his back. Still, his posture radiated respect for more than the length of my rapier...which *should* have filled me with much-deserved pride.

Unfortunately, my boss had been using the unlikely disconnect between my appearance and my skill level to her financial advantage for nearly a decade. It was a lucrative proposition—toss the tiny street girl out against a gang of heavy hitters, bet on the underdog, and watch the cash roll in. Since my ten percent of the take paid the rent, having members of the audience betting *for* me rather than against me could very well turn into a financial disaster for both Ma and myself.

Drat and blast! What did it take to be underestimated in this town?

Before I could decide which evasive action to take, though, I glanced toward the other side of the stadium where my opponents usually held court. Best to see what kind of warrior Ma Scrubbs had dug up before I decided between the damsel-in-distress routine and the fake-wound walk....

New fighters were always easy to pick out due to the contestants' banners slung across their chests. And I was ready for any number of them. After all, I'd faced down five opponents just last month, forgetting myself and knocking the quintet down like dominoes with a few short swipes of my sword.

But during that ill-matched contest, I hadn't been forced to hide my abilities. Had been facing humans only, without a single werewolf in sight.

Now, as I eyed one tall male and one erect-ruffed four-legger, I not only recognized the abilities of the shifters before me, I also knew immediately who they were. The man standing on two legs possessed uncannily familiar features for all that I'd never set eyes on his face before. And no wonder when he smelled identical to the wolf panting by his side, both boasting the same deep musk that lingered on my tongue despite every effort to wash their granite and ozone signature out of my brain.

No, these opponents weren't strangers. Or at least the wolf wasn't. Instead, this was the self-same shifter who had accosted my sister on the cemetery wall earlier in the afternoon.

Meanwhile, the two-legged shifter's words were just barely audible with the help of my own supernaturally assisted hearing. "Of course this is a good idea," the male murmured on the other side of the chattering crowd. His voice was gritty with rebellion, which struck me as strange since I could smell his dominance from fifty feet distant. "You know the evidence leads here."

Evidence? Were these werewolves hunting something? Could they possibly be seeking *me*?

Whether that conclusion was grounded in reality or in pure paranoia, I'd risk too much by fighting fellow shifters unaware of my closely held secret. So I turned on my heel and stalked off in the opposite direction.

It was time to hold a serious conversation with my boss.

"YOU'RE LATE."

Ma Scrubbs glowered at me across a table littered with dollar bills and scraps of hastily scrawled wagers. To the uninitiated, the mess looked like, well, a *mess*. But my second-shift supervisor memorized each offering, constantly recalculated the odds, and ensured the finances fell forever in her favor.

Not so difficult when she had a fighter like me in her back pocket.

Which, tonight, she most definitely did *not*. "I'm not doing it, Ma," I responded, slamming the door of my employer's office to block out the crowd so I could transition from Disney princess into hardened warrior and feel like myself once again. Only after stuffing both arms into the leather jacket waiting for me on the back of the door then buttoning the armor up to my chin did my heart calm sufficiently for me to fall into the empty seat waiting on the other side of Ma's desk.

"Cool it with the tantrums, girlie. And I'm not your mother. So don't call me 'Ma.'" As she spoke, the older woman's brows scrunched together into a glower that I was far too familiar with. Because, no, Ma Scrubbs wasn't my mother. But she'd let me play in her office dozens of times while my father fought, had offered me his vacated spot when I struggled to keep my tiny family afloat after being orphaned at age eighteen, and was the closest thing to a parental figure I had left.

So I obeyed her command and elaborated as best I could without mentioning supernatural elements that Ma Scrubbs may or may not have picked up on by now. "I can't win against those two," I explained. "It's just not possible. Pick someone else for the first fight then I'll go in for round two."

Ma Scrubbs considered me from the far side of the desktop, her head barely visible above the cluttered surface. If I was small, she was wizened, face so wrinkled it was impossible to guess what the seventy-year-old might have looked like when she was young. After a moment of consideration, she shrugged, pulling a battered notebook out of one pocket. "Go home then," she told me. "I'll call the Raven sisters in to fight."

"No!" The word burst from my lips before I could soften the rejection. "They're children! They'll be slaughtered!"

"Not against those two. Gunner and Ransom are boy scouts. First blood will be a nick on the cheek. Won't even scar. And next week, ticket sales will skyrocket out of sight."

So she *was* aware of the existence of werewolves. No human would refer to a four-legged shifter in the same breath as his two-legged companion unless she fully understood the former's ability to change forms.

Still, I had no time to further analyze that fact because Ma Scrubbs wasn't even looking at me any longer. Instead, she pulled out her cell phone and began thumbing through her address book, stopping only when the faces of Jessie and Charlie Raven popped into view. The twins were sweet young things who I'd mentored for a couple of summers. Despite my best efforts, though, the duo still thought fencing was a sport in which you didn't hit below the belt or above the neck. They had no concept werewolves existed and they were barely older than my kid sister. If I didn't allow Kira to sit in the Arena's audience, I certainly wasn't going to be responsible for Jessie and Charlie ending up within the Arena's cage.

So even though I knew I was being played, I reached out and blocked the phone's surface with my hand. "Okay, you win," I answered. Took a deep breath, considered the angles. I couldn't use my supernatural speed to its full advantage against a pair of werewolves, but there had to be a way to turn my opponents' cockiness against them.

If there was, Ma Scrubbs surely would have thought of it. "And you clearly have a plan," I continued. "So let's hear it."

"It's simple," my boss answered, her eyes twinkling with old-lady mirth. "You've been winning, winning, always winning. Nobody's gonna bet against you. So tonight, you'll reset the clock. Tonight...you'll lose."

Chapter 3

Losing, unfortunately, wasn't as easy as I'd expected. Oh, sure, when the cage door clanged shut, leaving me trapped within a small chain-link enclosure with two very large werewolves, the shiver running down my spine suggested the hard part would be merely staying alive. But my opponents—for all that they appeared to be brothers—combined to create the worst team imaginable.

Ransom—the human-form brother and the only one the announcer had introduced by name—turned out to be a run-of-the-mill opponent. He was fast and aggressive and out for my blood.

His brother, on the other hand, was not.

"Get out of my way!" Ransom muttered between gritted teeth the third time Gunner tangled himself between his sibling's legs and made it nearly impossible for the human sibling to dodge my blows...let alone get in one of his own. I would have laughed out loud if my goal hadn't been to lose the match subtly enough so the audience wouldn't wring my neck afterwards. As it was, my cheeks heated with frustration and I could almost feel next month's rent money slipping out of my grasp.

Meanwhile, the crowd was no more pleased than I was at my opponents' inability to put up a passable show. "Boo!" howled one angry bystander while fingers rattled the cage inches from my head. A beer bottle cleared the fence and shattered onto the mat a yard away from my booted feet, the glass shards turning into makeshift blades my opponents could pick up at any moment and use against my flesh.

In the midst of all this mayhem, I needed to not only survive but also to lose without appearing to throw over the fight. Time to implement my favorite weapon—my tongue.

"Ma Scrubbs told me you two were boy scouts," I said conversationally even as I danced through a series of warm-up exercises that appeared far more impressive than they really were. Had to keep the crowd happy while gearing up for the grand finale. "I'm thinking you look more like Brownies, though. Or maybe Daisies. Did you even earn enough merit badges to sell Girl Scout cookies yet?"

In response, Ransom growled between human teeth and took a single step forward, but I could have sworn Gunner was amused rather than provoked by my taunts. Whatever the reason, the latter's lupine jaws gaped open, his tongue lolling off to one side even as he blocked his brother as gracefully as if the two were dancing a minuet.

You-fight-like-a-girl jabs clearly weren't going to move this match along to the point where the audience would go home happy. So I assessed the way the two males worked in effort-filled non-harmony. Guessed reasons why one gamecock brother might choose to engage in battle while the other would undermine Ransom's authority at every turn...while still insisting upon guarding his sibling's back.

Then I opened my mouth and launched a second attack. "New alpha can't handle his own fights, can he?" I guessed, piecing together whispers I'd recently heard emerging from the few shifters I dared to speak with. "Just another dumb jock inheriting shoes too big for his puny feet. You know what they say about a guy with small feet...."

And just like that, the brothers glanced at each other in perfect harmony. Silent words streaked between them while the scents of fur and electricity filled the air.

At last, I'd gotten under their skins.

How like wolves to get riled up over issues of heredity...and shoe size. I let a smile crinkle my cheeks for a split second, but then it was time for battle.

Because both brothers were leaping toward me in synchronized splendor now. And above our heads, a surge of approval rolled out over the crowd.

FOR LONG SECONDS, MY world narrowed down to the simplicity of attack and parry. I hooked the hilt of my sword around one of Ransom's knives and pulled it out of his grip as easily as I disarmed raw beginners in my day job. But with Gunner circling slyly toward my blind spot, I was soon forced onto the defensive, spinning on my back foot and stabbing wildly to force the wolf into a retreat.

Whoosh. My sword cut deeper toward my lupine opponent than I'd intended, and I held my breath as hairs sprayed out around us both. If I'd misjudged my reach and pricked Gunner's skin, the match would be over before it really started...and not in a way that would please my picky boss.

Rent, I reminded myself as I scrambled backwards, glad there was no blood welling up where my blade had recently made contact with the four-legged werewolf. *Groceries. Bus money. More magic-trick paraphernalia for Kira's birthday next week. Tuition at her school in the nice part of town....*

Gradually, the roar of the crowd receded into the background and calm descended upon me just as it did every day during training. I grabbed the veil of control Dad had taught me to wield two decades earlier, slowed my attacks and parries until they matched my gasping breaths. *There.* The outer world meant nothing. Now I could be certain my blade would fly eternally true.

"I know what you are."

And to my eternal embarrassment, I stumbled, Ransom's words cutting through my hard-earned concentration far more admirably than my earlier verbal parry had interrupted his. The pack leader's knowledge of my identity was impossible. Because if werewolves were aware of my family's secret, their leader wouldn't be fighting me in a cage match. The whole pack would instead descend upon Kira and me as a unit, intent upon tearing out both of our throats.

As I tried to make sense of the nonsensical, Ransom took advantage of my turmoil. Swiping his sole remaining knife beneath my armpit, he opened up a nick in the jacket that had protected me year after year. And even though the cut didn't reach all the way to my skin, I was so shaken by the damage that I took a step backward...

...and promptly stumbled over Gunner, who'd poised himself in just the right spot to take advantage of my lapse. I teetered, nearly falling.

Then I decided not to fight the imminent collapse. Instead, I allowed the accidental momentum to propel me sideways as I slashed my sword in a Z pattern in front of the unruly wolf's nose.

The sword-waving warning gave me breathing room to come up behind the two-legger's unguarded back. And, okay, so maybe I called upon a little supernatural speed to get me there. Maybe I bent my sword slightly away from its target so the metal didn't come in contact with game-ending flesh. But, in the midst of combat, who would either know or care?

The sharp tang of success cleared my head the way it always did. And I realized as I set up the defeat I so badly needed that my opponent was merely accusing me of being an unaffiliated werewolf...not of something considerably worse. After all, I smelled as much like fur as the brothers with whom I shared the stage at the moment. And more than a century since our supposed eradication, most shifters probably didn't believe beings like myself and my sister continued to exist.

So I ran with it. "Yep, you're right. I'm outpack. That means I don't have to kowtow to the new alpha who thinks his farts don't stink," I bantered, knowing that my voice would prompt Ransom's body to swivel just the way I wanted it to. Knowing that his knife would spin through the air at precisely the same level as the hand I'd raised in supposed self-defense. The sharp blade would cut through the flesh of my palm deeper than the scratch Ma Scrubbs had promised these boy scouts would dole out in victory, but the searing pain was more than worth the result.

Because as red blood dripped toward the ground between us, the audience erupted into jubilation. They'd lost their hard-earned money on the match, but they'd enjoyed every minute of the tussle that had come before this bitter end. The crowd would be even larger next week...and in the meantime I'd take home a rather hefty ten percent for my surprise upset.

"Good fight," Ransom offered, holding out a hand to shake without any arrogance in his posture at all. He really was a boy scout. As gentlemanly in his win as he would have been after a loss.

"Good fight," I agreed, swapping the sword over to my bloody left hand so I could return the hand clasp. Only then did I turn toward Gunner and shiver as something darkly suspicious flickered behind sienna lupine eyes.

Maybe my lapses hadn't been quite as overlookable as I'd thought in the heat of the moment. Now, I decided, would be a good time to beat a hasty retreat.

Chapter 4

I lost myself in the crowd before Gunner could shift and find me. Nodded at a bouncer then slipped through a heavy fire door to enter the private hallway that led toward the quiet of my personal changing room. I was ready for thirty minutes of down time before returning home to my sleeping sister. Thirty minutes to relax while Ma Scrubbs counted dollars and divvied up my share of the take.

Unfortunately, there was a werewolf on the couch when I thrust the door open. And not just any werewolf, but the one who thought he ran the city I lived within.

"My dear," Jackal greeted me, remaining recumbent for one long moment before unfolding long limbs and springing gracefully to his feet. He wore a half-unbuttoned silk shirt that showed off hardened muscles and his hair curled dashingly over both ears. Despite the eye candy, though, my attention remained firmly focused upon the promised respite of the couch behind his back.

There should have been overtures to live through before I could achieve my destination, but lack of nearby underlings put a kibosh on our customary embrace. Instead, Jackal merely raised his eyebrows and waited until I'd sunk into the leathery cushions before taking the opposite end of the sofa and getting straight to the point.

"Two Atwoods in my city." In front of the drifters who made up his not-quite-pack, Jackal would have donned a mask of alpha invulnerability. But the understanding between the two of us was sufficient to prevent him from mincing words. As a result, his observation came out as less of an observation and more of a pout.

I shrugged, wishing for one split second that Jackal really was my significant other. The pretense propped up Jackal's alpha tendencies in public and protected me and my sister when we walked through the city alone. A mutually beneficial arrangement...but one that, unfortunately, left me without anyone to rub my weary feet.

Perhaps that's why my subsequent words came out harsher than I'd intended. "In *their* city," I countered. "The pack leaders might not have been around much lately, but technically it's Atwood land for another hundred miles south."

Which was entirely true. But apparently I'd gone a step too far in reminding Jackal that he was poaching on a more established clan's territory while lacking sufficient manpower to back up his claim.

"*I'm* the one who keeps this city stable. *I'm* the one who keeps you safe," my companion bit out, a droplet of spittle striking my jacket while his fist came down to pound the leather cushion an inch from my thigh.

Yep, I should have stopped while I was ahead. Accepting my own misstep, I attempted to fix the faux pas with a little male ego-stroking. "You're right," I agreed. "But the brothers are just passing through. They're probably scouting the edges of clan territory, getting their bearings. After all, their father just recently died."

I expected Jackal to relax back onto the cushions, to accept what he couldn't change. But instead, something dark and menacing rose within his eyes, and his muscles tensed with lupine alertness when next he spoke.

"Well, they'd better keep moving," he told me. "Because this city and everything in it is *mine*."

"BE CAREFUL OUT THERE," Ma Scrubbs warned as she led me to the back door half an hour later. The old woman had been alerting me about the city's hidden dangers ever since I'd started trailing along behind my father two decades earlier. But something in my employer's tone promised a rapier might not be enough to keep my skin intact tonight.

Still, I had a hard time taking the threat seriously when my pockets were full of cash and all three werewolves I'd run into this evening were long gone through the opposite entrance. So I offered a jaunty salute and strode away into the darkness, already counting the moments until I could fall into my warm bed. Just one last stop at the corner store for bread and milk to ensure Kira's cheery disposition, then I could rest easy in the knowledge that I'd raked in sufficient supplemental income to ensure our survival for another week at least....

Or so I thought for the few minutes it took to exit the Arena's alley and turn onto the wide but quiet avenue that formed the main artery of this part of town. Only after enough time had passed that Ma Scrubbs would have removed her hearing aids and descended into her basement apartment did a thread of sound cut through my thoughts of hearth and home.

And at first, I thought the auditory intrusion was merely a run-of-the-mill wolf whistle. But I couldn't make out a single human shape lingering in the shadowed doorsteps I was passing. And this sound was less a whistle and more a thread of barely discernible melody that sent a trickle of prey-like awareness skittering up my spine.

As much as I strained, though, I couldn't make sense of the disjointed notes. The night musician was quite a distance behind me, I estimated. Perhaps a block or two east as well....

But then the tones coalesced into a strangely familiar lullaby, the tune popping to life as if emerging from a dully remembered childhood. And even though my curiosity was piqued by the vague memory, my gut told me the sound represented danger rather than intrigue. So I sped up my footsteps, wishing I hadn't already shrunken my magical star ball away from its sword shape and down into its easy-to-carry energetic form. Now would be a good time to be holding onto a blade....

Even another human on the streets would have been appreciated at the present moment. Anything to jolt away the adrenaline-rush of terror that was flooding my body for no discernible reason. Was I really about to break into a sprint to escape from a *song*?

Unfortunately, the streets on every side of me were dark and empty. And the whistle continued at exactly the same volume even as I sped up my pace, as if my follower had increased his own footsteps in synchrony rather than falling behind as I would have hoped.

Yes, the tune's volume remained steady...but its tempo gradually lessened until both my star ball and my feet were pulsing in sympathy. Like Kira, I enjoyed moving quickly and silently. But now my instinctive press for speed felt akin to slogging through a sea of molasses. Meanwhile, my boots thudded against the pavement with every descending step.

What's wrong with me? Stifling a shiver, I glanced backwards, half expecting a fairy-tale monster to be following in my wake....

But my gaze met with nothing out of the ordinary. Just the usual potholed pavement, one streetlight vainly attempting to illuminate an entire block. Doors were locked, windows were grimed over, and a single rat was the only living being in sight.

There *was* light ahead of me though. The 7-Eleven came into view like an oasis in a desert, the brightest patch of safety around.

And sure, the establishment possessed grease-stained windows along with an air of declining profitability. But I knew from experience that the store also boasted a rifle-toting clerk and a back door that would spit me out into an untraveled alley. If necessary, the clerk would cover my back sufficiently so I could use my hidden abilities in safety, then I could slink home with my tail quite literally between my legs.

Or maybe I'd get lucky and my stalker would turn out to be a cheerful passerby who whistled his way past the plate-glass windows without so much as a glance in my direction. Kira could enjoy milk on her morning cereal with toast as a chaser, and all would be right in our little world.

Still, I flung open the 7-Eleven door with my head turned in search of my pursuer...and had no warning as I ran smack dab into a far too familiar chest.

Chapter 5

"**Y**ou and your sister don't look where you're going very often, do you?"

Gunner's fingers burned against my wrist as he restrained me from...what? Pulling a sword that didn't currently exist? Punching him in the eye or kneeing his balls in an effort to relax his grip?

Unfortunately, the tremor racing down my spine couldn't be entirely attributed to the grasp of a powerful opponent. And perhaps that's why my rebuttal came out with so much bite. "Oh, yes. The expert on sibling relations. Did you show your big brother to his room, sedate him with sleeping pills, then sneak out for a beer? Is that why you dared to leave his presence when the poor little pack leader might very well be stubbing his toe at this very instant?"

Only the slight twitch of Gunner's left eyebrow proved that my verbal attack had struck home. But he *did* release my wrists and take one small step backwards, the musk of predatory alpha thinning until I was finally able to think...

...and to remember that I had a friend here in the convenience store. Over the werewolf's shoulder, I caught the eye of a clerk I'd gone to high school with and shook my head briefly in response to his raised eyebrows. No, I didn't need help. Not against one annoying shifter whose worst fault was a tendency to show up in the wrong place at the wrong moment.

"A beer," Gunner answered, picking the least incendiary part of my tirade to fixate upon. "Good idea. How about I buy you a bottle and we can talk about why you purposefully lost tonight's match?"

His words followed me more closely than the whistled melody had as I slid away from his tantalizing body heat and stalked toward colder quarry. Bread—not the kind Kira liked the best but the cheaper sort she would still

23

smile upon. Life was all about compromise and tonight's Arena windfall wouldn't last long if I fed her tween appetite with name-brand morsels.

"I didn't lose on purpose," I lied vaguely, trying to decide whether my kid sister was still on a 1% kick or whether we could return to the whole milk we'd both enjoyed until the previous autumn. Unfortunately, the girls in her grade were brutal on body fat, and Kira embraced their barbed comments even though our kind required far more calories than the average couch-potato twelve-year-old.

Better safe than sorry, I decided with a grimace. Plucking out a gallon of low-fat, I froze as Gunner's warm breath counteracted the cold emanating from the refrigerated case.

"Or we could change the subject," the werewolf murmured, voice so low the clerk had no chance of overhearing. "My brother and I are hunting something very specific. My gut says you're the key to finding it. We'd pay very well if you helped us track it down."

I was the key to finding whatever these brothers were looking for here in a city their pack had ignored for several decades? A shiver far less enticing than the ones that had been impacting me previously ran down my spine. Slowly, unwillingly, I turned to meet Gunner's gaze. "What are you looking for?"

"Something," the werewolf answered unhelpfully before allowing silence to descend between the two of us. His face was as expressionless as a still pool of water, but I could smell his amusement that I'd risen to the bait.

Gritting my teeth, I tried to focus on lunch meat. Perhaps if I splurged on a hunk of salami my kid sister's eyes would light up at the treat like the noon-day sun....

But despite my best impulses to the contrary, Gunner's hook lodged itself in my gills and pulled me relentlessly out of the safely deep waters. What were these werewolves looking for? Did it have anything to do with Kira and my kind?

My inherent curiosity sent me leaning forward as I pondered, heart rate elevated more than it had been by my recent near miss. Still, I opened my mouth to give the smart answer, the correct answer. Because I shouldn't spend any more time than necessary around the new pack leader's brother.

Kira and I couldn't afford to risk our skins just to enjoy salami on a weekly rather than a yearly basis...or to douse inquisitiveness that was so painfully inflamed.

But before I could come up with an appropriately scathing comment, a trickle of melody slid beneath the crack in the door. The same strangely familiar tune I'd heard while walking down the street....

And in response I paled, dropping Kira's bread on top of a display of candy bars as my fingers abruptly lost their hold on the potential purchase. My instinct had been right and my pursuer hadn't given up. Which presented an even worse situation than I'd previously been in. Because I was now standing beside an eagle-eyed werewolf, unable to use my inherent abilities to gnaw my way out of the trap before it could close around my leg.

I bit my lip as I began lowering the jug of milk to the floor in instinctive disburdenment. But the liquid would rot there if the clerk didn't notice in time to slide the jug back into the case. And upcoming evasive maneuvers would be less obvious if I hung onto one potential purchase at least.

So I clutched the cold handle, fingers digging into plastic as I spoke to the werewolf who'd delayed me—purposefully? accidentally?—long enough for the whistler to catch up. "Hold that thought," I told him, offering Kira's full-blast-sunshine smile and hoping the expression was as heart-stopping on me as it was on her. After all, I needed every advantage I could muster if I intended to slide out the 7-Eleven's window right under a werewolf's nose.

Then, without further explanation, I padded into the filthy bathroom, twirled the lock to solidify the barrier...and hoisted myself plus my purloined jug of milk through the tiny opening set too high in the wall for an average human to clamber in or out.

"I'll pay you back tomorrow," I whispered into the night air, knowing the clerk would understand the delay in cash flow. Still, the debt squeezed at my star ball, dragging at my footsteps as I beat a hasty retreat.

Chapter 6

"Oof. Get off me!" I woke to fur in my face along with my sister's smug grin peering through the small gap between covers and red tail fluff.

Oh, and did I mention Kira was in fox form? I could feel the year's seventh tardy slip falling into my hands already.

"You need to shift and shower and eat and...did you finish your homework last night while I was fighting?"

The fox who was my sister leapt off my pillow a millisecond before my fingers would have closed around her snow-white belly. Soft feet landed on top of the tiny dorm-style refrigerator three feet away from my pull-out sofa-bed, and I decided to take that as a yes to the breakfast and a no to the shifting, showering, and homework. At least we'd get the bare necessities done today.

"Kira, I'm serious," I grumbled, even as I pulled out the wide cereal bowl that was easy for a snout to scoop food out of. Half a box of off-brand cheerios, a healthy glug of last night's stolen milk, and my sister was at least eating her breakfast...even if she was still perched on top of the fridge while doing so.

Of course, Kira was also a *fox*, so nothing came easily. Three bites later, my young charge lost interest in food and hummed a request instead, drawing our mother's star ball toward us out of the only bedroom our apartment boasted. The golden glow was the reason my sister was able to shift before coming of age, but it was also the last remnant of our dead mother's spirit. So I didn't argue as Kira leapt away from her half-finished meal and used the solidified magic as a platform, allowing her to dance across the room without touching the ground. Instead, I smiled fondly...then froze as I remembered the jolt of understanding that had run through my head as I succumbed to slumber the night before.

The whistle in the dark alley hadn't been just an eerily unfamiliar melody. Instead, it had matched the tinny sound made by our mother's nearly forgotten music box. Or so I thought. I'd need to rustle up long-packed-away possessions to be sure....

"I'm serious about that shower, Kira," I told my sister absently, turning away as my own star ball joined the circus without any explicit request to do so on my part. "And you know you have a test today in..." I racked my brain, gave up "...in *something*. So, please, at least bring the relevant book to school."

Kira *hadn't* done her homework and *had* forgotten her test—I could see the guilt in her beady eyes. But she was a fox who was snatching bites of a filling breakfast in between her capers, so she'd land—both literally and metaphorically—on her feet.

Confident that my sister was taken care of, I took the five steps to her bedroom in a rush. Clothes covered every available surface and it took longer than it should have to pick my way through to the rather empty closet. I'd need to find an hour this afternoon to tidy up just in case Social Services dropped by for a surprise inspection....

For now, though, I was more interested in the boxes on the closet's top shelf than in the clothes all over the floor. It had been so long since I'd been up there that dust bunnies gave even Kira's slovenly ways a run for their money.

And yet...the box I was looking for was swept as smooth as if it held a daily necessity. And when I pulled down the battered cardboard container, the item in my hands wasn't nearly as heavy as it should have been.

Inside, a few photos and childhood drawings fluttered against my fumbling fingers. But the music box, the jewelry, Mama's cherished possessions—every single one of them was gone without a trace.

"I'M SORRY," KIRA WHISPERED as her class poured into the gym for third-period PE. She'd clearly been working on this apology for the entirety of her first two classes, because the rest of it came out in a rush. "I should have talked to you first. But selling Mama's belongings was the only way I could think of to pay the water and electric bills. And it wasn't as if we were *using* any of that stuff."

"It's okay," I told my sister, even though it really wasn't. But I was disappointed in myself more than in Kira. Disappointed that my thirteen-years-younger sister had taken household expenses upon herself without me noticing...and, I'll admit it, disappointed that I'd never see our dead mother's possessions again. Just because Dad—and then I—had hidden the items away in a dusty box while avoiding all mention of our shadowed heritage didn't mean I was willing to sell the items on Ebay.

Still, my day brightened a little when Kira accepted my words at face value. She shot me a sunny smile before bouncing over to the opposite side of the room where three girls waited. And even though they were entirely human and dressed far better than I'd ever managed to deck out my ward, they still welcomed her into their midst with cheery greetings and sparkling eyes.

"Wanna see a magic trick?" my sister asked as she joined them, pulling out three scarves and a deck of cards before her companions could reply. And I'll admit it—I let the pre-class bustle linger longer than usual so Kira could enjoy her moment in the limelight. Gave everyone three long minutes to gab and gossip and make objects disappear.

But, finally, I could drag my heels no longer. "Line up in two rows. We're going to start with drills parrying four and six," I bellowed in a voice guaranteed to garner even argumentative sixth graders' attention.

The girls obeyed as sluggishly as Kira had caved to the necessity of her morning shower. But, eventually, clanging practice swords proved that nineteen over-indulged princesses—and my orphaned sister—would go to math class with hearts racing and endorphin levels elevated.

Which should have been good enough. But my skin itched and my eyes kept being drawn to the three students in front of and beside my kid sister. So I drifted closer to hear what kind of muttered secrets were being exchanged along with sword blows.

"Keep the tip of your blade pointed at your opponent's chest while you parry," I murmured to a rather over-excited redhead as I worked my way closer to the girls in question. "Hand parallel to the floor," I corrected another student, angling toward the girls upon whom the entirety of my attention now rested.

And then I could hear their chatter above the din...at which point I finally realized that Kira had been lying when she told me everything was just peachy at school. "Maybe you can use your *magic tricks* to get Jared's attention," Kira's current opponent sneered, eyeballing my sister's body in a way that made the shorter girl's cheeks flush crimson.

"Or maybe you could make *yourself* disappear. That'd be a good one." The girl on Kira's right was barely moving her sword while she indulged in a verbal offensive of her own.

"I don't know why they let gooks into our school," the third student interjected contemplatively. "Asian kids are supposed to be smart, but we can all tell from Kira's uniform that she's a scholarship student. She can't even pay her own way."

At which point, I stopped even pretending to pay attention to the rest of the class. Started sprinting toward my sister...even though I knew any intervention would come far too late.

Because Kira might have been abjectly apologetic at the beginning of class, but all foxes have a temper and Kira was no exception. Unlike me, however, she tended to save words for later and to dive straight into the physical when cornered and outmatched.

So I wasn't surprised when my nose caught the faintest hint of fur as Kira unleashed a tiny fraction of the vulpine agility she'd been holding back earlier in the session. I wasn't surprised when she knocked off each girl's face mask with a quick dip and jerk of her blunt-tipped sword. One, two, three helmets clanged onto the floor then one, two, three sets of manicured fingertips rose to feminine throats in unintentional unison.

Behind me, air pushed against my back as someone opened the door leading to the hallway. But I ignored whoever was coming or going, channeling all of my attention upon my sister as I turned my sprint into something a little faster. Because I'd learned the hard way that an angry Kira was unable to think through the consequences of her actions. And, like the rest of her family, my kid sister was remarkably good with a sword.

Sure enough, before I could interpose myself between the four battling students, my sister's practice blade rose for a fourth time. Thankfully, the swords I'd handed out to these children boasted unsharpened edges and a soft rubber ball protecting each tip. Still, any hunk of metal can do real damage if wielded by a pro.

Kira was well on her way to becoming such an expert.

"*Don't!*" I demanded, sending one curt word where my feet had failed to carry me.

But my sister's lashes didn't even flicker in response to my order. Instead, she slapped those bitchy girls with the flat of her blade so fast the first wasn't even crying before the third was being similarly assaulted. Within seconds, three red welts stood out against perfectly moisturized skin...then the floodgates opened up.

"I...I...I...." the leader of the posse stuttered, spinning to take in her damaged face in the mirror that covered one entire wall. "My face is ruuuiiiinnned!" another girl wailed. For her part, the third student was too overwhelmed to even emote verbally. Instead, she collapsed into a silent heap, cradling her injured cheek in both hands.

"Maybe you should grow up and shut up," Kira whispered in a voice blazing with passion. "Maybe you shouldn't talk about things you don't understand."

Meanwhile, behind me, an equally familiar tone cut through the room's hushed silence. "Mai, Kira, I'll see you both in my office immediately," the headmistress informed us. "Injured parties report to the nurse's station. And the rest of you, it's time to go to math."

Chapter 7

"I've been concerned for some time about the levels of violence in your classes," Ms. Underhill informed me as I sank into one of the two seats in front of her desk. The armchairs were obscenely comfortable...but they were also considerably lower to the floor than average. Given my already short stature, I felt like a child peering up at an adult from my present vantage point, precisely the effect the headmistress was going for.

"Fencing isn't about violence," Kira countered from the perch she'd taken on the edge of her seat, her chin level with the desk rather than hidden beneath it like mine was. "It's about control and restraint and..."

I could repeat our father's words just as glibly as my sister was currently doing, but something told me Ms. Underhill wasn't going to be impressed by the well-rehearsed refrain. Not when Kira had recently used her so-called control and restraint to mark the daughters of three major donors to the academy.

"We apologize," I said instead. "Kira was out of line and I should have been able to stop her." I swallowed, knowing the school had a zero-tolerance policy toward physical aggression. This wasn't my sister's first offense, so she would definitely be suspended. The question was—for how long? And when the suspension was over, would she be allowed to return to class?

As if sensing my distress, Kira rushed in to back me up as she always did. "Yes, I'm *so* sorry Ms. Underhill. I take complete responsibility for my actions. I'll apologize to Missy and Callie and Veronica too. I swear, nothing like this will *ever* happen again."

Her face was so open and candid, her tone so gushing. And the effect would have been believable too...if all three of us hadn't remembered the other incidents in vivid technicolor.

There was that time in the cafeteria when my sister had grown bored and started a food fight so severe the entire place had to be shut down for the rest of the afternoon for cleanup. The time she'd gotten tossed out of class after correcting her Latin teacher's pronunciation then reciting a very bawdy ballad in a language only she and he understood. And how could we forget the way my tiny sister had beaten up three over-sized football players who were trying to take advantage of a slip of a girl behind the bleachers?

Kira's heart was in the right place...but sometimes her brain didn't come along for the ride.

So my relief was palpable when the faintest hint of a smile pulled up the corners of Ms. Underhill's thin lips. "*You* will be spending one week thinking through your choices during an out-of-school suspension," the headmistress told my sister firmly before returning her attention to me.

"I appreciate your generosity." Only when my lungs expanded to their full extent for the first time in several minutes did I realize that oxygen hadn't been making its way to my lungs quite right ever since the headmistress's voice had shown up in my class at exactly the wrong moment. Kira needed structure in her life and someone other than me pushing her academically. She'd been bored out of her skull at the public school, and a bored Kira was like a grenade with the pin removed. Bystanders had better brace themselves and wait for the detonation.

The academy was our family's haz-mat suit. Being able to maintain that protection in light of Kira's recent actions was more than I'd dared to expect.

So I struggled up out of the depths of the armchair and met Ms. Underhill's eyes as best I could from two feet lower. Did she sit on a pillow back there to elevate her height? "I promise you that Kira will come back to school on her best behavior and ready to learn...."

"I'm sure she will be," the headmistress interjected. "But that's not the reason I brought you here today. As I mentioned earlier, I'm concerned that *swordplay* is an inappropriate activity for impressionable young minds. Control and restraint can be learned just as admirably at a gentler sport. Something like *ballet*."

I cringed, imagining myself in a pink leotard barking orders at a roomful of tutu-clad kindergartners. But this was what I'd signed on for when I promised my dying father that I'd raise Kira myself rather than losing her to the foster-care system. So I merely nodded, keeping my clenched fists hidden beneath the overhang of the desk. "I understand," I agreed. "I can do that."

"No, I don't think you *do* understand," Ms. Underhill contradicted. Her head tilted, her mouth pursed, and for a split second I thought the old battle ax felt sorry for me. "I'm afraid I've found someone else to fill your position. Your final paycheck will go out in the mail tomorrow...along with a bill for the rest of Kira's tuition at the normal rate."

"I'LL BE BETTER OFF without that school anyway." Kira was back on top of the cemetery wall, but she wasn't dancing through our walk home this time around. Instead, she was skulking, shoulders hunched and feet kicking out at every pebble that dared stray into her path.

Her words, in contrast, remained perfectly controlled as she laid out a plan that would have made our father weep if he wasn't rotting in his grave. "At the public school, I can land an A without any effort. Which means I can get a job. We'll be a two-breadwinner family. We can buy a TV and a better sofa. We can eat salami. That's how it *should* be. Really, Mrs. Underhill is doing us a favor. I'll write her a thank-you note as soon as we get home."

Despite the evenness of Kira's monologue, she clearly lamented the lost opportunity as much as I did. Because rocks went spraying out in every direction beneath a particularly virulent kick, and this time I had to dodge to prevent being struck.

"How about a milkshake?" I countered. "Or a candy bar? We can talk about school later."

After all, I'd learned the hard way that it was a recipe for failure trying to out-argue my sister once she'd dug her heels in. Kira *was* going back to the academy, but I wouldn't press the issue until I figured out how to pay the full-price tuition. Until then, I might as well keep us both calm so our fox natures didn't make us say things we'd later regret.

Kira, on the other hand, had no such compunction about speaking before thinking. "*You* said I needed to steer clear of sugar. *You* said it made me volatile."

I had to laugh at my sister's rebuttal...because, really, how much more volatile could Kira get after being kicked out of school for bitch-slapping three classmates? "I think just this once you can handle a sugar high," I started...

...then yelped as hard hands grabbed onto my shoulders while the sidewalk spun away from beneath my feet. There were male figures all around me now, the emergence of lanky legs and leering faces proving that I'd been too focused upon my sister's hurt feelings and not focused enough upon potential dangers impinging from the outside world.

But Kira was perched on top of a wall in a place of momentary safety. "*Run!*" I told her seconds before a hand landed atop my open mouth, strangling all further sound.

The teenager's palm tasted like grease and salt, and I was 99% certain my opponent hadn't washed after using the restroom. *Gross.* Still, the eyes that advanced toward me were entirely human. And the male's scent was more fast-food pickles than incipient fur.

So I didn't bother dulling my reflexes. Just hooked my knees around Pickle Breath's ankles and *pulled* so hard he hit the ground with an audible thud even as I struggled to regain my own footing.

Which didn't leave me in the clear, of course. Not with four other gang members still reaching toward me, their hands making up in number what they lacked in supernatural speed.

Despite the advancing front of heady testosterone, I stole a moment to peer at my sister as she perched atop the wall just where I'd left her. Predictably, Kira had completely ignored my previous commandment. If I didn't miss my guess, she was currently trying to decide which gang member to leap upon first.

"*Go home,*" I mouthed again, hoping our opponents had forgotten about the girl's presence. Just imagining what would happen if they grabbed my innocent sister sent my chest shrinking in on itself, forcing life-giving air out of my lungs....

So I let the barest hint of fox fill my features as I glared directly at her. Let Kira know from my sharpening teeth and darkening eyes that I was serious about being obeyed this time around.

And, to my relief, Kira hesitated only one more second before nodding. Then she spun on her heel and sprinted away so quickly none of the gang members would have been able to catch her even if they'd tried.

The distant shriek of a city bus's air brakes promised Kira would be safe within seconds if she played her cards right. Which left me with no one to worry about except my lonesome.

Good thing I had aggressions to work out of my own system since the field was currently rather overbalanced on my opponents' behalf.

Chapter 8

Five against one was a bit much even for me, but I didn't bother turning my star ball into a sword this time around. Not when goons like the ones before me measured the world in terms of greater and lesser forces. If I whipped a blade out of nowhere and vanquished them today, they'd just try again with weapons of their own tomorrow. On the other hand, if I beat up five bozos using nothing except my own body...well, maybe they'd leave my kid sister alone should she ever sneak out and walk down this street by herself in the future.

So I dipped beneath the closest male's grasping arms and used his own momentum to push him toward the pavement. Goon two received a kick to the chest and three didn't see the arm-twist coming. Which left only the tallest gang member standing...plus Pickle Breath, who was clambering back to his feet on my right-hand side.

The recent show of strength really should have been enough to dull their aggressions. After all, these teenagers were just kids barely older than my sister. So I gave them an opportunity to cut their losses without further bruising doled out by me.

"I recommend you walk away while you still can," I told the tall guy who apparently believed in leading from the rear. Then, glancing at the three teens still catching their breath atop the pavement, I added, "Or crawl. Whichever works best for you."

"You need to pay up if you want protection in our neighborhood," Tall Guy countered, acting as if he had a full posse behind him rather than being the only member of his gang with all body parts still intact. "We've carried your ass long enough. Stay and pay, or go and..."

I couldn't decide whether or not to roll my eyes as Tall Guy struggled to come up with a word that rhymed with "go." Because I'd felt bad about beating up gang members who were really just confused teenagers. But if their leader was going to force the issue...well, I hadn't enjoyed a good fight in over a week due to Ma Scrubbs' requirement that I lose my most recent Arena match.

"Go and owe?" I suggested, taking a single step forward. Now that I thought about it, I couldn't really blame Kira for beating up those girls earlier in the day. Not when my own feet were itching with the urge to leap and kick, not when my fingers tingled with the knowledge that battle was imminent....

"Let the water flow," my dead mother's voice warned me. And her words materializing in my brain shocked me just as much the second time around as they had the first.

Perhaps that's why I merely stood there as a faint scent of musky fur washed over me. Since when did werewolves follow me around day after day? And did my maternal ghost's sudden chattiness have anything to do with the presence of a shifter where one didn't belong?

Unfortunately, Tall Guy took advantage of my surprise to get the jump on me. The teenager wasn't willing to be laughed at in front of his comrades, and he was apparently willing to do something about that affront. I barely caught a flicker of movement before he was reaching into the back of his baggy trousers and pulling out a revolver that changed the odds in an instant.

The weapon reflected a beam of pure sunlight into my retinas before tilting so I stared down the dark barrel instead. "Die, ho," the gang leader said grimly.

Then he pulled the trigger.

WITH A WEREWOLF NEARBY, I couldn't dodge out of the way of the oncoming bullet. But I *could* use my star ball to protect myself.

Apparently it was too much to ask to manipulate magic into a solid barrier while also bracing myself against the impact though. Because the cartridge hit dead center in my chest so hard it sent me sprawling, the scab on my hand scraping loose against the pavement as I attempted to catch myself before my skull hit the ground.

And even though I didn't crack my head open, I *did* land with enough force that I ended up unable to do more than watch as the newcomer launched himself onto those poor goons with the full force of a pissed-off werewolf. My protector was outwardly human but inwardly bestial. And once I finally blinked tears out of my eyes sufficiently to make out my ally's identity, I found myself unsurprised by the realization that I was far too familiar with this ravening beast.

A swordsman's grace in an athlete's body. Gunner. Of course. Who else would be tailing me so slyly that he could come to my supposed rescue at just the wrong moment...yet again?

The werewolf-in-human-clothing wasn't even breathing heavily when he paused thirty seconds later to assess the damage. His opponents, on the other hand, were another matter entirely. Tall Guy whined like a nap-deprived toddler, his arm broken and his pistol kicked twenty yards away. Pickle Breath swore steadily, but even he kept his eyes down and his head bowed in instinctive submission to the beast within their midst.

And the other three kids? They'd run off the moment Gunner turned his attention elsewhere, proving they were smarter than their so-called boss.

"Mai is under my protection," Gunner growled then, words barely human as he knelt atop Tall Guy's prone figure with the teen's unbroken arm twisted up behind his back. The werewolf's muscles rippled with his attempt to maintain humanity, and his dark eyebrows lowered into a glowering frown. "You so much as look at her funny, and your future ends precipitously. Do you understand what I'm saying here?"

I wasn't so sure Tall Guy knew the meaning of the word "precipitously," but he certainly got the gist of the werewolf's threat anyway. Because the boy cringed in on himself so severely he appeared shorter than I was. And his breathing became so sporadic he managed no more than a frantic nod as I took advantage of the lull to pry myself off the pavement and pad over to their side.

Not that I wanted to put myself between an angry alpha and his quarry. But while Gunner might have seemed like a nice-enough guy in the Arena,

I didn't trust any werewolf to protect the innocent. And Tall Guy—despite his chosen profession—was innocent enough.

So I twisted half of my star ball into the shape of a dagger, secreting the weapon beneath my sleeve where it would be accessible if Gunner turned overly aggressive once I moved to interrupt. Then I opened my mouth and accepted the werewolf's annoying yet helpful support. "And my sister as well," I murmured just loudly enough for the shifter to hear me without impinging upon Tall Guy's attempts to smooth his gasps into words.

"And Mai's sister," Gunner added, driving his knee deeper into Tall Guy's kidneys while twisting the poor kid's arm up higher into the air. "The sister is mine also. *Swear it.*"

The scent of fur grew stronger as Gunner's humanity continued slipping. And I'd already opened my mouth to let the kid off the hook when Tall Guy finally forced out a babbling plea for mercy. "Yes, yes, yes, *yes!*" the teenager shrieked, writhing within the larger male's grip.

At which point I placed one hand on Gunner's shoulder to remind him that my former opponents were only human. If he broke them, they'd remain broke.

Alpha werewolves hate being contradicted, but Gunner's response was more extreme than I'd anticipated. Because before I could so much as skitter sideways, his hand reached out to grab my wrist with the speed of a striking cobra. Then his nostrils flared as he took in the liquid pooling across my palm.

"Blood," he noted. At which point his gaze landed on the hole in my sweatshirt and his eyes widened. "You've been shot."

Chapter 9

Gunner rose to his feet so abruptly I would have lost my balance if his hands hadn't been tearing at the neckline of my sweatshirt, attempting to rip fabric away from my skin. Out of the corner of one eye, I caught sight of the remaining gang members fleeing the scene of their defeat. But I wasn't concerned about teenage hoodlums any longer. Instead, I was fighting off a male who outweighed me by approximately a ton of muscle and who possessed supernatural speed and agility to boot.

"Stop!" I demanded, bringing one knee up to hit the male equivalent of an eject button. Because, yes, I'll admit it—I had previously found the alpha werewolf as enticing and dangerous as a shiny new rapier. But I didn't intend to assuage my curiosity on an open city street.

Unfortunately, Gunner's instincts proved far too well-honed to fall prey to the typical female self-defense moves. Instead, the alpha's easy twist out of my reach suggested that he was as adept at street fighting as he was at protecting his brother. And this time around, my throat tightened as I realized I was trapped within the vise-grip of werewolf arms.

Well, not quite trapped. The icy dagger slid down into my left fingers with facility despite the mandates of gravity begging it to move in the opposite direction. And my lips twitched into a smirk as I recalled how easily a lefty strike typically worked its way through an opponents' unwitting guard.

But before I could decide between the long-lasting damage of a stab and the shock value of a swipe, the fabric of my shirt tore at last with a resounding *riiiiip*. Then cold air rushed across my chest at the same moment Gunner flipped the dagger out of my hand with an almost-gentle bend of his wrist.

I was both disarmed and in dishabille. And while either state might have been enough to leave me shaken, it was the separation from my star ball that struck like a punch to my gut. The fragment of my soul soared away before I could beg it to change trajectory, and I bent inward as my strength fled right along with my blade.

"I need to see where you're *wounded*," Gunner growled, his words laden with more emotion than seemed justified by the ugly gray of my sports bra. Oh, right, the bullet hole. I shook my head woozily, trying to recall why showing the handsy alpha my holeless skin wasn't the obvious route out of this untenable situation.

And as I pondered, Gunner took matters into his own hands. "Easy does it," he murmured, voice hoarse with emotion. One huge hand slid down to press almost gently against my lower back while the other leveraged my shoulders up. Then chilly air gaped down the dramatically enlarged neckline of my sweatshirt, bringing my barely covered chest closer to the werewolf's searching eyes.

IT WAS HARD TO THINK with a third of my soul glinting against the pavement two body lengths away. So despite the sure knowledge that retrieving the star ball via magic was a bad idea, I nudged at the pseudo-metal with my mind's eye, dragging it inch by inch across the road as stealthily as an alley cat stalked a mouse.

And the mere change in direction of my soul fragment snapped the rest of my brain back into focus. *He can't know what I am,* I realized, hoping it wasn't already too late.

Luckily, I could work quickly when haste was necessary. Calling upon the rest of my magic with far less ceremony than usual, I molded the icy star-ball fragment into a medallion. Sent out a tendril of magic to solidify into a gold chain looped around my neck. Then mental fingers slipped the bulky disc into my left bra cup a split second before Gunner's hand-on-shoulders momentum bared my unclothed chest to view.

It turned out I needn't have hurried though. Because the werewolf who had been so aggressive one moment earlier paused before digging into my underwear. His fingers hovered atop the second layer of fabric while his scent grew subtly more human as he overcame the instincts of his beast.

"I need to look at...." He paused, averted his eyes, and didn't quite manage to complete the thought as the faintest tinge of red infused his cheeks.

The abrupt shyness from a formerly brash alpha was endearing. So rather than snapping back in retaliation for earlier abuses, I merely pulled the medallion out of its hiding place with a jerk to the chain that hadn't existed seconds before. "The bullet never hit me," I informed him, speaking as slowly as I did with the most annoying of my sixth graders. "It's the old Bible-in-the-breast-pocket routine. No wound. No blood. No reason for you to be pawing at my breasts."

Seconds after I spoke, though, I realized the error in my logic. Kira would have rolled her eyes at such an obvious continuity flaw in someone else's magic trick. Because if the medallion had been inside my bra cup from the get-go...why was there no hole in that second layer of fabric? Why wasn't there the bulge of a bullet breaking up the gentle curve of my breast?

Moving as swiftly as I could, I pulled a safety pin out of nowhere...or, rather, out of the back of the medallion, which shrank by half a centimeter as it lost a twentieth of its mass. Then I covered up the evidence quite literally, pinning my sweatshirt back together with hands that trembled only slightly.

Meanwhile, the boomeranged dagger nudged at my boot, its peregrinations complete. Just what I needed—to draw further attention to inconsistencies in my spur-of-the-moment solution. Still, I couldn't just leave it there.

So, neck prickling with danger, I bent down to collect the errant weapon, feeling absurd as I went through the motions of stashing a trickle of magic away in an imaginary sheath up one sleeve.

Up my *right* sleeve. Shit. Could I be more disingenuous?

Before me, the werewolf's brows furrowed in consideration. He knew something was cockeyed...which meant it was past time to make my escape.

"Thanks for nothing," I said grimly, turning away from a predator who possessed the means, motive, and opportunity to snap my neck between his long fingers. Then, forcing my feet not to break into a run, I headed blindly toward the far end of the block.

Chapter 10

Unfortunately, I'd only taken a single step when Gunner's hand came down upon my shoulder. And I hated myself for the tingle of awareness that had nothing to do with the werewolf tendency to hunt fox shifters as one of his fingers slid sideways to brush up against my bare skin.

"Wait," Gunner ordered. Or rather...requested? Because there was no electric tingle of alpha compulsion seasoning the single syllable this time. He wasn't telling. He was asking...well, as much as an alpha could bring himself to ask.

I was too much of a teacher not to reward good behavior. So I swiveled back to face him, arching an eyebrow even as I cocked my head. "What?"

"I wanted you to know the offer's still open." Confusion must have painted itself across my face because Gunner elaborated. "The job. My brother headed back to headquarters this morning, but I'm here for the duration. Well, not literally *here*. In town." He stopped himself before explanation turned into babble, held out what appeared to be a newly printed business card.

Curiosity forced me to accept the small rectangle of card stock. The werewolf had rented an office in the city while searching for a single Something? From the address, the space couldn't have come cheap.

"I'm not going to take a job I know nothing about," I countered, even as dollar signs danced through my head like moonbeams. How much, I wondered, might the werewolf in front of me spend hiring a local guide and investigative assistant? Enough to pay Kira's tuition? Enough to buy my voracious sibling salami every day of the week?

"I wouldn't ask you to do anything nefarious," the werewolf in front of me promised. His eyes were hooded, his voice sweet as honey. "There's something dangerous walking these streets and I intend to find it. To keep people like your sister safe. There are elements involved I think you might be familiar with...."

Only when his words trailed off did I realize that I'd been inching closer with each of his syllables, my chin tilting upward as if Gunner was a magnet and I was iron filings drawn toward him through no action of my own. *Bad idea, Mai*, I berated myself. Forcing myself to take one long step backward, I decided then and there that Kira and I would be better off living on ramen noodles rather than placing ourselves in the sight line of a seductively smooth alpha like this one.

Unfortunately, the star chain around my neck was unimpressed by my decision to be my own master. Instead, the mere thought of food was enough to remind it of last night's unpaid milk money, and now the magic sent cold trickles shivering over my shoulders and turning icier by the second. I *needed* to get to that 7-Eleven sooner rather than later. I *needed* to pay off my debt....

"Thanks but no thanks," I told the waiting werewolf, tucking his business card into one pocket while turning back in the direction from which I'd come. I'd hand over three bucks for the milk, then my star-ball-turned-conscience would leave me alone.

And even though my life was tricky enough without werewolves in it, I was subtly disappointed when Gunner's footsteps failed to follow me down the block. Apparently, though, lack of sound didn't equate to lack of movement. Because werewolf breath soon warmed the back of my neck despite the distance I'd moved since his last words.

"You can go straight home," the werewolf noted, apparently having realized why I'd switched directions without me having to explain the action in words. "I paid for your milk."

This time, the lizard of debt inside my chest cavity scrambled up my spine with scratchy claws even as Mama warned inside my brain: *"Specks of dust slowly accumulate into mountain ranges."*

"Let me pay you back," I started, knowing my mother was right. I couldn't afford to be indebted to a werewolf....

But this time Gunner was the one backing away, was refusing the bills I fumbled out toward him in an effort to stave off further star-ball compulsions. "It was my pleasure," my companion answered, the distance between us growing with every word. "Maybe next time you'll let me buy you a beer. Or at least we could drink some milk together. You have my card."

He was flirting. Sweetly almost. If only he wasn't a werewolf, perhaps I would have said yes.

Instead, I squashed the niggle of complaint from my star ball, shook my head once, then swiveled around yet again to head in my original direction. If the werewolf didn't want my money, then I'd save it for my sister. It was time to get home and check on Kira.

I SHOULD HAVE BEEN relieved to finally achieve the anteroom of my den, but I winced as I pushed open the heavy fire door that separated stairwell from hallway. Because my least favorite person was waiting on the faded welcome mat outside our apartment, and I really could have done without dealing with Simon tonight.

"Mai," the gangly social worker greeted me, his voice as droopy as the wrinkles around his eyes. "I've been waiting for twenty minutes."

"Shi—oot," I parried. "So sorry about that."

Meanwhile, my mind was running a mile a minute. What was Simon doing here? Had he found out about my lost job and about Kira's precarious school situation? Was he ready to live up to past insinuations that my sister would be better off placed in another home?

If our conversation had been a cage fight, I would have been backpedaling rapidly while hoping my hind end didn't end up against the chain-link before I came up with a strategy other than retreat. Luckily, Simon took pity on my confusion before I let anything particularly incriminating slip. "Did you forget we had a home visit planned for today?"

A home visit? That's all this was? "Yeah," I admitted, brushing past the state employee as I turned my key in the lock. I'd likely noted down the date in my planner, then lost the reminder during Kira's ill-fated magic trick last week. After a building evacuation, two hours of mopping up sprinkler water, and a furious tirade by the apartment supervisor, the fate of my planner—and the dates of any upcoming home visits—had been the least of my concern.

As if reading my mind, Kira's bushy tail flicking apologetically from her perch atop the bedroom lintel and I found myself smiling instead of fuming. At least my sister had made it home safe and sound.

"So," Simon said, walking in behind me without invitation and settling into one of our two dining chairs. "How is everything going here?"

As he spoke, his gaze flicked around the tiny apartment, and I scurried along in its wake, moving dirty cereal bowls into the sink and picking up place mats that had been knocked onto the floor by fox action. It wasn't as if we lived in a pig sty, but I worked two jobs and Kira was a shifter cooped up in a one-bedroom apartment. Our home wasn't exactly spic and span.

On the other hand, I loved my sister, I neither used nor dealt drugs, and I didn't bring home pervert boyfriends who snuck into her room to fondle Kira's underage body while she slept. It was hard to believe this was the worst fostering situation Simon came in contact with. So I mustered a smile and offered foodstuffs I didn't actually have on hand rather than remarking upon the financial upset threatening Kira's and my lives. "Would you like some tea? Or a cookie?"

"No." Simon's mouth pursed as if the mere idea of eating something inside my home gave him the willies. He paused, then added: "Thank you."

We stared at each other in silence for enough seconds that the meeting began to feel profoundly awkward. Then the social worker pinned me down with a specific question I didn't know how to sidestep. "What is it you're working so hard not to tell me?"

The man was too astute for my own good. And I couldn't risk being caught up in an untruth.

So I went ahead and spilled the beans. "I lost my job at the school," I admitted. Then, figuring a little white lie wouldn't kill me, I added: "I've got several leads on new ones though. I swear to you, Kira isn't going to end up starving or on the streets. I just need a little time to work things out."

Rather than answering immediately, the social worker clambered back to his feet so he could take my hand. His palm was faintly damp and chilly, but I forced myself not to jerk away from the contact. Instead, I met Simon's gaze head on as he spoke in what he probably thought was a compassionate manner.

"I'll return Monday with my supervisor," he told me. "Please have Kira packed and ready. If your work situation hasn't improved dramatically by that point, I'm afraid we'll need to move your sister to a more appropriate home."

Chapter 11

"**S**tay here," I ordered Kira fifteen minutes later while molding my star ball into its favorite shape—a long, slender sword hanging at my hip where it would be easily accessible. "Don't go out, don't open the door, and don't let anybody in."

As I spoke, I kicked off my PE teacher shoes, donning high leather boots instead. Off went the fitted gym pants, on went the knife-resistant leather. A school-themed hoodie electrified my hair as it slid off my slender frame, then I drew my favorite shiny, black jacket back up around my shoulders like a shield.

"Go over the next chapter in your math book," I continued. "Just because you're suspended doesn't mean you can afford falling behind."

"Where are you going?" Kira spoke as she shifted, a shimmer of light and air turning fox into girl with the effortlessness of magic. She hadn't bothered leaping down from the lintel before transforming, so she ended up chinning herself onto the floor, landing as silently as she would have in her animal form.

Unfortunately, my sibling was even more inquisitive on two feet than she had been on four. And no more interested in schoolwork either.

"Tonight's not an Arena night," Kira pointed out, padding in a circle around me as she completely ignored all preceding instructions. Her agile fingers twitched my hair out from under the collar of my jacket and straightened my sword in its sheathe even as her equally clever tongue pinned me down verbally as only a little sister could. "Where else can we get enough money to satisfy Simon?"

I wasn't in the habit of lying to my sister, so I told her the cold, hard true. "From werewolves," I answered, eyes closing as I made a decision I knew in my heart would lead to yet more trouble. But I couldn't lose Kira to the foster-care system. And Gunner possessed both the funds and the ability to make my upcoming employment appear legitimate enough to satisfy even our dour social worker's unattainable standards.

I'd just have to keep a tight rein on my abilities until Gunner left town. Easy enough.

As if she was reading my mind, my sister raised herself on tiptoe until she could look me in the eye. Then she parroted back words I'd tossed in her direction far too often over the years. "Foxes and wolves don't mix. You can't let them know what we are."

My chest expanded with pride as I gazed upon a young woman growing into wisdom by the moment. "I won't," I started. But Kira wasn't done with her efforts to rule the roost.

"You need backup. I'm coming with you," she decided, dropping butt-to-linoleum by the door while yanking on recently discarded tennis shoes. The math textbook beside her was nudged subtly aside as she dressed, a sprawl of notebooks turning dog-eared and rumpled as she used them to pry dirt out from between her cleats. "I can be a distraction."

She sure could. Right now, for instance, I was distracted with worry that Dad might think my sister was better off in a wealthier household than the one I was able to pay for, or in a family where textbooks weren't used as doorstops. After all, our father had believed in education just as firmly as he believed in kinship. What would he think if I was forced to yank Kira out of the academy just because I couldn't come up with enough cash to pay the bill?

"No, you're not coming with me," I countered, squashing second thoughts even as I pulled up Gunner's address on my cell phone. The closest bus stop was a mile from the alpha's office and I'd have to make two changes to even get that far. "Math is an essential life skill," I muttered both to myself and to my sister. For example, math told me I couldn't afford a taxi...which meant I'd take the bus for the first leg then walk the rest.

I should have realized that Kira's mercurial nature was shifting from helpful to fretful, but I was too busy plotting out my plan of attack to notice the symptoms. Now, though, the leggy tween eased between my phone and my face, forcing me to pay attention to her expression. And I winced as I caught the red flush of anger brightening her cheeks.

"Kira..." I started.

"I'm not a *child*," my sister countered. "I deserve to be involved. I deserve to know what I *am*."

"We're foxes..."

Kira didn't even wait for me to finish that particular sentence. Instead, she pressed closer into my personal space, standing on tiptoes not so much in solidarity this time around as in an attempt to intimidate. "We're fox *shifters*," she corrected as if she was the adult and I was the child. "But what does that even mean? Why do the werewolves hate us if we're just like them except with red fur and better style? It doesn't make any sense."

She was right, unfortunately. But Mama had been my only link to knowledge about our heritage and our mother was long gone...or was she?

Absurdly, I waited ten long seconds for a voice in my head to illuminate the darkness. And during that delay, my sister's stewing erupted into outright rage. "If you don't want to tell me..." she started.

"I don't *know*, okay?" I snapped back, ashamed of myself even as I lost my temper. "Do you think turning into a parent at age eighteen came with a handbook? It *didn't*. I'm doing the best I can and you're not helping matters. Now do your homework then go to bed."

And, predictably, Kira lashed right back with her own fox fury. "I hate you," my usually sunny sister emoted, family cohesiveness and math textbooks forgotten in the face of my badly chosen honesty. Then the girl fled to her bedroom without another word and slammed the door behind her back.

Chapter 12

I'd managed to make the switch onto the blue line and was relaxing as the third city bus of the evening wended its way into the good part of town before it occurred to me that I wasn't the only person in the vehicle's shadowy posterior. How had I missed that hint of fur beneath the stench of unwashed bodies and spilled soda pop when I boarded ten minutes earlier? My only defense—that I had more important matters on my mind than getting jumped by a stray werewolf—failed to hold water when my attempt to swivel in search of further information was stilled by a flash of silver flicking in front of my eyes one millisecond before cold steel came to settle beneath my chin.

"Eh, eh, eh. Not so fast."

I froze, running through possibilities in my mind. Was this an unaffiliated drifter, an Atwood underling, or one of Jackal's henchmen? My opponent's identity should have made a difference, but the male's subsequent words turned off my rational side and prompted me to throw caution to the winds. "Your sister...." the male started.

And without giving him time to spit out whatever thinly veiled threat he'd dreamed up, I acted. One hand rose to pry his blade-holding fingers back into a painful reverse stretch even as my other arm leveraged me off the seat sufficiently to get my feet underneath my butt.

Then I was the one attacking. My sword was less than useless in such a confined situation, but I could spring upwards holding onto my opponent's hand while leaping. No wonder his knife clattered to the floor between us even as the male—scruffy, badly dressed, older than I'd expected—exploded into the aisle with teeth sharpening within his still-human mouth.

"You little bitch," he started, shaking out his right hand even as his left inched toward what appeared to be another knife marring the drape of his Hawaiian shirt. And here Kira thought *my* clothing needed assistance....

Wardrobe aside, I refused to be intimidated by my opponent's bulk or by his small-space-appropriate weapons. Instead, I bought a little breathing room with a verbal attack. "Nice flowers," I started. "But I thought Casual Friday wasn't until tomorrow...."

Before I could finish, I was sliding sideways, the non-slip matting beneath my feet insufficient to hold me in place as the bus driver slammed on his brakes. My stomach hit the plastic of the nearest seat back, breath whooshing out of me even as I scrabbled against the floorboards in search of my opponent's dropped weapon.

But the male was no longer attacking. Was, I realized as I looked up, instead halfway down the aisle where he'd been slung by the vehicle's abrupt halt.

Which meant his second knife was now poised half an inch away from the eyeball of a boy too young to be out by himself after dark. Yes, *I* was now safe from the werewolf's weaponry. But based on the curl of the shifter's upper lip, he was well aware that harm to an innocent was just as damaging as harm to myself.

The boy whimpered as the scent of smug shifter filled the enclosed space so densely it choked my attempted inhale. "The brain is right behind the eyeball," my werewolf opponent observed smoothly. "I learned that from a Hawaiian medicine woman. Are you ready to deal yet?"

THE BASTARD THOUGHT he had me over a barrel. But he'd missed my fingers closing around the knife recently abandoned on the bus's floor, and he must have also missed the memo that street fighters never back down.

So, unlike him, I attacked without warning. Didn't open my mouth or even flick my eyes to give away my intentions. Just twisted and flung the knife in one unerring movement, gaze following the blade as it sliced through my opponent's sleeve and bicep, ripping him away from his current victim and pinning the male against the back of the seat in front of them both.

The werewolf howled in agony, the boy shrieked in terror...and I was slung around hard as handcuffs pinched shut around my left wrist. "Police! Don't move!" a human shouted in my ear. Then my face was squished up against a seat back while my right hand was wrenched up behind me, only the faint musk of receding werewolf suggesting what I'd see once I was finally allowed to stand erect.

My opponent had taken advantage of the tussle to flee, I noted. And the humans, predictably, took one look at my ragged clothing combined with the massive sword still belted at my waist and rewrote the past with chilling inaccuracy.

"She was attacking that boy!" a cane-wielding matron exclaimed, pointing at the child who'd survived the scuffle without a single scratch...thanks to me.

"She pulled a knife," the bus driver confirmed, watching as I was frog-marched down the aisle and out the front door of the bus. I'd nearly made it to my destination, I realized. Was standing in a residential neighborhood full of mansions and bigger mansions and vast expanses of emerald green grass.

And...werewolves. Because the scruffy male was long gone, but another shifter waited at the bottom of the bus steps. This one reminded me of a more wiry version of Gunner and Ransom with a wardrobe even Kira would have considered both stylish and smart. Another brother? A cousin? I couldn't be certain. Whatever his lineage, the mild-mannered shifter in his bespoke business suit was a good fit for talking the policeman off my back.

"Is there a problem, officer?" the not-quite-stranger asked, the query so clichéd it might as well have rolled off the lips of a B-rate movie actor. And yet, he managed to pull off the impression. Could almost have been readjusting a monocle as he superciliously stared the policeman down.

"This woman attacked a boy on a city bus..." the officer started. But the stranger cut him off with a single raised hand.

"Did you see the altercation in person? Was anyone injured?"

"Well, no...."

"Then I highly doubt you have your facts straight. Because this young woman is my house guest. Not a troublemaker in the least...although she *could* use a better tailor. I'll admit that part."

Together, the werewolf and the police officer looked me up and down, lips similarly pursed as they passed judgment on my thrift-store attire. Hey, it was better than a hot pink Hawaiian shirt....

And even though my escape from potential incarceration shouldn't have been that easy, the bus of witnesses was already rolling away down the street. Meanwhile, the officer before us apparently had no incentive to argue with a well-heeled resident of a top-tier neighborhood. "I apologize for any inconvenience," the official told me after a single second of consideration. Then air flowed in to replace the pinch of handcuffs, my former captor strolling away down the sidewalk before my rescuer could lodge an official complaint.

Which left me in the custody of a werewolf who had every reason to berate me at length for nearly revealing myself to humans. But the stranger just raised one eyebrow and shook his head slowly instead. "Not smart," he chided almost gently before adding: "Go home."

Then he left me there. Didn't ask what I was doing in his neighborhood or why I'd let myself fall into the hands of a human authority while looking only moderately human. Instead, the male swiveled away from me—who turns their back on an angry sword-woman?—then continued on his trajectory alone.

For half a second, I just stood there, shocked by the male's rudeness. But then I scurried after him, jogging slowly enough to appear human while following the shifter up the steps to the mansion that bore Gunner's address. I fully expected the male's chivalrous instincts to prompt him to wait for me at the entrance of the building, but instead the door literally clanged shut in my face.

Rubbing my bruised forehead with one hand, I reached out to turn the knob with the other. Only to find the barrier locked and unwilling to budge. Really? Nameless Dude was just going to retreat inside and shut me out behind him?

Which is when my fox nature took over entirely. Not bothering with the bell, I pounded on the wooden door with both fists. "Let me in!" I demanded, temper firing hotter with every blow.

"Just like a werewolf," I growled under my breath, so intent upon fuming and noisemaking that I didn't hear footsteps responding to my barrage of knocks. My hand was drawn back in preparation for further pounding when the door jerked open before me.

And that's how I came to punch an alpha werewolf in the nose.

Chapter 13

There was blood. And the scent of fur. And the wildest flash of rage in a broad-shouldered shifter's eyes.

Then I was being drawn inside, the door closing behind us, as Gunner grabbed a doily off a sideboard and held it up to his streaming nostrils. "You certainly know how to make an entrance," he said grimly, walking away from me just as quickly as his brother—cousin?—had.

Like the thinner werewolf I'd followed up the front steps, the one currently in front of me didn't bother glancing back to see if I followed as he sped through a series of rooms full of ebony furniture and Turkish rugs. Instead, he bellowed loudly enough for humans to hear from the sidewalk, calling out names of pack mates who came sprinting toward us from nooks and crannies I didn't have time to fully peruse as we rushed past.

"Liam," Gunner greeted my former savior as we reached a broad stairwell in the heart of the mansion. The alpha's voice was muffled by the table runner he'd snatched to replace the doily as he stopped barking out names and moved on to demands. "What else do we know?"

I wasn't sure how the dark-haired shifter had found time to reach the second story in the few short seconds I'd spent pounding on the door out front. But now Liam descended the stairs in a measured manner while answering the shifter who clearly outranked him by at least a bit. "We don't know much," Gunner's relative said, falling in beside his superior while subtly boxing me further away from the center of power. "And are you sure you want to talk in front of a ragamuffin off the streets?"

Ragamuffin? Did the male think he was living in Victorian-era England? And did that mean my potential job hadn't been okayed by the rest of the pack?

Gunner glanced at me for a split second only, his eyes piercing as he dropped the table runner to the floor and accepted the handkerchief another pack mate was thrusting into his hand. "Tell me," he ordered Liam without bothering to respond to the dig about my part in...whatever this was.

And this time, information was finally forthcoming. "The body was found in an alley," Liam offered, which snagged my attention in a way Gunner's vague job offers had not. A body didn't sound good. A body meant there was more going on than an overbearing alpha and my need to pay the bills.

"Unscented like the last one?" my maybe-boss queried.

Liam merely nodded by way of reply, leaving me to wonder if my understanding of the world was perhaps a smidge small-minded and naive. Because as best I could tell, everything in our world had a scent. After all, superior nostrils were half of my edge over human opponents in the Arena.

But I didn't have time to further ponder the issue, because Gunner was pushing through the back door and leading us all onto what appeared to be an industrial loading dock. "Address?" he queried as I took in the view.

There were two moving vans backed up to the elevated concrete porch, as if these shifters had settled into my home town for the duration rather than merely passing through on their way to greener pastures. In addition, a fleet of cars and SUVs promised the pack would have no problem getting around while they were in residence. Must be nice having so many wheels at your beck and call.

And, apparently, a driver. Because Liam angled ahead of his relative at last, opening the driver's side door of the closest SUV. "I'll take you there."

The move appeared properly obsequious. However, for the first time, Gunner slowed the pack's forward momentum as his hand closed upon the reedier male's forearm. "No," the alpha said quietly...but not quietly enough to keep any of the nearby shifter ears from picking up on the mild rebuke. "Ransom would be lost without his personal secretary. He expects you home tonight. Stick to the plan."

THE WORDS WEREN'T COMMANDING, nor were they overtly revealing. Yet I read volumes of information streaming between the two males as they locked identical sienna eyes. Both shifters were looking out for their relative. Both understood that Ransom possessed some weakness requiring a trusted advisor present at all times.

Or that's the way Gunner saw the matter. Liam, it seemed, had a different approach to dealing with a potentially problematic leader of their shared pack.

"*This* is where the action is," the slender shifter started. "*This* is more important than whatever business I'd be taking care of back home."

Liam's words weren't overtly insubordinate, but they were enough to evoke a growl of rage from his superior. And within seconds, the lower-ranking werewolf was rattling off directions with eyes averted then obediently slipping behind the wheel of a much smaller vehicle off to one side. Apparently Gunner's worries about Ransom trumped whatever crime scene the former was going to investigate. Equally apparent—Gunner's merest hint of displeasure was law within this pack.

I was similarly shunted out of the flow of werewolves as Gunner tossed out orders to his remaining crew members. Doors slammed as half the assemblage piled into vehicles. Meanwhile, half of the shifters present spread out, trotting down the block or back into the building to form a well-oiled security patrol.

Then Liam's car was rolling away down the alley, his headlights cutting through the gloom even as other engines sprang to life on my every side. Like his departing relative, Gunner was behind the wheel of his own SUV rather than depending upon a driver. Still, the male definitely played the stereotypical alpha role as he honked his horn so loudly I instinctively jumped backwards out of the way.

Tonight was not the night for a job interview, I decided. I'd return tomorrow and beg forgiveness for the nose bleed while stating my case. In the meantime, I could brainstorm other opportunities of gainful employment. This testosterone haze of a werewolf pack couldn't be the only way to keep Kira in math books and lunch meat.

Only, Gunner hadn't forgotten about my presence. When his horn honk didn't elicit the desired reaction, the tinted window between us rolled down to expose a tense and craggy face.

"Get in," the alpha ordered, blood-encrusted nostrils flaring. He jerked his chin sideways, and for the first time I noticed that, although the back seat was cramped with three cheek-to-jowl shifters, no one had elected to ride shotgun beside their boss.

If the feeling of handcuffs around my wrists had horrified my fox instincts, entering a small space with an angry werewolf seemed akin to committing suicide. But I'd run out of good ideas and was willing to jump at the bad. So, opening the door quickly before Gunner could change his mind, I hastened to obey.

Chapter 14

We rode to the crime scene in eerie silence, sword squeezed between my knees and the rest of my body pressed up against the door. I hated being so timid, but hungry eyes lingered on the back of my neck. And every time I opened my mouth to speak, the musk of alpha werewolf coated my tongue like moss. No wonder I clamped my lips together over incipient words every time I considered breaking the ice.

Meanwhile, my star-ball-turned-sword throbbed against my pant legs, sucking heat out of the air and forming ice crystals atop everything it touched. Twice, Gunner turned the heater up a notch, and each time he eyed me with probing consideration. In response, I used the most fox-like offensive imaginable. Despite flicking glances in the predatory alpha's direction, I made sure to be looking out the window every time he returned the favor.

Finally, though, the vehicle ground to a halt just off the edge of the highway, the buffeting wind of a passing tractor trailer shaking our SUV like a leaf. This wasn't a legal place to park. But if a highway patroller dropped by, I could imagine Gunner smiling his way out of probing questions as easily as Liam had recently gotten me off the hook.

Despite our precarious parking space, the werewolf behind the steering wheel seemed in no hurry to open his door, and the shifters behind us knew better than to disembark before their boss. "It won't be pretty," Gunner informed me when we'd been sitting there long enough that my sword was beginning to create a rime of ice on plastic surfaces nine inches away. I swiped at the dashboard as unobtrusively as I could with one finger, smudging frost into water. Then I reddened as my seat mate raised his brows at the dampness coating my hand.

Before Gunner could remark upon the inconsistency, though, a mutter emerged from the peanut gallery behind our backs. "He has to warn girls first," one noted.

"Of course he does. Otherwise, they'd run screaming as soon as he unzipped his fly."

I blinked, opened my mouth...and tasted amusement replacing the former aggression in the air. Gunner's underlings were making dirty jokes about their boss now...and he wasn't tearing them to bloody pieces with his bare hands? Perhaps I didn't understand werewolves as well as I'd thought I did.

And despite everything, I found myself playing along. "I can handle ugly," I answered, blinking aside enticing mental images with an effort. No matter what his pack mates were insinuating, Gunner's warning had referred not to portions of his own anatomy but to the rotting body of a corpse. "If," I added, remembering my priorities, "it's part of the job."

"So you want it now?" Gunner's scent twisted, lightened, teased my nostrils with the humor of yet another double entendre.

"I *need* it," I countered, then reddened as the murmurs from the back seat grew even more lewd. I might have been playing along earlier, but I hadn't meant my final sentence in *that* way. At least not consciously....

Rather than trying to pry my foot out of my mouth, I pushed open my door without regard for passing vehicles...or for whatever laws of shifter hierarchy were keeping everyone else penned up inside. And for half a second I allowed myself to bask in the flow of cold air across hot cheeks, to imagine what it might feel like to be part of a pack that teased each other with such blissful simplicity while still guarding each others' backs.

Unfortunately, I wasn't a werewolf. And an innocent sister depended upon my protection both today and always. So I inhaled deeply and took in the more far-flung aromas flowing toward me beneath car-exhaust fumes. Tinges of blood and even less savory bodily fluids slapped me in the face within seconds, reminding me why I was here.

Whatever Liam had been saying about "unscented" apparently didn't apply to decomposing corpses. Shrugging, I headed down the steep slope toward the stench of death.

THE BODY WAS STUFFED beneath an overpass, subtly illuminated by the vehicle lights Gunner's pack had left on when they left their SUVs and cars. And at first glance, it looked like a homeless person had merely succumbed to the elements. Our noses, however, told us a different story entirely.

"See the baking-soda bomb?" Gunner pointed up to the bridge above our heads, where a splintered black trash bag fluttered in the breeze. Every now and then, a few white particles drifted off its otherwise pristine surface, joining the scent-leaching compound that blew around our feet like desert sand. This was a shifter-specific cover-up, a sullying of evidence that only a being with super-powered nostrils would dream of. No wonder the local pack leader's representative considered the crime his personal duty to investigate.

"Smart move on the killer's part to counteract his scent," I agreed, trying to make a good impression as I picked my way through drifts of white powder on my way to the corpse's side. Because even though crime-scene investigation didn't top my list of potential professions, I was willing to showcase relevant cleverness if that's what it took to keep Kira enrolled in her fancy private school. "Let me guess. The bag was attached to a string that could be pulled from a vehicle's window after he covered up the rest of his trail?"

"Yep," Gunner agreed, joining me as I padded closer to the victim. Even with eddies of baking soda filling the air, I could smell my companion's personal aroma now. Pine needles and ozone and dew-dampened granite, as if the male by my side embodied the type of forest I wished I could set Kira loose to frolic amidst.

I must have inhaled a little too deeply though. Because I snorted up a blend of dust and death so intense that I started sneezing wildly enough to draw tears from my eyes. Perhaps the universe was trying to tell me something....

"Alright?" Gunner asked, his hand landing lightly on my forearm. Earlier, the male had seized me so violently I couldn't get away, ripping at my sweatshirt like a boy tearing away wrapping paper on Christmas morning. But now, strength flowed from his skin into my own, the mere touch burning with so much heat it made me shiver in protest.

And even though instinct begged me to lean into the werewolf's tantalizing body, eyes on the back of my neck promised that nearby shifters were judging both of our actions. So I took a step away from the alpha's warmth instead. Swiped tears off my cheeks almost angrily.

Then I skipped over any explanation for my weakness as I peered more carefully at the waiting corpse. I was here to do a job. Might as well get it over with.

Chapter 15

The recently departed looked even more like one of the city's lost souls up close and personal. His coat was a blue so faded it had turned gray while hair streamed down his shoulders and off his chin. The man himself could have been twenty or fifty. Whatever his age, he wouldn't see another year—not now that he was quite solidly dead.

"The other body you mentioned was the same?" I asked, squashing my instinctive urge to move further away from the corpse just as I'd previously tamped down the strange attraction to the male at my side. But even though my living mother had imbued in me a healthy hesitancy about touching dead bodies, her ghost was more interested in deciphering the puzzle before our eyes.

"Three people gathering can create wisdom," Mama whispered.

And at the same moment, Gunner replied: "Same baking soda, different setting. We're looking for a serial killer now."

As he spoke, he nudged the corpse with one boot tip, toppling the body over from its side onto its back. And in response, I lost all squeamishness as my eyes took in the discordant feature shining out of the corpse's porcelain skin.

To the unmagical eye, the lost soul was likely no paler than the average dead body. After all, crime shows had informed me that when the heart ceases to beat, blood pools at the lowest point and turns the body a dusty gray.

But this corpse was paler than it should have been. Was, to the shifter eye, not just devoid of blood but lacking in magic as well.

"Like the moon and the soft-shelled turtle," Mama murmured as I dropped to my knees and pried back the scarf knotted around the dead male's throat.

Sure enough, lines of glowing magic slid down the corpse's neck and beneath his clothing. The rivulets were pulsing, tantalizing....and I unbuttoned the tattered coat nearly as roughly as Gunner had gone after my sweatshirt earlier in the day.

I wasn't expecting the resulting view though. Wasn't expecting the circle of symbols that emerged, branded upon the dead man's chest.

Or, not branded, but rather *frozen*. *"Don't try to bite your own navel,"* my mother ordered. But whatever she was obliquely warning me against, I *had* to understand what was going on.

Reaching forward, my fingers brushed against the pattern with the lightness of a feather. And, as if the magic had been waiting for me to make contact, the glowing lines coalesced into a miniature replica of a star ball before shooting comet-like into the dark. Seconds later, the dead man's chest was left as pristine as age-spotted and dirt-encrusted skin could be.

Unfortunately, I wasn't the only one who had noted the transition from magically branded to simply dead and grungy. "What was that?" Gunner demanded, hand latching down upon my unprotected nape. There was no seduction in his touch now, only hard, demanding anger. "And why did the pattern exactly match the necklace you were wearing this afternoon?"

"YOU'RE SEEING THINGS," I countered, too shaken to realize until the words left my mouth that confusion would have been a more appropriate response to his astute remark. But I hadn't expected the magical brand to be visible to the uninitiated. Meanwhile, most of my mind was intent upon figuring out how Mama's possessions could have been used to kill a man.

Because the similarity between the burnt circle and my amulet was no coincidence. In my moment of instinctive terror earlier in the day, I'd modeled the pattern of my supposed bullet-protection after one of the few objects my mother left behind her. It was easier to recreate a known pattern than to dream up something new on the fly....

Only, that particular amulet was supposed to harness good, not evil. And Mama's stories to that effect were all just superstition anyway.

Or so I'd thought at the time.

Now I sincerely regretted not having materialized a Mickey Mouse medallion as the supposed bullet blocker. Because Gunner yanked me back onto my feet with complete disregard for personal space, hands sliding from neck to shoulders as he pulled me in so close we were standing eye to eye...or rather, eye to the middle of his chest.

"You're saying it's an illusion that both your necklace thing and the burnt circle on the dead man's chest were marked with Japanese characters?" the alpha werewolf demanded. "It's an illusion that light flew off that man like a fu..." he gritted his teeth, calmed his language with an effort "...like a *freaking* ball of flame?"

Before I could answer, one of the werewolves who'd ridden in a different vehicle called toward us from the far side of the underpass. "Everything okay, boss?" Apparently our current altercation had grown loud enough to impinge upon the other werewolves' search of the surrounding landscape. And from the way the male's eyes bit into me like daggers, he agreed with Liam that a stranger shouldn't be trusted with secrets more appropriate to pack.

But Gunner was too intent upon our conversation to give his underling's warning the air space it deserved. "I'm fine. Now go," Gunner responded, biting off the words so sharply that his underling's scent of submission overwhelmed even the nearby stench of death.

Despite the clear sign that he was taking his frustration one step too far, though, the alpha's eyes never left mine even as rustlings in the bushes promised all other shifters were hastily relocating into safer territory far from potential reprimand. And, once we were even more alone than previously, the alpha's voice turned ten times quieter while its intensity ratcheted up in equal measure. "*Explain,*" he ordered for my ears alone.

The compulsion would have drawn a flood of words out of a submissive werewolf, but my fox heritage cut the command's effects down to a mere itch atop my skin. Still, I didn't like being threatened, and I didn't like the way Gunner's hands turned into manacles biting into my upper arms either. So I found myself spitting out inappropriate comments without passing the idea first by the more rational centers of my brain.

"What makes you think those are Japanese symbols? Maybe they're Chinese. Or Korean. What, you took one look at my slanty eyes and assumed I was a geisha? Racist much?"

I'd found that most Caucasians grew stymied by the assertion that prejudice colored their thinking. Gunner, unfortunately, turned out to be the exception that proved the rule. "No circles or ovals, no complicated symbols," he growled, calling my bluff with knowledge that exceeded my own. "So the symbols weren't Chinese or Korean. They were Japanese, just like you."

Japanese like all fox shifters. Japanese like the bane of werewolves' existence. I shivered, wondering for the first time whether Gunner's interest in me had ever been attraction or if he'd been suspicious of my heritage from the moment we first met.

For his part, Gunner paused for only a moment, pushing further into my personal space until his nose nearly touched my suddenly sweaty forehead. "If you have nothing to hide," my companion murmured, his gravelly voice turning almost sweet with anticipation, "then show me your necklace thing so I can compare it to what was on the dead man's chest."

As if he expected there to be blood stains on the amulet. Or for the "necklace thing" to have gone missing during the several hours in which the corpse at our feet turned from living being into so much dead meat.

Unfortunately, I couldn't think of another way to get Gunner's hands off me. He'd proven already that I couldn't outfight him once his vise-like fingers bit down. And my vulpine disinclination to being constrained was already making it hard to breathe....

So I fought to keep my inhales steady, hoping the night was dark enough to hide both the red on my cheeks and the fist-sized mass I magically yanked out of the sword sheathed by my side. Only when the amulet materialized around my neck with a near-audible pop of displaced air particles did I wince, the ice of its recently used magic burning against my skin.

"It's an *amulet*," I informed the handsy alpha, pulling the heavy circle out from beneath my clothing while subtly pushing my companion just a little further away. "And it looks nothing like what was on that dead man's chest. The symbols must have been all Japanese to you."

Gunner ignored my weak attempt at humor, and he didn't give me time to pull the chain over my head either. Instead, his huge hand swiped the amulet out of my grasp, tilting it to take in the distant glow of passing headlights while drawing my neck closer to his own. "Hmmm," he murmured, seemingly oblivious to our heart-pounding proximity.

Well, if he could stick to business then so could I. To that end, I let my gaze brush over the raised symbols that covered the amulet's surface, wishing I wasn't so sure that the hash-marked lines *did* indeed match up to the ones that had recently disappeared from the dead man's chest. But before the overbearing alpha could debrief me further, another werewolf emerged out of the darkness inches from my left side.

"You'll want to see this, boss," the newcomer murmured, eyes narrowing only slightly as he took in my proximity to his alpha. "There's a footprint on the east side of the overpass. Scentless, small, but most definitely made by a wolf."

Chapter 16

Icould feel both my job…and possibly my skin-protecting secrets…slipping through my fingers no matter how hard I clenched said appendages into fists. Still, I stretched my legs to catch up as the two werewolves ahead of me strode up the steep hillside with complete disregard for darkness.

"I hear you, Allen," Gunner said, answering a murmur that I hadn't been able to make out as I lagged, trying to tease out the third shifter's signature scent. Allen was one of the males who'd ridden in the back seat of the SUV during the drive over, I gathered. Given how easily the trio had teased Gunner then, it was hard to imagine what might have provoked such a cool reaction from his boss now.

Giving up on the puzzle, I broke into a trot and broke out of the thicket just a step behind as the werewolves paused in an open area where a metal drainage pipe produced a flat, muddy area perfect for capturing passing animals' tracks. "But I've decided," Gunner continued, flicking a single glance in my direction that suggested I'd been the topic of conversation. Then his eyebrows rose, a clear signal that whatever conversation I'd missed was now over and done.

Shrugging, Allen got down to business, shining a flashlight between us to reveal indents of bird toes, pinpricks of insect feet…and one perfectly formed canine print just at the edge of the mud slick. The animal had traveled up the slope since the last rainfall, lacking the savvy to skirt around the muddy spot. As a result, its passing had been recorded as perfectly as any fossilized dinosaur track imprinted in Jurassic clay.

So, yes, the print definitely existed. Still, I couldn't imagine why Gunner's underling was so certain the imprint represented the foot of a werewolf. After all, its moderate size would have more closely matched a domestic canine like a Labrador retriever...or possibly a very large fox.

Did I mention that fox shifters out-mass the wild version by quite a wide margin? Kneeling down beside the track, I found my fingers stretching toward what might very well be the first sign of an unrelated fox shifter that I'd ever come in contact with.

"Don't touch that!" My hand was slapped back so abruptly I didn't even feel the sting before the shifter who had drawn us here began pointing out clues to his eagle-eyed alpha. "There's no scent," Allen informed us unnecessarily. "Note the white lines where baking soda stuck to his pads...."

"Or *her* pads," Gunner interjected, his voice so cold I cringed back away from his menacing form. Gone was the thoughtful protector who'd helped me stifle my sneezing only a few minutes earlier. Instead, Gunner had regressed into exactly the sort of terror-inducing alpha I'd assumed him to be at our first meeting.

So maybe I'd guessed wrong about Allen objecting to my presence. Perhaps Gunner was the one who wanted me gone ASAP.

"Yeah, I *guess* so," the lower-ranking shifter agreed, eyes lowered in instinctive submission as he responded to the same cues that triggered my own urge for flight. Still, the underling's tone didn't match his body language, the emphasis on "guess" suggesting he considered a female killer a profoundly unlikely hypothesis.

And after a moment of skin-saving silence, the male proved his courage by speaking up once again. "Should I run to the store for some plaster of Paris?" he asked, his voice becoming increasingly animated as Gunner's reproof faded from his memory. "I can take a casting to compare to the feet of shifters around town...."

For the first time in several minutes, I was tempted to smile. There was something so geeky about the enthusiasm infusing the underling's voice. As if arts and crafts were far more interesting than the blood and gore of a crime scene. He seemed to be envisioning a Cinderella-like hunt for our perpetrator...albeit with a much less fairy-tale ending. How surprisingly un-werewolf-like of him.

Unfortunately, Gunner shut the initiative down with the verbal equivalent of a slap. "No," the alpha growled, voice brooking no further debate. "We've learned all there is to learn here. Wrap it up and head back to base. I'm taking Mai home."

SO I GOT BACK INTO the vehicle with a surly werewolf...this time without the added buffer of teasing pack mates watching from the back seat. Only my problem wasn't the expected inability to run away from an angry alpha. Instead, Gunner opened my door like a gentleman then hesitated there on the roadside rather than slamming the barrier shut in my face.

"About earlier," he started. Then, running one hand through his hair, he shook his head as if his behavior was far too complicated to explain verbally.

"Gunner?" I asked when the silence between us had lengthened to awkward levels, half a dozen vehicles having whizzed past us on the highway. I only realized this was the first time I'd used his name aloud when my companion's scent shifted to dewy pleasure seconds before the door closed between us with a firm yet gentle snick.

Then the male was in the seat beside me, was pulling out into traffic as he headed in the direction of my neighborhood without bothering to ask where I lived. He'd clearly researched my statistics in the time we'd spent apart this afternoon. Which should have chilled me...but instead created a warm puddle of pleasure centering around the bottom of my gut.

"You need to get home to your sister," Gunner said finally, deftly switching lanes to zip past a slow-moving vehicle. "So I guess that gives us nine and a half minutes to discuss your pay rate."

"My pay rate?"

For the first time since entering the vehicle, I swiveled to face the confusing male beside me, not daring to hope that I'd heard him right. Because, possible two-sided attraction aside, I'd blown it multiple times over the course of our job-interview-turned-criminal-investigation. Why would Gunner still want me on his team?

"Funds provided for services rendered," the alpha elaborated, his tone turning honey smooth. Well, if Gunner was going to be flirtatious...then I could afford to push whatever slim advantage I might possess.

I cleared my throat then launched into the bare truth. "I need more than cash under the table," I informed him, the dour face of Kira's social worker rising up in my mind's eye. "I need a job description that sounds conventional and dependable, a weekly paycheck that I can report to Social Services. And I need seven thousand dollars on top of that, up front, to pay for Kira's school."

My requests were outrageous, but Gunner merely shrugged, taking one hand off the wheel long enough to toss his phone into my lap. "The passcode is 9653," he told me. "Text Allen and tell him what you need."

It was a good thing A came at the beginning of the alphabet, because Gunner's address book contained more contacts than I was likely to muster in ten lifetimes. Still, when I found the appropriate entry, I had to laugh. Because the plaster-of-Paris werewolf was apparently Gunner's accountant too.

"Tell him what you told me," Gunner prodded as my fingers hovered over the phone's touchscreen, unwilling to repeat my demands in print. "Five minutes until we arrive at our destination," he warned.

So I typed. I added a link to the payment portal for the academy, the email address of my least favorite social worker, and an explanation that it was me sending the text with Gunner's consent.

And the whole time I was doing so, a slender sliver of wishful thinking made me imagine what it might be like to revoke my outcast status, to have friends ready and willing to come to my aid. Perhaps that's why I knocked the previously requested seven thousand down to six thousand—surely I could come up with an extra grand from Arena fights before the deadline. It just seemed pushy to ask for so much money when my new employer was taking time out of his busy schedule to run me all the way home.

Not that the drive was a hardship in such a high-class vehicle. The faintest smile lingered on Gunner's lips when I glanced in his direction, and the SUV's brakes were silent as we pulled to a halt in front of my apartment complex seconds after I hit send. But Gunner stilled me with a hand on my arm before I could reach over to open the door and emerge from the vehicle.

"Your sister's sleeping," he noted, nodding toward the darkened window three floors above our far-too-close-together heads. "She won't know the difference if you come run with the pack tonight. I can get you home before dawn."

And with his attention turned directly upon me, the magnetism of Gunner's proximity flowed between us like the glowing magic of a star ball. I could imagine his fingers sliding across my cheekbone, his lips settling at the pulsing indentation at the base of my throat. There was so much more to this alpha than mere physical attraction. He was protective, funny, kind...

...And dangerous. So dangerous I didn't even trust myself to answer aloud as I shook my head and pushed my way out the door.

"Tomorrow then," Gunner answered before the metal barrier slipped out of my fingers and cut him off from view.

Then I was sprinting toward the dimly lit entrance of a building that suddenly felt more like a fox's underground and secretive lair than like a human's welcoming and airy residence. It took all the self-control I could muster not to turn my head and look back.

Chapter 17

I made it up two flights of stairs before the werewolves ambushed me. Was already dreaming of my sofa bed, in fact, imagining warm sheets and soft pillows while pretending there wasn't a hard bar that always ended up poking into the middle of my back. Then, in the midst of that waking hallucination, three sleek-furred four-leggers slid out of the shadows, ruffs raised and lips curled as they growled me back in the direction from which I'd come.

"Really?" I demanded, my voice a hiss as I tried to vent my displeasure without waking sleeping residents. "What do you want?"

A louder rebuttal might have done the job better. But knowing my sister, the girl would come running out of our apartment in her nightshirt if she heard a commotion. Plus, heaven forbid one of the complex's human residents stumbled out of their own residence then called the police upon sighting three wolves attacking a women so close to their home turf....

The image of Kira and cops and werewolves all mixed up into one steaming stew of catastrophe was enough to prevent me from resisting as I was herded downstairs past the entrance I'd come in through and toward the basement where a second exit opened onto the alley out back. There, though, I hesitated rather than pushing the heavy fire door open even though one of my herders lunged forward to nip at the air beside my knee.

After all, nothing good ever came out of that secluded cesspool by the dumpsters. Rushing out now with three werewolves at my back and nothing but darkness before me felt far too much like walking into a trap....

Luckily, I was now far enough away from both sister and human residents that I could afford to make a little noise. So I resisted the wolves' nudges and peered around me instead.

On my right was the laundry room, on the left was the resident storage area, and not a single human ear was close enough to hear what was about to go down. Which meant now was the perfect time to whirl and kick out at the closest shifter, grinning when he yelped at the bruise to both his dignity and to his sensitive nose.

"Back up," I gritted from between clenched teeth, dodging just in time to bypass the shifter leaping toward my unprotected neck from the other side. So maybe these werewolves weren't just here to mess with me? Maybe they were aiming for a more final end to our engagement than that?

Well, that put an entirely different spin on matters. I hadn't been willing to indulge in full-scale battle to salvage wounded pride, but I'd do a lot to protect my own skin.

Unfortunately, half of my star ball still hung around my neck where I'd left it to avert Gunner's suspicion. Which meant the sword I pulled out of its sheathe was really only half a sword, the jagged tip menacing but the internal structure flawed by its recent loss of mass. The weapon would be as likely to shatter as to stab if I thrust it into an attacking shifter....

Of course, the three wolves leaping toward me as a single unit didn't have to know that. So I bought time with pageantry, whirling the sword in complicated circles while adding in kicks and leaps possessing no function beyond looking pretty and—I hoped—intimidating my trio of foes.

All I needed was a few seconds to strengthen the metal of my sword, a few seconds to bring its molecules back into alignment....

Ah. There.

The weapon still lacked a tip, but now it rang with resilience as I tested its prowess against one of the metal bars separating the hallway from the storage room. And my opponents must have sensed the change in my body posture, because they abruptly backed away from the true menace glinting out of my eyes.

Until, that is, the fire door disappeared behind me. And before I could dodge, a hard male arm settled vise-like across my chest.

THE SCENT OF ALPHA werewolf burned like ammonia against the exposed membranes of my nostrils, and yet I found myself relaxing rather than further tensing up. Because while this wasn't the best opponent to grab me in a near chokehold, he wasn't the worst either. "Jackal," I greeted the male behind my back.

I expected the werewolf to release me, having fulfilled whatever charade he was playing out for the sake of his men. But, instead, he pulled me in closer, the subtle slide of fingers across my fabric-covered breasts suggested I wasn't quite out of the woods just yet.

And while I was willing to go quite a distance for the sake of public appearances, groping was where I drew the line. So I pulled at my star ball's magic ever so subtly, sharpening one of the buttons on my jacket until the metal boasted a razor edge. The next time my assailant's finger slid in that general direction....

Jackal stumbled backwards, a much larger cut than I'd intended splitting open the pad of his thumb. "What the—?" he started. Then, recalling our rapt audience, he straightened from his attempt to peer at my fastener, running out his tongue instead to take one long lick along his own bleeding wound.

Within seconds, crimson stained a grinning mouthful of wolf-sharp fangs while fur sprang out in a circle around both of his eyes. The male was seconds away from shifting. And, predictably, his show of bestial dominance knocked the other werewolves off the trail of any potential weakness, sending them stumbling over each other as they retreated from us both.

I, on the other hand, had been busy figuring out how to wrangle a decent conversation without our audience turning Jackal into even more of a dick than he usually was. "If you'll excuse us for a moment...." I told the room at large, batting my eyelashes as flirtatiously as I could manage. Then I grabbed Jackal's lapels and drew him into the laundry room, kicking the door closed behind our backs. A quarter in the dryer, and soon I was confident that we could speak without being overheard.

"What do you want now?" I demanded, dropping all pretense at toadying up to the male I usually thought of as one of my few allies within my home turf. "I'm tired. Tell me whatever you have to tell me, then let me get some sleep."

I expected a request or a warning, not the ammonia-scented rage that came rolling off Jackal in waves. "You're playing with fire, pup," he told me. And even though there were no underlings present, he pushed in closer, glaring down at me with teeth that were still as sharp as any wolf's. "Being seen entering the Atwood mansion after dark then leaving with that filth. What were you thinking? No wolf waltzes in here and takes over my town and my girl."

The emphatic words rolled around in my head like so many pinballs, knocking down my defenses and abruptly pushing any soothing response out of my reach. "But it's *their* territory, not yours," I countered. "Just because they've been staying close to home for the last decade doesn't mean they don't have dibs on this land."

"If you know what's good for you, you'll change that fact," Jackal answered back just as fast. His fingers were similarly speedy when he yanked a cell phone out of his pocket, tilting the screen so I could look over the crook of his elbow and catch photo after photo of my sister's smiling face.

Kira out behind the school with no one to protect her except clawless humans. Kira walking to the corner store, a time stamp proving her expedition had occurred this evening after I'd explicitly warned her to stay at home.

The pictures were a visceral reminder that my kid sister could either be helped or harmed by this werewolf who depended upon my supposed romantic interest to solidify his precarious grasp on power. The trouble was, I couldn't just lock Kira away in her room to keep her safe.

"You've enjoyed years of protection," Jackal told me as I rearranged my understanding of the situation, realizing too late that this male I'd thought my staunch ally was both more fickle and more dangerous than he'd initially appeared. "Now it's time for you to pony up. Get rid of those trespassers by the end of the week or I'll be forced to transfer my affections to a more malleable female. Your sister, I think, might just do the trick."

Chapter 18

Anger and fear carried me back up the same flights of stairs I'd traversed twice already in the last half hour. Rage turned my key in the apartment's lock and powered me through the darkened room on fox-soft feet. But once I tiptoed up to Kira's bed and found the girl snoring on her pillow, the events of the night all caught up with me at once.

An intriguing—and far too astute—alpha. A well-named Jackal nipping at the heels of those stronger than himself. A serial killer on the loose who appeared to possess my mother's missing possessions. And Kira, caught in the middle, with only me to defend her from the horrors of the outside world.

At least I still had my sword...and whatever information I could glean by tapping into my neighbor's unprotected wireless connection.

To that end, I booted up the laptop so ancient it had been discarded as useless by Kira's school a semester earlier. The power cord was frayed and only worked if bent at just the right angle—I folded the appropriate loop into place and tacked it down against the kitchen table with the weight of the computer itself. Similarly, the right-hand hinge was broken from being manhandled by one too many students, so I had to use two hands when opening the screen so as not to damage the machine beyond repair.

Finally, though, I had a browser in front of me, the colors blinding against the darkness of the otherwise unlit room. Tapping F9 with a fox's instinct for stealth, I continued dimming the screen until I was able to see again using my peripheral vision. Only then did I begin to type.

Luckily for me, Kira had saved passwords on the same device I was currently accessing. So it was the work of only a few minutes to discover that Mama's possessions had been sold off in three batches to three separate buyers. The closest purchaser was in Michigan, the furthest in California, and the amulet had been included in the latter lot.

It seemed hard to believe that someone had traveled halfway across the country to return items I'd considered junk to their original location then had used the self-same amulet to commit murder in a manner seemingly designed to implicate werewolves after the fact. Still, the listing was one of the few leads I'd come up with to date, so I noted down each address and Ebay handle to be analyzed once my brain was less desperately in need of sleep.

By that point, my eyelids were starting to slide closed and I knew I'd hate myself in the morning for failing to go to bed in a timely manner. Still, there were so many questions circling through my mind that I doubted my ability to sleep even if I succumbed to my current state of exhaustion.

Specifically, I wanted to know more about fox shifters, to answer the questions Kira had recently been asking. Mama had sworn me to secrecy as soon as I was old enough to say my own name, and I'd somehow carried that promise through to adulthood. But what could it hurt to google the concept and find out what the wider world knew about my kind? What would it hurt to educate myself about my abilities as well as the risks that threatened my sister and me?

So I pulled the screen closer toward me, placed my hands on the keyboard...then swore under my breath as the formerly lit surface went abruptly blank.

"I know better than that," I berated myself while fiddling with a funky hinge full of rather important cables. Had I pulled out an internal wire while trying to make the words on the screen a little easier to read? Or did the cranky laptop just need a little TLC to bring it back to life?

Only after several minutes of frustration did I realize that it wasn't the hinge that had caused the problem in the first place. Instead, my touch to the upper corner of the laptop had caused the power cord to unravel...and of course the battery no longer held a charge.

4:44 read the glowing numbers in the upper right-hand corner of the rejuvenated screen when the operating system finally booted back up. I waited for my mother to toss out a proverb about bad luck. After all, I remembered her warning me repeatedly as a child about the ill-fated nature of the number four.

But her ghost voice remained silent. So I pushed the memory aside, typing in my query with two fingers and a thumb.

"What are fox shifters?" I whispered aloud as words slowly materialized on the screen before me. And Google answered immediately, a single word popping up in a box above all other search results.

"Kitsune." The foreign word sent a jolt through the star-ball-turned-sword still scabbarded at my back. But when I nudged at my mother's ghost, she remained resolutely silent.

Well, if Mama wasn't going to explain my genealogy, then I'd have to do research on my own. Because familial secrets had already killed two innocent humans. For all I knew, Kira and I were next.

So I clicked through to the first website and slowly I began to read.

SOMETIME BEFORE DAWN, I collapsed onto the softest bed in our apartment...the one that already contained my comatose sister. "Ge' offme," Kira complained, words running together muzzily. Then she growled sleepily as my cold fingers snuck up against her warm scalp to thaw.

"So shift," I answered only a little less groggily. There had been so many stories on the internet, myth and supposed fact and tales labeled modern fiction. Kitsune were Japanese fox shifters—that part I could vouch for myself. But were we tricksters who only appeared human in moonlight? Or beautiful and loyal women whose reflections showcased the fox within? So many stories, and none of them seemed to reference an amulet able to suck a human's life force out of his body then leave said two-legger with a miniature star ball frozen into his chest.

So I took the easy way out and decided to deal with my heritage tomorrow. Instead of mulling over the issue further, I snuggled closer to my sister, waiting for her to pull upon her fur form and make a little extra space for me on the bed. After all, the bar in the sofa bed was brutal. I ended up here more often than not, and Kira was always willing to shift and snuggle.

Only, apparently, she was feeling argumentative tonight. "*You* shift," my sister countered, sounding more awake than previously as she elbowed me in the kidneys. Her bones were sharp and her tone was surprisingly adamant, so this time I shrugged and obeyed.

One moment I was a women frozen and exhausted, mind running in endless circles that all centered around the child hugged within my arms. The next, I was a fox, moist nose the only part of me exposed to the chilly air in our barely-heated apartment. Tucking my snout beneath my tail solved that problem, and soon I was as toasty as if Kira had let me under the covers in the first place. This was the life....

With that thought, I drifted off and slept the sleep of an innocent animal. The bed was soft, my sister was close, and vague threats could be dealt with at a later date.

Too bad "later" came far too prematurely when the kitchen door crashed open and werewolves poured into our previously solitary den.

Chapter 19

Laptop, fox, sister. Three potential weaknesses, none of which I could currently guard against displaying to the outside world. Not when my own body represented the second danger, my red fur glimmering in the full-noon sunlight that bathed our small but well-lit room.

Kira, on the other hand, was currently human and quite capable of diving directly into muddy waters without measuring the distance to rock bottom first. "What are you doing here?" she demanded while stalking toward our uninvited guests in half-dressed tween splendor. "Have you ever heard of knocking? Didn't you realize a locked door means *Keep out*?"

I itched to protect rather than hide and continue being protected, but rationality pushed me flat against the bed instead. Because if these werewolves became aware of my identity, they'd know what Kira was as well....

A heart that always beat faster in vulpine form now pounded so hard against my throat that I could barely breathe. Meanwhile, the rumpled covers that stood between me and discovery felt far thinner than they had in the darkness last night.

Kira, get back here! I wanted to scream the words, wanted to drag my sister out of harm's way. But all I actually managed was a twitch of my whiskers before an unexpectedly familiar voice soothed the worst of the terror out of my skin.

"I apologize, ma'am." I sighed out the reediest whine of relief as I realized this was Allen, Gunner's geekiest assistant. Still a werewolf and perhaps suspicious of me...but at least not currently slavering after my blood.

"We tried to call and we tried to knock," the male continued, unaware of my near meltdown, "but there was no answer. Gunner was concerned something might have happened, so he gave us permission to force entry. If you want to put on some clothes and get your sister, we'll wait...."

Terror gradually gave way to curiosity, allowing me to sniff the air and assess the situation more fully. Astonishingly, embarrassment was the key emotion rolling off these home-invading werewolves. So I risked a peek around a corner of my cover barricade, noting the way Allen looked at everything other than my sister while his cheeks turned from faintly flushed to boiled-beet red.

Aw. A baby-doll nightie on an underage female was apparently a better weapon than the one I itched to grasp into my not-yet-present hand. Kira *was* rather well developed for a twelve year old....

Still, Allen wasn't the only werewolf present. There were two bulky shifters behind him, one of whom seemed far more interested in his cell phone than in his surroundings. The other, though, was nosing around the laptop I'd been using as night faded into morning, the exact same device I couldn't quite remember shutting down properly before I stumbled off to bed.

Had the browser still been up when I abandoned the computer? Would the screen flicker to life full of damning evidence if Nosy's fingers hit the proper key sequence? Now more than ever, I needed Kira to close the bedroom door so I could regain my humanity and shut this party down....

And as if I'd called her attention to me by the force of willpower alone, my sister swiveled slightly to glance in my direction. Then her head tilted in a query I hoped was too subtle for the werewolves to make out.

The door, I tried to communicate with widened eyes and flaring nostrils. And the motion must have caught Allen's attention, because he took a step forward...only to disappear from view as Kira got the message and slammed the much-needed barrier between uninvited werewolves and myself.

"Mai's in the bathroom," my sister prattled as I yanked hard on my magic, shifting in less than a second into shivering human form. *Clothes, clothes, clothes,* I reminded myself, hopping into yesterday's wrinkled outerwear without bothering to don undergarments first. After all, forming the brilliant ball of frigid magic currently streaming out of my body into sword form was more important than panties if my goal was rushing to my sister's aid.

"Nobody's in *this* bathroom," Allen was saying as I pushed my way out into the kitchen-living-room combo.

"Well, we've got two," my sister lied through her teeth.

And before the accountant could argue about the unlikelihood of a one-bedroom, two-bathroom apartment, I was shoving my sister behind my back and slamming the laptop screen down inches from Nosy's furtive fingers. I think I heard the hinge crack all the way through in the process. But as best I could tell, no secrets had as yet been revealed.

"I'm here. My sister is none of your business," I told them. Then, dividing my glare equally between all three werewolf faces: "Now get out of our house."

"THIS ISN'T A HOUSE, actually," Allen countered. "More like an apartment. Or, if you're British, a flat."

"Your lips are moving but your feet aren't," I observed, doing my best to usher all three werewolves toward the open door via physical intimidation alone. Unfortunately, Allen was the smallest of the three shifters and even he topped me by a good six inches at a conservative guess. No wonder none of the werewolves budged in response to my attempted loom.

The phone-obsessed shifter, on the other hand, *did* deign to speak...even though his eyes remained glued to his cell screen. "Boss says to tell chica here that he's tied up at the moment but that he'll see her this evening. In the meantime, she's in charge of the investigation today."

I was in charge of three home-breaking werewolves? Something didn't quite add up. "What were Gunner's exact words?" I demanded, angling closer in hopes I could see what was so engrossing about that tiny screen.

"I don't think..." Phone Dude hemmed. At which point Nosy snatched the device out of his pack mate's hand and read the contents aloud.

"*Tell Mai I'm busy measuring my brother's cock. Back tonight. Until then, she's the boss.*"

"Told you it wasn't appropriate for the ears of a lady," Phone Dude grumbled.

"What could be more appropriate for a lady than cock measuring?" Nosy countered.

"Crow, Tank, that's *enough*."

And while I should have been laughing right along with Kira at Allen's attempt to squash his pack mates' hilarity, something warm began unfurling in my stomach instead.

"You know what they say about a guy with small feet," I'd teased two nights prior at the Arena. No wonder Gunner had turned so grumpy yesterday evening when we stumbled across an extra-small canine track near the site of the murder. Had the alpha really taken my jab so literally? And if he believed Ransom to be responsible for the killing...why would Gunner risk his most important relationship by relaying that information to a near stranger like me?

Those questions could be dealt with later. For now—"If I'm in charge, then let's investigate," I said at last, trying not to read too much into Gunner's show of trust. Yet again, I waved my hands toward the still-open door leading into the hallway...and yet again no one bothered to so much as shuffle their feet in the indicated direction.

"Sure thing, bossette," Nosy—aka Crow—answered. "Just tell us who's gonna stay here to take care of the kid and the rest of us will be on our way."

As I glanced at three waiting faces, I realized this must have been yet another order meted out by their absent leader. And while I would have scoffed at Gunner's over-protectiveness yesterday, in light of Jackal's recent comments I found myself both relieved and ready to accept.

"Allen can stay," I decided, figuring the smartest werewolf was also the one least likely to lose track of Kira if she got it into her head to play hide and seek with her bodyguard. Then, turning to my sister, I laid down the law. "You've got enough homework to keep you busy all day," I informed her. "I want to see you parked on the sofa when I get home."

Kira glanced at me, raised an eyebrow, then turned the full force of her charm upon her designated keeper. "Wanna learn a magic trick?" she asked Allen, tilting her head down until she was peering up from between dark lashes. "I'm excellent at making things disappear."

I turned to the door to hide my smile. Allen would be lucky if he made it out of this babysitting session with wallet and dignity intact.

Chapter 20

I didn't remember what day it was until hours later. Friday. The last work day of the week, when fights began early and crowds at the Arena doubled in size. I couldn't afford to miss the match this evening, not when the whole point of Wednesday's loss had been setting up a resounding Friday win.

Which gave me a limited window in which to discharge the duties of my new day job then get rid of Tank and Crow. Unfortunately, neither task looked like it was going to be easy to accomplish in haste.

"Well that was a waste of time," I groused once we'd finished nosing around the crime-scene site a second time and had returned to cruising down random city streets. Given the lack of information found at the now-cleaned-up underpass, I was beginning to think Gunner had hoped I'd spend the day spinning my wheels with the sole purpose of taking the heat off his own spur-of-the-moment trip.

And I would have been glad to oblige if I'd thought Ransom was the culprit. Unfortunately, that conclusion seemed dramatically premature. From the little bit I'd seen of the Atwood pack leader, Ransom was hotheaded and not a terribly good fighter...but none of that added up to a serial killer using Ebay-purchased heirlooms to somehow magic humans to death. I mean—what was the point? And did Ransom really possess the gumption to figure out a puzzle that continued to elude my own grasp?

Not likely. Which meant there was an actual miscreant on the loose in my city. And from the way Tank and Crow peered at me like puppy dogs expecting their master to pull a bag of treats out of her pocket, it was up to me to guide the exploration onto the proper path.

"I think we should take a look at the original body," I decided aloud, feeling my way through potential alternative avenues of investigation. After all, what better way to track down the twisted personality we were seeking than to assess his initial foray into life taking? Maybe there was a magical signature on his body that the werewolves had missed....

Unfortunately, my supposed backup turned into minders as soon as I spat out an actual game plan. "No can do," Crow said tersely, swinging into a fast-food drive-through. Then, completely changing the subject from what we were meant to be discussing: "Anybody else want a snack?"

Tank looked up from his cell phone long enough to shoot off a list of items that amounted to half a cow plus an extra-large potato field. Crow ordered all of the above plus enough sugar to rot out his teeth. And I tacked on a grilled chicken sandwich, hold the mayonnaise, plus a large ice water on the side.

"What?" I demanded once we were parked and eating. Or, rather, once *I* was eating. The guys just stared at me from beneath their mountains of food as if I'd grown an extra arm.

"You don't have to pretend to be human around us, chica," Tank told me after a moment. He patted me on the head as if *I* was the puppy...which made it hard not to snap at his patronizing hand.

"Here, have some of my fries," Crow added, holding out the cardboard carton...then pulling it back before I had time to so much as shake my head. "Or...Tank can go back in and get you your own fries maybe. Boss won't be happy if you faint from lack of food."

I scrunched my eyes shut, astonished at how drastically the reality of werewolves differed from my expectations. Here I'd spent decades shivering at werewolf shadows only to find that the sole threat from their presence was death by frustration...or perhaps exploding when I followed their lead and ate way too much.

"I have food," I growled once I finally trusted myself enough to speak. Then, remembering what I'd asked before Crow sidetracked me, I pressed my earlier point. "We *can't* go see the body? Or you *won't* take me there?"

"Can't," Tank answered.

"Won't," Crow added.

Both males spoke with their mouths full, and I had to avert my eyes before I was willing to take a bite of my own lunch. "Explain," I ordered after chewing and swallowing. Single words sometimes worked with Kira.

Perhaps similar simplicity would do the trick while attempting to whip my unlikely assistants into shape.

Sure enough, the males seemed willing enough to expand upon their earlier answers when pinned down. "We disposed of it," Tank elaborated. "Weighed it down and sunk it in the middle of the river. Can't have pesky bodies floating around for the human cops to find."

"Plus, the boss said to keep you safe," Crow added once his partner had finished. "First murder was two weeks ago. That corpse has moved on from dead to wrigglin', if you know what I mean."

I *did* know what he meant. And suddenly the grainy texture of the reconstituted chicken meat in front of me looked far too much like maggots for my peace of mind.

Closing the paper wrapper back up around the rest of my sandwich, I did my best to hold onto my temper. "So what *are* we allowed to do today?"

"Investigate," Crow answered.

"Drive around and look for shit," Tank suggested.

The pair had somehow managed to scarf down 99% of their lunch while I was nibbling through a quarter of my own small meal. Now, Crow pulled back onto the road, one last double bacon cheeseburger in his hand...well, until he shoved the entire thing into his mouth that is. "Where to, bossette?" the long-haired shifter asked around chunks of beef and pork.

As if I was the one actually in charge of this disaster. And as if we weren't wasting precious hours when I had better things to do...like preparing for a very lucrative fight.

"Turn right," I decided. "Then left at the stoplight...."

In short order, I'd found what I was looking for. A thoroughfare so packed that parking was unlikely within a ten-block radius. Even slowing down here would risk the driver's life...or at least the structural integrity of his wheels.

Which is when I opened my door and leapt from the moving vehicle, ignoring the shouts of distress behind me and the blaring of nearby horns. Sprinting for an alley, I barely caught Tank's recriminations before I shook the pesky babysitters off my tail.

"Chica! The boss won't like this!" the burly shifter howled.

But "the boss" was far too engrossed in determining whether his brother was a murderer to worry about me at the moment. So I slipped behind the awning of a bustling street cafe, ran down a set up steps, sprang over a wall, and was soon back within my comfort zone—entirely on my own.

Chapter 21

"She who chases two rabbits catches neither."

"And she who talks to the voices in her head gets locked up," I muttered back to my mother's ghost as I wound my way through the unsavory streets of the Warren on the way to my ultimate goal. I'd tugged on as many investigative threads as possible without straying far from my path over the last couple of hours. And, no, I hadn't come up with any blinding flashes of insight in the process. But it was better than trying to do the same work while dragging around two gruffly overprotective werewolves. Plus, I still held out hope that some of the seeds I'd planted might bear fruit...after the upcoming fight.

Now I paused in a shadowy alcove just outside the Arena, hasty fingers running through tangled hair while my magical senses performed the more important preparation—materializing my sword within the sheathe along my spine. The match was due to begin in a matter of minutes, and I didn't need a Japanese proverb to know I'd better get my head into the game before dashing through that door.

So, pushing away Mama's memory, I closed my eyes and focused on Dad's voice instead. My father had fought in the Arena as long as I could remember, and he'd passed along many of his tricks to me. The most important, he'd always asserted, was preparation. *"Before you start fighting,"* he'd always told me, *"remember to center on your breath."*

Closing my eyes now, I obeyed the oft-repeated admonition. Sucked in a deep lungful of air through my nose then gently relaxed the carbon dioxide away between loosely parted teeth. Whoever Ma Scrubbs had chosen as today's opponent would be more bark than bite. As long as I ignored their bluster, chances were good that I'd win...and pay the rest of Kira's tuition in the process.

"Darkness lies one inch in front of your nose."

My eyelids burst open at Mama's shrill interjection, breath coming faster as I peered around the dim alley in search of potential danger. Her words had seemed so ominous at first blush...but now that I thought about it, I was pretty sure that proverb was merely telling me to expect the unexpected. Perhaps this was Ghost Mama's attempt to help out?

Whatever the reason, I wasn't quite in the zone when I slipped in the back entrance of the Arena moments later. Sure, my sword was in my hand and my muscles were loose and ready. But the roar of the crowd made me wince as I left the shadows behind and walked out under the blinding floodlights.

Meanwhile, the words of the announcer didn't help matters either. "Please welcome Wednesday's competitors back to the Arena! Ladies and gentleman, introducing Mai Fairchild and Ransom Atwood!"

IT WASN'T RANSOM, THOUGH, who appeared on the other side of the small cage as my eyes adjusted to the over-illumination. Instead, resembling his brother enough to make the false identity work from a distance, Gunner greeted me with a grin that did odd things to my stomach. Then, taking advantage of my unconscious lean in his general direction, my opponent opened the fight with a forward lunge transitioning into a slashing stroke of the sword clasped in one long-fingered fist.

In response, I dropped to the ground and somersaulted past him, rolling upwards even as the alpha spun to trace my path. I told myself it was just Mama's unhelpful words of encouragement that made Gunner's reappearance hit me like a punch to the gut the moment I set eyes upon him. But his verbal greeting both deepened my reaction and illuminated my lie.

"I was worried," the big, scary alpha told me, a subtle tightening around his eyes suggesting he was actually telling the truth even though his sword continued to parry mine stroke for stroke. "Crow and Tank called two hours ago. Said you'd slipped your leash. The whole pack's been tearing the city apart ever since. I figured you could take care of yourself. But..."—he feinted then struck at my knees, a blow I easily blocked—"...I'm glad to see your face."

"Aw, you missed me," I countered, finding it easy to keep my words light when my feet felt as if they were walking on rainbows. Taking advantage of the emotion-fueled energy, in fact, I transitioned into one of Dad's favorite combo moves then. Bing, bang, boom. Feint, parry, attack. Gunner must have had more experience with swordsmanship than I'd expected or he would have ended up with a game-ending scratch right then.

Instead, the male proved his prowess by nearly catching me on the rebound, swiping low a second time and forcing me to leap to evade his sword. "I did miss you," he agreed, not even out of breath as he offered a stab that could easily have pierced my stomach lining. "And I'm glad to be back. Not least because we have a mystery to solve."

I inhaled as I twisted sideways, windmilling my arms then using the change in balance to launch my own attack. "I could have told you Ransom's feet weren't that little," I puffed, finally losing a bit of my composure as Gunner's blade caught mine and nearly ripped said object out of my grasp.

The scrape of metal against metal provoked a cheer from bystanders I'd nearly forgotten, widening my tunnel vision at last. The crowd members were standing on their seats now, pounding fists against the cage that locked me and Gunner in. Calls of "Ransom" and "Mai" rang out across the Arena in equal measure, and I wasted half a second hoping Ma Scrubbs was right and fewer watchers had bet in my favor this time around.

Because I was going to win. Never mind what a smirking Gunner thought as a flick of his wrist ripped my sword away to send it flying toward the chain link behind my back. My opponent might be bigger and stronger. But I needed the cash far more than he did...and I'd never promised to fight fair.

So even as the sword left my fingers, I sucked as hard as I could against the retreating magic, feeling icy tentacles sliding into the darkness up my sleeve. The shell of my former weapon clanged dully against the cage wall even as I formed a slightly smaller rapier in the same sheathe the original sword had occupied five minutes earlier.

"Never bet against a Fairchild," I told Gunner. At the same time, I reached behind my back to grab the replacement blade even as I danced forward to swipe the tiniest pinprick of a line above my opponent's brow.

If he'd seen the move coming, he could have dodged or even parried. But Gunner had thought I was out of weapons. So he stood like a rock, the widening of his eyes nearly as satisfying as the adulation of the crowd.

Unlike Gunner, I knew how to play to my audience. So I turned, bowed, turned again. And I would have bowed yet another time had I not caught a glimpse of an unexpectedly familiar face pressing up against the chain-link door.

"*She's gone*," Allen mouthed, face as white as mine was suddenly growing. The accountant didn't need to elaborate for me to realize he referred to the girl I'd left in his charge several hours earlier.

Someone had snatched Kira right out from under my nose.

Chapter 22

"Mai, wait!"

I ignored both Gunner's command and the rational knowledge that my sister might have just slipped her leash the same way I'd done a few hours earlier. Because I trusted my gut, and my gut told me Kira wouldn't risk throwing off my game on fight night just because she felt cooped up in our apartment with a werewolf babysitter.

No, if Allen was unable to find my sister, that meant someone had taken the child against her will.

So, delaying only long enough to swipe my now-hollow sword off the ground, I sprinted out of the cage and toward the nearest exit. Behind me, I could hear the alpha debriefing his underling. And while Allen's quiet words were swallowed up by the noise of the crowd, I didn't need to hear answers to Gunner's increasingly frantic "Where?" and "Who?" and "How do you know?" to send me in the right direction.

Jackal had threatened my sister yesterday and now Kira had disappeared. I knew precisely where to look to get her back.

Getting there, however, was another matter entirely. Hard elbows and heavy feet pummeled my extremities as I forced my way through a sea of human bodies that seemed uninterested in parting to let me through. And for once, I regretted being smaller than average. Because one glance over my shoulder proved that Gunner was having no problem keeping pace, the werewolf's bulk preventing the tide of humanity from sucking him under the way it threatened to do me. Too bad he wasn't willing to act as a battering ram to help me achieve my destination in a timely manner.

In fact, Gunner was not only failing to help, he was actively working against me. Or so it seemed seconds later when raised hairs on the back of my neck proved that the alpha had closed the gap between us just as a hand on my shoulder swung me around to face back in the direction from which I'd come.

"Mai, I know you're worried. But you can't run off half-cocked before we figure out what's happening...."

Werewolf platitudes. I bared my teeth, wondering if the surprise of fangs piercing flesh would be enough to remove the restraining hand so I could continue on my way....

Then a human larger even than Gunner was looming over me. The newcomer's bulk pushed the alpha backwards before the latter even realized what was happening, at which point a wad of folded bills slipped from the human's fingers into my own beneath the eddies of the crowd.

"She doesn't need to talk to me?" I asked the doorman, surprised that Ma Scrubbs was resisting her usual impulse to haggle me down from our agreed-upon percentage. Tonight, though, the sheets of doubled-over paper were an inch thick. And, for once, I had more important matters at hand than pinching pennies and counting every bill.

So I accepted the doorman's silence as implicit agreement then turned and sped through the open tunnel he'd left behind him as he pushed his way through the crowd to reach my side. Breaking out into the alley at last, I breathed in one huge gulp of much-needed oxygen. And, finally, I turned to face the alpha who I still hadn't managed to shake off my tail.

Which, apparently, was a good thing. Because no matter how I poked at the issue, one fox shifter against a couple dozen werewolves wasn't good odds for freeing my sister. So I closed my eyes, sighed, and accepted the inevitable.

"I need your help," I admitted. "Your help, and the help of your most trustworthy men."

"*These* are your most trustworthy men?"

"*This* is where you think your sister is being held?"

We were talking at cross-purposes...and, honestly, I could see Gunner's point. The local Walmart didn't top most werewolves' lists for hostage-negotiation venues. Of course, Jackal wasn't most werewolves either.

Still...Tank, Crow, and Allen were Gunner's chosen backup? I'd thought the Atwood pack's second-in-command was able to call upon more skilled manpower than the three oddballs he'd sent to my apartment to wake me earlier in the day. If I'd known we were going in with jokers as backup, I would have skipped negotiating with werewolves and instead hired a pair of human fighters off the street.

Because all I really needed for this job was two dependable allies. Too bad I wasn't so sure any of my companions were up to the task.

"I trust Tank, Crow, and Allen with my life," Gunner said levelly as he and his trio of pack mates followed me through Walmart's automatic doors, past the pharmacy section, and out into the open air of the screened-in garden center. "I don't think you heard Allen's full report, though. He lost Kira at the cemetery...."

Willingly, the spectacled werewolf began repeating the same story I'd gathered from bits and pieces tossed out during the rush to reach our current location. Since I'd already guessed the details before I heard them, though, I tuned out the male's repetition and began navigating by scent alone.

Not many people visited the garden center in early March, so I wasn't surprised to be able to pick out Jackal's trail as easily as ever. Actually, there were half a dozen pathways leading to the same location, the amount of time the male spent browsing likely dependent upon how many humans were around when he initially arrived.

And, sure enough, the freshest trail had been made mere hours earlier. No sign of Kira, but it was hard to get a handle on what exactly had happened with dozens of bags of mulch and fertilizer exuding their own overwhelming scents. I forced myself not to dream up reasons my sister's aroma might be absent, but the baking-soda-influenced paw print at the crime scene rose unerringly into my mind without my consent. If anyone had small feet, that someone would be a pack-leader-wannabe like Jackal....

"Mai, you're not even listening." Gunner was in front of me now, a wall of alpha preventing me from prying up the loose flagstone that covered the tunnel to Jackal's lair. I'd found this spot years earlier when the male first came courting, his honeyed words prompting me to tail my supposed paramour and figure out what made him tick. What I'd discovered was an underground chamber accessed via Walmart's garden center, the place he went to be alone. Since Jackal apparently thought he was the only one aware of the den's existence, this seemed like the perfect spot to stash a girl he wanted no one else to discover.

Unfortunately, there was currently an alpha werewolf standing between me and my intended destination. Meanwhile, hair-raising electricity proved that Gunner's patience was wearing thin. "Mai," he growled so intently that I gave in and wasted thirty precious seconds getting the doubter off my back.

"Kira wanted to go to the cemetery," I recited, repeating Allen's words back to them in a much condensed form. "To the pond in the middle with the huge weeping willow and the spring-fed waterfall covered in moss. That's where she always wants to go. That's where we spread our father's ashes."

"I'm sorry." The tremendous werewolf before me deflated visibly...which just made me madder since his pity was wasting yet more time during which my sister was stuck beneath our feet terrified and hopefully alone.

"Allen let her play hide and seek," I continued, managing the barest hint of a smile for the accountant-turned-babysitter who was clearly berating himself for losing track of his charge. Now that I took in my entire audience, I realized Gunner was forcing this issue for more than my sake. Allen needed to be let off the hook if he was going to be any use during the battle ahead.

"It was clever, Allen," I continued. "Don't let your boss tell you otherwise. Making Kira finish one math problem every quarter hour was a good way to keep her on track and ensure she was still hanging around while giving her a bit of breathing space at the same time. Kira doesn't like being forced to sit still and she *loves* disappearing into that tree."

Despite my words, the male in question still hung his head. "I should have kept a closer eye on her...."

"You did nothing wrong," I said honestly. "Someone snatched my sister. And now we're going to get her back."

I turned around then to face that all-important flagstone, ready to push Gunner out of the way if necessary. But it turned out my words had achieved their original goal as well as softening Allen's penchant toward self-chastisement. Because the argumentative alpha was no longer standing atop the hidden entrance, and he even knelt down to help me slide the covering aside without being asked.

The hole we revealed was barely large enough to crawl through, dirt-lined and dark as far as the eye could see. Predictably, my fox nature perked up at the close, dank confines. The wolves behind me, on the other hand, sucked in one united, claustrophobic breath.

"This is why you didn't want more backup," Gunner murmured. Like me, he was now understanding that whoever waited on the other end of the tunnel could pick off invaders at his leisure. There was no point in bringing an army to a battle that, by necessity, had to be fought one on one. I needed a single dependable wolf at my back and a few more guarding the exit. After that, the battle would turn on skill level alone....

"Correct," I answered. Then, drawing my sword, I dove into the tunnel before Gunner was able to start an argument about who'd go through first.

Chapter 23

The tunnel was worn smooth by repeated passage, but dirt still scraped off the ceiling from time to time and filtered through my hair. I ignored the itch, however, trying instead to figure out why I couldn't smell my sister's distinctive odor no matter how hard I sniffed.

Would Jackal have pushed his prisoner or pulled her? The male was lazy, I reasoned, so he'd likely kept Kira conscious so she could crawl into the darkness under her own volition. Still, my ferocious sister would have fought rather than giving in easily. She would have clawed, maybe even shifted form and bit at her captor's hand. So why hadn't her efforts left behind traces of her existence? Why didn't I smell even the faintest hint of blood?

Behind us, the scrape of stone on pavement coincided with the extinguishing of the last faint glimmer of light shining over my shoulder. And, in response, my star ball pulsed against my fingers, begging to be let out of its weaponized form so it could illuminate the pathway ahead.

"Mai?" Werewolf fingers closed around my ankle and a shiver ran up my spine. But the reaction wasn't terror. Instead, Gunner's warmth gave me the courage to continue crawling forward into the darkness, holding my star ball's illuminatory impulses in check. After all, we couldn't risk alerting Jackal to our impending entrance with a blaze of magical starlight. Our only real chance was to burst out of the hole so quickly our opponent lacked all opportunity to block the gap....

If you do not enter the tiger's cave, you will not catch its cub, Mama murmured. And this time my skull thunked into the top of the tunnel in reaction to the ghost's sudden arrival inside my mind.

"Now isn't a good time for proverbs," I retorted...then cringed as I smelled Gunner's interest behind my back. There would be questions later,

I gathered. For now, all I could manage was to push onward while ignoring both my mother's talkative ghost and the fact that I was willingly leading one very powerful alpha werewolf toward a sister who might currently inhabit the skin of a fox.

It felt like we crawled for hours after that. The space heated and dampened around us, and my pupils dilated so dramatically they began to strain against the absence of light. Then I pushed my sword forward just as I'd done a second earlier and a second before that...and the weapon slipped away from me, crashing against a hard surface within a much larger room.

Was Kira sitting with that darkness scared out of her mind by the clatter? Or was Jackal lying in wait beside his captive, crouched and smiling as he used the lack of illumination to give him the upper hand?

My sword, unfortunately, had taken the element of surprise out of our court already. So I didn't assess the danger further. Just pushed myself out of the hole with all my might, rolling sideways as I snatched at where I guessed the blade had fallen.

And it was a good thing my star ball refused to cut me or I would have ended up with a gash through my right palm to match the scab on my left. As it was, I banged my shin hard against a chair leg as I came to standing then spun in a circle as light emerged from behind my back.

"It's me," Gunner grunted as my blade cut through the air half a centimeter from his cell-phone-turned-flashlight. Not bothering to defend himself further, he lifted the device above his head and looked around.

Together, we took in a lair well furnished with stolen Walmart chic. Just like last time, the space was clean and almost cozy...if you ignored the cave crickets and spiders crawling across the uneven floor. There were rugs atop the dirt, a folded chair plus a mound of pillows in one corner, even an electric camp stove off to one side.

Unfortunately, the space was also entirely empty of anyone except me and Gunner. Neither my sister nor Jackal was there.

GUNNER RAISED ONE EYEBROW as he took in my shock and devastation. I'd been so sure Kira would be here to greet me. Had been so sure that saving her skin was worth risking our secret around this far too astute werewolf...who was even now opening his mouth to begin a debrief I couldn't afford.

But before my companion could spit out a single word, a werewolf leapt out of the tunnel behind us, shifting midair so he landed naked but human by his alpha's side. "Jackal's been sighted on the other side of the city," Crow reported, holding out a cell phone he'd carried through the tunnel in his lupine mouth. The device was wet with spittle, but I grabbed it before Gunner could close his fingers around the damp plastic. Then I peered down at the picture on the screen.

Jackal in his home turf. Two shifters I didn't recognize behind his left shoulder. No sign of my sister in sight.

"If we go into the Warren after him, he'll slip through our fingers," I observed, already considering the hundreds of exit points surrounding the city's underbelly. "He could have stashed Kira anywhere. We'll have to tempt him out by offering something in exchange."

But what? Myself as mate was the only obvious bargaining chip, but Jackal had clearly tired of sniffing after me. What he wanted was territorial rights to the city...something an alpha werewolf like Gunner would never provide.

As if reading my mind, Gunner smiled faintly. "I can think of several somethings Jackal would like to have. None of which he's getting. But it won't hurt to pretend."

The alpha nodded his chin toward the tunnel then, and Crow shivered down into lupine form before leaping back into the small space he'd come in through. Only after we were once more alone in the otherwise empty lair did Gunner take a step toward me, bending over slightly so he could peer more intently into my eyes.

"I need to understand the bigger picture if I'm going to help your sister," my companion rumbled, his voice so deep it vibrated against my bones. His proximity felt like sticking my finger into an electric socket while teetering above a bathtub—a burst of shock and awareness wrapped up in the knowledge that even greater danger lay mere inches away.

In response, I tried—and failed—to pry my lips open, expecting every minute for the male to push harder against my obvious reservations. After all, he was an alpha werewolf, used to taking whatever he wanted. And even though my fox nature made verbal compulsions roll off my back like so much rainwater, my milk-money debt worked in the opposite direction, urging me to give this particular werewolf anything he cared to request.

The wave-like crash was almost audible as the inconsistencies in my various stories collided together in Jackal's abandoned den. Lies, lies, and more lies leading to questions beyond my ability to brush off. Like—how did my half-Japanese heritage relate to the murderer on the loose in our city? And why did my sister and I choose to live on our own when female werewolves would have been welcomed with open arms by any pack...

...assuming, that is, I was actually a werewolf and that my sister was the same.

Rather than voicing the obvious, though, Gunner merely stood over me and waited. His scent embraced my body, clearing my sinuses and at the same time tightening my chest until I could barely breathe.

And as if in response to that two-sided reaction, my star ball disobeyed my earlier commandment and began glowing gently. It was only the faintest flicker of illumination, and Gunner now held two cell phones to beat back the darkness. Still, I knew he noticed when the scent in the den turned from salty dominance into spicy intrigue.

"Mai?" the male murmured at last. "Is there something going on with your sword?"

I couldn't answer, but I also couldn't lie while my debt held me within its power. So I broke the moment in the only way I was capable of. I ignored the way his gaze raised hairs up and down my spine, stashed my disobedient weapon away beneath my clothing, then padded toward the tunnel in three quick strides. After that, I crawled into the hole so quickly I bruised both elbows and knees against the hard earthen ground.

Gunner slipped in right behind me, his broad shoulders catching on the walls and slowing him down in areas where I could slither straight on through. Still, I didn't take advantage of the opportunity to flee when I emerged amid a ring of interested faces.

After all, while Gunner might suspect everything, he knew nothing. And until Kira was safe, the watchful werewolf was still the best ally I currently had on hand.

Chapter 24

"*The talented hawk hides its claws,*" my mother noted as Gunner's SUV pulled to a halt in front of my apartment complex. And despite my best attempt at maintaining a poker face, I was pretty sure I jolted visibly at the internal commentary yet again. So it was a good thing any astute alpha questions were cut off by an interjection from the back seat.

"One hour," Tank informed us, looking up from his phone for the first time since we'd entered the vehicle. "Jackal says he'll meet us at the southside McDonald's at 11 pm. He wants Mai there."

I nodded, already pushing open the SUV door in relief. I'd be too frazzled to think straight if I spent the next sixty minutes in these wolves' presence...especially with the ghost of a mother hovering at the back of my mind. So a little time to stuff Mama back in the corner where she belonged—and to finally pull on a pair of panties to stop the chaffing—seemed like a gift from the gods.

Unfortunately, a hand reached out to close around my left wrist before I could make good on my escape. "You're not going to run," Gunner informed me, the words a question disguised as an order.

"I just need time to shower and catch my breath," I replied honestly. Well, that, plus the leeway to pull my brain back together. Mental hygiene, physical hygiene—it amounted to pretty much the same thing. "I'll meet you there."

"We'll pick you up," Gunner countered, but he *did* release my wrist. And even though I could feel the alpha's eyes boring into my back as I strode to the apartment building's entrance, the vehicle was gone when I peered back through the fogged glass from inside.

Only then did I lean my forehead against the tiny square of window, close my eyes, and speak to the ghost who seemed intent upon hounding my every move. "Any ideas, Mama? On how to get Kira back?"

"A frog in a well does not know..." my mother began, only to lapse into silence rather than finishing the phrase.

"Doesn't know what, Mama?"

I was talking to myself in an empty stairwell, I realized as I spun in a circle hoping for more words of wisdom from someone who had died soon after Kira was born. Despite that self-awareness, however, I waited longer than I cared to consider, hoping the ghost would return and at least finish her sentence if nothing else.

But, at last, I was forced to admit my solitude. So I walked up the stairs alone, padded down the hallway with my hand on my star-ball-turned-sword...then froze as I took in a small rectangle of paper tacked to the outside of my apartment door.

FOR HALF A SECOND, I thought Kira had come back and left me a note so I wouldn't worry. That she'd just been teasing Allen, had forgotten tonight was fight night, had let her mercurial fox nature get the better of her considerate human mind.

Then I stepped closer, took in scrawled handwriting nothing like my sister's looping script. Knew Kira was well and truly taken and wasn't going to be returned easily or willingly to her home.

Because I couldn't smell my sister here any more than I had done in Jackal's underground hideout. Couldn't smell anything, actually, except the metallic bite of baking soda that matched the trail of human-shaped footprints following the path I'd just taken from stairwell to door.

Then, behind me, the trickle of a melody. Not a whistle this time, but the actual tinkle of Mama's music box emerging from the stairs I'd just walked up.

The killer was here, in my apartment building. And not bothering to think through the fact that, even in my frazzled state, I wouldn't have overlooked someone standing in the stairwell, I sprinted back in the direction from which I'd come. Thundered down the stairs so loudly residents pounded on their walls and swore at being woken. Pushed through the heavy fire door at the front entrance...and peered out into a seemingly empty street.

There was no one there. No one to match the trail of baking-soda footprints that disappeared as soon as it hit uneven pavement. No scent of shifter, no sound of music box, no magic tugging at my star ball and leading me toward the sister who should have been safely snuggled in her bed upstairs.

So, shoulders slumping, I looked in both directions one last time then climbed back up the stairs far more quietly than I'd rushed down them. And as I did so, I paid attention this time to the footprints, measuring their length in my mind's eye. The tracks were larger than my own feet but not so large they were definitively male...nor so small they were definitively female. The tread screamed athletic shoes but the stride was shorter than my own, suggesting whoever wore those sneakers didn't often use their gear to work out.

Which meant my visitor could have been about 80% of the people in the city. Good luck using that evidence to make an arrest.

Refusing to be disheartened by the lack of information, I made a beeline for my apartment as soon as I stepped out onto the third floor once again. The note was still there, the words gradually materializing as I puzzled out the pointy handwriting that had initially resembled nothing more than bird tracks in the snow.

And as I read, I gradually sank forward until my forehead rested on the scuffed surface of the door frame. Because the message was worse than expected, nothing like the overt threat Jackal would have offered. Instead, the words were polite, cultured...and marked the death knell of the secrecy that had protected me and my sister for the last twenty-five years.

"The artifacts aren't working as advertised," the note-writer informed me. *"The young fox is not an adequate guide. Come to the South Street bridge at midnight to renegotiate. Don't make this poor child suffer by bringing werewolves along."*

Chapter 25

I unlocked my door like an automaton, leaving it hanging open behind me as I headed into the kitchen in a daze. *It's happening.* The exposure I'd guarded against for decades hovered over my head like a storm cloud.

Good thing I'd gathered everything necessary to guard against the impending rain.

So I didn't enter Kira's bedroom to rail against her absence or take a much-needed shower. Instead, I climbed atop a wobbly kitchen chair and rooted around in the back of the cupboard for several long minutes, seeking the coffee neither Kira nor I drank.

Ah, there it was. Pre-ground crystals, still aromatic within their unsealed container. Pouring out the entire mess into the sink, I snatched up the ziplock bag of fake IDs that was revealed as the coffee grounds flowed out.

"Am I interrupting something?"

Good thing I was a fox or I would have fallen flat on my face when the lanky social worker waltzed through my door without bothering to knock first. As it was, the ziplock bag slid from suddenly nerveless fingers and I had to use a tendril of my star ball to nab the slippery plastic before it fluttered toward the floor.

Still, my voice was serene as I denied the truth to Simon's face. "Of course not. Just making coffee. Want some?"

As I spoke, I jumped down off the chair just a little too lightly to appear human...then made up for that lapse by scraping the wooden legs loudly across the floor while tucking the article of furniture back into its usual spot. I could almost hear Mr. Grouchy downstairs growling into his comforter, wanting to know why I couldn't keep banker's hours like everyone else...which might have explained why Simon was here. Had an ornery neighbor called Social Services just because I'd been too loud after dark?

I wasn't given time to pursue that supposition, though, because Simon responded with an easy "Sure," catching me off guard as he called my hospitality bluff for the very first time. What, now he wanted coffee? After years of politely evading my offers of tea and cookies? Of lifting his hands off the table when he accidentally brushed the surface, as if my bad housekeeping would rub off at a touch?

Unfortunately, while the sink was full of coffee crystals, the apartment possessed no brewing apparatus. And I wasn't even sure we still had a mug after Kira's most recent juggling attempt.

So I utilized one of my favorite game plans—when in doubt, go on the offensive. "What are you really here for?" I demanded, realizing as I spoke that there was no need to toady up to this social worker any longer regardless of his current reason for invading my home. Because, sure, for the last decade Simon had held the key to my happiness in his clammy fists. But Kira and I would shortly be starting over in a new community...and this time her ID would say she was over eighteen.

"To see your sister," the social worker replied, then proceeded to drawl out more explanation than he really needed. "I realized Kira wasn't here last time I spoke with you. Doesn't look like she's here now. Where is your ward?"

As he spoke, the male's eyes trailed across the combined kitchen and living room. And as Simon searched for a girl who was very obviously not present, my brain caught up with the adrenaline that had been coursing through my veins ever since the social worker barged in.

Wasn't his current behavior a little beyond the pale, even if the neighbors had called to report me? Since when did city workers make house calls late on a Friday evening? And why was he suddenly so intent upon seeing Kira?

My gut told me to get out of there, the sooner the better. And I trusted my gut. So I pasted on a smile and lied between my teeth.

"At a sleepover with a friend," I answered, mentally shuffling through the contents of the apartment as I spoke. Was there anything else Kira and I couldn't live without? Not really. My sister had sold Mama's last possessions, I kept all of our cash in my pockets, and our mother's star ball had recently been hanging out on my sister's person. Everything else was just so much jetsam ready to be thrown overboard as we abandoned ship.

"I'll go see her there then," Simon answered, breaking into my musings and accepting the deflection more easily than I'd expected. "What's the address?"

I was tempted to rattle off a fake street number then push the human out the door. But instinct told me he wasn't going to leave so easily. Might call in a coworker to check out my story while he kept me talking, wasting time I could use to get my sister back.

So I parried rather than feinting. "Give me a minute. I'll hunt it down for you," I offered before slipping into the bedroom and closing the door in his face.

Then, just as I'd done two nights earlier, I gave into my fox's urge to flee the premises. It was ten times easier to do so in Kira's bedroom than it had been in that gas-station restroom, the window here a little larger and the fire escape on the outside providing an easy pathway to the ground.

"Hey! Wait!" Simon's face appeared at the window sooner than anticipated. But I didn't pause or answer, knowing his long arms and legs would take far too long to slip through the small gap after me. Instead, I just ran down the metal steps with heavy footfalls that once again wakened the neighbors. Then, knowing I was irredeemably cutting off all possibility of retreat, I slunk into the shadows and disappeared into the night.

Chapter 26

Unfortunately, I'd traversed only half a block when the scent of werewolf rose up around me. "Going somewhere?" Gunner demanded as he stepped out of an alcove to block my path.

I flinched backwards, wishing I could pretend I was still the same person I'd been one hour earlier. Then, I'd been glad for this male to join me. Yes, he was trouble. But he also seemed to possess a gentlemanly willingness to set aside my secrets in an effort to bring Kira back.

Now, though, my cards were face up on the table and I couldn't afford dragging an alpha werewolf along for the ride. So I hesitated one second longer than I should have...at which point Gunner struck.

Between one eye blink and the next, his hand was inside my pocket. Then the ziplock of fake IDs emerged squeezed between skillful fingers despite my attempt to twist away. "I..." I started...only to freeze as his other arm landed like a manacle around my waist while the first pried open the plastic bag.

"You're running," the alpha growled, his breath hot against the top of my head. He paged through paper and plastic that Kira and I would need to create a new life together, his voice turning chillier with each flipped over item. "Is your sister even missing? Or is that just another lie?"

"I've never lied to you," I countered, contemplating ways to free myself from my captor's handhold. Despite our size difference, I could have used his ill-considered grip to throw Gunner over my back so I could flee while he lay winded on the pavement. Or my star-ball-turned-dagger could stab the pesky werewolf in the gut for a more final form of freedom than that.

And yet I hovered indecisively, kicking myself for being unwilling to make a move against Gunner. My Arena fights had gone south many times over the last decade, with dozens of matches ending in hospitalizations rather than a simple scratch on the cheek. So why did the mere thought of injuring a werewolf make me shiver uncontrollably now?

No matter the reason, my opponent didn't miss the change in mood. His arm softened as he pulled me in closer, and his next words were midway between human speech and werewolf growl. "Tell me what's wrong and I'll fix it," the male murmured.

He sounded so solid, so dependable. But before I could answer, the decision was taken out of my hands. First came a yip followed by a single howl...then the cacophony grew until lupine voices were erupting all around us from over a dozen throats.

The newcomers must have scouted the scene before announcing themselves, because they weren't coming from one direction alone. Instead, they'd blocked passage down the street in both directions, north and south pathways equally cut off from the potential for retreat.

I spared one quick glance toward the alpha who still held me up against him, hoping this was merely Atwood backup finally making themselves known. But, of course, Gunner would never have allowed such overt wolfishness in a human neighborhood. So I wasn't at all surprised to see the alpha's eyebrow's rising while the air around us filled with the unmistakable tang of fur.

Nope, the encroaching pack wasn't friendly. And, based on their numbers, Gunner and I were dramatically outmatched.

"PUT THIS SOMEWHERE safe, then shift."

The ziplock of IDs whizzed toward me even as Gunner spun away to peer down the darkened street in both directions. And while I *did* take the time to carefully stash the bag into an inside pocket, I just as overtly disobeyed the alpha's second command. After all, donning my fox form would have been sure suicide. So I molded my star ball into a sword instead and came to stand beside Gunner on two human feet.

"You'd be safer as a wolf," he observed, although I noticed the male made no move to follow his own advice. Then, when I didn't answer: "I don't suppose you have another sword I could borrow?"

"Here." I hoped the darkness was deep enough so my companion couldn't see my rapier narrowing by half as I pulled a second weapon out of the sheathe along my spine. Star-ball metal was strong if formed properly, so I wasn't worried that even a half-width blade might fail to do its job.

What was more concerning was whether being separated from so much of my magic would dull my reaction time. Strangely, I felt stronger rather than weaker as the not-quite-solid weapon slipped into my companion's waiting hand.

Gunner nodded his thanks briefly before calling out into the darkness as the click of nails on pavement grew audible against the night. "Last chance to talk out our differences. Don't start something you're going to regret."

It was a nice gesture on his part, but none of the enemy shifters currently possessed human vocal cords with which to reply to him. Nor did they have any interest in backing down. Instead, they sprang upon us in two synchronized waves, yips and snarls preceding fur and claws by barely enough seconds to allow me to angle my sword toward the shadows rushing toward me out of the night.

After that, nothing but fangs and growls mattered. And I had to admit that even my star ball wouldn't have been enough to keep me afloat had I been flying solo. But, back to back with Gunner, we were able to fend off the attackers even if we failed to gain actual ground.

The night was dark and the wolves were many, so it took me quite a while to figure out who we were fighting against. *Jackal*, I realized, picking out the white-ruffed wolf even as I sliced a wicked wound through the hamstring of his second in command. Had I been wrong in my reassessing of the situation? Was my pretend boyfriend the strangely polite note-leaver who had snatched my sister off the street in pursuit of an agenda of his own?

As if sensing my confusion, Jackal shimmered upward into humanity even as two of his pack mates attempted to take me down from the left and right. Good thing Gunner had eyes in the back of his head...or at least the alpha fought as if he did. Knocking one wolf onto its tail with a rather impressive side kick, my partner opened up enough space so I could swipe a welt across the other wolf's nose.

Then Jackal was standing naked in the middle of the street without concern for shifter secrecy or human modesty. "You made the wrong decision, little girl," he told me, advancing forward until he stood just beyond the reach of my sword. "I would have protected you. This filth will not."

In reaction, Gunner growled deep in his throat, his back muscles tightening where they pressed up against my own. But my companion didn't turn his head to answer, just kept attacking and parrying while providing leeway in which I could speak.

"I want my sister back," I demanded, ignoring Jackal's insults and cutting straight to the heart of the matter. "What is it you want in exchange?"

And to my surprise, my opponent's brow furrowed while his head tilted to one side. "You want your sister *back*?"

I had just enough time to realize Jackal had no idea what I was talking about—that he hadn't been the kidnapper and note-writer and presumably had no notion that I shifted into the form of a fox rather than that of a wolf. But before I could decide how that understanding changed the face of the current battle, Gunner roared behind me...and a strange lethargy flooded my limbs.

Meanwhile, a gleaming *something* whizzed away into the darkness even as my legs began trembling with their effort to hold me erect. I whimpered like a puppy, my vision turned muddy, then—to my eternal chagrin—I fell onto my knees.

Chapter 27

I was vaguely aware of an unpadded shoulder cutting into my belly as blood rushed to my upside-down head. Then I was lying flat on my back atop a foul-smelling dumpster, Gunner's hands rubbing heat back into my limbs.

"Damn it, wake up!"

I wasn't unconscious and I tried to tell him as much. But the attempted words instead came out as a moan even as the scent of fur dampened into bitter-almond concern.

Gunner dropped his sword, I realized, the words materializing far more slowly than they should have as my own star-ball-turned-weapon throbbed in my clenched right fist. Which explained why I was suddenly weak as a newborn kitten, unable to do more than roll over onto my side and strain against the darkness in search of the other half of my soul.

To my relief, the second sword hadn't entirely disappeared into the night. Instead, it was clearly visible twenty feet distant, lying at the feet of a snarling werewolf. If I could just....

Before I could muster sufficient energy to do anything, though, Gunner was tilting my torso upright and piercing me with the intensity of his gaze. "Mai, talk to me."

He sounded so desperately worried. And even though I knew I had more important matters to contend with, I succumbed to the fuzzy need within my belly. Raised my left hand. Trailed two fingers along the knife edge of his jaw...

...then jerked aside as skin-on-skin contact hit me like an electric shock. Even the mud in my brain settled in that moment. And this time when I yanked at the distant sword with all of my remaining vigor, the weapon gradually dislodged itself from the ground and began dragging itself toward my wiggling fingers.

Meanwhile, I did my best to stem Gunner's angst by letting him know I wasn't actually perishing at his feet. "I'm fine," I told him...the words coming out more like "I fie." Unfortunately, from the whiteness surrounding the alpha's lips, my consolation hadn't hit its intended mark.

But I'd be able to mollify my companion with fully-formed words sooner rather than later. Because the sword was arcing up toward us now, slicing through the ear of a werewolf who had been attempting to scramble up the sheer side of the dumpster protecting us from the melee below. The four-legger yelped and Gunner whirled...and I did the only thing I could think of to prevent my companion from seeing a sword break the laws of physics as it flew upward toward our perch.

I allowed the weapon in my right hand to dissolve into starlight then used those freed digits to pull my companion's head down toward me. After that, I kissed him, our lips merging together even as metal-turned-magic reunited with my grasping left hand.

Hot and sweet and rough all at once, enchantment and sensation exploded inside me in a jumbled mixture that could have been pure passion or might have just been the energetic reunion with my star-ball-turned-sword.

Either way, I didn't have long to ponder the issue. Because Jackal was no dummy and his henchmen had access to human fingers if they chose them. So it didn't take long for several two-leggers to build a ramp of debris leading to our aerial retreat while others maintained their four-legged forms to serve as the vanguard. Now, muzzles mounted the dumpster, hot breath sneaking down the top of my boots while blood-crazed eyes glowed against the night.

"Shift!" I ordered Gunner, breaking our connection as quickly as it had begun and pushing backwards out of his arms. For half a second he continued to hold me. But then the alpha's eyes cleared and sharpened as the air filled with incipient fur.

Gunner must have assumed I intended to join him in four-legged battle. Because he didn't spare me a second glance, just dropped down into the form of his wolf, fragments of shredded clothing spraying out around him. And while I would have liked to once again stand back to back with the alpha and fend off Jackal's underlings, our kiss had re-awoken the count-down timer inside my head.

If Jackal wasn't the kidnapper, then someone else was out there threatening the life of my sister. And that someone had left me a very small window in which to reach the South Street bridge.

There was no world in which I chose to ignore the mandated meeting. And, given the contents of that note, it was safer to do so without being trailed by even a friendly wolf. So as Jackal's army leapt up onto the dumpster one after another, I backed away rather than raising my sword and diving into battle. Gunner growled at the intruders, protecting me with his body...and I took advantage of his lapse of attention to slide through the cracked window behind us and leave my overprotective companion-at-arms behind.

I WAS USED TO TRAVERSING the city in solitude. So why did I suddenly feel so queasy as I left the alpha to fight off a dozen werewolves with nothing but his claws and teeth?

"Gunner can take care of himself," I muttered under my breath, guilt dogging my footsteps as I ran down graffitied steps and entered the nearest subway station. I'd evaded Pickle Breath and three of his cronies along the way, the teenager's presence suggesting he'd been dogging my footsteps earlier as a paid lackey of the werewolf I'd recently fought against. But neither shifter nor human would be able to follow after metal wheels and the press of humanity eradicated my trail.

I pulled out bills to feed the fare machine...then inhaled sharply as I realized what I held within my hand. Ma Scrubbs' doorman hadn't presented me with a big wad of twenties this afternoon the way I'd expected. No, these were hundred-dollar bills, far more than I would have expected to rake in over the course of a month, let alone from a single night's work.

I hesitated, but a far-too-close howl returned me to my senses. There was a train incoming and I needed to be through those doors before anyone caught up and followed on my heels....

So I pushed the bills deeper into my pocket, zipped the closure, then rushed through the turnstile at a sprint. And twenty minutes and two transfers later, I was emerging from the underground maze with the breeze off the river ruffling through my hair.

I'd made it. Ten minutes early even, the brightly lit bridge arching over water that flowed endlessly underneath. And sure, I lacked a game plan. But I trusted my fox senses and my star ball to get me out of any pinch.

Plus, there was always the Arena windfall to consider. Maybe Kira's kidnapper would be willing to trade my sister for cold, hard cash?

Padding away from my destination rather than toward it, I took in the bridge a second time out of the corner of one eye. The kidnapper would have arrived hours earlier, I suspected, both to scout the area and to ensure I didn't appear at the head of an army of werewolves. So I wasn't surprised when flickers of movement materialized into dark-coated figures scattered hither and yon across the open expanse...wasn't surprised but was prompted toward deeper stealth.

There were half a dozen of the watchers. One pretended to read a newspaper on a bench by the bus stop, one walked a dog down the sidewalk, and two lingered on nearby rooftops.

It was the sixth waiting figure, however, who gave me the clue that my initial read of the situation had been dramatically off kilter. His sedan idled down by the river, the glow of a cigarette lighting his stubbled face. The male looked like any hardened criminal, but his car was too blocky and well-maintained to mesh with that disguise....

I took a step back, adrenaline flooding my bloodstream. Because while I'd thought I was walking into one kind of trap, it appeared I had instead nearly stumbled into another.

These men weren't aligned with Kira's kidnapper. No, these figures keeping eyes peeled for newcomers were instead entirely human. They were city cops.

Chapter 28

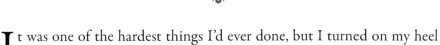

It was one of the hardest things I'd ever done, but I turned on my heel and walked away from the only clue I possessed pertaining to my sister's current location. I maintained a disingenuous saunter until I rounded the corner, then I broke into a slightly superhuman run.

The note on the door. I saw the small, white square in my mind's eye as vividly as if I was actually standing on the well-worn carpet in the apartment building's third-floor hallway. I'd read the kidnapper's missive, had hurried inside to hunt down forged identification documents...then had forgotten all about the scrap of paper when Simon's presence sent me scurrying down the fire escape to beat my retreat.

Of course Kira's pesky social worker would have found the note. His broad shoulders had no chance of fitting through that window, which meant Simon would have left via the more traditional route. When he closed the door, the square of paper would have been staring him in the face, adding mentions of werewolves and artifacts to my earlier evasions about Kira's current whereabouts. No wonder he'd contacted the police department and set up an amber alert, then sent out a net of officials to scoop me up.

It all made perfect sense...and, unfortunately, turned Kira's future even murkier than it had been before. Because human authority figures sniffing around my trail meant that the one open channel of communication between myself and my sister's kidnappers had just slammed shut in my face.

Inhaling deeply through my nostrils, I reminded myself that I wasn't entirely out of resources just yet. The city was dark but far from sleeping as I angled my way into the red-light district, planning to hit up acquaintances who kept their ear trained to the street. Unfortunately, a string of prostitutes and black-market thiefspawns slammed their doors in my face one after another. And at the end of the block, the fear widening Joe Sly's face as soon as I entered his establishment suggested my usual resources had a more unified reason to clam up.

"Just let anyone who's interested know that I'm willing to negotiate," I told the bartender rather than bothering with a question he was clearly unwilling to answer. "I won't be reachable through the usual channels. But they *can* call me on this cell." I rattled off the numbers of a newly bought burner phone then waited impatiently as Joe failed to write even a single digit down.

"I don't know who I'd give this to," the vertically challenged old-timer muttered, glowering up at me from beneath bushy brows. He was lying through his teeth, I noted...which confused the issue further. After all, as best I could tell, Joe was entirely human and didn't have a clue about shifters' existence. If it wasn't sharp-toothed werewolves putting the fear of death into him, then what sort of terror would keep this leathery survivor from even passing along a measly note?

Kira's round face rose in my mind, and this time I succumbed to the urge to beg. "Please," I said. "I'm hunting for my sister...."

Joe gave me the fish eye, but the male *did* eventually write down my digits. Still, I had a sinking suspicion he was going to ditch the napkin as soon as I turned my back.

The pulsing neon lights strobed behind me as I stepped outside, tucking my chin deeper into my coat. It was turning colder by the minute, so I wasn't entirely surprised to feel the soft chill of snow landing atop my cheekbones as I turned my face up toward the sky.

"Now would be a good time for vague hints, Mama," I whispered starward, figuring the drunken teenagers behind my back were too engrossed in whooping it up to notice I was speaking to nobody but myself. Unfortunately, I really did seem to be talking to snowflakes only. Because no answers were forthcoming even from inside my own head.

I WANDERED FOR HOURS after that until the first glint of dawn overcame the glow of half-strength streetlights. A businessman had offered to pay me for sex, two frat boys had made an even less successful attempt at pushing me to the pavement, and I'd been roundly ignored by all permanent residents of my home turf. All told, I was exhausted, frustrated...and scared to death that Kira's kidnapper would harm my sister due to circumstances beyond my ability to control.

"Don't make this poor child suffer..." The polished nature of the written words didn't lower their threat value one iota, and I shivered as I remembered the homeless guy hidden beneath the bridge with the imprint of Mama's medallion frozen into his chest. That could be Kira if I didn't find her quickly....

But I'd twisted metaphorical arms all night, and now my contact information was almost certainly flowing down the grapevine between myself and whoever held my sister hostage. Which meant I might as well take cover and ensure no nosy cops found me while I waited for the kidnapper to call.

To that end, I ducked into a dank public bathroom, tucking clothes and personal belongings into a star-ball-created yoke around my stomach before donning the body of my fox. Nosing out from under the stall door in red-furred splendor, it was easy to hop up onto the sink then slither out the broken window placed just underneath the eaves.

For half a second, I teetered there atop the chipped concrete, breathing in the freedom of becoming a fox. Snow was falling harder now, the white blanket covering up grime and making the city appear both clean and new. And I couldn't help thinking how much Kira would have loved the snow storm, how her eyes would sparkle while her cheeks turned pleasure-pink.

Today, though, Kira would enjoy neither snowmen nor hot chocolate. Instead, she was caught in the grasp of a shadowy force dark enough to make even Joe Sly run scared. No wonder focusing on my sister resulted in a sharp pain within my gut.

But...wait...was that ache merely remorseful wallowing? Or was something else going on?

Because between one gust of snow-laden wind and the next, the burn had gained a direction that tugged my vulpine feet forward. Merely swiveling my body to face north lessened the agony momentarily. And when I hopped to the ground and took one tentative step in that direction, my stomach warmed and the pain lessened...only to bubble back to burning agony when I planted my furry feet rather than continuing along the indicated route.

It was never a good idea to get caught up in unknown magic. But I'd been wandering aimlessly for hours and was glad to be pulled in any direction, even a bad one. So I didn't try to resist the tug further. Instead, I sprinted north out of the Warrens, twisting and turning down curvy alleys guided by the compass within my stomach.

I stopped only once to bite ice balls out from between my paw pads. The snow was growing deeper now and the day had warmed just enough for the heat of my skin to melt fluff into ice. But my muscles tensed and I barely managed to pause long enough to catch my breath before the tug in my gut yanked me forward. And I somehow wasn't surprised when Mama's voice sprang to life with yet another warning I couldn't puzzle out.

"Hang out a sheep head to sell dog meat," my mother's voice noted. And as I panted, pressed against the side of a building, I realized I knew exactly where I was for the first time in over an hour.

The nearby houses had turned huge several moments earlier, but my tired brain hadn't made the obvious connection until I recognized the cavalcade of parked cars half-covered by blankets of white. In my defense, snow stifled scents and blowing particles obstructed vision, so it was hard to tell I was walking directly into danger until werewolves rose out of the white haze before me while the overwhelming scent of Atwood finally filtered into my nose.

So that's what Mama meant. Walking up to the ruling werewolf's den in the body of a fox was a recipe for disaster, and I could only hope it wasn't already too late to hide whatever secrets I had left. So I pushed upwards into humanity then shivered as bare feet froze upon contact with an ankle-deep layer of snow and ice.

Chapter 29

"Tank, Allen, Crow," I greeted the trio, tension melting off my shoulders as I took in the identities of the males emerging out of the swirling snow. Unfortunately, my relief was short-lived because none of Gunner's pack mates returned the greeting. Instead, Tank and Crow shifted into fur form without bothering to remove their clothing first, while Allen lunged sideways on human feet to cut off my easiest avenue of escape.

They know what I am. To my eternal chagrin, I neither fled nor attacked in the face of this culmination of my recurring nightmare. Instead, I stood there, naked save for the not-quite-fanny-pack around my waist, trying to decide whether I could get away with yanking a sword out of the ether without sealing Kira's fate as well as my own.

After all, it was still possible the trio hadn't noted my white-tipped tail and vulpine whiskers when they first came upon me in the snow....

While I hesitated, the pack's accountant cleared the air. "The boss was disappointed you ran off and left him," Allen informed me, his words a rough growl backed up by the hard knock of his shoulder against my own. And maybe the night spent scouring the city in search of my sister had exhausted me more than I realized, or maybe I was just shocked by the bitter violence emanating from a once-gentle shifter. Whatever the reason, Allen's blow threw me off balance...then a wolf to the back of my knees sent me toppling over into a drift of snow.

Frozen water crystals molded around my body like a not-so-warm trenchcoat. But it was the increasing pain within my gut that left me doubled over...that plus a realization of why I'd been drawn to this mansion in the first place.

My debt to Gunner. Of course. I owed the alpha three bucks plus interest. And whether he'd called in the tab intentionally or by accident,

I still found myself crawling away from my attackers and toward the building's rear entrance rather than saving my skin by beating a hasty retreat.

Unfortunately, the werewolves around me must have thought I was trying to flee rather than accepting my comeuppance. Because snarls tunneled through the snow clogging my ear canals, then wolf teeth scraped against the naked skin of my calf.

In response, my star ball pulsed against frozen fingers. The magic wasn't subtle enough to understand the consequences of forming armored long johns or spiked garters when I was currently buck naked. Instead, it pushed me to provide guidance. Should we attack or defend?

"Neither," I began, the stab of agony spreading from my belly into my temples making it nearly impossible to speak. But the word didn't entirely materialize since my cheek was now pressed against a snow drift. Instead, I coughed as I inhaled a mouthful of solid snow.

I lay there spluttering, unable to twist aside as a second wolf pounced upon what little bit of my face was currently accessible. Foul breath wafted into my nostrils even as the wound in my leg deepened sufficiently to impinge upon the pounding in my head and gut. These weren't the same cheerful pack mates who had ferried me around the city yesterday. Instead, I was facing angry werewolves out for enemy blood....

Which is when I lost track of self-preservation and let instinct take over. Yanking at my fox nature in terror, I prepared to disengage and flee in my agile vulpine form.

But my shift was blocked by the debt dragging me toward the now invisible mansion, and I wasn't able to so much as twist out of the duo's tightening grasp.

"I'm sorry, Kira," I murmured as I stopped straining against the impossible. It was finally time to admit defeat.

"LET HER UP."

Gunner's command would have been more welcome if his tone hadn't been as cold as the snow packed between my butt cheeks. So it wasn't terribly surprising that his underlings obeyed the spirit rather than the actual letter of his order. Tank and Crow *did* let me go long enough to regain their own humanity, but Allen took advantage of the lull to haul me up by my hair. Then naked two-leggers regained the holds recently relinquished by lupine jaws, this time grabbing my arms in a vise-like grip that was no more yielding than their teeth had been.

Meanwhile, the snowfall was easing up around us, which made it easier than it would have been previously to see the tall male figure stalking down the mansion's rear path toward our circle of trampled snow. And I cringed as I took in the bandage crossing Gunner's cheekbone, the bruises around his throat, and the way the alpha walked with an ill-disguised limp.

The odds *had* been badly stacked against him back by my apartment, especially after I'd abandoned the male to duke it out alone. Gunner was lucky he'd made it out of that dog pile alive, and his current existence was no thanks to me.

"I'm sorry," I started...only to lose track of apologies as the phone in my fanny pack buzzed angrily against my belly. Of all the moments for my trails of bread crumbs to finally bear fruit, now was *not* the time for Kira's kidnapper to call.

Unfortunately, the hands gripping my arms only bit in tighter as I attempted to reach for the potential lifeline. And there was no warmth in Gunner's eyes as he watched me struggle in silence for one long second before I accepted the futility of the attempt.

"Someone more important you need to talk to?" the alpha asked as I stilled, proving that his shifter ears made him well aware of the call that would soon be shunted over to voice mail. He stalked one step closer until I was sandwiched between so many male bodies my breath caught within my throat. And, despite everything, my skin still tingled as the alpha's warm breath blew miniature tornadoes through my ice-streaked hair.

"I was wrong about Jackal," I answered as quickly as I could while trying to remember how many times the phone had buzzed at me already. Three, four? Would Kira's kidnapper try again if I didn't pick up, or would this be my second strike that knocked my sister's rescue off the table for good? "This call is..."

I didn't even manage to get out the rest of my sentence before Gunner reached toward my belly, feeling for the zipper that didn't actually exist. *Open,* I bade the star ball, and the alpha's scent sharpened as the cell jumped out into his extended hand.

Then the screen was glowing between us, *"Unknown name, unknown number"* filling the small rectangle. I stretched toward it even though I knew Tank and Crow wouldn't release me. And secretiveness or no secretiveness, if I'd been able I would have pressed the appropriate button with the power of my mind.

Unfortunately, I wasn't that powerful. And the alpha before me didn't appear ready to soften his stance anytime soon either. "If you want to answer, you'll promise to stop running," Gunner growled, still up in my face.

The air between us was so full of fur and electricity that I nearly choked on my next inhale. Still, I managed to nod. And when Gunner raised his eyebrows, clearly requiring verbal confirmation, I breathed out a vow that dug debt-bearing claws yet deeper into my gut. "I promise."

At which point the fingers holding back my right arm loosened, allowing me to snatch the cell phone out of my companion's extended hand. I slid damp fingers across the slick surface, relieved when the call picked up. Then I turned my back for the barest illusion of privacy while pressing the cold plastic up against my ear. "Yes?" I answered, the single word all I could muster using long pent-up air.

"You've just about blown it." Ma Scrubbs' creaky old voice was the last one I'd expected to wend its way out of the speaker. But as she continued, the entire charade suddenly made far too much sense. "I've turned Kira over to the client," the old woman who loved money above all else informed me, "so you'd better turn up fast."

Chapter 30

"Ma, don't do it!"

"I've told you before that I'm not your mother." I could imagine the old woman puffing herself up the way she used to when I trailed into the Arena on my father's heels, a lanky teenager with dreams even larger than my sword. Ma Scrubbs had doled out tough love then, but there was no affection mixed into the harshness of her voice when she continued now. "I'm looking out for number one. About damn time you did the same."

Then the cell phone was no longer pressed up against my chilled cartilage. Gunner had snatched the device away, transferring the call over to speaker phone in the process. "Where is Kira?" he demanded.

My companion's words were so full of alpha electricity that they would have easily compelled a werewolf to reply. But Ma Scrubbs merely laughed. "Hey there, boy scout. Whatcha gonna offer me in exchange?"

"What do you want?" I couldn't believe it, but Gunner was negotiating with the woman. Was apparently willing to offer any of his rather astonishingly large array of assets in exchange for my sister's life. Within my belly, the milk-money debt grew into a dragon...and I willingly allowed its foothold to increase.

Ma Scrubbs, unfortunately, was less impressed by the offer. "Naw, naw, I got what I wanted. The client's funding my retirement. I'm off to the Caribbean. Or maybe the Mediterranean. Never could keep those warm-water oceans straight...."

"Ma!" I couldn't help myself. Because Kira was in the hands of someone who'd used kitsune magic to murder at least two people recently. Given the obvious danger of that situation, Ma Scrubbs couldn't just offer a vague warning then hang up on me....

Unfortunately, the only response I came up with beyond her name was a strangled growl. So it was probably a good thing Gunner continued his negotiations without any loss of steam. "But think of how nice it would be to live in a mansion rather than in a straw hut during your golden years. Give me a routing number and I'll transfer over a million bucks. All you have to do is tell me where Kira is right now."

"Money first," Ma countered. "And you'd better hurry. The client is already on his way to pick her up."

Nails bit into my palms, but I forced myself to remain silent. I wasn't helping matters by emoting. Somehow the werewolf beside me was able to able to speak the old woman's language better than I could, so I might as well let him continue blazing the path.

"You give me an address and we'll transfer funds during the drive over," Gunner replied smoothly, proving my point even as he began pushing me toward one of the waiting vehicles. Without requiring nudges of their own, the alpha's three underlings slid into seats while pulling on clothes soppy with melted snow. Tank and Crow got in the front, Allen aimed for the third tier, and the middle row sat open and waiting to thaw my frozen skin.

But rather than joining the other werewolves inside the steaming vehicle, I found myself shifting from foot to foot in ankle-deep snow while Gunner completed the deal-making aspect of the morning. "I'm a boy scout, remember. You know I'll keep my word," the alpha growled when Ma Scrubbs' silence proved her unwillingness to pony up before she was paid.

"Better hold him to that, girlie," Ma said after one last moment of endless consideration. And I could hear in her voice that she, at least, understood the secrets I didn't want revealed.

"Yes," I answered, voice catching in a way that caused all four werewolves to eye me oddly. But then Ma Scrubbs was rattling off an address that was far too familiar, giving me something new to worry about.

Because the old woman hadn't stashed Kira anywhere easy to access. Instead, she'd stuck my sister in the Warren, where Jackal's riled-up wolves ruled the roost.

THERE WERE SO MANY zeros on the screen of Allen's cell phone that I gulped. Still, I'd accepted the debt already. So I busied myself pulling my leather jacket out of the star-ball-turned-fanny-pack, hoping no one noticed that the space was far too small to contain such a bulky object without the assistance of magic. Meanwhile, I promised aloud what my kitsune nature required as recompense to the alpha pressed far too close against my side. "I'll pay you back."

Was I just imagining the faint smile quirking up the corner of Gunner's lips as the debt within my belly ballooned from draconic to sea-monster size? Probably. Because all he said was: "Let's worry about that later." Then his eyes widened as they returned to the road.

"*Stop*," he ordered, his alpha command causing the male behind the wheel to slam on the brakes before easing up his foot and pulling into an empty parking space.

"Boss?" Allen asked from behind us, leaning over the seats to peer over his alpha's shoulder. "I thought we were in a hurry...."

"Cops," Gunner noted succinctly. And now that he mentioned it, I *could* just barely make out the taillights of stalled traffic three blocks ahead. Still, the leap from there to a police barricade...wasn't really that great once I remembered that every policeman in the city was likely staring at pictures of Kira's and my faces at the present moment. A fact Gunner now knew as well as I did since I'd clued him in to all relevant details during the five minutes we'd spent on the road.

"*The weak are meat. The strong eat,*" my mother murmured inside my head. And even though I only narrowed my eyes slightly, I was pretty sure Gunner didn't miss the fact that I'd just been graced with another missive from my maternal spirit. Instead, his eyes bored into mine like icicles. And despite the heat blowing out of the vent above my head, I felt very much as if I was back outside, standing naked in the snow.

Yes, I hadn't mentioned my kitsune nature or the dead-mother-voices-in-my-head during the hurried debrief. So sue me. At least I wasn't actively running away.

"We can park here and get there easily as wolves," Tank noted when no one else suggested a game plan. "The destination is only four blocks away."

For a werewolf, the idea was a good one. But for a kitsune.... I needed to arrive two-legged if there was to be a single sliver of hope that Kira and I might survive our upcoming meeting with skins intact.

So I pushed open the car door without speaking, preparing to make tracks away from the werewolf who represented both my greatest asset and my greatest weakness wrapped up together in one overbearing package. I had no plan. Just an instinctive urge to reach my sister before anyone could threaten her further.

But I wasn't actually able to force a single foot outside the vehicle. My debt was holding me far too strongly within its grip.

"No, we'll walk there two-legged," Gunner decided after what felt like an eternity. "Crow, you take point. Allen and Tank bring up the rear. Whatever happens, your top priority is to protect Kira and Mai."

Chapter 31

Something about Gunner's command unstuck my feet and allowed me to slip out of the SUV without waiting for my companions to follow. But electricity pulsing against my skin promised werewolves were fast on my heels as I turned into the first of several alleys too narrow for a vehicle to traverse. I'd have little time to cover up any fox-related lapses before the quartet reached my sister's side....

And, in the end, Gunner's proximity turned out to be an asset rather than a hindrance. Because as I barreled around a corner without bothering to scout for danger, a growling werewolf stepped directly into my path. His distinctive scent of strawberries and asphalt was entirely unfamiliar, suggesting he wasn't one of the dozen or so shifters I'd smelled within Gunner's compound. Meanwhile, the greedy smile on his face suggested he had a very specific idea of what to do with me.

But whether the male was a new initiate into Jackal's army or merely a drifter with murder on his mind, I wasn't a lone fox any longer. Instead, pounding footsteps behind me soon turned into four angry shifters surrounding me in their midst. And before I could speak, Gunner reached out and smacked the strange male upside the head.

"What are you *doing*?" The strawberry-asphalt shifter sounded more surprised than angry, although Gunner's answer had enough rage embedded in his tone for both of their sakes.

"Preventing you from making a very unfortunate mistake," the alpha answered. Gunner's body seemed to double in size as he loomed over the other shifter, and—predictably—the weaker wolf cringed away from his alpha's disdain. "I told you to keep Ransom back home in safety. And the backup I requested was meant to block off the Warren's perimeter only. Why are you here rather than with him?"

"Chief Ransom decided…"

I didn't bother waiting for what seemed inclined to turn into a string of excuses. Because if this male was an Atwood werewolf, then I had no need to hang around and listen to the dressing down of a subordinate. Kira's life hung in the balance and I had more important places to be.

So I slunk sideways, unsurprised when Gunner's eyes flicked away from his underling to latch onto me. He didn't call me back, though. Just nodded at his men to stick to my heels as he finished his own task.

"The early one wins," Mama murmured as my feet once again slid silently over snow-lined pavement. And I didn't even flinch this time, just continued winding through the maze of alleys that stood between me and my ultimate goal.

Because I was beginning to guess where the twists and turns were leading me. Sure enough, moments later a grand old opera building rose mid-block, its slightly decaying edifice elegant against the snow. I didn't need to check the address to know this was where Ma Scrubbs had stashed my sister. Not when the derelict structure should have been empty…and yet a string of large footprints led up to and away from the front door.

An equal number of people appeared to have walked out as had initially entered, but I didn't take that assumption for fact. After all, I was frantic rather than stupid. And I was pretty sure I'd caught the scent of Pickle Breath a mere block distant, the teenage hoodlum's presence in the wrong place at the right moment suggesting Jackal wasn't far away.

I didn't want to draw attention to myself so close to where—I hoped—my sister waited. So instead of taking the direct approach, I slipped around the side, found an unlocked window, and shimmied my way through. My werewolf bodyguards swore beneath their breath, too large to follow. But I ignored their recriminations, tiptoeing out of the changing room without pause and heading down a narrow hall.

"…shift for me and we'll call it even." The voice emerged as I neared the stage entrance. Robotic, uninflected, as if someone had used a computer to anonymize their existence. Meanwhile, I smelled my sister's terror…but caught nothing else beyond stale notes of long-absent beings filling the massive space.

My fox senses bade me to scout the surroundings further, to spend time figuring out what kind of trap waited for me atop the stage. But Kira gasped, and I didn't hesitate. Instead, I stepped out into the open...and saw the sister I'd sworn to protect dangling twenty feet above my head at the end of a rapidly fraying rope.

"KIRA, SHIFT!" I YELLED up at her, vaguely taking in the laptop lying near my feet. The screen was blank, the webcam pointed toward the ceiling. Someone had gone to a great deal of effort to capture the visual of a shifting kitsune...and yet that still appeared to be the only way for my sister to escape from the deteriorating harness that rucked up beneath her armpits.

"I can't," Kira moaned, her face so white it might as well have been coated with the snow still falling outside the theater. "I sold the star ball to Ma Scrubbs so we could pay our bills. I *trusted* her, so I followed her out of the park like an idiot when she came up to me today...." Kira caught her breath against a sob, straightened her spine, then returned to the matter at hand. "So I *can't* shift now," she informed me. "Not without Mama's star ball. I *could* untie the knot, but then I'd just *fall*...."

And now the entire messy endeavor finally made sense. *That* was what Ma Scrubbs had initially pawned off on the killer. *That* was what the shadowy being was trying to find a way to unleash—the true power of a kitsune's star ball. Magic that could move at least metaphorical mountains if placed in the wrong hands.

The repercussions of fox-shifter magic entering the mainstream were potentially earth-shattering, but I couldn't find it within my heart to care at the moment. Instead, I eyed the series of catwalks that would allow moderately easy access to the space near the ceiling. Ma Scrubbs' people must have used the elevated walkways to hook Kira onto the end of a fly-line in the first place. I could just follow their lead and reel my sister in using the reverse of their actions....

Or so I guessed in the split second I spent taking in the setup. Unfortunately, the rope my sister dangled from had been sawed three-quarters of the way through, and her weight now tested its limits. Even as I watched, yet another strand broke free.

"Mai!"

I'd been responding to my sister's distress cries since she was an infant. So I didn't need the tug on my gut to send me scurrying toward the ladder leading upward. My feet thundered across the first catwalk even as I was plotting my approach, and I turned left to angle closer...only to find twenty feet of open air gaping between myself and the suspended child.

Clever, Ma. The old woman's helpers had strung Kira up, then dismantled the most relevant part of the catwalk behind them. Of course they had. They wanted to ensure that the only way out of Kira's conundrum was to leap away in the body of a fox.

Which my sister couldn't do...but *I* could.

"Untie the knots," I told Kira, knowing as I spoke that she would make short work of even pulled-tight tangles. After all, replicating Houdini's coffin-in-the-river trick had been one of her favorite afternoon activities in lieu of homework...well, without the underwater part. I'd had to put my foot down somewhere.

Ignoring the urge to leap without looking, I gauged the distance even as I slipped out of my clothing piece by piece. I couldn't jump that far as a human, but it would be easy in vulpine form. Assuming Kira untied herself in the interim, my body slamming into hers should take us both to the catwalk on the other side. And, after that, we'd be home free....

"Look down!" my sister demanded one second before I tugged at my star ball and seized my animal form. My eyes flicked in the indicated direction, and I swore beneath my breath as I noted five faces peering up out of what had formerly been an entirely empty audience hall.

Gunner and his trio of pack mates stood just inside the main entrance as a unit...and if they'd been the only ones present I might have come out on the other side of my upcoming transformation alive. After all, my employer had proven himself thoughtful and trustworthy. Surely he'd understand that I wasn't evil merely because I'd been born allied with an inner fox.

So it was really the fifth face that pulled the breath out of me. Ransom. I recognized Gunner's brother from our fight at the Arena. Knew even though the distance was too great to pick out his features that the male's brow was lowered as he tried to understand what I meant to do.

Because a wolf couldn't make the leap from catwalk to child. Nor could a human. I'd only manage to save my sister if I took on the body of a fox.

Gunner might give me time to explain before tearing me to pieces. But his brother was a pack leader in charge of hundreds of werewolves. He'd toe the party line and sign my death warrant himself.

On the other hand, a nearly inaudible snap promised that Kira's rope was fraying rapidly. And she was suspended above a spine-shattering expanse of unyielding floorboards.

By my estimate, we had less than ten seconds to save her. So I shrugged off the future, ignored my audience...and, at long last, I found my fur.

Chapter 32

Foxes are world-class climbers and pretty good jumpers. But I wasn't just a fox. I was kitsune—ten times better than that.

So my muscles vibrated with tension as I ignored the chatter beneath me. I breathed into my stomach as Dad had taught me. Then I pushed off, nails snagging on gridded metal as I launched myself into the air.

Wind rushed past my fur and my sister giggled in delight before me. She could feel the buzz of woken star ball expanding my lungs, could sense the pure freedom that filled my heart as I embraced the form I was meant to wear.

I was a fox for five short seconds only. Had rebuilt myself into a naked woman even before slamming into a blessedly unhindered Kira. Our arms melded, our forms twisting sideways. Then we were landing half on, half off the exact catwalk I'd been aiming toward.

Or make that Kira three-quarters on and me three-quarters off the unyielding metal. "Don't fall!" my sister cried, clutching at my shoulders as I slid over the edge until only fingertips kept me aloft.

And, with a pop of returning air, vision that had narrowed into catwalk-sister-catwalk expanded back out to include the rest of the world. Snow blew in a broken window, the metal platform vibrated beneath me, and twenty feet below the world erupted into snaps and snarls of a dozen werewolves at least.

I couldn't afford to glance down, though. Not when Kira was clinging to my arms while the sway of the catwalk suggested someone rushed upward to finish the job gravity and overconfidence had begun. Clawing against the metal, I attempted to drag myself back onto the horizontal surface. After all, if I lost my nerve and my grip, who would keep my sister safe?

A broken fingernail sent a streak of agony shuddering up my spine as gravity stretched fingers closer and closer to the edge of the metal. Now I was clinging by one and a half hands only, the pain of ripped keratin causing two fingers to slip loose.

Meanwhile, the shouts from below had grown louder, as if I was already falling toward the pitched battle beneath my feet. I wasn't going to be able to chin my way back onto the catwalk, I realized. Not from this awkward angle more beneath than to one side of the surface I was attempting to attain.

"Stand back, Kira," I gritted out as my sister once again tried to help me rise and nearly toppled over the edge in the process. If I fell, I'd shift to fox form and survive, damn the consequences. On the other hand, if Kira fell then this entire rescue would have been for naught. I knew which scenario I preferred.

Of course, my sister was a pro at ignoring things she didn't want to hear. Laying down on her belly, she managed to reach all the way under my armpits this time. "You're not falling," Kira proclaimed, her voice angry even though a stream of tears dripped from both eyes to plop onto my chin.

"Kira, I'm serious," I started. "It's not going to kill me...."

And then Crow was there behind her. Was pushing my sister aside as he lifted me back onto the catwalk as easily as if I was a child. "Come," the werewolf told us, not even out of breath as he lashed out to grip both me and Kira by one arm apiece.

The hand in question latched down with predictable werewolf firmness...then Crow's fingers twitched away as if the ability to become a fox was somehow contagious and likely to rub off on him. The male eventually forced himself to regain his grip, but I took advantage of the lapse in order to glance below.

As earlier sounds had suggested, the theater was now filled to the brim with shifters, some in human and some in lupine form. There were so many that they'd pushed the building's earlier occupants out of the aisle and onto the stage then surrounded Gunner and his compatriots within a nearly seamless wall of human hands and lupine teeth. Still, despite the milling mass of movement, my eye was immediately drawn to the four small figures who had watched in horror as I shifted several moments before.

Ransom, Tank, Allen...and Gunner, whose earlier bruises were now hidden beneath streams of blood running down his arms and face.

Just as in the Arena, my employer was intent upon protecting his brother at his own expense. Unfortunately, this wasn't a battle to first blood. Instead, as I watched far-too-familiar werewolves attack in a badly coordinated yet still overwhelming wave, I winced at the growing carnage beneath my feet.

Jackal's not-quite-pack had found us. And they seemed intent upon taking Gunner and his brother down.

I SHOULD HAVE CHEERED at the realization that most of the males who knew my secret were floundering beneath enemy attack. But, instead, I ripped myself out of Crow's still-lax handhold, assessing my options as I backed away from my captor's advance.

There were two ladders extending down from this particular section of the catwalk, I noted. The one Crow had been pulling us toward led left toward a rear entrance currently devoid of battling shifters. The other led right directly into the heart of the melee.

My fox nature suggested that turning left was a fine idea. Flee, protect my sister, and live to fight another day.

But I couldn't tear my eyes away from Gunner, who was now grunting out a muddled combination of battle rage and breathless agony. And no wonder since two wolves were latched onto his ankles while a human-form shifter layered punch after punch upon the alpha's unprotected chest and neck. Gunner was putting every ounce of energy he had into shielding his brother, which meant his own body was taking a beating even a werewolf couldn't stand up against for long.

It was four against approximately four million. And Kira was safe, Crow's arm encircling the girl's shoulders not to restrain her motion but rather to ensure the girl wouldn't tumble over the edge of the catwalk should she lose her footing on the descent.

For a split second, I couldn't understand why Crow thought touching me was akin to picking up dung with his bare hands while Kira was a porcelain doll in need of protection. Then I remembered that no one had seen my sister shifting. That given her lack of a star ball, Kira wouldn't be showing off her fox form in the near future either. Surely a pack of boy scouts wouldn't let an innocent twelve-year-old come to harm....

So I chose the un-fox-like path of helping the precise male slated to execute me. Chose the right ladder instead of the left.

"Wait, I'm coming with you!" Kira cried, properly assessing my decision one instant before my feet began to move.

But she was currently safe and Gunner wasn't. So sprinting toward the proper ladder, I slid down the rungs like a firefighter and landed directly in the heart of the melee.

Chapter 33

I was vastly outnumbered, but I'd also brought a sword to a wolf fight. No wonder the furry bodies parted before me like so many rabbits fleeing from a sharp-taloned hawk.

Unfortunately, I'd left my clothes up on that catwalk, and wolf teeth are quite effective against unprotected human flesh. Fangs clamped down around my ankle one instant before I whirled and sliced a gash along the biter's hipbone. And even though he released me with a yelp, I could feel the blood puddling atop my foot as I continued on my path.

The pain was minimal, though, compared to the agony of those before me. Because I could still see Ransom and Gunner, their heads barely visible across the sea of two-legged and four-legged opponents who had them so badly outmatched. Allen and Tank must have both donned their animal shapes for protection, but their pack leaders stood tall above the others...or as tall as they could be while fighting off dozens of werewolves with what appeared to be the a pipe wrench and the leg of a wooden chair.

They weren't just outnumbered; they were drowning. No wonder Ransom's left arm hung limply against his side while Gunner appeared to be favoring his opposite leg. I redoubled my efforts to reach them, pushing forward one slow step at a time even as I kept my ears open for any hint that Kira wasn't making good on her escape.

Slice and stab, duck and lunge. At first, only the closest members of Jackal's pack had realized I existed. But now half a dozen enemies peeled away from the Atwood brothers, arrowing directly for me instead. *Spilt water will not return to the tray,* Mama noted unhelpfully, breaking into my realization that coming down here by my lonesome hadn't been the brightest idea after all.

We were losing. Of course my sword wasn't enough to make up for a horde of enemies. Ransom bellowed as a wolf broke through his brother's defenses, an agonizing scream sounded far too much like it had come from Allen's lips, and I was still too distant to make any difference in the end game that was about to go down....

But then the front doors were flung wide open and twice as many werewolves entered with Tank at the head of the charge. So the rough-featured shifter hadn't gone lupine. He'd instead fled to rustle up far more backup than I'd thought the Atwood brothers had waiting on their beck and call.

And just like that, the tide shifted. Now it was the Atwood pack who outnumbered the enemy. Meanwhile, the newcomers were also better trained in working together, their force splitting seamlessly into two groups that looped around the perimeter of the stage area while a third arrowed directly toward their bosses in the center of the action.

"And I guess I'm not needed here anymore," I murmured, leaping up onto a piece of stage furniture that had been left behind after the theater's final production. I'd avoided the high ground previously because it led away from the center of action rather than toward it. But Gunner didn't appear to need me after all....

Before relief could relax tensed muscles, though, the floor shuddered beneath my feet as something huge thundered into the outside of the building. A quieter clink of metal against tiles sent my head swiveling in yet another direction, then smoke erupted at floor level as black-clad figures raced in through every entrance point.

Wolves and two-leggers alike gagged and yelled in confusion as a gas-masked human emerged from the haze. "Call off your dogs and come out with your hands up!" the spokesman demanded, his words expanding out from a bullhorn to take over the entire space. "This is the police. You're all under arrest."

BOTH FOLLOWERS OF JACKAL and of the Atwoods fell to the ground without regard to alliances, hacking and coughing as tear gas broke through the battle fervor that had previously held them in its grip. Luckily, the air was clearer atop the scuffed table. So I held my breath, leapt, and barely managed to land on the closest ladder as police in riot gear streamed in every door.

"Stand down!" Gunner called across the roiling mass of mist and bodies beneath me, his voice breaking off into a desperate coughing fit halfway through the final word. But the simple knowledge that the alpha was well enough to give orders spurred my footsteps, and I managed to reach catwalk level before being forced to inhale a breath of my own.

Up here, the air was just barely breathable...and my sister, I noted was still very much present rather than having been rustled out the back door as I'd hoped she would have been. "They're fine," she told me, pointing toward the center of the battlefield where Gunner and Ransom were currently being cuffed and frog-marched out along with all the other two-legged shifters.

Unfortunately, Kira's reassurance hadn't reached only my own ears. "There's the kid!" a cop yelled from beneath us. And while his words really should have been lost amid the whines of teary-eyed werewolves, several other officials peered upwards as he spoke and moved to join in the charge.

Meanwhile, next to the wide-open front door, one tall, lean figure pushed through the sea of ailing werewolves toward us. I tried to tell myself this was just another police officer heeding the call of his compatriots, but the male's excessive height and skinny frame provoked the sinking suspicion that Kira's social worker had caught up with us at last.

It was time to get the hell out of there. But even though I turned in a frantic circle, I found no windows through which we could escape. No doors had been left unbarricaded either. And each ladder now had multiple cops streaming up its rungs.

"The bamboo that bends is stronger than the oak that resists," Mama murmured. Bending? She probably meant not only surrendering but also appearing human. So, sucking in my breath, I relinquished my weapon and donned clothes the magical way, transforming myself from naked warrior into no-really-I'm-just-an-average-civilian as quickly as I could.

Beside me, Crow's eyes widened as my weapon poofed into nonexistence. Then his fists clenched as thin filaments of magic streamed across my skin before coalescing into a cream-colored garment that might have been overlooked from ten or twenty feet away.

Up close, though, the effect was in no way overlookable. Crow had been sent to watch over me and Kira, but I could tell he was now second-guessing the decision to help me back up onto the catwalk rather than pushing me off its edge earlier. What his alpha would do when Crow reported my lapses remained to be seen....

Then the police were ripping Kira away from us, were slamming me and Crow face down into the catwalk and snapping handcuffs around our wrists. "You have the right to remain silent. Anything you say can and will be held against you in a court of law."

Too bad Gunner's mild-mannered cousin wasn't present this time to talk us out of our current predicament.

Chapter 34

We reconvened on the pavement outside, policemen working their way through the crowd and handing out tickets right and left. There was no way to take all of us into custody, but I figured we'd each end up with hefty fines. The lucky combatants were the ones who'd remained four-legged and were released into the custody of a supposed "owner" with no more than a pat on the head.

I, on the other hand, wasn't so fortunate. "What were you trying to do with the child?" one policeman demanded, wrenching me back around to face him when all I wanted was to enfold my sister in yet another well-earned hug. Kira hadn't been wearing either a coat or hat when she was taken yesterday, and I didn't like the way her teeth were chattering now.

"I'm her guardian," I countered...then paused as the same lanky figure I'd seen earlier stalked toward me out of the crowd. Sure enough, when the male ripped off his gas mask, the social worker I'd eluded one day prior emerged from behind the covering.

"You *were* her guardian," Simon countered. "No longer. I'm taking Kira into protective custody."

"But..." I started, only to be cut off once again, this time by the sound of a shifter's voice emerging from behind my back.

"You're taking a child away from her only living family? For what reason, may I ask?"

I turned, half expecting Liam to have arrived after all. But, instead, Tank stalked forward, looking no more prepossessing than he had when I saw him last. The male's nose had been broken then reset improperly many years earlier, his eyebrows fuzzed upward to take over half his forehead, and he weighed more than both the cop and the social worker combined.

Despite those facts, however, the male's voice was urbane as he pushed his way into our little grouping, placing one hand possessively upon my back.

"Who are you?" Simon demanded, attempting to separate me from the intruding werewolf. Tank was approximately as movable as a brick wall, however, so the social worker had little luck tearing us apart.

"Ms. Fairchild's lawyer," Tank answered easily. He pulled out his billfold, removed a card that did, indeed, list his job title as "Attorney-at-law." The paper was heavily textured, the letters gold-embossed and well-scripted, and I could see the cop measuring up the likelihood of ending up on the wrong side of a civil case...and finding the odds not at all to his liking. Perhaps that's why the uniformed officer took one huge step backward, leaving me alone with the social worker and the wolf.

Unfortunately, Simon was less easily intimidated. Sometime between last night and this morning, he'd apparently decided that I was an unfit guardian for a child, and he wasn't any more willing to back down now. "Social services has the right to withdraw any foster child from temporary custody without notice," he started.

"And Ms. Fairchild has the right to sue your ass back into the Stone Age," Tank replied. This time, I could smell the waves of fury radiating off the male shifter, and I wasn't surprised when Simon's fight-or-flight instincts kicked in at last. After all, humans might not be aware of the existence of werewolves...but their lizard brains knew how to protect their own skins.

"I'll be bringing this matter to my supervisor's attention," Simon said after one long moment of loaded silence, snatching the business card out from between Tank's extended fingers. But he didn't argue the matter further. Just stalked away, leaving me alone with yet another werewolf who'd recently seen me shift into vulpine form.

LUCKILY FOR THE SAKE of my skin, Tank seemed even less interested in my secrets than Crow had been earlier. So instead of tearing into me verbally, the male left without another word, fancy business cards spreading through the crowd like confetti as he squared away matters with officer after officer until every Atwood wolf had been released from custody.

Which left me to warm up my chilled sister...who, I belatedly realized, was no longer hovering by my side. I vaguely recalled an EMT pulling Kira away to check her vitals a few minutes earlier. But now the tween was invisible, lost within the milling crowd.

And the number of bystanders appeared to be growing larger by the minute. I didn't recognize even half the faces around me, suggesting that Ransom's backup forces had been even more extensive than they'd appeared from my elevated perch in the theater. No wonder Jackal stuffed his driver's license back into his wallet after a policemen relinquished the rectangle of plastic, glaring at me only once before leading his underlings stiff-leggedly away into the snow.

I had little interest in future battles, though. Instead, I pushed between rock-hard shifters, searching for a sister who resolutely refused to be found. "Kira!" I called, not wanting to bring any more attention to myself than was absolutely necessary but driven to desperation by the absence of a sister who had disappeared without a trace only a day before.

I smelled her before I saw her. Caught a hint of caramelized sugar seconds before a raised hand waving in my direction from the other side of the street. "I'm fine!" Kira told me, voice filled with just as much wounded dignity as if I'd forgotten her age and had warned her to look both ways before crossing the street in front of her sixth-grade compatriots.

And despite everything, my lips curled upward in response. Kira was the ultimate tween, certain of her own abilities and craving independence. I loved the fact that even dangling from a rope in an abandoned theater hadn't robbed her of that trait.

Unfortunately, my own resilience wasn't through being tested. Because the search for my sister had drawn the exact sort of attention I'd been hoping to avoid.

"Mai." My name slid across the crowd like a snake stalking its dinner. And I was pretty sure that in this scenario, I was the featherless baby bird.

Chapter 35

Unwillingly, I turned away from Kira and sought out the alpha who had watched me shift less than an hour earlier. Gunner must have heard Crow's side of the story already, must be rewriting all of our past interactions in light of recent events....

Only, it wasn't just Gunner glowering at me from across the thinning gathering. Instead, both siblings stood shoulder to shoulder, their features so similar a stranger might have found it hard to tell them apart.

To me, though, the males were night-and-day different. Because Ransom's eyes were filled with amusement—had he somehow missed my fox fur party before all hell broke loose? Gunner, on the other hand, boasted muscles clenched so tightly I was pretty sure nobody would have been able to pull the stick out of his ass.

"Come here," Gunner growled once he saw he'd gotten my attention. And to my despair, my feet began moving in his direction no matter how hard I fought the impulse with my rational mind. It was the debt, I realized. The dragon of an owing that I'd willingly allowed to sink its claws into my flesh while Kira was caught in the grasp of someone who'd already murdered two innocents at least.

The more I fought, though, the more control slipped through my fingers. So I wasn't even able to glance sideways by the time we three settled beneath an awning and out of the snow. Instead, I peered straight ahead, noting that the huge male bodies raising my heart rate also blocked the entrance to a pawnshop. Unfortunately, it was far past closing time. So no one came out to drive the werewolves away and set me free.

"Well," Ransom said at last, breaking the silence after we'd stood there for several long seconds, nothing but white breath flowing between us in the cold. "A fox."

He paused, and for the space of one hopeful breath I thought maybe the local pack leader didn't know whatever secrets made bearing star-ball magic so dangerous for me and my kin. After all, I wasn't privy to that information. Why should a werewolf be more knowledgeable about my own heritage than I was?

But then he continued: "A kitsune. An offense punishable by death."

"My sister isn't like me," I started, lying about the one thing that truly mattered. My own fate had already hardened into certainty, but I could at least ensure Kira slipped out from beneath the descending ton of bricks before they landed on her head. "We're half-sisters. Same mother, different fathers...."

"...strange, then that fox nature travels down through the mother's line." Ransom smiled at me then, his teeth so sharp they gleamed despite the gray of incipient snowfall. He'd apparently researched this subject, or perhaps had been raised to hunt foxes at his father's knee.

Wherever Ransom's savvy came from, it was clearly bad news for me and Kira. And my first impulse, as always, was to count on fox agility to ensure my escape. To run through the crowd and snatch my sister then flee together until both Atwood brothers faded into a vague memory from our past.

But the debt didn't let me twitch a single muscle away from my current companions. And now Gunner was sliding closer to back up his sibling, fist clenched and brow lowered as pure aggression radiated off his skin.

ONLY, GUNNER DIDN'T face me when he finally interjected himself into the conversation. Instead, his shoulder slid between me and his brother, making promises that contradicted his unwillingness to meet my eye. "I'll take care of this."

"Hmm, yes, I do believe you will." Ransom had appeared to possess a weak underbelly in the Arena, where his brother persisted in protecting him at every turn. But now I began second-guessing the notion that Ransom was the underdog. Because the elder sibling appeared plenty authoritative at the moment, his mere presence making it difficult for me to breathe. "If you don't want me to deal with these two kitsune in the traditional manner," he informed his brother, "then you'll keep them far away from the heart of our pack."

"Of course." Gunner pushed himself further between me and the pack leader as he spoke, the wall of flesh allowing me to suck in a much-needed lungful of air. "I'll make sure they do no damage..."

"...And you'll keep an eye on them *personally*."

"Brother?" Gunner's question was careful, his eyes averted so far I could make out the pained crinkling above his cheekbones. This level of submission was traditional when speaking to a stronger werewolf, but I'd always gotten the impression that power flowed in the opposite direction between the two brothers.

Apparently I'd been wrong about a lot.

"Let me be more clear." Now I could once again smell the fur of Ransom's presence, could see the older male's eyes piercing me over his brother's shoulder as he stepped up into Gunner's personal space. "I'm done being mollycoddled. You're not the pack leader. I am. And now you'll take one huge step backwards as I stand in my rightful place at the head of the clan."

"Of course you're the pack leader." I could have told Gunner that such a placating tone wouldn't work against his brother. But apparently the younger alpha felt the need to at least try.

"*Silence.*" Whether or not Ransom was powerful enough to make that command stick, the male between us subsided instantly. And we both listened as the Atwood pack leader laid down the law. "You'll stay here until I call for you. No more manipulations to avert my orders. No more undermining my commands."

"Yes, Chief." Gunner's head bowed in acceptance. But his fists clenched when his brother refused to accept a simple affirmative.

"You'll swear it."

I kept expecting Gunner to sell me out, to decide that Kira and I weren't worthy of such a severe loss of face. But, instead, he dropped down onto one knee in the slush of snow melt without hesitation, the ice that currently froze my toes surely sliding through his clothes to bite at his skin as well.

But Gunner's feet were warmer than mine, metaphorically at least. Because he spoke so clearly that even I could feel the magic imbuing his promise. "I swear to obey you, brother, in this as in all things. From this moment forward, I am your man."

"Good," Ransom answered. Then, without a hint of compassion for the profound concession he'd dragged out of his sibling, he turned on his heel and left us both alone.

Chapter 36

Gunner's ensuing silence was oppressive, but I had more important matters on my mind than a glowering alpha's injured pride. Matters like Kira, whose facade of spunky indifference faded the instant the last police officer rolled away in his patrol car, leaving us alone with one painfully silent alpha and the three pack mates who'd chosen self-imposed exile over returning to the heart of their clan.

"Let's go home," I suggested, taking in the way my sister's lower lip was beginning to quiver while the arm I'd slung around her waist did most of the work of holding the girl upright. Kira sagged in silent acceptance of my game plan, and I hugged her tighter in lieu of wrapping the shivering child in the jacket I no longer possessed.

Meanwhile, I glanced over Kira's shoulder at the boarded-up theater. The owner had finally arrived to lock the doors and cover broken windows, so there was no slipping inside now to grab the possessions I'd left on the catwalk. Plus, the officer in charge had warned us to get moving, the glint in his eye suggesting he'd be driving back around in a few short minutes to make sure everyone had dispersed.

So—back to our apartment, where Kira could snuggle up under the covers and I could change into non-magical garb. Unfortunately, my companions weren't impressed by my proposed retreat.

"Not a good idea," Crow offered before kneeling down to assess Allen's injuries. The accountant perching on the curb below us hadn't been one of the two males who'd died in wolf form this evening, but he hadn't come through the battle unscathed either. Instead, he hissed as Crow rolled up his left pant leg, the swelling and mottling above Allen's knee suggested he'd either broken a bone or pulled something serious on the inside.

"Yeah, stupid to go back where Kira's kidnapper can find her so easily," Tank agreed, glowering at me from under lowered brows as he joined his pack mates in the snow. Then, turning his attention to Allen, he added, "This is going to hurt" one second before wrenching the accountant's swollen leg back into place.

So, a displaced bone rather than a broken one. I pressed Kira's nose into my neck, covering her ears with my hands in an effort to cut off Allen's agonizing scream. "You could have at least offered him a sip of whiskey," I growled at the lawyer-turned-medic, surprising myself with how much Allen's pain had cut into my gut.

But werewolves were resilient. Allen offered me a reassuring smile at the same time Gunner finally reentered the conversation, stalking over to join us after seeing the last of his brother's men off. "Mai and Kira will come home with us," the alpha stated, proving that he hadn't missed our conversation even though he'd been talking to someone else a dozen yards away. With the effortless grace of a predator, he pulled Allen upright, draped a jacket around Kira's shoulders, then turned in the direction of the SUV without bothering to wait for our reply.

And I should have argued. Should have asserted my independence. But I was bone weary, any confidence that I could protect Kira on my own thoroughly shaken by recent events.

So we went. Accepted two bedrooms on the second story of the mansion—although the wrinkling of Kira's brow foreshadowed the moment five minutes later when she snuck back down the hall to bunk with me. The two of us listened to computerized gunfire emanating from the far end of the hallway where the guys were winding down to the tune of a highly violent video game, then we allowed our eyelids to gradually lower into sleep.

When I woke, five minutes or five hours later, the mansion was silent around us, my skin cold against the late-night air. Kira had rolled sideways and pulled the blankets along with her, but it wasn't just lack of bedding that sent goosebumps shivering across my skin.

The laptop. In the relief of surviving a pitched battle and police standoff, I'd forgotten the serial killer's MO. Had assumed that whoever initially wanted my sister was now gone without a trace, a few hours of shuteye making no difference to our own search.

But our opponent was a cat-like predator, one who enjoyed playing with his prey. Why else dangle Kira so theatrically when he could have simply tortured any secrets out of her? Why lure me in with a note on my door rather than snatching me off the street?

And what would a cat do when partially successful but cheated of the full prize he thought he deserved? He'd wait and hope the mouse would crawl back into the trap so he could snap the jaws the rest of the way shut.

I wasn't a mouse, though. I was a fox. And if I got to that laptop while the killer was still connected, perhaps I could use his own cockiness to figure out exactly who he was.

Chapter 37

I slipped out of bed silently, pulling on the baggy jogging outfit Allen had lent me in lieu of absent clothing of my own. Even though the accountant was the smallest of the werewolves living in this mansion, I could barely draw the string tight enough to keep the pants up around my waist. But at least I'd stay warm this time around...and could carry my star ball in the far more useful form of a sword.

I didn't leave immediately, though. Instead, I hovered over Kira, loathe to be away from her for even an hour. Not that I thought someone would sneak into the mansion and snatch the child while she was sleeping. Our enemy didn't seem idiotic enough to break into an alpha werewolf's lair while Gunner was in residence. Still, if my sister woke and guessed where I'd gone off to...well, experience proved she'd dive into the fray without bothering to look before she leapt.

It was the cold of floorboards chilling my bare feet that suggested the solution to that particular conundrum. Sneakers. I needed shoes anyway if I was going to walk through the city two-legged, and surely even Kira would turn back to the warmth of the mansion the moment her toes froze into blocks of ice.

My feet were half an inch longer than Kira's, but I managed to stuff them into my sister's shoes anyway. Then I was gone, out the door, through the hallway, sliding down the banister in a burst of joy at the unfettered freedom I'd wrapped around myself.

Because Kira was safe and I was finally going on the offensive rather than acting like a night-blind chicken fleeing a fox in the hen house. *I* was the fox this time. And I was ready to hunt.

But my mother's ghost wasn't so sure. *"Stepping into a melon field, standing under a plum tree,"* she warned me, her words so adamant that I turned in a circle to make sure she wasn't actually present. But, no, I was alone in the entranceway of the mansion, only five feet distant from the freedom represented by the gargantuan front door.

Unfortunately, I remembered this particular proverb from my childhood. Remembered how I'd argued that I wasn't stealing sweets when Mama came in and found me with my hand literally stuck in the cookie jar at five years old. Gunner would judge my actions similarly if he woke in the night and found my bed empty save for Kira. I wasn't running away this time...but how was he to know that?

The resultant twinge of guilt—plus something far less identifiable—sent me creeping back up the same stairs I'd recently slid down, continuing to backtrack until I hovered indecisively outside the alpha's bedroom door. Something about this moment felt like a turning point. Like an admission that I no longer hunted solo, that I needed someone to watch my back.

That thought nearly sent me scurrying back in the opposite direction as fast as my legs would carry me. But I needed to be rational here. Needed to remember that there was more at stake than my fox-sensitive pride. Ensuring I captured our opponent rather than being captured by him was more important than asserting prickly independence when Kira was the one who'd suffer if I failed.

So I didn't flee. Still, I turned the doorknob thief-in-the-dark slowly, not quite willing to commit to this path by waking Gunner up. And...he heard me anyway. Heard and was across the room before I'd caught more than the barest hint of movement out of the dark.

"I was wondering if you'd leave without me," the alpha rumbled. And when he smiled, I caught a glimpse of wickedly pointed, wolf-sharp teeth.

I MUST HAVE SQUEAKED, because Gunner stepped backwards, cold air rushing in to cool my suddenly heated cheeks. And as he moved, the moonlight played across his bare chest, sliding over muscles that my fingers suddenly itched to stroke.

So *that's* why my subconscious had been strangely willing for me to accept a hunting partner. Apparently my instinctive side wanted to do more than *hunt* with this wolf.

Dropping my eyes, I clenched my hand over the hilt of my sword but found little comfort in the cold weight beneath my fingers. A bladed weapon wasn't going to cut through the confusion and embarrassment that now rioted beneath my skin.

As if sensing my discomfort, Gunner's chuckle rolled over me like a warm-fingered caress, so different from the cold silence with which we'd parted earlier in the evening. "I'll put on clothes if that'll make you feel better," he offered, his voice receding into the darkness. And my feet followed after him without consideration for the self-preservation instinct that should have made me wait out in the hall.

Gunner's bedroom smelled like a jungle. Like male and power and seduction wrapped up in the crispness of fresh dew on pine needles. "I remembered the laptop," I called into the silence, hating the fact that I had to clear my throat halfway through my first sentence to ensure the rest of the words came out clear. "It's a long shot, but Kira's kidnapper might still be linked to it. He was talking to Kira through the speakers when I showed up."

"He?" And Gunner's attention was trained once again upon the mystery, the almost tangible sway he'd held over my body receding as quickly as it had begun. I was disappointed in myself for regretting the absence, which might explain why I offered more information than my companion had really asked for.

"It was a computerized voice," I answered, catching a glimpse of hard muscles rippling across Gunner's abdomen as he pulled a shirt on over his head. "Anonymous. But, yes, my gut says it was a he."

"Speaking in real time?"

"Do you really still think the killer is your brother?" I countered, attention finally snagged by the puzzling dynamics flowing between the two males. "Ransom was fighting by your side against Jackal's wolves yesterday. He let you take charge of me and Kira without batting an eye."

For a moment, I thought I'd pushed too hard. Because the granite of Gunner's aroma rose up to overtake the fresh, leafy odor, and he sank down onto the bed to lace up his boots without bothering with a reply.

But then Gunner laughed out a short "Heh" beneath his breath, glancing up at me with an almost hangdog droop to his features. "I'm still figuring out my brother," he answered, the words coming slowly as if they were just now coalescing for the very first time.

For my part, it was dawning upon me that this alpha's earlier silent treatment hadn't been anger at my actions. Gunner's instinct outside the theater had been to protect me...which had likely confused him as much as it did everybody else. So I hummed out a question, gave my companion the space to speak or not as he saw fit.

"When we were kids, Ransom was the rash one," Gunner continued after a long moment. "He made...mistakes...and was glad to have me as his compass. But maybe he's grown out of that. Maybe he doesn't need me any longer."

The pain in Gunner's voice was palpable, so I did my best to brush his worries aside. "Siblings always need one another," I countered, unable to imagine a day when Kira and I would be glad to see the other's taillights receding in our respective rear-view mirrors.

"Well," Gunner answered, neither overtly agreeing nor disagreeing. He was fully dressed now, cloth covering every delectable surface before I'd had a chance to really see any of it in the light. "Are you ready? We're less likely to wake the household if we go out the back."

Chapter 38

The snow had nearly melted by the time our headlights swept across the face of the abandoned theater, illuminating the marquee. *The Importance of Being Earnest.* Were even long-ago playwrights giving me tips on how to live my life now?

"I brought a crowbar," Gunner started, then swore beneath his breath as a police cruiser came toward us from the opposite direction. I'd never known the cops to have such a presence in the Warren, but perhaps they figured an event serious enough to make the local papers merited a follow up visit...or three.

So we couldn't park out front as originally intended. Instead, we continued past our destination and waited to pull into a side alley once the police car was long out of sight. We hugged the shadows, walking like octogenarians on the way back as the previous evening's tight muscles and scabbed-over wounds hindered our progress. But aches and pains were forgotten when Gunner slipped his crowbar under the edge of a board-covered window, prompting me to stop him with one hand lightly touching his arm.

"That's going to be crazy loud," I protested, remembering the awful screech of a pried-up nail the one time I'd tried—and failed—to make our shabby apartment a little bit spiffier.

"Alternatives?" Gunner countered, cocking his head and waiting for me to come up with another way in.

Rather than answering, I tilted my chin to gaze at the barely-visible stars, trying to remember when I'd started telling alpha werewolves what to do. And as I forcibly relaxed my neck muscles, I caught a square of darkness in the third story, a broken window too high for the owner to have bothered boarding up.

"Look." I pointed upward, only realizing as I did so that neither a human nor a wolf would have even considered making such a climb.

But Gunner had already seen firsthand what I was able to shift into. So I ignored decades of conditioning and spoke openly about my secret for the very first time. "It'll be easy to get up there as a fox. Then I'll come downstairs and let you in."

I expected Gunner to growl at the overtness of my offer. But, instead, his voice was almost too level to be natural as he answered me after a short pause. "You'll fall."

"I won't. The climb is easy. Especially if you give me a boost onto that ledge."

There was something flowing between us that I couldn't quite put my finger on, and I held my breath waiting for the other shoe to drop. But instead of acting the way I'd always been told werewolves would respond to my foxishness, the alpha merely waved one hand. "Be my guest."

Which is when I remembered the prerequisite for donning red fur. Getting naked. Right here in front of Gunner, with no other eyes present to depersonalize the effect.

It took three throat clearings before I managed to spit out the solution. "Turn around," I demanded.

Gunner was amused, I could smell that in the air between us. Still, he obeyed me, and I quickly slid out of Allen's jogging suit and Kira's sneakers before assuming my animal form.

Only then did I realize my companion had been peeking. Caught the glint of his eyes skimming across my completely un-wolf-like fur and body. The contact was nearly tangible in its intensity....

But Gunner didn't growl or move to attack. Instead the big, scary alpha werewolf got down on one knee and offered his left arm as a ramp leading up onto his shoulder. "Come on. I'll give you a leg up."

I SLIPPED THROUGH THE window as easily as if I spent hours every day four-legged rather than donning my fur once every other blue moon. No wonder Kira seized every opportunity to frolic as a fox. Light-assisting vulpine pupils made it a breeze to scamper through the upper story in near darkness, and I barely managed to force myself back into human form upon reaching the closed door at the top of the stairs.

Thumbs, I reminded myself. *Doorknobs require thumbs.*

Shivering out of my fur, I came to stand two-legged atop the rough floorboards. And, at first, I thought the goose bumps breaking out on my skin were the result of unheated air brushing up against abruptly furless skin.

But my seldom-utilized animal nature refused to go back to sleep now that it had been wakened. And the stairs yawned dark and cavernous before my dilated eyes.

Shaking off the strange case of the willies, I tiptoed down without calling upon my star ball for illumination. There was always a slight chance an enemy remained in the building, or that one had returned after the police sweep to mop up curious foxes like myself. Better to stub my toe than to arrive heralded by the glow of a magical flashlight....

Unfortunately, walking blind resulted in more than toe stubbing. I was halfway down the stairs when my heel brushed against soft fur in the darkness. And I'm ashamed to admit I emitted a rather feminine "Eek!" as I leapt a foot into the air.

The mouse—it *was* only a mouse—ran chittering into the darkness. *Get a grip*, I told myself firmly. After multiple police sweeps, the theater was unlikely to house critters larger than a rodent.

So I pushed open the door at the bottom of the stairs at a normal pace and strode directly out onto the back of the stage area. *Huh.* This wasn't where I'd expected to end up when I started down the stairwell. Still, I was here, so I might as well poke around a little. Grab the laptop. Maybe even head up to the catwalk and collect my discarded clothing so I didn't end up facing Gunner a second time in my birthday suit.

But the laptop wasn't present. Instead, the thinnest trickle of sound caught at the edge of my consciousness as I batted aside dusty curtains and got down on my belly to peer at the floor below the stage. I didn't even realize I was hearing something, actually, until I found myself humming along to a tune from both my distant and recent past.

Mama's music box. For the first time all night, my teeth sharpened into the fox equivalent of a werewolf's hunting instinct and I padded silently toward the dressing rooms from which the trail of melody had emerged.

He'd come back. Of course the serial killer hadn't depended upon an anonymous computer voice to make contact. Not when my vulpine curiosity was bound to bring me here before the sun rose....

Which meant I was finally going to get a chance to vanquish Kira's kidnapper, to ensure that my sister never again worried when she walked the streets alone.

There was a light before me now. The flickering glow of a candle visible as I entered the hallway leading to a series of changing rooms. My prey must have grown tired of waiting in the darkness, choosing to camp out in the room at the end of the line. This was almost too easy....

I took one step forward...then spun faster than mere human muscles would have been capable of as I felt the presence of something much larger than a mouse materializing behind my back.

Of course he wasn't waiting by the candle. Any good warrior knows you feint before you attack.

Sure enough, the cloaked figure who arose out of the shadows before me was as anonymous as he was dangerous. His face was hidden beneath a pitch-black hood, the enveloping fabric preventing me from telling anything other than his height—which, as usual, was considerably taller than my own.

But I didn't spend long trying to eke out the being's identity. Because he held in his hand the root of this entire hassle—my mother's star ball converted into a glowing sword.

Chapter 39

"The light distraction was clever," I admitted even as I brought my own magical weapon up into an on-guard position. "But you can't sneak up on a fox."

Predictably, my enemy failed to answer, just lunged forward with speed that proved he was more than human. And even though my well-honed reaction should have been a parry, some instinct told me to twist out of the way instead.

Dodging, unfortunately, wasn't the best move against a sword-wielding opponent. But at least I managed to twist far enough away so his blade snagged a lock of hair rather than slicing through living flesh. And as I pivoted in preparation for the hooded figure's next movement, Mama spoke for the first time in over an hour.

"Even monkeys fall from trees."

"I *am* being careful," I hissed in response, wishing my dead mother would speak plainly and tell me what I was missing here. Was I just jumping at mice when I chose not to engage with my attacker...or was there a real reason not to counter his lunge with my sword?

Unfortunately, I had no time to prod at my mother's ghostly warning. Because my opponent was dancing sideways in a move far too similar to Mama's signature sidle to be coincidence. And I found myself backpedaling rapidly while memories flowed fast and furious through my brain.

The park. My parents. Swordplay and laughter, practice merging into dancing. Dad was straightforward and powerful, light on his feet but not the best feinter if you were familiar with his favorite moves. In contrast, Mama's motions were akin to a leaf dancing along invisible air currents, totally erratic for those of us unable to see the wind.

And this person before me was moving just like Mama had. Was twisting and leaping so mercurially I didn't know where he was going to end up next. Only my vulpine senses helped me dodge a second blow, and this time my enemy's blade flicked sideways just in time to nick my bare hip.

It burned. Not like the usual slice of a blade through muscle; more like running into a flaming torch with the sensitive skin of a cheek or a hand. Was this why both Mama and my gut had both warned me not to touch the stolen star ball? Had Kira's kidnapper tapped into kitsune powers I wasn't even aware of...or was there something deeper at work?

As I pondered, the figure before me drifted sideways, forcing me to pivot to keep him in my sights. Or should that be "her"? Because with the cloak covering my opponent's body, there was no way to tell whether I faced a tall woman or an average-height man. The only visible flesh was long fingers wrapped around the sword hilt, and even those appendages could have belonged to a member of either sex....

Suddenly, I had to know who my opponent was. If Mama's sword bit me again in the process so be it. But I couldn't keep fighting while wondering whether this being might be the parent I thought long dead.

So I went on the offensive. Eyed a folded chair leaning against the wall as I skipped sideways. Then took a running leap, using the top of the chair to fuel my forward motion before pivoting midair to aim toward my opponent's head.

The chair clattered against hard floor tiles. And, vaguely, I noted the sound of a crowbar prying at a window-covering in the distance, the result just as teeth-clenchingly loud as I'd known it would be.

Looked like Gunner had lost patience and decided to break in after all. Not good news with cops patrolling the street.

I didn't possess a single spare breath, though, to suggest that Gunner cool it on the screeching. Because Mama's sword was swiping toward me, proving the error of my original plan.

After all my trajectory had been decided by the way I'd pushed off the wall seconds earlier. No amount of twisting or flailing of my arms now would send me scudding sideways to prevent my opponent's blow from hitting home.

So I did the only thing I could think of. I shifted midair, flickering into my smaller fox form and sliding unharmed under the sword thrust before landing atop my opponent's cloth-covered head.

AS I REGAINED MY EQUILIBRIUM, the sword whizzed past so close that it nearly nicked one of my long red ear tips. Air buffeted, claws dug for traction, and Mama screeched inside my head: *"The broken mirror cannot be made to shine!"*

If I'd possessed human vocal cords, I would have yelled back that it was unhelpful to toss out oblique warnings to someone in the middle of a pitched battle. But, instead, I scrabbled at the fabric beneath my pads, yanking the hood with my teeth then leaping away before my enemy could decide whether it was safe to bring that stolen blade closer to his or her forehead.

And this time, my move was successful. I didn't glance back over my shoulder to peer at my receding enemy, but I could feel the hood fluttering down upon my tail as I darted away. Soon, I'd know exactly who had bought my mother's star ball then paid Ma Scrubbs to have my sister kidnapped....

Unfortunately, my opponent only laughed in reaction to being disrobed. And I could see why as I spun back around, understanding at the same time why the evidence of amusement had come out so muffled and low.

Because my enemy had taken his or her cover-up seriously. Beneath the hood was a black ski mask, the only flashes of humanity revealed by my action being two dark eyes and a tiny circle of a mouth. Meanwhile, I spat out the bitterness of baking soda, understanding why I'd failed to pick up even the barest hint of an odor while standing on my enemy's head.

The laugh itself might have been a clue, but unfortunately I wasn't that lucky. Instead, the low-pitched sound was entirely androgynous even as my opponent continued to chortle beneath his or her breath.

And this time I'd had enough. Jumping upward into humanity, I staggered once due to the speed and frequency of my recent shifts. But then I was screaming out my anger, sword raised as I mimicked a samurai swooping in for the kill.

I was done with caution. It was time to use my skills to take this enemy down.

Chapter 40

"**M**ai!" Gunner's voice threaded toward me through the otherwise empty building. Vaguely, I noted that my recent yell might have sounded like pain rather than aggression to a distant werewolf. But I could ease the alpha's worries later. For now, I had a fight to win.

Spinning on the balls of my feet, I dodged beneath my opponent's sword, continuing to pretend my only impulse was defense. It wasn't, though. Because I'd stopped worrying about my sword touching my opponent's the moment I lost my temper. Which opened up an endless array of opportunities in the fight ahead.

In the end, I chose the simplest game plan—feigning a stumble in order to bait my cloaked enemy to attack. Predictably, my opponent responded just as I'd expected. He or she easily bypassed my flailing sword arm then lunged toward my left shoulder. All I had to do was wait until the last moment then raise my own weapon in three...two...one....

"No!" Mama started, the word perhaps the beginning of a proverb or perhaps her first attempt at giving it to me straight.

And then images flickered behind my eyeballs. Mama on her deathbed, hands shaking as they reached out to fold my much smaller hands around the hilt of a sword so similar to my own. *"This is yours now. Keep it safe until your sister is old enough to understand its power."*

Even though the memory was twelve years old, I still remembered the tingle that ran through me...and the way clinging to Mama's glowing star ball had eased my grief over the months afterwards. Because while my mother's physical body had faded into absence, her spirit had remained beside me for more than a decade. The warm security of her presence had wandered afield to help Kira shift at frequent intervals, but it had always flowed back in my direction whenever I cared to call.

Except the warmth was fading fast now that I actively fought against that beloved connection. The chill began in my feet and quickly engulfed my entire body as I placed my own sword right where it needed to go to slice Mama's star ball violently aside.

I tried to mitigate the offensive at the last moment, understanding too late that magic works on intention first and foremost. I'd launched this attack from a place of rage and hatred, and that might just be enough to finally split my dead mother and me apart.

Which wasn't at all want I wanted. I hoped to cling to the tiny fragment of Mama's undying spirit, to keep her close and listen to pesky proverbs if that was the only way she could communicate from beyond the grave.

But my change of heart came too late. Two thin streams of magical weaponry met for the very first time with a bell-like tone rather than with the usual clang of reverberating metal. And as they did so, an electrical jolt racked my body, the shock hitting me one instant before the connection to my mother's memories winked abruptly out.

I hadn't appreciated what I possessed until it was gone, I now realized. Hadn't appreciated how much I depended upon Mama's silent—and recently not-so-silent—presence to buoy me up. Had I thrust her spirit into the void without a life boat? Or—worse—was she now being forced to empower my opponent, a free spirit turned into a prisoner within the enemy's cloaked form?

No wonder the hooded figure's eyes crinkled with pleasure. No wonder my muscles turned to water even as my opponent's hardened into stone.

The shock at losing a part of myself that I hadn't fully realized was present loosened my grip until it was all I could do to cling onto my sword as I was pushed backward against the wall. I couldn't even struggle. Lacked the presence of mind to duck down and out of my opponent's grasp before being pinned by someone considerably larger and stronger than myself.

I was trapped between a serial killer and a hard place....

Then I was spinning sideways. My neck whiplashed, my limbs flailed in a vain attempt to catch my balance.

And when I came at last to stillness, the back of my skull was pressing hard against the floorboards while I peered up into the panting face of a tremendous male wolf.

Chapter 41

The werewolf's breath was hot against my forehead, his teeth inches away from the soft spot beneath my chin. No wonder I shifted into fox form, depending on animal instinct to wriggle free before I could be eaten alive.

But the wolf was having none of it. He grabbed my newly materialized ruff and shook me so severely my teeth clattered together. And even after I was suitably chastised, the male continued standing stiff-legged atop my crumpled body while a deep growl rumbled up out of his massively broad chest.

Which is about the time I realized this wasn't my sword-wielding opponent. This was Gunner, turned guardian while letting our true quarry escape behind his back. I'd always known alpha werewolves were idiots, but I hadn't expected behavior as ass-backwardly overprotective as this.

Unfortunately, I couldn't shift forms in order to berate him. Not when the reservoir of magic within my belly had gone quiescent with exhaustion, refusing to even create a minor electrical shock to tingle against Gunner's skin. Without Mama's star ball to strengthen me, I apparently had far less stamina than I was accustomed to possessing.

So I lay there panting, unable to so much as twitch without provoking another growl from the alpha straddling my body. Meanwhile, the anonymous being who had paid for my sister's kidnapping after killing two innocent humans disappeared without a trace.

We might have remained stuck in that stalemate all night, too, had a trickle of smoke not emerged from the changing room at the end of the hall. *The candle,* I thought at first, shoulders relaxing back down away from around my ears.

But the stench flowing over us was too foul to have emerged from one small chunk of wax and cotton. Meanwhile, beneath the smoke, I caught the unmistakable scent of gasoline, suggesting our enemy had left us with a parting gift far more serious than one overturned candlestick.

Gunner must have smelled it too because his eyes widened, his signature scent of unyielding granite giving way to the more malleable aroma of ozone and dew. Then my captor became my herder. Nudging me erect then chivvying my footsteps, he pushed me down the hall then out onto the stage proper. And when I veered toward my favorite leather jacket, he hip-bumped me away before literally pushing me out through the unboarded window he'd recently used to enter the building.

In the semi-fresh air of the outdoors, my companion finally managed to shift while I merely dragged my feet a few inches further from the theater that I suspected would soon go up in flames. There was no sign of the conflagration on the exterior just yet, but the building was so very old and built almost entirely out of wood....

"There's a fire," Gunner growled into his cell phone just as the first brilliant streak of orange rose into the barely lit neighborhood. "The theater. Find a burner phone then call 911."

So it was his pack he'd contacted rather than the fire department. "*Clever wolf,*" I mumbled, realizing only after I'd spoken that, of course, I was in vulpine form. So the words came out as a thready whine rather than as understandable human communication.

Gunner didn't look down, but his hand dropped onto my forehead even as his scent hardened further in reaction to whatever his pack mate was relaying over the phone. "The whole apartment?" He paused, listened to something I should have been able to hear in my fox form but couldn't quite manage to focus upon while my body was melting into the watery slush beneath my feet. "And the Ebay account was wiped also?"

Wait, they were talking about *my* apartment and *Kira's* Ebay account. Did that mean the last possible trail leading to our serial killer had iced over during the night?

Forcing myself erect with an effort, I realized only after raising a hand to my aching head that I was standing on two human feet rather than on four furry ones. No wonder I was shivering, the effort of the shift creating a watery haze that obstructed my view.

Those weren't tears, I told myself. Not over a rented space that had formed the bare minimum shelter necessary to keep body and soul together rather than representing any sort of home.

By the time I'd blinked the obstruction out of my eyes, Gunner was already slipping into his clothes and turning off his phone. "Here," my companion told me, pulling Allen's sweatshirt over my head far more gently than I'd thought him capable of before thrusting the matching sweatpants and Kira's shoes into my arms. "We need to make tracks."

So we ran away from the flaming theater together. Fled toward a shiny SUV that promised to carry us to a tremendous mansion nothing like the rat-infested apartment I was used to...and all I really noticed along the way was the fact that the vehicle's heated seats eased a tiny bit of the chill away from my frozen heart.

It would have taken a full-fledged sauna to heat me through at that moment though. And I reached into my mind, hoping for a proverb—*any* proverb—instead of the terrible silence that resolutely filled my brain like a thick blanket of snow. "I think I made a terrible mistake," I murmured, only realizing I'd spoken aloud when Gunner glanced toward me, cocking his head in question.

"Your sister's safe," he offered when my flood of self-recrimination became dammed into silence by the dryness of my throat.

"For now," I countered, voice croaking as I forced further explanation out through parched lips. "But I just gave a serial killer power over my mother's star ball. And if I lose custody of Kira...."

Then a water bottle was being inserted between my trembling fingers, a large hand guiding mine up to tilt the much-needed moisture into my mouth. "You're among wolves now," Gunner promised, the words far less ominous than they would have been one week prior. "Our pack will solve this together."

And even though I'd been trained since birth to catch sight of a werewolf then run in the opposite direction as quickly and stealthily as possible, I believed the words of the alpha beside me. Sank back against the buttery leather seat and relaxed into acceptance.

I was no longer alone. Together, Gunner and I would figure this out.

Shadow Wolf

Chapter 1

Dried blood coated my cuticles and I blinked, unable to make sense of the unexpected sight. Safely sheltered by werewolves, I'd gone on frequent fur-form expeditions in recent weeks. So maybe that explained the dark circles beneath my fingernails...but since when did I pounce upon unwary rabbits and rip open their throats while I was sleeping?

Seeking clues, I tipped my head upwards to take in the crescent moon then stamped bare feet against bent and splintered grass blades. The strands caught against my toes, clinging as if coated with glue...or with some other halfway-dried and considerably less savory substance.

Blood?

I leapt sideways, the harsh tang of copper following me away from the trampled circle of earth. From the amount of bodily fluids I'd brought along with me, I could only assume I'd waded through the same carcass that had sullied the grass and soil...or had been the one to spill those bodily fluids myself.

There has to be a rational explanation for all of this. Closing my gaping mouth and forcing air to flow more naturally through flaring nostrils, I peered out at the darkened landscape in which I found myself. I was perched atop a rounded knoll, encircled on four sides by tree silhouettes while the moon shone down through a gap in the canopy to illuminate the spot where I now stood...

...Where I stood beside a cloaked figure all too familiar despite the three months since I'd seen him or her last. The being had bought Mama's star ball and absconded with it last spring despite all of my efforts to reclaim the magic....

So I *was* dreaming. I exhaled in relief, pinching my forearm. Unfortunately, the sharp burst of pain failed to wake me back up.

Well, if I had to repeat a three-month-old battle against the owner of my mother's star ball, perhaps this time I'd win the fight. Change the rules, change the game....

To that end, I yanked at the source of my magic, the glow of a sword arcing through the air between me and my enemy. And in instant response, lightning bugs rose in a wave of green-hued reaction, their sheer numbers proving that this was not memory but rather dream. I'd never known so many of the bioluminescent fliers to exist in one location...had rarely even seen a smattering of their neon lights at the wooded edge of the city park where I sometimes went to be alone.

But I wasn't located in my home city any longer. Instead, forest stretched out around me, lacking streetlights, porch lights, even the barest hint of asphalt and diesel fumes to pinpoint a nearby a road.

Where was I? And why had I moved this frequently remembered battle from the abandoned theater in which it had actually occurred to an idyllic spot lifted from a fairy tale?

All of these thoughts flooded my neurons in the time it took for the lightning bugs to wink out and return the scene to near darkness. Meanwhile, as if my enemy had been waiting for the return of my attention, cloaked arms rose in a flicker of black on black. Then a shining orb levitated out of the being's right sleeve.

Now I could see my opponent easily as he—she?—beckoned me forward with one curving finger. *Come*, the gesture demanded as Mama's star ball winked at me from around the being's gloved hand. I cocked my head in response to the magic's odd behavior. Then the glowing star ball shifted, stretched...and turned into a whip that lashed out faster than a cobra to encircle my arms and chest.

The magic *burned*. Cut through my silk kimono and almost—but not quite—prevented me from noticing how dramatically this nightmare had gone off the rails of its usual script.

Since when was there a lasso involved in our battle? Since when did I wear kimonos? Since when did the anonymous being I fought against wield magic I had yet to understand?

"Who are you?" I demanded, not even trying to bring up my magical sword to sever the imprisoning connection that pulled me one step closer to my nemesis, then another. Because I could feel my mother's essence within the glowing rope restraining me—who knew what would happen if I cut that soul-bound magic in half to free myself?

The words had been a parry, meant only to win me another moment in which to think. But, to my surprise, my opponent didn't ignore them. Instead, lasso pressure on my stomach eased as a hooded head cocked to one side in mimicry of my own earlier gesture. I could almost smell the being's confusion as he or she paused rather than continuing to reel me in.

Scent. Yes, of course I should use every weapon at my disposal if this really was a face-to-face meeting with my nemesis rather than a rehashed memory-turned-nightmare.

But the breeze was flowing from behind me, the air too dry to be redolent with identifying scents. And as the wind whipped unbound hair against my cheekbones, I flinched, realizing what I should have gathered from the start.

The body I inhabited wasn't my own—how could I have missed that? Instead, I stood in the skin of my dead mother. More slender than my real body, a trifle shorter, and enfolded in the subtle haze of jasmine that always preceded my mother whenever she entered a room.

Then my lips opened and Mama's voice spoke through me. "Master..." she started, chilling me to my core. So the cloaked being had figured out how to use Mama's star ball since I'd last been in his or her presence. Had figured out how to use her magic...and her as well.

But before Mama could bow to the Master further, before I could beg forgiveness for letting her fall into such a trap, my earlier wish was granted. I slipped out of my mother's body and woke in my own bed with a start.

Chapter 2

It was half past four in the morning, but I couldn't close my eyes, let alone return to slumber. Not even after examining now-clean fingers and toes to reassure myself that the strange confrontation had only been a figment of my dreaming mind's imagination.

Instead, I lay between soft sheets, listening to the silence of Gunner's mansion. During the day, the halls filled with chatter and laughter. But in the wee hours of night, the place became positively peaceful with everyone sleeping.

Well, everyone except for me.

It wasn't the first time I'd risen before dawn, unable to accept a wolf pack's confining safety. So I pushed out of bed, pulled on clothes, and headed downstairs to the empty courtyard. There I drew upon my star ball and dueling against nobody, stretching muscles well toned from previously insomniacal bouts.

Fighting, at least, tired me enough so the questions and worries circling through my mind lowered their volume. Was I doing the right thing choosing momentary safety for Kira while going against every instinct toward self preservation that our parents had taught? *Slash, lunge.* Would I come to regret accepting a so-called "job" that involved doing whatever I wanted while being paid more than I'd previously made as a teacher and cage-fighter combined? *Riposte, retreat.*

There were no more answers this morning than there had been last Tuesday or two weeks ago Wednesday or any other time I'd come out here to fight shadows rather than snuggle up in my bed like a good little wolf. Still, I couldn't help smiling despite the sweat burning my eyeballs when the inevitable morning bickering rose with the sun, proving that my sister was now wide awake and much perkier than she'd been the day before.

"So you think it's *funny* to let me fall into the toilet first thing in the morning?" Kira snarked from the east end of the first floor—the massive kitchen where everyone except me tended to congregate as soon as they got up.

"Come on, pipsqueak. Today's the big day. Give me a break."

Looked like my kid sister was back on task as self-appointed toilet monitor. And one of our house mates—Tank this time—had relieved himself in the night without remembering to re-lower that all-important white seat.

Kira grows more wolf-like and less fox-like every day, I noted, not sure how I felt about the matter. Foxes were reserved and elusive. But wolves, I'd found, expressed their affections best in the physical realm.

Sure enough, the crack of a snapping towel evoked a squeak from my sister even as another house mate, Crow this time, stated the obvious: "That's *our* bathroom, puppy. You and Mai have your own on the third floor. So if you fell in, it's your own da...ahem...*darn* fault."

Logic, apparently, had no impact upon my sister. "I live in this entire *house*, not locked in the attic like a crazy auntie. For example, I spend a lot of time in the kitchen *cooking*. So if you want any of my bacon, you'll start putting down the toilet seat *everywhere*."

"Ooh, *burn*," Allen murmured, far too quietly for the neighbors to hear him. My fox senses, on the other hand, caught the comment quite ably...along with a salty sweet scent that had me slowing my morning exercise into a cool down. Perhaps being part of a wolf pack wasn't so terrible if it came with bacon at the exact moment my stomach started growling....

Except even as I started imagining breakfast, the hairs on the back of my neck prickled. My nostrils flared, my muscles tightened. There was something nearing, something watching....

Bacon abruptly forgotten, I whirled in reaction, raising my sword as I turned to face the stalking wolf.

OR, RATHER, TO FACE the two-legged wolf in human clothing. Gunner raised one eyebrow at the pointy blade just barely indenting the skin beneath his Adam's apple. Then, ignoring my weapon, he held out a mug of chamomile tea, the sweetness of honey curling off the surface as the leader of the wolf pack I lived amidst greeted me aloud.

"Tough night?"

I shook my head, not so much in denial as in a refusal to rehash my dream landscape verbally. And in response, Gunner's open face shuttered ever so slightly as if he was more disappointed by my evasion than at being greeted by the sharp tip of a sword.

But just as quickly, Gunner regained his customary smile, jiggling the mug between us so the ceramic clanked against my magically-created weapon. "We should do something fun before Kira's custody hearing," the ever-patient werewolf suggested. "Go for a run somewhere wild before we're due in court. Or...shopping? Does Kira like shopping?"

"My sister loves nothing better then spending other people's money," I admitted, allowing my sword to diffuse back into a magical blob that slid along my skin to form a bracelet, a belt, a sheathed knife at my left ankle. In front of me, Gunner didn't even twitch at this evidence of my kitsune nature. "But we shouldn't spoil her," I added. "And, anyway, I've got other plans."

"Plans?"

This time I accepted the mug my companion brandished in my direction, pretending that I needed to all of my attention to prevent a spill. Taking a sip, I noted that Gunner had steeped the tea just the way I liked it, not so long it turned bitter but not so short that it was simply sweetened water with a hint of aroma to turn hot liquid into soothing tea water.

The flavor was perfect...but my gut clenched anyway. Because it was time for our inevitable weekly ritual. No one managed to slip away from the pack without extensive explanation, but I couldn't afford to let any of the werewolves I lived with know where I went on Tuesday afternoons. In lieu of the truth, I always ended up stuttering through an entirely unbelievable explanation, and the wolves around me always smiled grimly and allowed me to lie.

As usual, my body language broadcast my mistruth before I even opened my mouth to speak it. "Girl stuff," I said stiffly, turning away from the piercing eyes of the far too astute werewolf who was providing food, housing, protection, and now the likelihood of ripping Kira out of the foster system permanently.

Gunner had done everything he could think of to enfold me into his pack...and yet I remained at heart a solitary kitsune.

"It might take a while," I continued. "So I'll meet you and Kira at the courthouse. If you don't mind bringing her there for me...."

"Of course, I'll take care of Kira," Gunner agreed quietly. "She's part of our pack."

The unspoken addendum—that I lacked that distinction due to actions just like this one—separated us more effectively than my now-absent weapon.

But there was nothing I could do about the sad sag to my companion's shoulders. Nothing except the impossible—turn myself into a wolf.

So, stepping backwards, I nodded once. "Thank you," I murmured, eyes downcast in wordless apology, "for the tea."

Chapter 3

As if the universe was intent upon repaying my bad karma, there were human-form werewolves everywhere when I finally wriggled free of the mansion and began working my way downtown. Two sniffed in my general direction as I hesitated at the top of the stairs descending toward a subway station. And now two more patrolled the crest of the river bridge when I opted to travel across the city on foot.

No wonder it had taken twice as long as expected to reach my destination.

I was there now, though—or *nearly* there. Narrowing my eyes, I assessed the pair of two-leggers leaning up against the bridge railing fifty feet distant. It was unusual to see any member of the Atwood pack other than my four house mates, but these males' ozone-laden scent promised they were Ransom's underlings. Which begged the question—what were they doing so close to Gunner's place of exile when their pack leader had not-so-subtly discouraged visits to this southern outpost of his territory back in the spring?

I hesitated despite myself, the question of who the males were and what they were doing here nibbling at my concentration. It wouldn't do to let Gunner be blindsided....

Fox, not wolf, I reminded myself. The important matter here wasn't these shifters' identity. It was reaching my destination without catching their eye.

Luckily, the street was crowded and I found it easy to slide in behind a group of laughing ladies, pressing forward until I was just barely inside their personal space. The quartet was too animated to notice the intrusion as they recounted some past adventure involving beaches and dancing and far too many margaritas...all while striding toward the foot of the bridge I very much needed to find a way across.

"...and then Doug took off his shirt! Bared everything! Potbelly and all!" one woman crowed, and I threw my head back and laughed right alongside them...the gesture doubling as a show of solidarity and an easy way to hide my face from sight.

Unfortunately, the ladies didn't cross the bridge I wanted to go over, and there was no way I could veer away from the group without being noticed at this point. So I flowed down the block along with the chattering humans. Slipped through the doorway of a high-end boutique when the women whooshed inside in a close-knit cluster. Then, glancing back over one shoulder and noting the werewolves' lack of attention, I yanked the door back open and sprinted toward the river behind the nearby row of shops.

"Hey!" The shout was redolent with alpha compulsion, but it didn't faze me. Not when the command was aimed at werewolves and even more at those who belonged to a pack.

Instead, I was a fox. So the order rolled over me like water off a duck's back.

"Stop!" the wolf continued. But his word didn't even slow my footsteps. Instead, I leapt onto the horizontal limb of a sycamore, raced across smooth bark until I was directly above deep water, then I dove directly in.

I REMEMBERED ONE MILLISECOND before breaching the surface that I couldn't soak my current outfit. Not when I'd donned my best clothes for Kira's custody hearing and lacked the time to drop by a laundromat and bake the pant suit dry on my way back.

Good thing I'd spent the last few weeks learning to better manage my magic.

Yanking at my star ball with a facility I hadn't possessed three months earlier, I was encased in a skin of water-repellant magic by the time I slid beneath the river's murky surface. And while a more experienced kitsune might have been able to sequester an air pocket for ease of breathing, I was content to simply block out encroaching liquid as I allowed the river to carry me slowly downstream.

I *did* produce a cone-shaped protrusion around each ear, though. And I was gratified to find that the spur-of-the-moment hearing aids were quite efficient at picking up sound emanating from the nearby shoreline.

"The boss didn't send us here to track down strays," one voice growled. "If the bastard wants to swim the river, he'll be a Claremont problem on the other side."

Smiling as the river flowed around me, I couldn't help but agree. Another benefit of being a fox around werewolves—the latter were so rigid in their pack structure that it was remarkably easy to wriggle my way beneath the rules.

For example, meeting my mentor outside Atwood territory and without Gunner's permission meant Ransom wouldn't be able to argue his brother had broken his promise. The convoluted reasoning was immensely satisfying...but the second shifter's words wiped all amusement off my lips.

"That wasn't a 'he', you idiot. It was a female." This voice sounded vaguely familiar, as if the second watcher might have been one of the shifters who'd turned the tide at the showdown in the theater three months earlier. And his scent? Had there been more to it than the mantle of Atwood ozone rising through the stench of city garbage?

I racked my brain but came up with nothing else by way of memory. I could only hope that meant my own flavor had been similarly muted by distance, and just as generically werewolf-like as I'd been led to believe.

With an effort, I turned my body around to push back upstream against the current. Wolves might not be curious, but foxes were. And I had a feeling the duo might let drop identifying information if I hovered here long enough.

"If it's a female," the first male started....

But now my lungs were burning, the opposite shore seeming an impossible distance away from where I hovered. If I popped back up in the river so close to where I'd gone under, this pair of werewolves might risk the gray area of the boundary and come in after me.

So, reluctantly, I relinquished my spot in the river. Changed my ear cones into flippers. And pushed toward my original destination with all my strength.

Whoever these shifters answered to, they weren't my problem. Not when I was, and always would be, a lone fox rather than a wolf.

Chapter 4

I emerged, gasping, beneath the overhang of a bushy outcrop on the Claremont side of the watercourse. The watchers had lost interest, I noticed, retreating back to their bridge-side vantage point. Relieved that their tenacity was so subpar, I rose out of the water, pushed through the brush to the open area further from the river...then felt myself spinning sideways as hands grabbed and tugged on my left arm.

Shifter. My sense of smell was still catching up to my reeling balance, but I could tell I was being manhandled by a werewolf due to the superhuman speed my attacker possessed. Too bad my diffusely dispersed star ball meant a sword refused to materialize in a timely manner....

I couldn't afford to shift into fox form, either. Not when kitsunes were verboten everywhere other than in Gunner's mansion.

That didn't make me entirely helpless, however.

Instead, I let momentum carry me groundward, curling in upon myself as I fell so I hit the leaf litter already spinning into a somersault. With any luck, my opponent would still be shuffling backwards into two-footed stability after such an all-out attack, a lapse I planned to take full advantage of by ramming into his knees....

Or, rather, into *her* knees. I identified my teacher's signature scent of spring rain, roses, and ozone even as I bowled her over, was apologizing profusely before she thudded butt-first atop the hard ground.

"Elle, I'm so sorry. Did I hurt you?"

My roll had carried me past my opponent and back to my feet, so it was an easy matter to reach down in preparation for pulling the slender brunette erect beside me. And as I did so, I felt my forehead furrow in confusion. Why was my teacher—Crow's mate, a resident of Ransom's pack—waiting for me here rather than half a mile down river where we usually met each other? Had Crow received a message that he failed to deliver? Had our illicit meetings finally been found out?

"You were late," my mentor answered the question I should have asked rather than the one I'd actually managed even as her hand clamping down on mine. "I was worried."

Not so worried that her lupine nature didn't show through, however. One moment she was my smart, protective teacher. The next, her eyes glistened with amusement and I braced myself against the inevitable yank intended to tumble me onto the ground.

Strangely, though, Elle merely scratched my palm rather than pulling me downward. A tiny trickle of blood welled up even as she retreated, her expression more fox-like than wolf-like as she licked her fingernail clean.

"What?" I started as icy cold ran up my arm and across my shoulder. My mentor's eyes glowed red, my stomach lurched in answer...

...Then I was bending over backwards, twisting my body into a series of contortions that might have amused an audience but felt torturous from the inside. I hadn't actually known I could hook my leg around my neck, and now that I'd been pretzelified I sure hoped Elle planned to untangle me...

...then the possession that had forced gymnastics upon me dissipated. I was once again alone inside my body while Elle hooted out her laughter at my struggles to shake out the newly-created kinks.

"And that," my teacher told me, "is why you need to practice defensive magic." Then, thrusting a photocopied document toward me: "Now read."

IT TOOK A SOLID MINUTE to loosen my muscles sufficiently so I could take the paper from her fingers. But when I did so, I was immediately sucked in. Because this new historical document provided much more than the vague hints offered by Elle's previous findings.

Or so I guessed while poring over the bad handwriting and worse grammar that had passed for literacy a couple of hundred years before. As best I could tell, the writer had seen werewolves seize kitsune magic and use that power to perform terrible feats of subterfuge....

"Your trust is what left you open to manipulation," Elle confirmed as my gaze rose from the paper. "Me taking your blood is only part of the reason it worked."

"But I trust you because you're trustworthy," I countered, trying not to cringe at tossing such high praise at a wolf.

"Oh, and you always know to trust the good guys and distrust the bad guys?" Elle shot back. "You're a fox among werewolves. You'll never really know who your enemies are."

Chilling...but true. And, at the same time, shifter faces flowed before me. Gunner, Tank, Crow, and Allen—how could I not trust werewolves who provided a better life for my sister and myself?

The contradictions were giving me a headache, so I forced myself to relinquish them and focus upon what really mattered. "Point taken," I said simply, running my hand through tangled locks and grimacing at the dirt stains on both of my knees as the day's deadline reasserted itself. "I'll work on defensive magic...but not right this minute. I'm sorry I was late, but now I have to go."

"To Kira's hearing. I understand." And just like that, Elle turned from hard-nosed teacher into loyal pack mate. Her hand settled on my arm in an example of werewolf touchy-feeliness, and the gesture actually felt natural. "I hope she's doing better than she was?"

I shrugged, wishing I had something better to report about Kira's strange crankiness. Because my sister hadn't been quite herself for weeks now. The symptoms were mild but tenacious, and I was considering a visit to a human doctor to figure out what was going on. I just wasn't sure if the risk was worth the potential payoff....

"Tell me if I can help in any way," Elle continued, rather than prying further. And something about the kindness in her voice flowed across the city alongside me as I returned to the husband she hadn't seen in three long months. Elle refused to risk the guys by cluing them in to her proximity during our meetings, which I knew created a wedge in her relationship that shouldn't rightfully have been there.

Now, as I rushed up the courthouse steps and found the mate in question pacing anxiously, I somehow lost track of the plausible deniability Elle had worked so hard to create. Because Crow was clearly worried by my lateness...and not because he distrusted my ability to guard my own skin. No, the male had seen through the charade Elle and I created and he was anxious about his life partner.

So even though I shouldn't have, I broke my mentor's rule of secrecy. "She misses you but she's fine," I murmured, heartened by the way the male's eyes lit up with instant pleasure.

Then I was pushing past the werewolf and running up marble steps toward the tremendous, column-lined entrance. Was sliding through the metal detector without removing anything other than my keychain—another benefit of carrying my star ball in a diffuse manner rather than as its customary sword.

And I was only two minutes late when I slid into the back of the courtroom...just as the judge banged his gavel and prepared to decide my sister's fate.

Chapter 5

"Kira's grades improved dramatically toward the end of the school year," our current social worker, Stephanie Baumgartner, noted. "On the other hand, I'll admit that her living situation is a trifle on the unconventional side...."

At this point, the middle-aged human glanced up from her paperwork and slid a glance toward the five of us flanking Kira in the front row. Yes, for those unaware of the existence of werewolves, a teenager living with her sister and four cute guys was likely a bit surprising. The judge, unfortunately, had more weighty reservations than that.

"Unconventional is one thing," he interjected. "Undependable is another. I see here that you are Ms. Fairchild's employer as well as her landlord," he continued, spearing Gunner with a far less forgiving gaze than Stephanie had offered. "What's to prevent you from firing your employee and evicting the child all in the same day?"

"Nothing," Gunner started, pausing just long enough for my fingernails to dig painfully into my palms in reaction. Then my companion's left hand was engulfing my right, his huge paw teasing my clenched fist apart even as he added another word to his answer: "Yet."

The judge raised both brows, clearly unimpressed by Gunner's theatricality. Before the official could voice further objections, though, Tank was standing. "Permission to approach the bench?"

At the judge's impatient nod, our personal lawyer—and the worst toilet-seat offender—strode forward and slapped a heavy packet of papers down in front of the older human. "As you can see," Tank continued, "Mr. Atwood is intent upon ensuring the well-being of the underage child regardless of the sister's employment status."

The judge hummed his interest, but unlike him *I* couldn't see whatever made Kira cover her mouth in an attempt to stifle a giggle. My kid sister had apparently been in on this sneak attack from the beginning. I, on the other hand, was left leaning forward and vainly attempting to read the fine print from twenty feet away.

"This document is ten pages long," the judge complained after a moment, flipping through legalese that I likely couldn't have deciphered even if I'd been close enough to make out letters and numbers. "This should have been presented weeks ago so I could read it in my chambers."

"Please allow me to sum up the matter, then, Your Honor," Gunner interjected mildly without removing his hand from mine or approaching the bench the way his pack mate had. "It's really quite simple. I'm promising to maintain monthly support for the child financially, physically, and emotionally until she turns eighteen, no matter what happens with Ms. Fairchild's employment or our relationship."

Despite myself, I retreated away from Gunner's body as I parsed his offer, my fingers sliding out from beneath the heavy weight of his palm. I'd known the alpha had a soft spot for Kira from the first time he met her. But we were foxes and he was a werewolf. Offering me the bullshit job as his personal secretary seemed like a nice gesture while we were all stuck in limbo...but I didn't really expect the alpha to continue involving himself in our lives after he inevitably made up with his brother and was allowed back into their clan home.

The judge, of course, knew nothing of this convoluted family drama. However, he joined me in sharing major reservations about a gesture that seemed too big and too bold. "You do realize that by presenting this contract during a custody hearing, you will be in violation of state law if you renege upon it?"

"I realize that," Gunner answered, kindling a strange fire within my belly. "I have no plans to go back on my word."

"Even though, in essence, you are promising to become this girl's father," the judge translated.

"No," Gunner countered. "I'm angling for a slightly different role in her family. Big brother, to be precise."

THEN THE ALPHA WEREWOLF turned to face me, the gesture drying my mouth so thoroughly I gaped like a fish rather than forcing out any words. Which was likely a good thing given that my instincts consisted of a strange mixture of fleeing...and melting into Gunner's protective arms.

"Mai..." he started. But before I learned whether my companion intended to finally bring whatever had been simmering between us up to the surface, a voice I'd almost forgotten spoke up from the back of the room.

"This is all very sweet," Kira's original social worker stated wryly, "but it is clearly antithetical to the case at hand."

Swiveling in my seat, I sighed at the abrupt appearance of Simon's gloomy visage. The lanky human must have slipped in even later than I had, and unfortunately his professional opinion as a social worker was likely to hold more weight than a grand gesture on Gunner's part. Especially with a judge who was now *smiling* despite the entirely out-of-line discussion taking place in his court of law.

"Because...?" the judge prodded.

"The point being—as always in these cases—the well-being of the child." Simon glanced in my direction briefly, his grimace suggesting that he hadn't forgotten the glimpse of paranormal happenings he'd been privy to three months earlier. The social worker had seen just enough to fuel wild guesses...but I could tell the conclusions he'd come to made him even less impressed by the idea of me raising an innocent child than he had been before.

Luckily, Simon wasn't our social worker any longer. Because the move to Gunner's mansion had changed the district overseeing our case...a point which Stephanie was quick to point out. "I'm the one making a recommendation on behalf of the state," the middle-aged woman said loudly, half-rising as she turned her attention back and forth between Simon and the judge.

I held my breath, half expecting her to make another dig about a teenage girl living among so many unattached and unrelated male personages. But Gunner had worked his magic on Stephanie over the last few months just as thoroughly he had tamed everyone else in his vicinity. There had been cookouts, thoughtful questions about her family, and in the end the alpha had ingratiated himself so thoroughly that the social worker had started inviting *us* into *her* home.

So I shouldn't have been surprised when Stephanie barked back at Simon without hesitation, her tone as fierce as that of any territorial wolf. "I am entirely in favor of this adoption being carried out as requested. The Fairchild family deserves to remain intact."

"Hmm," the judge answered, not even glancing at Stephanie as he jerked his chin toward Simon, giving the latter an opening in which to elaborate.

And Simon didn't fail him either. "After watching Kira live on pasta and peanut butter, start fights with little or no provocation, and get kicked out of two schools over the past six months," Simon intoned gloomily, "I strongly believe the opposite. Kira would be better off living in a halfway house rather than remaining under her sister's inappropriate care."

Chapter 6

Reprieve came from an unexpected the direction. The judge, who I'd thought was looking for the slimmest excuse to wrest Kira out of my custody, banged his gavel before Stephanie could do more than open her mouth for what was bound to be a heated rebuttal.

"As much as I'm enjoying this farce, I have a dinner date," the man said dryly. "So we'll conclude this case on Friday. If anyone has additional evidence they hope to discuss at that time, I recommend you file it *in advance*."

Then we were rising, watching the judge sweep out the back door while Simon stormed out the front. It wasn't a success, but at least we'd been granted a stay of execution. And after thanking Stephanie for her support, the fun-loving werewolves around me immediately leapt onto the idea of a celebratory hunt.

"Wildacres?" Allen suggested, naming the former retreat center that had become the pack's customary hunting grounds in the months since Kira and I been folded into their pack-in-exile. Because the loss of Mama's star ball meant Kira wouldn't be able to shift until she materialized magic of her own making. Good thing Gunner just so happened to have purchased a two-hundred-acre retreat complex, complete with trails wide enough for a teen-driven golf cart to speed along beside wolves and one lone kitsune.

I glanced at my sister, expecting her to take the choice of venue as her due. But Kira wasn't even following the conversation, I realized. Instead, her legs wobbled and her lips quivered, giving me just enough warning to encircle her waist with one supportive arm before she sagged.

"Kira?" I asked, trying to remember if I'd fed her lunch. No, I hadn't. But my sister had been in the middle of the pack at the noon hour—surely the guys had stuffed her to the gills.

"I'm *fine*." Now Kira sounded like herself...and looked like herself as she batted away my supporting arm too. "And you guys don't have to go to Wildacres just for me either. I'd rather read in the car than hang out with you losers anyway."

Now every eye was focused on my sister, four sets of werewolf eyebrows lowering in synchronicity that owed much more to their attachment to Kira than it did to the bonds of pack. "Losers, huh?" Tank countered while I was still trying to decide if the legal setback was really what had shaken up my sister so thoroughly or whether her health had faded so much so quickly. "You can't even beat us with an engine under your a...butt. You want to beg off because you're *afraid*."

For all of his wolfishness, Tank was surprisingly subtle when he wanted to be. Okay, so maybe "subtle" wasn't quite the right word for it. But, whatever the proper adjective, Tank's jibe effectively staved off Kira's emotional retreat and tempted her to engage with her usual flourish.

"Am not!" the child countered.

"Are too!" came the lawyer's skillful repartee.

As our other companions cheerfully joined into the bickering, we all ambled together out to Gunner's SUV then rode through rush hour traffic to Wildacres. And if an odd hole opened up in my stomach as I watched my sister's easy camaraderie with the werewolves, it was worth it for the smile that ended up on her formerly grumpy face.

WE STRIPPED AND SHIFTED outside the abandoned retreat center's main building, in a parking lot surrounded by trees that reminded me for one split second of the setting of my nightmare. Perhaps that's why I hesitated before transforming, stood for ten long seconds absolutely naked but with my panties still dangling from lax fingertips.

"Mai?" Gunner's warm presence pulled me out of my brown study, his eyes searing into my own. Unlike me, he and the guys were accustomed to shifting in company. In fact, the other three werewolves were already in lupine form, frolicking beside my sister who had thoroughly regained her usual good humor during the preceding ride.

"Sorry." I shook my head and dropped the scrap of fabric onto the pile of clothing between us, trying to keep my gaze as carefully face-oriented as Gunner's was. I was a fox, though, not a werewolf. So perhaps it was merely vulpine curiosity that made my eyes drift south....

Whatever the reason, I couldn't stop myself from assessing the alpha's corded muscles and sun-warmed angles. My gaze stroked skin that I would have liked to follow with my hands....

Well, that's not happening. Covering up my illicit daydream, I acted as I should have minutes earlier. I closed my eyes for one split second, then I exploded into the form of my fox.

Fur itched as it pushed out of a human body. Fingernails yanked themselves forward into claw points. My tail grew lightning quickly into a fifth appendage, its fluffy bulk providing an acrobatic grace I could never muster on two legs.

And as I gave in to the fox's body, the preceding awkwardness faded in the face of the challenge of a slanted tree trunk. Rough bark on paw pads. The scrabble of claws against wood as I almost slipped but didn't fall.

Then I was laughing down at my companion from five feet above him...just as the low whir of the golf cart's electric engine started the race.

Immediately, every head turned toward Kira's conveyance. This was why we came here. To hunt sometimes, but more often just to run. And with Kira zipping down the path already, every wolf was hard-wired to give chase.

Foxes, on the other hand, have more choice in the matter. Yes, I craved a triumph...but I was more flexible about how I achieved that goal. Cutting down into a ravine then back up the other side might have been cheating by werewolf standards, but how can you cheat when there are no rules?

Wind, fur, mud, rush. This was the best part of denning with werewolves—the opportunity and ability to race.

Which is how I came to be diving out of the woods to rejoin the others as Kira sped toward the finish line. Behind her, a line of panting werewolves jockeyed for position, Gunner in the lead as his claws tore up the soft earth.

Only nobody in our pack triumphed. Instead, the golf cart skidded sideways as it stopped prematurely, the wolves between me and Kira growling as they picked up on clues I was unable to see or smell from my spot on the other side of the ditch.

Then a tall figure rose up beside my sister's shoulder. A grimly smiling werewolf, but not a stranger unfortunately.

"Well met, brother," offered the pack leader who had sent Gunner into exile. Then his hand came down upon Kira's unprotected neck.

Chapter 7

Mud squished between my toes and my sword tingled to life in abruptly human hands as I lunged toward the male threatening my sister. I half expected Gunner to get there first, frowned as I saw him instead shift and sink into the mud with human shoulders bent earthward. "Pack leader," my former protector murmured. "I have done everything you requested. I ask that you do the same."

The brothers' compromise. Of course. Ransom had ignored the fact that I was a kitsune three months earlier in exchange for Gunner's fealty. Now it appeared that the time had come for the latter to pay up.

A rock dug into my left instep as I swerved sideways to steer clear of the alpha I'd thought was on my side but who might actually be forced to do Ransom's bidding. No matter. I could trust Kira to roll sideways at the proper moment. So all I had to do was...

...twist away from the five wolves who had slid out of the trees and into my sight line while my attention was riveted upon Gunner and his brother. The newcomers reeked of Atwood ozone, their trajectory clearly intended to cut me off from their leader's unprotected backside. And, based on the way they lunged forward without even glancing toward Ransom for permission, I had to guess they'd also caught a glimpse of my illicit fox-related shifting....

Suddenly, I couldn't spare a thought for Kira's predicament or for Gunner's precarious loyalty. Instead, it was all I could do to push off the mud-slick pathway and slip between two teeth-bared muzzles as sharp fangs grazed the skin of my unclad thigh.

Now they growled, the sounds smug with imminent triumph. No wonder when I was entirely surrounded, five wolves spreading in a tight circle that pushed me toward a laughing enemy each time I backed away from one of his pack mates. My sword could only do so much in tight quarters and I was surprised the quintet hadn't already leapt forward and taken me down into the muck.

Their strange reluctance to finish what they'd started, however, couldn't last forever. So I hacked desperately, the flurry of blows insufficient to break me free of the circle but enough to send my enemies back a single step.

A whimper. The scent of Kira's terror. I couldn't spare a glance in her direction, but she was clearly in distress now.

So I tried something I'd been pondering ever since Elle bested me with a scratch from her finger. I flicked my sword back instead of forward, seared a larger cut than I'd intended onto my left forearm.

My own blood tasted nothing like a rabbit's. Instead, it was sweet and at the same time peppery, full of magic I'd yet to learn how to tap.

Necessity is the mother of invention, I decided, closing my eyes for one split second and pulling every burst of power down my spine and into my feet.

Mud splattered around me, slipping through my parted lips and onto my tongue. The soil was gritty and vile, tasting strangely of iron even though the scarlet seeping from my leg and arm shouldn't have made it all the way to the ground so quickly.

Unfortunately, a mouthful of mud was all I got out of the endeavor. No shards of star ball pushed my enemies backwards. No wall of magic prevented their approach. Instead, the wolves pressed in closer, the fear in their eyes promising danger.

Because frightened wolves tend to react predictably. They squash their terror, then they attack.

"DON'T TOUCH ME!"

Kira's voice rang out as I tried—and failed—to rebuild my sword from a lax and diffuse star ball. Her silence up until this point had been carefully calculated, I knew, to prevent distraction. The fact she was now speaking, her voice more shriek than words, proved that the situation was growing worse outside my circle of werewolves even as I edged closer and closer to losing the current fight.

Desperation hadn't been enough to turn the tables in my favor, but worry over my sister pushed me forward where the impulse for self-preservation had been insufficient. Giving up on rematerializing a physical weapon, I instead slid into my fox skin as easily as a swimmer dives beneath the water. And, like a swimmer, I immediately felt gravity recede beneath my feet.

Human, I'd been unable to escape the ring of werewolves. Vulpine, I leapt over the closest wolf's head and landed atop his well-padded rump light as an errant sunbeam.

Unfortunately, my opponent wasn't a fan of sunbeams on his butt. He whirled, teeth snapping shut a millimeter from my fox tail...or perhaps he *did* end up with a mouthful of white-tipped hairs after all. The small loss of bodily matter was irrelevant, however, when I was already ten feet distant, scampering toward a sister who I now saw was engaged in a struggle of her own with two familiar-scented Atwood males.

Ah, the bridge watchers had made a reappearance. So Ransom had kept an eye on us after all. Hadn't been as hands-off about Gunner's exile as he'd initially appeared.

And as if my puzzle-piecing had caught the pack leader's attention, Ransom's eyes abruptly bored into me from only a few feet distant. Meanwhile, Tank, Allen, and Crow were all belly down in the mud in wolf form, resolutely peering the other way as one of the bridge watchers wrenched Kira's right arm up behind her back.

They aren't going to help her. This sign of cowardice on the part of my supposed allies hit me strangely, deep and low like a punch in the gut. For the last three months, every one of our house mates had treated Kira like a beloved kid sister. But now, when push came to shove, they were just going to let her be manhandled without batting a lash?

Well, *I* wasn't so fickle with my loyalties. I bared my teeth, unsure what a single fox could do against masses of wolves but ready to make a stab at some sort of offensive anyway.

Only, before I could act, Ransom growled out an order. "Rein in your woman," he demanded, gaze turning now to his kneeling, naked sibling.

And Gunner didn't even attempt to disobey his brother. Didn't jerk his chin and give his men the right to help us out of our predicament.

Instead, he lifted his head from perusing the mud. Met my eyes. Used my debt against me.

"Mai, stop," Gunner said curtly. And, predictably, the kitsune necessity to repay all of the kindness Gunner had showed me and Kira froze my body mid-swivel. Wrenched me back to humanity. Knocked me into the mud so hard that I didn't get back up.

Chapter 8

Despite dark glares from my former enemies, the wolves I landed amidst didn't tear into me. Instead, they glanced once at Gunner, his verbal claim sufficient to mark me as ineligible for use as lunch meat. Then they shifted in tandem, revealing long scratches up their backs and shoulders that looked far more like the effects of human nails than like any wound I might have inflicted during the battle that came before.

I didn't have long to puzzle over that inconsistency however. Because the werewolves I'd spent the last three months sharing a house with had risen to human feet at the same moment, stepping forward to take up where Ransom's underlings had left off. Allen, Crow, and Tank had always treated me and Kira with gentlemanly deference back at the Atwood mansion. Now, though, the first two grabbed hold of my arms while Tank took custody of my sister on the far side of the racetrack-turned-battlefield.

"I have your word," Gunner growled between us, his back still bent in deference to his brother even though I could taste the former's frustration permeating the air. "The sisters are mine to manage. As ordered, I kept them far away from your pack."

Rather than replying, Ransom gazed at my unclad breasts in a very unshifter-like show of lasciviousness. Not that he seemed particularly interested in me as a sex object or even as a potential enemy. Instead, I got the distinct impression he was staring in an effort to draw his brother's attention to himself.

Gunner, however, kept his gaze carefully trained on the mud. So Ransom was forced to move on to words.

"Are you still sniffing after unwilling tail, brother?" the pack leader asked after one long moment during which my skin prickled with the intensity of his perusal. "If she hasn't put out by now, she's just using you for your money. You're no Casanova, but surely even you know that."

Gunner raised his head in response and I winced, surprised to find that this jab at the younger brother's manhood—or perhaps at my honor—had succeeded where Ransom's earlier efforts at breaking through his brother's illusory show of submission had resoundingly failed. The already loaded air vibrated with electricity now as the younger brother leveraged himself upright, the mud caking his legs from knees to ankles doing nothing to diminish the power of his broad-shouldered stance.

Gunner was magnificent, I noted. A pack leader in bearing if not by birth order. In contrast, Ransom looked like an upstart, no less dangerous but lacking the restraint and maturity his younger brother had in spades.

No wonder Ransom flared his nostrils and continued with his verbal parries. "I've invited two dozen pack princesses to this year's gathering," he said, smirking so broadly his final word was distorted. "They've all accepted, of course, because I'm the world's most eligible bachelor. I plan to try them on for size this week, in ones and twos and threes if you know what I mean." He wiggled dark eyebrows before finishing. "I'm sure a few of the discards will give you the time of day, though, brother. It's painfully obvious you can't get laid on your own."

And that was *almost* the last straw. Around us, werewolf shoulders bent down beneath the force of Gunner's displeasure, the concept of Ransom running through virginal innocents like kleenexes hitting the alpha where it hurt. Any second now, Gunner's already stretched nerves would snap and he'd say something that neither he nor his brother were capable of forgetting.

Which was a shame since I was beginning to understand the point of the preceding banter. Ransom was attempting, in the least efficient way possible, to rewind the brothers' relationship into the past.

After all, Gunner and Ransom had been a solid team when I first met them. The elder brother led the pair on wild goose chases while the younger brother propped up his sibling at all costs.

Which made Ransom's choice to assert his independence three months ago nonsensical. Apparently now the pack leader had returned to his right mind.

Unfortunately, an alpha werewolf can't just ask for assistance. So I sighed, pulled free of my supposed jailers, then took one step toward Ransom with diplomatic words waiting on my lips.

The male I faced, though, was nothing like his brother. He didn't raise brows in question and treat me like an equal when I inserted myself into a conversation that didn't apply to me.

Instead, the pack leader's eyes skimmed over my mud-covered body, a smirk rising onto his lips. "Can't resist a real man, can you, baby?"

Baby, really? And, to my eternal regret, the words I pushed into the ensuing silence came out cockeyed, less like a fox's smooth sidestep and more like a sally led by a werewolf's bared teeth. "My favors aren't for sale," I started. "But you think your brother's are, don't you? What do you need Gunner to do for you now?"

Five minutes ago, I'd thought the situation had already hit rock bottom. But, yep, I'd managed to make it significantly worse. Because Gunner's arm twitched as if he wanted to press between me and his brother...or possibly to wring my ornery neck.

For his part, Ransom *did* turn his attention away from needling Gunner. But as the pack leader's shoulders expanded with alpha aggression, I felt far less capable than Gunner had been of standing up beneath his brother's discontent.

Only...the pack leader didn't eviscerate me, either verbally or otherwise. Instead, his eyes slid sideways to land on the male guarding my back. "Actually, Crow, I came to talk about my cousin. Since when do you let Elle cross into Claremont territory and train kitsunes on the sly?"

Chapter 9

The mention of kitsunes startled a growl from my former assailants, but none of the five moved to act on their ire. So I took a deep breath and accepted that it was time to live up to the promise I'd made Elle when we first started getting together just beyond the edge of Atwood land.

"Are you going to get into trouble for meeting me here?" I'd asked tentatively the first time we'd slipped our minders and visited Claremont territory on the down low. I didn't want to lose my teacher before lessons even started...but I also didn't want to be responsible for a werewolf getting tossed out of her pack if she wanted to stay.

"I'm Ransom's favorite cousin. He wouldn't do anything to me," Elle had promised with a soothing smile. *"But Gunner and Crow aren't currently in his good graces. We have to play this carefully to protect the guys."*

So we'd met in secret, Elle passing along coded messages through her mate that Crow pretended not to understand the meaning of. For my part, I'd evaded Gunner's questions with far less agility, but the plausible deniability was still very much there.

And now the time had finally come to deny the males' involvement. After everything Elle had done for me, I refused to let my mentor down.

"Crow had no idea what was happening," I proclaimed, striding past far too many narrow-eyed shifters as I forced myself to approach the angry Atwood pack leader one step at a time. "No one here knew where I was going. The fault was entirely mine."

"Mai..." Kira started, her voice suddenly young and scared as the reality of our predicament broke through her youthful belief that no harm could come to those she cared about. I hated to worry her, but I trusted Gunner to protect my sister. And I didn't want Ransom's attention focused on Kira for any longer than it already had.

So I pulled out a metaphorical red cape and waved it in front of the bull—or is that bully? "If you want to punish someone for training me," I continued, standing tall at my full five foot zero inches, "surely you're not afraid to tackle a kitsune on your own."

THE WORDS WERE PURE bravado, and I braced myself to be punished by the pack leader now that he had an actual offense to lay at my doorstep. But I'd underestimated Gunner's protective instincts. Because his proximity warmed my backside mere seconds before his hands gently moved me out of his path.

Then the two brothers were facing each other directly, only a few inches of air standing between shoulders that were equally broad and features so similar they were almost twin-like. "An alpha knows what happens in his territory," Gunner growled, completely ruining my efforts to keep him out of harm's way. "It was my choice to allow Mai and Elle to spend time together. I wanted my kitsune to be properly trained."

I half expected Ransom to laugh at both of us. After all, Gunner and I were naked, muddy, and sorely outnumbered. But, instead, the Atwood pack leader puffed himself up further as if facing a rival, his muscles tensing as he attempted—and failed—to stare his brother down.

"*Your* territory?" Ransom muttered finally. Even I could tell that the words had been ill-chosen on Gunner's part. Because the younger brother was still on Atwood land despite having been exiled from clan central. And no pack leader likes having his property impinged upon in front of his men.

"*My* corner of *your* territory," Gunner corrected himself. He cleared his throat, remembered at last to avert his eyes from the supposedly un-meetable gaze of his older sibling. "I've finished clearing the city of malcontents as ordered, pack leader. Are you ready to put me to use so I can quit twiddling my thumbs?"

There. *That* was the answer Ransom had come here to draw out of his sibling. Gunner's head bowed in submission, and the tension between the pack leader and his brother dissipated like fog beneath summer sun.

Still, Ransom waited a moment before accepting his brother's rewording. But then he clapped his sibling on the back...just a little too hard.

"Oh, are you ready to end your vacation, brother? Ready to help me manage our entire territory...and reap the sweet rewards?"

The reminder of the waiting pack princesses made something dark flare within Gunner's eyes for one split second. But his words were pure docility.

"Of course, pack leader," Gunner answered, speaking to the mud rather than to his brother's face. "I come whenever you care to call."

Chapter 10

"Wildacres is safer than the city," Gunner whispered rapidly once we'd all donned clothes and had begun our preparations to depart. The alpha had drawn me aside at the edge of the trees where we could keep an eye on Kira without being in the thick of the action. And while his need to bid me farewell was heartening, any potential coziness was diminished by the fact that two other shifters currently hung on their alpha's every word.

"I can have the electricity on within the hour," Allen noted, tapping at his smart phone's screen, his eyes carefully steering clear of mine.

"Can't do much about the state of the buildings but food delivery is easily achievable," Crow agreed. "Clothing too. And the water comes from a well, so that should work right now."

It was as if I'd become a problem to be managed rather than an honorary pack mate. Which, combined with the way Gunner continued to stare me down like an alpha dominating a recalcitrant underling, made me tempted to rewrite my understanding of our shared past.

After all, Gunner told his brother he'd merely been "twiddling his thumbs" during the preceding season. Which begged the question—had he really become attached to me and Kira, or was his assistance nothing more than the actions of a bored alpha latching onto the nearest available task?

"Stay put," Gunner commanded now, gaze flicking over my shoulder for one split second while he continued barking orders. "Don't give Ransom any reason to go back on his word. Keep your sister close to you."

Well, if Gunner could stick to business then I could also. The trouble was—having Gunner leave us didn't only tug at my heart strings, it also threatened the safe future I thought we'd built for Kira during the preceding months. After all, without Gunner protecting us in person, what was to prevent other werewolves from poaching on his claim? How were we going to win the judge and social worker over to our point of view?

"I *promise* no harm will come to you within my territory," Gunner said, as if he was able to read the doubt in my posture. "I..." he continued. Then, shaking his head, he turned his attention to his hovering lackeys. "Give us a minute."

They didn't flee as quickly as Ransom's underlings would have. Instead, for the first time since the Atwood pack leader had shown up where he wasn't invited, a hint of amusement filtered into Allen's eyes. Meanwhile, Crow coughed into his hand as if smothering amusement, and I had to restrain an urge to kick both bozos in the knees.

Was our separation just a big joke to them? Had our inclusion in their pack for three full months meant nothing that it could be so easily set aside now?

Then—"Look at me," Gunner demanded, drawing my attention away from his receding pack mates. But rather than continuing to relay orders, he reached out slow as molasses. Let fingers trace my cheekbones as he cupped my face in both of his hands.

He's just a touchy-feely werewolf trying to keep me focused, I told myself. But it was hard to believe the lie when my companion leaned in close enough so his breath hovered above my lips like skittish butterflies.

For half a second, I inhaled Gunner's exhale. Smelled his rich, warm aroma. Felt his proximity heating my skin.

Then his mouth landed, hard as a sword thrust.

If our first kiss had been a subtle feint on my part, our second kiss was a ploy of ownership on his. Later, I would realize that every shifter present watched the claiming. Later, I would realize that Gunner was backing up his earlier words with a show of possession that no werewolf could fail to comprehend.

At the time, though, the kiss came and went so quickly I was left reeling and unsure of gravity. And by the time I'd regained my balance, Gunner was already twenty feet distant, his long, lean back the only part of his body visible to my searching eyes.

"Don't let your sister do anything stupid," he told Kira in passing. Then, without a single farewell glance in my direction, he gathered up his pack mates, rejoined his brother, and disappeared into one of the waiting minivans.

TOGETHER, KIRA AND I watched the last taillight recede from the parking area. Darkness was descending rapidly, the sprawling complex that had once housed a busy retreat center looming above us rather than inviting us inside.

"We're staying here?" my sister asked, her voice higher-pitched than usual. She sounded younger now than when wolves had first come into our lives three months earlier. As if becoming part of a pack then losing that protection had lowered her toughness quotient by 100%.

Or maybe it was my sister's unexplained weakness that sagged her shoulders and slowed her footsteps. Whatever the problem, it wasn't going to be solved by waiting here for an absent alpha to remember we continued to exist.

So—"No," I answered, letting my hand linger on the teen's shoulder for one long moment as I pondered next steps forward. I wasn't sure exactly how I was going to manage it, but I intended to find the source of Kira's malaise and solve it, even if—as I suspected—the effort involved hunting down the cloaked figure who had bought and absconded with Mama's star ball.

Which might take a while, given the fact that neither Gunner nor I had found any trace of our enemy's trail in the three months since we'd last seen the being. I'd cross that bridge when I came to it, however. First, I pulled out my cell phone to call the sole person who might miss us if we didn't make it home in the next few days.

While waiting for Kira's social worker to answer, I circled the SUV Gunner and his pack mates had left behind them. It was a nice gesture on their part...or so I thought until I realized the vehicle was locked up tight.

"...then leave a message after the beep," Stephanie's voice mail told me even as Kira offered up a suggestion on the vehicle front.

"We could hot-wire it," my kid sister noted, her eyes trained on her own cell phone, which currently played a video her social worker would very much *not* approve of. "But we'd have to break a window to get at the steering column and we'd need a screwdriver and some other tools...."

I shushed her rapidly as a strident beep promised Stephanie's phone was now recording every word we uttered. "Hey, this is Mai Fairchild," I answered on autopilot while mulling over my sister's suggestion. We *might* be able to break into the vehicle and hot-wire it, but we'd stand out like a sore thumb driving down the interstate with splintered glass in place of a window pane.

Not that I knew where we were going. But I trusted that once we had wheels under us, the path forward would become more clear.

"Kira and I decided to go camping for a couple of days," I continued, patting at my pockets in hopes a multi-tool would suddenly materialize. No such luck. Which left the golf cart as our more realistic option. Too bad the battery-operated vehicle would likely traverse no more than twenty miles before stranding us in an even less habitable spot.

So...maybe we should trust Gunner and stay here after all. His underlings were nothing if not efficient, which meant we'd soon possess both electricity and food. If Kira and I had actually been camping, we would have enjoyed far fewer amenities. Too bad the hairs on the back of my neck begged me to get the hell out of there...and fast.

"Mai," Kira started, all but tugging on my sleeve as she attempted to grab my attention. Once again I shushed her, rattled off farewells to her social worker's answering machine before ending the call.

Only when I removed the phone from my ear did I realize why my sister's eyes had widened in horror. She wasn't nudging me onward out of ordinary teen impatience. Instead, she was alerting me to the fact that we weren't alone after all.

No, there were wolves howling in the distance. And, by the sound of it, they were heading our way.

Chapter 11

"Take the battery out of your phone," I said evenly while matching actions to words with my own device. I couldn't be sure that these shifters had used technology to track us, but I certainly didn't intend to leave that particular barn door wide open for the next time....

Unfortunately, my fingernail caught and bent on the hard plastic in the process, and I swore using language I'd been trying to eradicate from my vocabulary while putting on a good face for Stephanie and her ilk. Not that invective was going to harm Kira more than the wolves now close enough so scents of fur and electricity pressed hard against my nose linings. Brushing aside my brain's wild attempts to think of anything other than the upcoming battle, I fumbled at the key of the only mode of transportation we had at our disposal—the slow and not-so-steady golf cart.

Only that *wasn't* our only mode of transportation, as I realized when Kira's battery slid into her pocket and landed with a soft metallic *clink*. "What?" I started. But my sister was way ahead of me, digging into the denim at her hip with slender fingers then hoisting a key fob erect.

"Tank must have put it there," she crowed, her words tumbling over themselves even as we changed trajectories, running now toward the opposite side of the lot. "I've been teaching him magic tricks, but I didn't realize he'd gotten so *good* at it. Way to go, Tank!"

For the first time in over an hour, Kira's eyes sparkled, reflecting my own rekindling hope. Because if we could outrun the wolves and flee the property that was beginning to feel like a death trap, perhaps we'd survive this ambush after all....

Then we were piling inside the vehicle Gunner had left behind him, slamming the doors, and twisting the engine into roaring life. Back wheels spun on gravel as I pushed the SUV into a three-point turn far faster than was advisable....

Not quite fast enough, though, since eyes were materializing behind us, pupils glowing yellow against the descending dark.

There were at least a dozen werewolves loping out of the forest now. From inside the vehicle, I couldn't smell whether they were Atwood shifters or strangers. All I knew was that they were hungry and *huge.*

Which meant we should be burning rubber in our haste to escape them. Only...my foot slipped sideways rather than punching into the gas pedal. And Gunner's order—*"Stay put"*—rang through my head like a tolling bell.

My debt, it appeared, was working against me. Rather than rushing to evade our attackers, I only managed to clench white-knuckled fingers around the steering wheel as the vehicle beneath me rolled to a gravel-crunching halt.

I wasn't alone, however. Instead—"Gunner always said you were an idiot!" Kira roared, the second-hand insult strangely effective at loosening my debt's hold. Meanwhile, my sister's hands pushed down on my knee even as my muscles reasserted themselves. Then we were speeding out of the parking lot, racing away from wolves howling angrily in our wake.

"He said that?" I asked the back of Kira's head as she turned to raise her middle finger and stick out her tongue at our rapidly receding pursuers. I would have worried that she'd make them even hungrier for our blood...but we had a vehicle and they didn't, so the point was now moot.

"Naw," Kira answered, turning back to face forward. She was panting and sweaty, I noted. Nothing like the teenager who could have run twice that distance without batting a lash. "But I thought a bit of anger might get you moving," she continued, proving that even if her body was oddly weak nothing had happened to her quick mind.

Then, changing gears in an instant, my sister bombarded me with questions of her own. "Where are we going?" she demanded. "Shouldn't we call Gunner to pick us up?"

And I *wanted* to drop the mess into an alpha's lap, I really did. I craved a life so simple I could depend upon werewolves to enfold us into their pack and bail us out of all predicaments.

But Gunner's bond to his brother had proven more resilient than any ties he'd built to us over a single season. And whatever was wrong with Kira seemed to be getting worse and worse.

So I shook my head, stilled Kira's fingers when she went to replace the battery in her cell phone. "No, we'll just drive for a while," I decided. Drive...and see if my instinctive fox nature could come up with a solution to Kira's malaise that my rational side hadn't discovered quite yet.

Loosening my stranglehold on the steering wheel, I let my fox have her head.

Chapter 12

A while turned into five long hours, the beginning of which was just high-speed meandering, attempting not to drive around in circles while ensuring the wolves at Wildacres had lost our trail. But then Kira conked out beside me and I had time to fully consider the impossibility of the task I'd set for myself.

I needed to figure out the source of and solution to the illness that had beset my sister. To track down the owner of my mother's star ball and vanquish the being who had won out over me three months earlier. Those mysteries had seemed unsolvable with Gunner's vast resources at my disposal. What chance did I have of finding the answers on my own now?

While thinking, I raised my left forearm to my mouth, sucking at the wound I'd self-inflicted in an attempt to escape from Ransom's lackeys earlier. The sore was no longer bleeding, but fox nature prompted me to purify the gash with the healing power of good, clean saliva. The task wasn't very palatable from a human perspective, but at least it soothed my nerves.

Soothed my nerves...and reminded me of how awful I probably looked. Glancing at myself in the rear-view mirror, I had to laugh at the mud and gunk splattering my clothes and skin from head to foot. One dirty wound down, ten thousand cuts and scratches still to go.

I wasn't about to lick my entire body, which meant most me of me would remain filthy. But at least I could drive without smearing the steering wheel with drying blood....

To that end, I switched to my sword hand to clean the red speckles off my thumb and forefinger. Only this blood wasn't of my own making. Instead, the particles bit into my tongue, sharp as pepper...then filled me with an epiphany-laden euphoria that came and went in the time it took to release a single breath.

This was the magic Elle had tapped into. This was the boost I needed to figure out where the solution to my dilemmas lay.

This was also likely highly dangerous. Why else would my mentor have warned about the ability of a werewolf to use kitsune blood without mentioning the reverse possibility?

Still.... Beside me, Kira curled in on herself as if shielding an aching belly. Outside, strangers rolled past in their cars. There was no one left but me to protect my sister. So, before I could rethink the avenue of exploration, I sucked up the last of the wolf blood on my finger....

"Take me to the solution to Kira's problem," I said aloud even as my head threatened to float out of the vehicle like a helium balloon. In response, the power channeled inward, hardened, pointed...pulled the steering wheel toward the north.

I FOLLOWED THE VAGUE hints of directions for the rest of afternoon and evening, until our SUV crunched to a halt in a tree-lined dead end. Kira was still soundly sleeping, and her fetal-position body looked so childlike that I hated to wake her up. Still, the niggle of intuition in my stomach urged me onward, so I shook Kira's shoulder gently then a little harder yet.

"Is it morning?" my sister murmured, voice hoarse and raspy. Back when Kira enjoyed access to our mother's star ball, she used to leap from bed to mischief in less time than it took for me to open my eyes and wipe away the sleepy dust. Now, though, my sister was groggy and grumpy, barely willing to follow me out of the SUV and into the night.

"I miss my star ball," the teenager complained as we picked our way across the roadbed and into the richly scented woodland beyond it. As if proving her point, a low-hanging limb smacked into her face, evoking a string of those exact same words my sister wasn't supposed to know the meaning of.

I started to laugh at her drama-queen impersonation—after all, moonlight illuminated the forest quite sufficiently for fox-assisted eyes. But there was actual blood on my sister's cheekbone, suggesting this was more than an act intended to send us back to the SUV to sleep.

No, my sister really was floundering without Mama's star ball, humanity reasserting itself as the borrowed magic faded away. Luckily, I could see well enough for the both of us. Readjusting our positions, I tucked Kira's fingers into one of my belt loops then began holding each limb carefully sideways until we were both long past.

We continued that way for perhaps three quarters of a mile, the traveling made easier once we latched onto a game trail that had been beaten into the earth. Here and there, I caught faint hints of canine. But the scents were old and might have been made by farm dogs rather than by wolves...or so I let myself believe.

Finally, the ground rose beneath our feet, giving us the option of turning sideways as the deer had done or smashing our own path through blackberry thickets up to the crest. My fox instinct whispered *upward*, and my human nature agreed that the rise would be an easily defensible location just in case the afore-mentioned scents belonged to shifters rather than to pets.

"Just a little further," I promised, easing Kira through the tangle. She whimpered as thorns snagged in her hair and tore at her cheekbones, but the girl didn't complain as I less than agilely untangled strand after strand.

A Kira too tired to even protest being manhandled was a sad sight indeed, and in desperation I turned to stories to keep her there with me. "Did I ever tell you what it was like when I got my star ball?" I asked, feeling her head shake slightly from side to side as I picked a thorny twig out of her hair.

Taking that motion as an indication of moderate interest, I dove straight into an anecdote from my past. "It appeared above my pillow the morning I turned thirteen," I offered, gently pressing Kira back onto the path as the thorn let loose its hold on her head. "You've gotta remember, I wasn't lucky enough to have a borrowed star ball from the time I was a toddler the way you did. So this was the first time I'd been able to change into fox form."

My sister murmured understanding, which was enough to keep me leading her on up hill while telling a story I'd never relayed to anyone previously. "It was scary and exciting to be an animal," I told her. "And, I'm ashamed to say, I ended up barfing all over my birthday cake...."

The tiniest trickle of a giggle was the nicest sound I'd heard all day. Then we were out of the briers, sinking down to sit side by side on a soft bed of tall grasses.

"But my birthday was *two months ago*," Kira rebutted after a moment, the impatience in her voice making her sound almost like her old self again. "And I *don't* have a star ball. I *can't* shift."

"So maybe biology doesn't always operate by the calendar," I answered. Then, ignoring the twinge of conscience in my stomach, I voiced a vow I had no way to keep. "Your magic will show up soon, I promise. And, if not, I'll find a way to get Mama's star ball back."

Chapter 13

I fell asleep begging my mother for answers, and maybe that explained my dream. A dream of fingers raking across rippling muscles, a male convulsing above and within me as I shivered in triumph and disgust.

Disgust because I was prostituting my body. And triumph because I'd harvested enough blood this time to sedate my Master...and also to empower myself.

"Stay," the male murmured as I disentangled myself from his body. "You're a wildcat. I dig it. There's more where that came from."

"Another night," I purred, licking scarlet liquid from beneath my fingernails and watching as the werewolf beside me slipped down into unbreachable slumber. Like the others, he'd remember nothing more than sharp-edged pleasure the following morning. Once again, the harvest had been a success.

I might as well have been alone now as the moon shone in through a screened tent window, the male's slumber a reprieve from possession and pretend. But the Master wouldn't like it if I lingered here indefinitely. So I licked more blood from around my cuticles, daintily spitting the liquid into a tiny bottle provided for this exact purpose before moving on to the next.

Without my star ball, I couldn't outright disobey direct orders...but my jailer didn't know enough to hedge every potential gap in the defensive wall that hemmed me in. So after cleaning my right hand and moving on to my left index finger, this time I swallowed instead of spitting.

And, immediately, the body I was inhabiting melded deeper around me. The world, which had been muffled and distant, roared closer in a haze of cricket song and hazy moonlight. Werewolf energy blossomed beneath my skin, and for one short moment my abilities amped up so far I was able to not only grasp blindly for my daughter but also to speak.

"If you can hear me, Mai, know this is your heritage," I murmured, feeling blindly through the void that separated us. "Your soul in someone else's body. It takes werewolf blood, but it is possible to achieve...."

I wanted to show her, to turn my head toward a mirror and let the red of possessed eyes shine out of someone else's features. After all, Mai likely couldn't hear me, but maybe she could see the potential if I tried....

Unfortunately, there were no mirrors present, and the closest body of water was too far for me to reach before the Master's will tugged me back onto the accepted path. Already, I could feel this dozenth try at communication failing. Could feel a tug in my belly drawing me away from the tent, across closely shorn grass, to the drop-off point at the edge of the field.

I tucked the bottle of liquid behind a rock in the designated area, pain coursing through me as I tried once again to disobey. Because I knew the Master's use of this magic would be worse than the possession that had harvested it. I knew...

...nothing as my conscious began to fade. The body I was inhabiting shuddered as my soul wisped into static. But I clung on with incorporeal fingers, unwilling to disappear before righting my own wrong.

Because I'd wrenched my star ball from my body to protect my daughters. How bold I'd been to think I might change the course of history when the trail into the future branched and branched and branched again.

And yet...I continued to be bold. Because every peek I mustered past the veil of the present promised dangers to my offspring. And I refused to leave them walking blindly into the mists.

So I used the last drop of werewolf blood still embedded in my palm to power one final attempt. "Be careful," I tried...and failed...to warn them.

Then, once again, I lost myself into the dark.

I WOKE WITH COPPER on my tongue and the vile memory of my mother—myself?—having sex with a stranger. My shoulders hunched in horror as I spat red-tinged liquid out onto the grass.

"Mai?" Kira murmured beside me. She woke slowly, the same dawn light that had broken me out of the nightmare prompting her to unfold, stretch, leverage her slender torso semi-upright.

She looked terrible this morning. Her lips were gray around the edges. Her eyes were barely slitted open. Her voice sounded like a fox's moan of discontent.

And there was nothing I could do about it except mimic werewolves. So I slipped my hand onto her shoulder for a quick dose of comfort then pulled her upright to follow the path my gut suggested downhill through the trees. *The Master is this way*, a voice in my head seemed to murmur, its tone midway between Mama's and my own.

But as much as I wanted to find our enemy and settle this issue once and for all, we had to pass through the forest to get to that point. And my life in a concrete jungle had left me with few wildcrafting skills to call upon. Perhaps that's why it took pretty much the entire day to pick our way through a forest that seemed to fold in on itself and grow larger by the hour, every passing moment making me doubt my instincts more and more.

"I'm thirsty," Kira whined as hot afternoon sunlight turned the forest into a sauna. Then she brightened, pointed—"Look! There's a stream..."

"...Which you're not drinking out of." I grabbed the teen's arm and pulled her away from the enticing rivulet of water. Wildcrafting wasn't my strong suit, but even I knew that imbibing untreated water in a forest full of deer poop was a recipe for disaster. This trek would be significantly less pleasant if we both came down with the runs.

Of course, I could have shifted into fox form and drunk from the creek without repercussions, but that would have been akin to smacking my kid sister in the face with her loss. Instead, I swallowed against the scratchiness in my throat, turned resolutely away from the water, then beat a path straight up a forty-five degree hillside in the direction my gut told me led toward the solution for my sister's malaise.

We walked forever, until my head pounded from the heat, drowning out cicadas, my thoughts, and even Kira's dismal panting in my wake. "I really think if we'd stayed in that valley, that creek would have led us right here eventually," my companion groused after we'd crested a rise, gone down the other side, and ended up beside a creek eerily similar to the one we'd started out beside.

I opened my mouth to agree, then hesitated as strongly scented air flowed across my palate and down into my throat. The breeze was sharp with ozone, and now that our feet weren't shuffling through leaf litter I was positive I heard something unusual rising over the insects' relentless song.

Yep, there it was again—a yelp piercing the thrum of the cicadas, a growl so deep it vibrated against my very bones.

Kira's dark eyes met mine, hers wide with worry. So she'd heard the same thing I had. Had heard, and was reacting in the way any smart fox would when facing predators larger than themselves—with the urge to flee.

But Kira looked like death warmed over and the tug in my gut told me the solution lay before us rather than behind. So, taking my sister's hand, I tugged her around a curve in the hillside...and straight into an amphitheater full of wolves.

Chapter 14

The indentation in the earth was massive, big enough to seat perhaps a thousand audience members upon the grassy steps that led from where we were standing down toward a similarly open and grass-lined stage. Which meant the two hundred or so shifters lounging both two-legged and four-legged before us should have been a measly showing barely sufficient to tempt the entertainment—two battling werewolves—out of bed.

But the air was electric with excitement. The fighters moved so quickly I couldn't tell one from the other. And every audience member leaned forward with such intensity that none noticed when Kira and I stepped out through the trees behind their backs.

Which was a good thing since it gave me time to scan the audience, seeking the solution to Kira's increasing weakness. The answer must be here somewhere—surely it wasn't coincidence that we'd come all this way and ended up right back within the ozone-scented Atwood pack....

There, my instincts whispered, the tug in my gut pulling me one step further out into the open before fading away entirely. Whatever was aiming me had turned my chin a little left of center, and I saw at once what I'd been guided toward.

Ransom lounged upon a gilded throne at the edge of the stage area, one leg flung up over the armrest and an empty goblet dangling laxly from the opposite hand. A male whispered in his left ear while a simpering female topped up whatever he was drinking. And as the battling wolves before him tumbled and growled with such ferocity that even my bloodthirsty sister winced in sympathy, Ransom just smiled wider and lifted his goblet back to his lips.

"When we were kids, Ransom was the rash one," Gunner had told me many months earlier. *"He made...mistakes...and was glad to have me as his compass."*

Now, as a chill ran up my spine, I suddenly regretted never digging into what those mistakes consisted of. Why hadn't I found time to ask the reason the younger brother acted in many ways like the older son?

Because Gunner was unshakably loyal to his brother, that's why. Because I trusted the alpha who had protected Kira so selflessly. Trusted him...and didn't want to see him hurt.

There in the amphitheater, Ransom's eyes met mine with gleeful malice. And I accepted at last that I might have let the younger sibling's trust cloud the instinctive judgment of my fox.

Because the brows of the Atwood pack leader lifted sardonically, then his eyes flitted sideways to take in Kira sagging beside me. The gesture was a clear warning, and I wished by all that was holy that I'd thought to stash my sister in the forest before walking boldly into the evening entertainment of the Atwood pack.

Hoping to correct my mistake, I scanned the crowd in search of familiar faces. Tank, Allen, Crow, and Elle were present, I noted thankfully. All four were clustered on a back step, close enough so Kira could likely reach them before Ransom's men had time to attack.

But I made no move to push her toward them, not wanting to relinquish my sister to second-tier protectors no matter how loyal they might be. Instead, I scanned the crowd again, hoping Gunner would materialize and use his strength to ensure Kira remained entirely safe.

If the alpha was present, though, his large form was lost amid the watching shifters. And now the wolf battle amped up to the point where it drew even Ransom's jaded eye...and my own skittish attention.

There was fur in the air as the combatants rolled together across the stage area. The growls turned so fierce that I wanted to spray them with a water hose, and the front row of the audience scuttled backwards as the fighters impinged upon their personal space. I couldn't understand why any pack leader in his right mind would allow such a battle to continue unhindered...

...and as if sensing my concern the pair froze, one wolf clamped down upon the other's jugular. So this was it. The bloody end that a suddenly silent audience had been anticipating.

"Mai, that's..." Kira whispered. But I already knew what she was trying to point out. After all, I'd been smelling Gunner for several long minutes—the only surprise was that he was the losing wolf on the bottom rather than the triumphant wolf on top.

Then the tables turned...or rather the wolves.

The pause, it turned out, had been a gathering of energy rather than incipient submission. Because without regard to his enemy's knife-sharp canines, Gunner shifted as he lunged upward. Muscled arms twisted, one behind his back and the other out in front. He heaved the black wolf through the air to thud so hard against Ransom's throne that the latter lay still where he'd fallen. Then straightening, Gunner stood tall and naked, appearing more like a pack leader than his brother did upon his throne.

The crowd erupted into an exuberant roar of shouts and clapping, but Gunner didn't even acknowledge the noisy jubilation. Instead, his gaze me mine, the touch hard hard like the kiss we'd shared back at Wildacres...then soft like a hand on my back guiding me through an open door.

Warmth, greeting, appreciation...then fear on my behalf. All of that flickered across Gunner's features one second before all expression faded away.

Unfortunately, Ransom was just as sharp as his brother and I doubted he'd missed the preceding exchange. But the pack leader didn't remark upon our wordless greeting, merely clapped slowly and sarcastically as the losing combatant clambered to his feet and slunk, still four-legged, away into the crowd.

"Well done, little brother," Ransom broadcast loudly enough for me to hear from the top step. Clearly, the preceding battle had merely been a game in his estimation, and as he motioned toward the audience I saw for the first time what had been intended as the prize.

Because a woman in a translucent white dress hovered at the edge of the assembled shifters. She was all pack princess—young and beautiful. And, apparently, for sale to the highest bidder now.

"Congratulations," Ransom continued. "You have won a night with the lovely Lucinda by your side."

Chapter 15

I think I must have gasped. Whatever the reason, Kira's right hand clamped down upon my left arm so hard I lost all circulation. And, in reaction, I forced my spine to straighten, my face to remain as serene as Gunner's still was.

But Ransom wasn't done teasing us. "Stay, stay, the show's not over!" he proclaimed, halting shifters who had begun standing and shaking tension out of their bodies in preparation for departure. Obediently, they stilled and sank back down upon the grass even as I pushed Kira toward the promised safety of Tank and his companions.

Because something was about to happen. I felt it, knew Ransom's trouble centered around me rather than around the brother he loved to hate.

And, sure enough, this time Ransom gestured across the audience in my direction. "Tonight will be a double header," he continued. "Who wants to fight for the right to take Mai Fairchild to his bed?"

Two hundred werewolves swiveled and stared at me, their eyes hungry, interested...and not friendly in the least. They were all young, I noticed, nearly all males too. As if the families and oldsters had opted out of Ransom's summer gathering, knowing what sort of craziness was likely to occur therein.

But Gunner rained on their parade quite admirably. Although already half entangled in Lucinda, he still managed to step forward and proclaim "Mai is *mine*" around the female shifter's curly updo.

Everyone else quaked before the younger sibling's growl, but Ransom merely laughed. "Don't get greedy, little brother. You already hold one bitch in heat. What use would you have for a fox?"

And, just like that, the cat came thoroughly out of the bag. *"Kitsune"..."Fox"..."Magic"*—words rose above the crowd in waves of whispers. I caught only hints of the ensuing conversation, but what I heard was pretty much what I'd come expect.

Only their pack leader's presence was preventing the crowd from turning into a mob intent upon tearing me to pieces. So this seemed like the perfect opportunity to raise my voice and announce: "I fight for myself."

Just like that, the few males who had stood when Ransom asked for takers promptly flopped back down onto the ground. "What, nobody?" Ransom laughed even as he raised one eyebrow. "Well, if none of you are brave enough to fight a kitsune, I'm game. No weapons, though. Skin and fur only. I'll beat you fair and square, little vixen. Then you'll scream with pleasure inside my tent."

I GLANCED AT NEITHER Gunner nor Kira, knowing the horror that would be displayed on both of their faces. Because Ransom had placed me in an impossible position. If I won, the pack would assume I'd used kitsune powers and disembowel me...and my sister also. If I lost, I'd be forced to sleep with a male I found distasteful—a matter worsened by my sister's wide eyes and Gunner's apparent inclination to tear his brother apart.

Buying time, I descended slowly, letting my sword dissipate into a ball of glowing magic and noting in the process which nearby werewolves stood their ground and which fell subtly back before my approach. There were more of the latter than the former...but winning still didn't seem like the smartest path to saving Kira's life.

For his part, Ransom was shucking off his clothing as if performing a strip tease, one slow article at a time. His eyes were on his brother instead of me, however. And as Gunner's color rose, I hastened my own steps.

"I'm ready," I told the nearly naked pack leader upon reaching the recessed stage. I hadn't shifted...I didn't particularly want to wave my fox tail in front of a pack of wolves when so severely outnumbered. Instead, I spread my legs and braced myself, lowering my weight a little and preparing for whatever attack Ransom chose to dish out.

I'd braced myself...but I still wasn't ready for the speed of my opponent's charge. One moment the pack leader was stepping out of boxers, the next he was spinning toward me, four-legged and covered in fur. I barely had time to leap out of his path before he barreled into the spot where I'd been standing. Then he twisted sideways and bit at my leg so unexpectedly that I only had one second to ponder whether to cheat and use my star ball for protection or not.

No, I decided. A fox would. A wolf wouldn't. So, instead of materializing the metallic cuff that could have saved my skin quite literally, I leapt upward and kicked out at my opponent's face.

Of course, magic aside, the move was the only one at my disposal. No wonder Ransom was prepared for my evasive jump. His head whipped sideways even as he flung himself airborne after me. And I yelped as sharp teeth bit into the skin of my hip.

Gunner's growl rent the air even as Ransom released me. And I knew without being told that, the next time my enemy's teeth contacted, the younger brother would join the fight.

Which couldn't happen. Not when Gunner was doing everything he could to maintain a relationship with his brother. Not when I was still unsure whether my instinct was right and the male I fought against was the Master and the solution to Kira's malaise.

But I couldn't turn fox or utilize my magic. So what alternative did I really have?

For his part, Ransom was enjoying the hunt. Rather than attacking again directly, he pushed me backwards subtly but unerringly, guiding my footsteps toward the first line of seating in an effort to trip me up.

Despite knowing what was happening, I had no real alternative. So I took another step backward...then something seared across my stomach like a combination of ice and fire. As if the magic guiding me here had rematerialized three times stronger than when it had left me. Only, tiredness now dragged down my body rather than the euphoria of wolf blood buoying me up.

"What?" I murmured, glancing down at my own belly. Ransom was too far away to have done the damage, but whatever had hit me was sharp and effective. Because a thin line of blood now pushed up through my clothing.

Meanwhile, behind my back, the audience's reaction was out of proportion to the minor wound.

While my attention had been focused elsewhere, whispers from the crowd had turned into a cacophony. A man grunted, a woman screamed.

Leaping sideways, I bought enough leeway to peer back at the watching shifters. To my surprise, it wasn't the prospect of a kitsune fighting their pack leader that had the werewolves riled up. In fact, they weren't even gazing in our direction at all.

Instead, shifters batted at themselves wildly. First they hit their own arms and legs as if trying to squash a biting insect. Then they pushed against each other, descending into an unruly snarl like dogs with cans tied around their tails.

One male turned to face the forest, revealing a long line of blood dripping through his shirt much like mine was doing. Meanwhile, at the edge of the stage only twenty feet distant, Lucinda leapt out of Gunner's arms and onto the grass.

Or, rather, she appeared to have been *pushed* out, slung sideways by a being we could neither smell nor see. I could sense the spirit, though. Could almost taste its barely contained anger....

So Mama *had* been the one guiding me after all. The unexplainable wound in my belly matched the location of the instinct that had led me to this location in the first place. Had her daughter's blood been sufficient to turn her corporeal? Was that why she was now able to come to my aid?

Whatever the nuts and bolts of the matter, I appreciated Mama's attempt to break up the fighting. It was just too bad she'd chosen to show herself so thoroughly right in front of a pack of angry wolves.

Chapter 16

"Stop!" I yelled, forgetting I was supposed to defend myself from Ransom as I instead dove toward the younger Atwood who appeared to be next in line for my mother's wrath. Because I wasn't so sure Mama understood who was and wasn't her enemy. And I couldn't bear the thought of harm coming to the alpha who had protected me and my sister for so long.

Only...I appeared to be moving in the wrong direction. Because Ransom—now human—roared like a stuck pig, slapping himself in the face as a scratch rose along the side of his jaw. Then another cut opened up the skin half an inch away from his eyeball, which raised the pitch of the shifter's roar into a scream.

"Mai, grab it!" Elle yelled from the top step of the amphitheater. Kira was gone—one glance told me that—hopefully spirited away by one or all of the guys we'd lived with back in the city. But my mentor was trying to push her way toward me...an attempt doomed to failure given the state of the milling crowd.

Her words, however, were enough to provide direction. If Elle thought grabbing my mother would make a difference, then I'd do everything in my power to touch Mama's spirit self.

Unfortunately, the ghost in the amphitheater was still invisible. And her attack upon Ransom was so erratic—hitting his feet, his head, and his buttocks in short order—that I didn't even know where to begin my defense.

Or my human self didn't. Sliding out of my clothes and into my fox skin, however, opened up new avenues to explore. Whiskers twitched with shifting air currents. Superior nostrils caught the faintest hint of my mother's favorite jasmine perfume winding around my nose.

She was hovering in a tornado of fury around the pack leader's head, I gathered. Too high for me to reach even if I regained my human stature.

On the other hand....

Leaping onto Ransom's shoulders was the work of a single second, fox paws spreading to catch my balance even as the werewolf attempted to bat me aside. Mama was close enough now that I could have reached out and touched her. But there was one more thing I needed to do first.

Because blood, I gathered, was the key to kitsune powers. Good thing I just so happened to be standing atop a bleeding werewolf.

I lowered my head and licked up a scarlet trail oozing out of Ransom's scalp, the first sustenance I'd imbibed in nearly twenty-four hours sitting rich and salty on my tongue. The effects, however, went far beyond squashing the low-blood-sugar wooziness in my noggin. Instead, a jolt of energy flowed through me like lightning, empowering my muscles and also providing a sixth sense I'd never experienced before.

Abruptly, I knew exactly where Mama was without needing to twitch my whiskers and make wild guesses. She'd slid lower in preparation for another strike to Ransom's belly. But before she could scratch, I leapt.

I shifted as I fell, landing with arms around my mother's neck as if I was once again a child. And in response, her face materialized before me, so familiar that it seemed like merely a day rather than over a decade since I'd seen her last.

"You're all grown up. My beautiful daughter." I wasn't sure if the words came out of her throat or simply flew into my head without the need for sound waves. Either way, almost-tears squeezed my throat so hard I could barely speak.

"Mama," I whispered after one dry-throated swallow. "You can't do this. You have to *stop.*"

Her eyes met mine, so much like peering into my own reflection that I shivered. Then—long before I was ready to lose her—she was gone, disappearing back into the void from which she'd come.

For my part, I was tumbling to the stage, no longer supported by my mother's barely corporeal body. Was listening to the shifters who—now that it was safe—had converged upon the recent battleground.

"She grabbed herself?" one asked, confused.

"Kitsunes can have two bodies," another answered, seeming sure of something that definitely didn't match up with my understanding.

Then the mutters merged into one endless stream of anger. And the sky disappeared above my head as the pack dove as one on top of my prone and winded form.

Chapter 17

"*Step back, go to your tents, and stay there!*"
The words were clearly an alpha commandment given the speed with which my attackers disengaged from the fight. On the other hand, the alpha tossing around orders was just as clearly Gunner rather than Ransom based on the way my debt tugged at me to follow in the receding werewolves' footsteps.

"I don't have a tent to go to," I muttered under my breath, getting ahold of my body with an effort. And when I was finally able to look around me, I noted that most of the werewolves seemed to be engaged in a similar battle of willpower. Only, in their case, the issue appeared to be whether to accede to the younger brother's wishes...or to continue protecting their wounded pack leader by killing the obvious kitsune in their midst.

Lucinda alone had no such ambivalence about which action to engage in. She picked herself off the ground where Mama had flung her, marched up to Gunner, and slapped him hard across the face. "You *bastard*!" the female hissed. "You won me and now you're angling for fox booty in addition?" Then she stalked out of the amphitheater with a sway to her walk intended to show Gunner precisely what opportunity he'd tossed aside.

And, to be honest, I couldn't really blame the other female for her anger. After all, from what I understood about the battle I'd walked in during, Gunner had as good as taken one girl to the dance then prepared to leave with another. As the side piece in question, I wasn't particularly thrilled.

Ransom was quick to agree with my assessment. "Brother, you have a *lot* to learn about women," the pack leader noted, blotting at his bloody face with the shirt he'd discarded a few moments before. And he looked so prosaic in that moment that I suddenly doubted the instinct that had made me conclude he was the Master. Could Mama really have broken through her minder's magical bonds so thoroughly as to attack him if that had been the case?

"On the other hand"—Ransom's voice broke through my thoughts as his eyes scanned the ambivalent shifters—"my brother speaks for me on matters that don't pertain to women. This fight is over. Now *go.*"

I turned to follow the other shifters, my mind already racing with ideas about how to track down my sister. Because finding her had to be my top priority, even above ferreting the Master's identity out. The guys would have brought her somewhere safe but would have assumed I'd know how to find them. So...

"Not *you.*" Ransom's words, while not impacting my footsteps the way Gunner's had, froze me in place nonetheless. Because what the pack leader might lack in overt dominance, he clearly made up for in wiles....

Only, Ransom wasn't speaking to me. His gaze was instead intent upon his brother, and now Elle was tugging at my arm.

"Mai," she murmured, pulling me along behind her until we stopped in front of a nicely dressed male that I'd met once previously. Was he Lincoln, Leonard? Whatever his name, this was the same shifter who'd slammed the door in my face the first time I'd visited the Atwood mansion, the male who had filled Ransom's goblet while Gunner was fighting...and, apparently, the twin Elle had spoken of so fondly of during our riverside lessons.

Because—"Go with my brother," my mentor murmured before sliding away from me and back toward the sibling standoff. The electricity in the air was raising the hairs on my arms, but she slid between the duo as if there was no danger, removing the shirt from Ransom's fist and bringing the fabric up to dab gingerly at her pack leader's face. "You're going to have a shiner..." she berated him.

Then I was being drawn up the stairs behind her brother, away from everyone I knew within this strangely combative pack.

"I JUST WANT TO FIND my sister," I offered once we were out of the amphitheater and away from the danger Ransom's presence represented. Unfortunately, the male beside me seemed disinclined to offer any direction. Instead, he thrust out his hand in a distinctly unwerewolf-like gesture of greeting.

"I'm Liam, in case you don't remember," he said.

"Mai," I answered, accepting a grip that was firm but not overpowering. Despite the unpleasantness of our initial introduction, Liam seemed less like the stereotypical werewolf and more like his easy-going sister. A definite relief given that he was the sole familiar face in the swirl of werewolfishness that surrounded us both.

"And now I know where Elle's been running off to," Liam continued, his words mirroring my pondering. "I'd thought all the secrecy meant she was stepping out on her boyfriend...."

"Her husband, you mean." I frowned. "Or mate, rather. I thought werewolves chose a partner for life."

"You've been reading too many novels." Something dark and wounded flickered across Liam's face as he answered, then he turned on his heel and led me downhill and deeper into the forest without another word.

So—mates, not a good topic. I grimaced, deciding that holding my tongue was a good decision when faced with a prickly shifter whose sore spots were impossible for a stranger to suss out.

After that, we walked for several minutes in silence, signs of werewolves dissipating until we might as well have been wandering through an uninhabited wilderness rather than skirting around the edges of the shifter equivalent of a professional networking convention. Still, there was no sign of Kira. So, eventually, I caved and asked again.

"My sister..." I started, having to speak up this time to be heard over the sound of a nearby waterfall. Rather than answering, though, Liam held up one hand in a request for patience then pulled me off the deer trail we'd been following and straight through a thicket of thorns.

In a minute, I decided, I'd turn back and find someone more likely to lead me to my sister. In a minute....

Due to the dim evening lighting or my own rushed thinking, I didn't realize we were on a clifftop until Liam paused...then dropped right over the edge. Only when I picked my way to the cliff edge after him did I see that Liam was holding onto the side of the rock face with one hand while leveraging himself down a series of ungainly but apparently human-created steps that led to a flat ledge of rock at the base of a waterfall.

How handy, I noted. *To have a hideaway close to but at the same time unrelated to the gathering....*

The existence of this secluded spot, however, became irrelevant as soon as my eyes drifted down to the cluster of shifters gathered at the shadowed cliff base. Allen, Tank, and Crow were all huddled so close together that I could barely distinguish one from the other. Then a shifter leaned backwards and I clearly saw the comatose form of my sister lying at their feet.

Chapter 18

"What happened?" I gasped out as I broke into their cluster. Pebbles were still tumbling down the staircase behind me, but I didn't actually remember working my way through the intervening space. Somehow, though, I'd ended up at the bottom while Liam was still nearly at the top. Meanwhile, the roar of the waterfall must have muffled the clatter of my approach because Tank and Crow responded as if I was an enemy, leaping to their feet and arraying themselves protectively between Kira and myself.

Allen, on the other hand, remained seated, cradling the teen's sweat-sodden head in his lap. "She collapsed," he said simply, recognizing me before the others did. Then he scooted sideways and let me take over his position, Kira's limbs flopping doll-like as she was transferred from his embrace to my own.

"No wonder. She's starving and thirsty," I explained aloud, trying not to berate myself for dragging a thirteen-year-old along on a journey that would have stressed a full-grown human. But even while latching onto a rational explanation, I knew there was likely more to it. Because Kira's stamina, until this summer, had been better than that of a marathon-running horse.

"Here." A bottle of water pressed into my left shoulder blade, one of the shifters having come prepared for a thirsty and comatose kid. But I lost track of both bottle and companions as my sister's eyelids fluttered open, the dark orbs below watery with unshed tears.

"Mai?" she whispered, trying and failing to sit up under her own volition. "Ow," she mouthed as she gave up on the motion, falling back against my knee while cradling her own head.

Then two shifters were leveraging her halfway vertical, a third was unscrewing the cap and tilting water between her barely parted lips. The liquid seemed to do the trick, too, because Mai's breath started coming a bit easier, the sweat I wiped away from her forehead failing to immediately reform beneath my hovering hand.

"Do you guys have a granola bar? Some beef jerky? Crackers?" I couldn't quite understand why Allen, Tank, and Crow averted their eyes at this question, so I continued listing what I considered readily available snack food. "Cereal would work also. Or a sandwich. It's been almost a day since Kira ate last."

"You're starving too," my sister murmured, her eyes squinting as if the dusky light of evening was instead the glaring sun of midday. In fact, her words weren't even audible over the roar of the waterfall—I was forced to read the rebuttal in the motion of her lips.

"I'm fine," I promised, placing both of my hands on my sister's shoulders, barely finding a spot around Allen and Tank's supporting fingers and arms. "Well?" I asked again, meeting the eyes of each male, one after the other.

They were silent for one long second. Then: "We don't bring food to the gathering," Allen explained. "We hunt as a pack...."

"Even when there's a sick child who recently fainted due to hunger?" I raised both eyebrows, unable to believe that we'd need Ransom's say-so before giving my sister food.

The guys' lack of answer served as confirmation and I wanted to shake them. But *I* didn't have to kowtow to the Atwood pack leader. Better to solve my problem than to vent my spleen.

So, gently releasing Kira, I rose to my feet and turned back toward the forest. "If anyone wants to help me, I'm going to find food for my sister. If not, I hope you'll at least keep her safe while I hunt."

LIAM WAS THE ONLY SHIFTER who offered to join me, and even he was more trouble than he was worth. Oh, the male willingly dropped his shorts at the cliff top and shifted into fur form just as I did. But every time I thought I was close enough to pounce upon a critter, the blundering werewolf scared my prey into flight.

"What are you doing?" I demanded half an hour later, curling into my human body after a particularly plump squirrel had scrambled away up a tree trunk to escape our approach. I'd lapped up a couple of sips of water at a stream we'd run alongside a few minutes earlier, but I still felt like I could have drunken an ocean and swallowed a whale without stopping. That measly squirrel had looked pretty darn good to me.

Apparently not to my companion. "You want to eat a rodent?" Liam asked, joining me on two feet and standing just a hair too close for comfort. I'd become accustomed to the lupine disregard for personal space while spending time around Gunner and his pack mates, but I was still a little squeamish about having a near stranger—and werewolf—inches away from my unprotected neck.

And perhaps that discomfort is why my words came out sharper than I'd intended. "I want to find something *edible* for my *sister*," I bit out, magic sparkling around my fingertips as my star ball responded to my adrenaline-fueled reaction. Then I sighed, expecting Liam to retreat at this evidence of my kitsune nature.

But, instead, he merely cocked his head and apologized. "I'm sorry. I wasn't thinking. Which way should we go next?"

Liam sounded so much like his twin in that moment that I couldn't hold onto my anger. Instead, I offered an apologetic smile of my own before turning away, scanning our surroundings in search of something small enough to capture with vulpine jaws.

Fresh deer scat peppered the leaf litter beside me, but I dismissed the evidence of an animal far too large for my fur form to bring down unaided. The sulfurous stink of stagnant water from the south, on the other hand, suggested a pond might be within easy walking distance. The evening was nearly dark already...surely birds would now be roosting for the night?

They must be called sitting ducks for a reason, I decided, hunger making my mouth start to fill with digestive juices. Sleepy waterfowl should be well within my abilities, even though I'd apparently wasted my childhood becoming an expert at swordplay rather than learning how to hunt.

"Let's head...." I started, then spun as a strangled yelp emerged from the spot where I'd last seen Liam.

Where Liam still was...only in wolf form instead of on two legs. He wasn't the sole wolf present, however. Instead, another beast had joined us while I was gazing in the opposite direction. Had joined us...and leapt upon Liam as if intent upon tearing out my companion's throat.

Chapter 19

I recognized Gunner one moment before the magically created spear left my fingertips. So rather than skewering my protector, I let the star ball diffuse back into pure magic as it flew toward the battling wolves.

I wasn't exactly sure what I expected to accomplish using incorporeal magic. But I have to admit, the net of blue light that landed atop the duo, yanking them out of their fur forms and back into humanity, was inspiring...and something I didn't think I'd been capable of before licking up Ransom's blood.

Gunner, on the other hand, was still intent upon his aggressions. "Stay away from Mai," the alpha growled out of newly humanized vocal cords. Despite his speech, he didn't appear to realize he was two-legged since his teeth then proceeded to clamp down upon the other male's furless neck.

In contrast, Liam was quick to acknowledge their shared humanity. Perhaps it was the blunt human dentition that tipped him off?

"What's wrong with you?" the slighter male countered, twisting away from his cousin and pulling himself up onto his knees in the process. "I was watching her back, you idiot. You should thank me, not jump me from behind."

I didn't consider myself an expert at werewolf relations, but even I could tell that "idiot" wasn't the brightest word to use around an angry alpha. Sure enough, Gunner didn't respond verbally, the air instead tightening with electricity. It was only a matter of time before he shifted back into lupine form and continued the fight...

...A fight that was delaying Kira's much-needed nourishment every moment it continued. So, rather than letting the males duke it out the way I usually would have, I gave the thread of star ball attached to my fingers another yank and watched the net of blue light around the males' shoulders snuff out the sharp bite of electricity once again.

So this *is kitsune power*, I thought, smugly amused by my ability to manipulate werewolves...

...then my legs collapsed out from under me as the last of my stolen energy fled in a whoosh.

That got Gunner's attention the way Liam's words hadn't. Supportive hands grabbed me one millisecond before my head struck the rocky ground. And even though my eyes were squinted closed against painful dizziness, the scent of dew-soaked granite proved Gunner was once again back in his right mind.

His warm arms enfolded me, pulling me close up against him as he lowered us both onto the ground. "Mai," he murmured, breath teasing tendrils of hair so one flirted ticklishly with my cheekbone. "We need to feed you. Kira is already enjoying roasted deer meat...."

"With Ransom's permission?" I murmured, keeping my eyes firmly closed in an attempt to prevent the world from spinning out of control once again.

"I speak for my brother in all matters that don't pertain to women, if you'll recall."

His words were amused; his smile pressed against my skin like sunshine. *Why,* I pondered into the darkness behind my eyelids, *am I making such an effort to keep this alpha at arm's length?*

"And, on that note, I think I'll head back to the campground," Liam interrupted, reminding us both of his recently forgotten presence. "You can thank me later, cousin, once you're feeling a little more sane."

In answer, Gunner growled, the rumble vibrating through his entire body before entering mine by proxy. His lack of control, however, recalled my own abilities. Unlike prideful werewolves, I knew how to be appreciative of provided help.

So I forced myself to push out of the warm darkness, opening my eyes and turning to meet Liam's gaze before the latter had time to depart. "*I'll* thank you, Liam," I offered. "I appreciate all you've done for me."

And I got the distinct impression that no one in the Atwood pack had ever noticed Liam's behind-the-scenes efforts previously. Because his lips quirked upward on one side and he saluted me sardonically. Then, dropping down into his lupine form, he trotted away into the trees.

"I WISH YOU HADN'T COME."

The warmth in my belly dissipated as Gunner's words hit me like a slap in the face, and I rocked back on my heels to escape from the unexpected reprimand. But before I could think of an audible answer, the fickle alpha had pulled me into the deepest bear hug I'd ever been a part of. And the explanation he whispered in my ear definitely softened the sting of the preceding words.

"You would have been so much safer if you'd stayed put at Wildacres. And yet, I'm selfishly glad to see your face."

Gunner couldn't actually *see* my face at the present moment, not when my cheek pressed into his naked shoulder, one large hand cupping the back of my head. All it would have taken to turn this hug of concern into an actual embrace was the slightest twist to our bodies, an alignment he and I never quite seemed to manage at the same time.

Now, for instance, there was information I needed to relay that trumped the demands of my libido. So I didn't turn my torso toward him. Just drew my head away from Gunner's shoulder sufficiently so I could speak.

"I wasn't trying to come here," I admitted. "At first, Kira and I were just fleeing the wolves who showed up on our doorstep after you left with your brother...."

"Wolves?" Whatever thread of romantic interest had previously been forming between us snapped as Gunner leaned away, his neck bending so he could peer into my face. There was only starlight above us, but I could still make out his pupils, so dilated they looked like caverns I could have plummeted into. I wasn't so sure that, once falling, I'd ever be able to halt my descent.

So I turned away, spoke to the trees as I finished my telling. "Werewolves," I elaborated. "I didn't recognize any of them, and they didn't get close enough for me to smell whether they belonged to your pack or to someone else's. At the time, all I could think about was getting Kira to safety."

Gunner hummed his understanding. "So you decided there was strength in numbers."

"Actually, no." I wished I could have said that my immediate reaction had been to track down my allies and stand united in the face of unknown dangers. But I was still far more of a lone fox than a pack wolf, regardless of my companions. So, haltingly, I admitted the truth.

I told Gunner how Kira's tiredness had spooked me. How I'd lapped up dried werewolf blood then let the tug in my gut lead me here, where dreams of my dead mother suggested the stealer of Mama's star ball currently resided. How I'd tried to contact Mama in the waking world, but had every attempt in that direction resoundingly rebuffed until the big fight in the amphitheater.

I *didn't* tell him who I thought was the culprit, however. Couldn't quite talk myself into hurting Gunner further until I was 100% sure.

"I need to figure out what's going on with Kira, but then I'll get out of your hair..." I finished, knowing the werewolf beside me had unfinished business of his own to tie up and that my presence would only get in the way.

Only, before I could complete my promise, Gunner raised his hand as if to halt the outpouring of words. He wasn't gesturing me into silence, however. Instead, he grabbed the skin of his wrist between sharp wolf teeth, grabbed it and *tore.*

Then, holding the bleeding appendage out toward me, the werewolf beside me ordered, "Drink."

Chapter 20

In the near darkness, the blood sliding across Gunner's skin and puddling in the crook of his elbow appeared black as swamp muck. Unappetizing in color but salty sweet in scent. No wonder my stomach growled hungrily at the sight.

Still, I was more than a mere animal. So rather than licking up the blood the way I'd done atop Ransom's shoulders, I instead peered into the eyes of the alpha who appeared to be offering his own ichor as fuel...for what exactly? Surely it would have been easier to lead me back to the waterfall and provide a chunk of well-cooked meat to satiate my hunger.

"Werewolf blood appears to be a kitsune's turbo-pack," Gunner rumbled by way of explanation. "If that's what you need, I'm more than willing to provide."

The offer appeared to be limited-time-only however. Because, before I could answer, my companion sighed and pressed his right hand atop the wound to slow the flowing blood.

Except, when my eyes managed to leave the tantalizing liquid and instead latch onto Gunner's face, I realized that he was giving me an even greater gift—time in which to think. It was hard, though, to hash out implications when the ooze collecting beneath my companion's fingers drew me as seductively as his kiss had stolen my breath back at Wildacres. Hard to hash out a pro-con list when I could almost feel the power surging through me, the potential so great I didn't know where the limits of werewolf-fueled kitsune magic might end.

I only realized I'd leaned in closer when a stray droplet splashed up to land on my cheekbone. It burned colder than ice...and yet my tongue rather than my fingers licked out to lap at the blood.

What had been frozen agony on my skin melted like chocolate when worked upon by digestive juices. Tensed muscles eased, aching stomach softened. That single drop of blood was as good as chugging a gallon of energy drinks at revitalizing my flagging strength, and my head cleared even as my muscles relaxed.

Which meant I was finally able to speak, even if the words sounded stilted to my own ears. "I don't know what will happen if I accept your offer. For all I know, this would tie us together in ways you might later regret."

"Or it might help you speak with your mother and save your sister." Gunner paused, the hand he had clamped upon his opposite wrist loosening, preparing to once again release the flow of blood. "The future is, by definition, unknowable. But it's better to dive in than to give up."

Bold wolf words, but my fox brain chose to accept them. So, reaching forward, I drew his bleeding arm toward me. Then I dipped my head and sucked his life force in.

MAMA'S FINGERS SLIPPED hair behind my ears as she tugged me away from Gunner. Or was that my own fingers slipping hair behind the ears of my oldest child?

I rose to my knees, lost in the joining. Felt ice suffuse my skin as Mama's dead spirit merged with my living body. Love poured between us, a deluge that threatened my breathing. But why should I even need oxygen if I was a spirit and already dead?

"Mai." I didn't hear Gunner's word at first. Didn't remember it referred to me, in fact, until his bloody hand clamped down upon our—my—forearm.

He smelled strongly of fur, earth, and ozone. Meanwhile, the warmth of his body as he pulled me up against him reminded me vaguely that my heart still beat and blood continued to flow through my veins.

Words cascaded over me, harsh and guttural. At first, they were only meaningless syllables. Then they materialized into a sentence. "Is she there?" Gunner asked.

"I'm here," my mother and I responded together. "He's cute," we continued—or, rather, that was Mama entirely, not me.

I caught the faintest whiff of amusement floating toward me through the darkness. "I'm glad you approve, Mrs. Fairchild," the werewolf murmured, his voice so deep it was almost a growl. "But let's stay focused, shall we? Who is your Master? And what does he have to do with Kira growing more and more weak?"

I whimpered, the agony of Mama wrenching herself from my body hitting me so hard that I barely managed to lunge forward and grab onto her wrist before she disappeared into thin air. "Don't," I croaked, understanding without having to be told that Mama's Master wouldn't allow this line of questioning. Then, in her words: "I can't speak about the Master. Please, don't ask."

"Not even if he's a male or a female? Human or werewolf? Maybe even a fox?"

Shivers racked my body and the pain of losing my mother was so intense I could barely uncurl my fingers. She was almost gone and we hadn't yet found out anything about Kira. So, reacting instinctively, I slapped one hand over Gunner's mouth, not realizing until too late that I was entrusting my fingers to a werewolf's fangs.

"Quiet," I ordered. Or maybe Mama ordered? Because as Gunner's words faded, I once again lost the distinction between spirit and self.

This time, Mama enfolded me from the outside. An icy hug that nonetheless warmed me from head to toe.

Meanwhile, huge werewolf paws rose to move my fingers so they no longer blocked Gunner's nostrils. But my companion remained silent as Mama and I, together, spoke.

"A kitsune can only have one daughter," we whispered. And now I saw images flickering through my mind's eye that I'd never been privy to before. The combined joy and sorrow when Mama realized she was pregnant a second time. Her decision to sacrifice herself to allow Kira to come into existence. I felt the pain and resoluteness as a star ball was wrenched from her own body to give her second daughter a chance at life.

"I gave Kira my star ball to use when she grew older," Mama continued, speaking through my lips. But we were separating now, my own throat aching with suppressed tears as my mother slipped out of my skin and drifted outward until only our fingers were touching.

She couldn't tell us the next part—couldn't mention the shadowy being who controlled my mother's spirit and magic so completely. I struggled to think of a question that would help Kira without eradicating my mother's presence entirely. And as I pondered, Gunner spoke.

"What can we do to keep Kira safe without a star ball?"

"Nothing," Mama murmured. And now her voice was a whisper on the breeze rather than an utterance from my body. "Kira fades as my magic is used elsewhere. Without a star ball, a kitsune cannot continue to exist."

Chapter 21

I swayed, shaken by the realization that my mother had died of her own volition in an effort to keep Kira from doing the same. Nearly as bad was the fact that I'd dropped the protective-guardian ball quite literally. Still, at least I knew how to begin correcting my mistake.

"Whoever bought Mama's star ball must be here at the gathering." In fact, I had a very good guess who the Master might be. I just didn't want to speak the words aloud in front of Gunner until I had more evidence that Ransom was the one with the rotten core. "I just need..."

Gunner cut off my words before I could state the obvious—that I needed to ingratiate myself to the larger group of Atwood werewolves in order to sleuth out the identity of the 'Master.' The werewolf beside me, unfortunately, had a different take on the matter at hand.

"You and Kira need to be somewhere off the radar," he finished for me. "But Ransom will balk at any of us going along to protect you. And we've already discovered that Wildacres isn't as safe as we'd initially presumed...."

His over-protectiveness was sweet in a way, but it also raised my independent fox ruff like nobody's business. "So you want me and Kira to run away while, what? While you do the hunting for us?"

The vision of Lucinda clinging to Gunner rose, at that exact moment, in my mind. Only to be followed by the more realistic image of Gunner trusting his brother, trusting someone who only wished him ill....

I wasn't the only one irritated by our lack of like-mindedness. My flaring nostrils picked up Gunner's burst of alpha aggression, and the loaded silence between us was so tangible I could have cut it with a knife.

Then Gunner—despite being a dominant werewolf used to getting whatever he wanted—backpedaled quite gracefully. "I'm not trying to tell you what to do," he offered. "You're your own woman. I get that. I just want to help."

"So help by telling me what I can do to get a toehold in this pack without compromising my sister's safety," I suggested. "Help by promising that you won't let Kira out of your sight while I'm gone."

I rose as I spoke, my feet carrying me back and forth between the trees that surrounded us. I didn't want to stand here arguing with my supposed ally. Instead, I itched to run back and check on my sister, while at the same time I also wanted to forge ahead and keep Kira from weakening further yet.

Luckily for my patience—or lack thereof—Gunner didn't wait long before he made a suggestion. Apparently the high point of the gathering was a Solstice Hunt, a time to restructure pack hierarchy without killing anything except local wildlife. "You'll be accepted into the pack if you do well in the Hunt tomorrow," Gunner admitted, voice low and reluctant. "But to be part of the chase, you'll have to swear fealty to my brother...."

"Fealty like the oath that sent you to your knees?" A bad idea if the Master really was who I thought he was.

Air currents swirling between us as Gunner nodded rather than elaborating. He didn't have to tell me that a bond like that to his fickle older brother was the height of lunacy for a lone fox like myself.

Or was it?

For one split second, a very different image flitted through my head. Not me submitting to a power-hungry alpha and possible serial killer. Instead, I saw Allen, Crow, Tank, and Elle running beside Gunner in wolf form...with my fox tail leading the chase.

Shaking my head against the daydream, I pushed myself back into the dangers of the present. No, I didn't relish the idea of pinning myself down beneath Ransom's thumb willingly. But if an oath was what it took to save my sister, I'd figure out the specifics on the fly.

"Alright. I'll do it," I decided. "And you'll watch my sister every minute? All of you? Everyone you trust?"

I tasted the electricity of Gunner's displeasure. Smelled his urge to gainsay me, to take over this hunt and manage it on his own terms...or at least send half of his trusted comrades along to guard my back.

But, again, the faintest breeze of a sigh flowed between us. "The pack will meet at dawn on a rounded hill west of here. It's open to the air, grassy. You can't miss the spot."

Of course I couldn't miss it when Kira and I had come from there that same morning. I shivered, suddenly remembering the dream of blood on grass that had been set on a hill so much like that one. Then I shook my head, thinking three steps ahead.

It would take half the night to return to the hilltop. And I needed food in my belly and at least a few hours of sleep if I hoped to win a place in the Atwood pack....

Still I lingered, not wanting to leave while a barrier hovered between me and Gunner. I was shunting the male aside through my own fox nature as much as to protect my sister, and we both knew it. But I couldn't quite turn myself into a wolf and act like any other pack mate.

So—"Thank you," I told him one second before shifting into my fleet-footed animal. But I heard no answer before I lost myself to the darkness of the night.

SITTING DUCKS WERE, indeed, easy to slaughter. Their feathers, on the other hand, took an eternity to gnaw off with vulpine teeth. So I ended up shifting into human form to skin the waterfowl, shifting back to fox form to chew raw meat off bones, then collapsing in exhaustion not far from the spot where Gunner and I had split up.

Kira's court date is tomorrow. I woke hours later instant alertness. And if I'd had human vocal cords to swear with, I would definitely have used one of the words Kira's social worker hated so much.

No two ways about it, I was burning bridges back in the city. And I was running late for my intended goal of making a good impression on Ransom's pack as well.

Luckily, I was a fox and my animal instincts left little room for self-recrimination. Instead, I rose, stretched once to ease aching muscles...then I ran like the fires of hell were licking at my heels.

Kira was right—sticking to the stream made the journey from campground valley to meeting hill far less strenuous. Meanwhile, the dim pre-dawn light was plenty sufficient to let me pick out easy routes I'd been unable to follow with a sick and weary human child dragging along behind. I scampered across a gully on a fallen tree trunk, listening to bird songs growing louder by the second in the woodland version of a bedroom alarm clock.

I was nearly there though. Meanwhile, the howl of excited wolves flowing downhill toward me promised that the pack hadn't divided up into hunting parties quite yet.

So I wasn't too late after all. I wasn't too late...but I wasn't paying sufficient attention to my surroundings either. One moment I was sprinting flat out to join up with the gathered werewolves. The next I was yelping as huge fangs cut into the soft skin of my flank.

Perhaps, I noted even as I spun sideways, *the pack is no more excited to meet me than I am to meet them.*

Chapter 22

Only, apparently I was wrong. Because even as I twisted upwards and lashed out at the attacking shifter with my newly materialized sword, someone behind my back noted, "Not too bad on the reaction front."

Meanwhile, another voice was less approving. "Still not good enough to be an Atwood wolf."

So I was being judged. Or hazed. Or perhaps there was really no difference between the two motivations. Because the wolf-form shifter in front of me didn't pull his subsequent attack one iota. Instead, he dove under my sword so rapidly that I was hard-pressed to force him back.

Or I would have been hard-pressed had Gunner's blood not fueled my footsteps. As it was, my feet pivoted and lunged faster than I'd thought possible, my muscles flexing even more quickly than kitsune strength should have allowed. Unfortunately, the boost could only do so much against an uncountable sea of attackers.

Because I was no longer facing a single werewolf intent upon disemboweling me. No, there were dozens of ozone-tainted opponents, their sharp scents biting into my skin as I whirled to stab at a werewolf leaping toward my unprotected back.

Instinct told me to play dirty and end this, to lower the odds against me by hook or by crook. To that end, I *could* have twisted my sword to the right and turned a scratch into a serious injury, taking my opponent out of the fight for good.

But, instead, I pulled the thrust after it skimmed epidermis, uncertain whether I'd lose my place in the Atwood pack if I disemboweled one of these wolves. If this was a test, I intended to pass it. Too bad evading my attackers without causing serious injury was akin to fighting with one arm tied behind me.

There were so many opponents moving so quickly now that I could barely make out anything beyond a blur of fur and fangs. Speaking of fangs, one set bit down into my ankle, knocking me off my stride. Instinctively, I pushed a shard of magic out of my sword and into an ankle cuff to protect me. Was relieved when my opponent erupted into humanity, his dull incisors glancing off my skin.

"You bitch," the shifter growled, wiping my blood away from his mouth with the back of one hand. "You'll regret..."

I didn't have time to listen to further recriminations, however. Because the other Atwood shifters were still four-legged, still slobbering with the urge to fight. And they now appeared to be banding together. Joining up into pairs and trios in preparation for hitting me from multiple fronts.

As much as I hated to change my tactics, Kira's face rose in front of my mind at that point. When given a choice between dying or killing, I had to chose the latter for my sister's sake. I couldn't simply surrender and hope for the best.

So I took a deep breath and selected my first quarry. I'd start with the small wolf on my left side, proceed to his partner then work my way through the wolf pack.

Before I could put my plan into action, however, warm skin slid up against my naked backside. Large fingers settled over my sword hand, clenching down and freezing my weapon into place.

Once again, someone had slipped through a gap in my defenses. And this time I was quite thoroughly caught.

"IT'S ME. LIAM," MY jailer offered as I tried and failed to elbow him in the kidneys. Then, when my tensed muscles proved I had no clue who he was referring to, the male sighed and elaborated even as he released my sword-bearing hand: "Elle's brother. I have your back."

Right. My brain unfroze as terror slid off my shoulders. For some reason, Liam's name was eminently forgettable, but I found myself glad that Gunner had disregarded my orders to keep everyone watching over Kira and had instead sent his cousin to ensure I made it through the day intact.

Because it was ten times easier to fend off attackers using teamwork, especially since a flicker of movement out of the corner of my eye promised that Liam had come prepared with a weapon much like my own. For thirty seconds, we both attacked and parried, the yelping of wounded four-leggers proving that my sword mate wasn't being as sparing as I'd been with his slashes. Apparently I'd misunderstood the level of injury allowed within a pack.

"Since when do werewolves carry weapons?" I asked after a few moments, when my panting had eased into regular inhales and exhales. Meanwhile, without looking back over my shoulder, I twisted counter-clockwise to jab at a white-furred shifter who was attempting to sneak up on Liam's right side.

"Since Atwood tempers made fighting in fur form a threat to pack cohesivity," Liam answered, pivoting right alongside me while his words flowed as easily as his sword hand had.

"You're an Atwood? Related to Gunner and Ransom on your father's side?"

I'd meant the questions to be idle conversation, but something about the silence behind me suggested I'd struck yet another nerve. *Yes, great idea. Insult your sole ally*, I berated myself, kicking out at one werewolf while swiping a great puff of fur off the back of another. "I'm sorry," I offered as I riposted. "None of my business. I'm just glad you've had sword training and are willing to help me out."

I half expected that to be the end of our partnership. But, to my relief, the close-mouthed shifter accepted my apology and opened up to me far more than he'd ever done before. "Gunner, Ransom, and I are double cousins," he offered. "Two sisters married two brothers. Very romantic...until you ask yourself who ended up with the consolation prize."

The haze of fur, I noted, now came from my human companion as much as from the werewolves behind us. "Liam..." I started, trying to remember every trick I'd developed to soothe ruffled lupine fur over the last three months spent in wolf company.

But before I could put my new skills to the test, yet another shifter stepped out of the trees beside us. I was half-turned away from him, yet I still recognized the Ransom by his size and bearing one second before the pack leader opened his mouth to berate us.

And despite my best intentions to stand tall, my shoulders hunched against the tongue-lashing I knew would be forthcoming. After all, our brawl had made a significant proportion of the pack—not just myself—quite definitively late. Meanwhile, Liam had just told me that Atwoods couldn't stomach being disrespected....

Sure enough, the pack leader flattened his underlings against the soil in a wordless burst of pure, unadulterated rage. Then, turning to face me—the only one still standing—he demanded, "Why do you disrupt my Hunt?"

Chapter 23

I knew that cowering would have eased the pack leader's displeasure, but a fox can't afford to submit in the face of a larger predator. Instead, I squared my shoulders and stood a little taller. Then I told Ransom—and all of the werewolves arrayed around us: "I didn't come to disrupt. I came to join."

Bracing myself for another eardrum-shattering roar, I was surprised to instead see Ransom's lips curling upward into the same subtle smile Gunner graced me with whenever I fell for one of his practical jokes. Only, the younger sibling had always been laughing *with* me during those past episodes. At the moment, I got the distinct impression I was about to become the butt of the older brother's joke.

"Did you now?" the pack leader purred, pacing toward me and slipping one finger beneath my chin so he could tip my head from side to side until the intensity of his gaze heated my features. "Because my brother couldn't get the job done, eh? Left you cold last night just as he did with Mirabelle and would have with Lucinda had she stuck around to go home with the victor after our little game."

A feminine growl emerged from behind me—Lucinda if I didn't miss my guess. But I was instead struggling against a grin that wanted to split my features. Of course Gunner wouldn't fight to bed a pack princess. But he *would* fight to ensure she didn't end up stuck having sex with some male against her will. The realization that Gunner's actions had been honorable rather than caddish the previous evening made me want to laugh and dance.

"Hmm?" Ransom nudged me verbally, hand still on my chin. And this time I mustered up a jerky nod in response.

"I'm here to join, alpha," I reiterated. And my answer must have been sufficient. Because, releasing my chin, Ransom turned his back on all of us and strode off in the direction from which he'd initially come.

Which left me and the lesser werewolves scrambling to keep pace with their leader, some rubbing shoulders in human form while others slunk forward in the skins of their beasts. Several knocked against my shins in the process, trying to topple me over subtly enough that they could swear the jab had been accidental. But I was too elated to take offense.

Because not only had Gunner been absolved, I'd also succeeded in my mission. I was *in,* and without having to swear an oath to the unpredictable pack leader either. Now I just had to determine whether Ransom was also the Master....

In search of confirmation, I felt for a sign from Mama in my belly, only to be met with complete silence on that front. Not that the Master in question was likely to let his servant off her leash again after such a show the previous evening. Instead, I'd need to use my wits to regain Mama's star ball. But at least I was here in the midst of the action where the solution to the mystery was within reach.

By this point, we'd reached the hill where the Solstice Hunt began and ended, a rounded knoll lit by sunlight that had brightened several lumens past official dawn. The orange on the horizon was already softening into true morning so the mass of werewolves arrayed before me showed up as individuals rather than as silhouettes. There were so many of them, though, and most were strangers. The chances of picking out the Master in this milling crowd of not-quite-humanity seemed far less possible than it had one moment before.

Of course, I wasn't entirely human. So I closed my eyes, pulled up my fox instincts, and proceeded to hunt with my nose.

Because shouldn't the Master smell a little like Mama? If Ransom was utilizing a kitsune's magic, shouldn't her jasmine perfume wreath the pack leader just as it always had my mother?

And, sure enough, the faintest aroma of jasmine drifted in over my left shoulder even as Ransom's voice broke into my thoughts. "I know you're all excited to determine who will serve as my second-in-command for the year ahead of us," he called, proving that he was the kind of leader who liked giving speeches. I wasn't particularly surprised by that realization either. In fact, I was glad of the leeway to squint my eyes more tightly shut and continue working on the tricky puzzle of instinct and scent.

"But we have another item on our agenda before I turn you loose to hunt this morning," Ransom continued. His voice, I noted, was deep and mellifluous when not competing with his brother's. As if he really was a pack leader as long as Gunner wasn't there to throw him off his stride.

Unfortunately, Ransom's pack-leader potential showed itself in more ways than oratory smoothness. Because while I'd forgotten the male's teasing smile, he hadn't forgotten my precarious position here in the territory he commanded.

"Mai Fairchild."

My eyes shot open as my name rolled across the sea of shifters between us. All around me, werewolves murmured, swiveled, turned as a unit to peer into my face.

I, on the other hand, was gazing directly at their pack leader. His lips, I noted, had curled back up into that faint, mocking smile. His neck bowed ever so gently like a king overseeing his subjects. And his words were soft as he told me: "I'm now ready to receive your oath."

Chapter 24

My oath. "I..." I cleared my throat, blinking furiously as I struggled to find a way out of the trap that had closed around me while my attention was focused inward. Somehow, when I'd told Gunner I was willing to swear myself to his brother, I'd assumed I'd think of some clever compromise during the intervening hours before I was forced to actually live up to my boast.

But Ransom's eyebrows rose as he eyed me impatiently. And any ingenuity I might have once possessed refused to show itself upon command.

So, thinking of Mama's recent bombshell and the precariousness of Kira's hold on reality, I accepted the inevitable and took the only path I could see toward my destination. "I, Mai Fairchild, swear to protect and uphold the Atwood pack to the best of my ability...."

The words gushed forth as if they'd been waiting for an outlet for weeks on end rather than being forced awkwardly from my lips by a force greater than myself. I *was* willing to protect the Atwood pack, I realized...at least the portion of it I'd spent the last few months living amidst.

Because Gunner and Tank and Ransom and Allen and Elle and Liam had been more than mere companions. They'd hunted with me and trained me and protected my sister with their lives.

Pack mates. They were pack mates and I was glad to acknowledge that connection with an oath.

And as I spoke, the debt-bound tie that had clenched my gut for months gradually loosened. As if promising to be part of Gunner's pack was all that had been required to allow my first full breath in several days.

For half a second, in fact, I could almost see the younger brother there beside me. Could sense Gunner's delight as he accepted the binding I'd created and offered a similar oath of his own in return.

"I swear to protect you and yours also," the alpha murmured, the warmth of his promise soothing skin pebbled by the morning chilliness. *"I welcome you into our pack."*

Then I was back in the forest, one very unimpressed pack leader glowering down at me from the crest of the hill. While Gunner had taken my oath as a heart-felt promise aimed at a group he cared for, Ransom understood my verbal slipperiness to be a personal affront.

And that was the difference between the brothers, wasn't it? Gunner had no need to make others feel smaller to increase his own stature...while Ransom had literally perched himself on the highest point in the forest in an effort to dominate his clan.

Means, motive, and opportunity. I shivered as the likelihood that Ransom really was the Master punched me in the gut.

But before I could follow that thought path any further, Ransom dismissed my evasion with a curt: "Enough of this." His eyes flashed but his tone remained full and firm as if he'd gotten exactly what he desired when he continued. "We'll meet back here to compare our kills at sunset. Ladies, I assume you want to hunt together. As the weaker sex, you deserve a fifteen-minute head start."

I WOULD HAVE CHAFFED at the chauvinistic send-off if the aroma of jasmine hadn't begun dissipating at that exact same moment. The owner of the scent appeared to be moving away from me rather than standing before me. Which meant...maybe Ransom wasn't the Master after all?

Gladly, I leapt upon any thread leading me away from tying guilt to Gunner's brother. The speed with which the pack princesses fled, however, left me little energy to quibble over who might have spilled Mama's jasmine perfume all over herself. Instead, we were deep in the forest before I caught up to the slowest female, fox agility barely making up for my shorter stride as we pressed through tangles of weeds and bushes as a pack.

Then, finally, wolf tails were slapping at my muzzle, which meant I was close enough to search for the floral odor's source. Not that my fellow runners let me. First a clawed foot struck my eye as I veered away from a thicket of brambles. Then, blinking furiously to regain full vision, I changed my trajectory, was pushed sideways a second time, and realized the females were actively attempting to exclude me from their midst.

Which suggested...they were all in cahoots with the Master? The idea didn't sit right, not when I knew that these females had left several different clans quite recently in hopes of becoming Ransom's designated mate. One *might* be my shadowy nemesis, but the chance that all twenty-odd females were working together to wreak havoc using my mother's star ball seemed so slender as to be nonexistent.

All of these thoughts flitted through my head in the time it took for us to descend a steep hill and start back up the other side. I still smelled jasmine quite strongly—the only reason I hadn't turned around to hunt more likely prey. So, pushing a hair more speed out of my dragging muscles, I leapt onto a tumble of massive boulders that allowed me to cut across the path of the earth-bound pack princesses, knowing even as I did so that I'd have no better luck invading the cluster from the front.

Only, the pack princesses were no longer pressing forward. Instead, as if reacting to an unspoken signal, the triangle of werewolves opened up into a circle at the base of the boulders, the lead wolf trotting backwards to sniff at a newly shifted female lying naked on the earth. The girl—because she probably hadn't yet reached her twentieth birthday—was sobbing furiously. And for a moment, I lost the thread of my thoughts and decided the Master could wait until we discovered whatever had set the poor teenager off.

I was too far away to soothe anyone, but the lead wolf was shifting and pulling the younger woman into her arms already. "Shh, it's alright," Lucinda murmured. Because, of course, the female who had glared daggers at me the previous evening *would* turn out to be the unofficial leader of this temporary pack.

"But it happened *again*." The girl's voice quavered, her tone nasal and rough due to stopped-up nostrils. Meanwhile, my own nostrils flared as I noted the strong presence of Mama's jasmine aroma emanating from the center of the circle of werewolves.

"Are you *sure?*" one of the other females asked dubiously. But I wasn't really listening. Instead, I'd leapt down from my perch and padded past the milling wolves who were too intent upon the teenager's story to hinder my approach.

Because I had a sinking suspicion I knew what the girl was so upset about. Especially given the evidence of Mama's blood-gathering tactics from my dream....

Sure enough, the child answered with a gesture, lifting up both hands in front of her face palm-sides outward. "There's no mistaking this," she whispered.

And she was right. Because I'd seen those same blood-rimmed fingernails on my own hands when joining Mama's hunt in my dream.

Chapter 25

"**Y**ou need to leave." I regretted the words as soon as they left my mouth. Because I should have been debriefing the child to figure out how my mother had possessed her, should have been figuring out whether there was an obvious connection between the Master and his prey.

On the other hand, I didn't really regret my instinctive reaction. Because this poor child couldn't stay here to be used as some sort of magic-harvesting sex slave without her knowledge and consent.

Only now Lucinda was in my face, her long nails biting into the bare skin of my shoulder. "What have you done to my sister?" she demanded, clearly drawing kitsune-related conclusions that were more grounded in reality than I cared to admit.

"*I* haven't done anything," I countered, forcing my star ball to remain quiescent despite the danger of two dozen angry werewolves pressing closer and closer upon me. "But it's not safe for her to be here. It's not safe here for any of you."

Because while Lucinda's sister was likely the easiest mark among them, I saw no reason Mama couldn't slip into someone else's skin if her Master so commanded. Even if I couldn't find our shadowed enemy in this cluster of pack princesses, at least I could protect them...and cut off the Master's easy access to werewolf blood at the same time.

And that quickly, Lucinda dismissed me as irrelevant. "Go tell your grandmother how to suck eggs," she rebutted while turning away as if I'd ceased existing. The female dropped to her knees then scrabbled through the leaf litter, and for one split second I thought she might have lost her mind...

...Until a ziplock-coated cellphone emerged from the hole she'd so recently dug with her manicured fingers. "You were right," Lucinda said into the microphone after two short rings ended with the sound of heavy breathing. "I need a pickup."

"You and Gloria and anyone else?" The voice on the other end was masculine, hard—an unhappy werewolf. But Lucinda wasn't cowed. Instead, she raised her eyebrows and surveyed the faces that surrounded us on every side.

"My brother will take anyone who wants away from this shithole," she informed her audience. And, honestly, I couldn't blame her for breaking up what should have been a carefully choreographed werewolf courtship and had instead turned into a frat-boy party minus the beers. Not even when her final words promised Ransom would be raging in the near future: "Who wants in?"

A moment of silence...then the rest of the pack princesses agreed in a flood of relieved acquiescence. To no one's astonishment, Lucinda didn't offer me the same pickup service she'd granted to the others. But, as the other females turned away in preparation to depart, she *did* toss me the powered-down cell phone in a gesture that came very much as a surprise.

"If you have anyone you can call for backup, I recommend you do so," Lucinda told me. Then she, her sister, and the rest of the pack princesses shivered back down to four legs and set off north, toward what I assumed was the closest road.

UNFORTUNATELY, I WASN'T a werewolf with backup waiting. That said, there *was* one loose thread I'd left dangling that could be cleared up with a simple call.

"Stephanie Baumgartner, Social Services," Kira's social worker answered, her voice less effusive than I was used to. But, of course, Stephanie wouldn't recognize this number. Wouldn't know who was calling her out of the blue.

"It's me, Mai," I started before leaving honesty behind entirely. "My phone's battery died, so I'm using a friend's. Guess I wasn't quite prepared for camping after all...."

Thinking of all of the events of the last twenty-four hours that I'd been totally unprepared for teased out a chuckle. And Stephanie softened, laughing right alongside me.

"Well, that's the point of camping," she responded, all grandmotherly wisdom. "It's good for young people to learn there's more to life than the internet. Fish to catch. Naps to take."

"Mm hm," I agreed. So I needn't have worried. My hurried voice mail had done the trick to keep Stephanie happy and Kira's court case on track after all.

But before I could get off the phone, the arbiter of my sister's future continued onward with her litany of summer-vacation perks. "Hot dogs cooked over an open fire. S'mores! I think it's been at least a decade since I've tasted s'mores."

A tendency to ramble was one of Stephanie's few flaws. Luckily, I was able to pull up the mapping feature on Lucinda's phone while half listening and take advantage of the lull to determine where Kira and I had ended up. Unsurprisingly, this vast wilderness turned out to be part of Atwood clan central. If we just walked west far enough, we'd end up in the more conventional settlement most of these shifters called home....

"In fact, I think I'll come up and join you. I've got the afternoon off and need to squeeze in one more home visit before the big day tomorrow. How does that sound?"

I'd already hummed my agreement before I realized what Stephanie had suggested. "Wait...what? No! We'll be back in plenty of time for a home visit. And we're not car camping. You'd have to hike in quite a ways to get to our site..."

"I'm old but I'm not feeble! Don't worry—I can be there before dinner. What's the address?"

I hesitated, imagining Stephanie waltzing up to a werewolf gathering to check how Kira was getting along. It sounded like a disaster, and I wished for the first time that Gunner hadn't been so inclusive about including Kira's social worker in pack events previously.

Because we'd taken Stephanie and her daughter with us to the movies one day. Had attended her youngest grandchild's birthday party with presents in hand. The line between professional and personal had blurred proportionally...which was likely part of the reason Stephanie had gone to bat for us so firmly in court.

Now, though, she'd wonder if I rejected her offer to join us. Would wonder...and might change her tune at the final custody hearing we still had a thread of a chance of managing to attend.

"Mai? Are still there? These newfangled phones have terrible connections...."

"I'm here," I answered, buying just a little more time in which to ponder options. We'd have to set up a fake camp somewhere far from the gathering for Stephanie's own protection. Gunner would be game, I knew that. And he could definitely make things work....

So I caved and told her: "We'd love to have you join us." Then I rattled off the coordinates and hung up the phone.

Chapter 26

N ot wanting to tempt my luck further, I re-hid Lucinda's cellphone as quickly as possible before slipping into my fur form and sprinting into the trees. Because if an innocent human was coming to visit this evening, it had become even more imperative that I track down the Master *now*.

Unfortunately, the world was working against me. At first, the diffuse sprinkles making their way through the canopy felt good against my heated fur and the skin underneath it. But then the sky darkened to twilight, and abruptly it began to pour.

So, okay, I'd navigate back to the meeting spot based on landmarks rather than on scent trails. Over the hill behind me, past that gnarled mammoth of a something-or-other tree, then across the abruptly raging creek....

There had been at least a tendril of fur-flavor to the air guiding me up until this point. But now, as sodden branches drooped wetly against my backbone, I was forced to rely on eyesight alone. Turning in a slow circle, I realized I had no idea where I'd ended up.

Because the map on the phone had made the green blob of wilderness appear not much larger than my neighborhood back in the city. On the ground, however, the forest felt like an inimical being intent upon swallowing me whole.

In fact, I was almost certain I recognized the tree dominating this small clearing. Wasn't that the same gnarled monster I'd passed by when scrambling up the scree slope on the other side of the creek earlier? Either I was walking in circles or....

I padded forward, reaching out one paw to tap at what should have been wet, scaly bark. Only...there was nothing there to pause my forward momentum. Nothing to prevent me from losing my balance and falling forward into the space where my eyes said a tree should have been.

Ice enfolded me. Darkness surrounded me. And when I pulled desperately at my star ball...I found only a weak spark of magic willing to answer my call.

Hopping backwards, I fell over my own four feet in a desperate attempt to escape the illusion. And now that I wasn't in the middle of the magic, I could pick out a shape where the tree had previously stood.

A shape...who turned as I watched materialized into a slender, Asian woman. My mother, or at least a fragment of her through which raindrops continued to fall.

"*I'm sorry,*" Mama mouthed. "*He made me do it.*"

Then she wisped into nothing just as a wolf stepped toward me out of the trees.

HE. Of course the Master was Ransom. I wasn't sure how I could have doubted my initial supposition, despite the thread of jasmine leading me away into the female subpack. Not when Mama had as good as pointed me at the clan leader the moment I stepped out of the woods and into the amphitheater. Not when Ransom himself had proven his sliminess every time we'd had a chance to interact.

Sure enough, the wolf stalking toward me now was rain-drenched but still distinctly cinnamon, the distinctive Atwood streak forming white eyebrows on his lupine forehead. Meanwhile, his ozone aroma carried toward me so strongly it proved the wolf wasn't a run-of-the-mill member of the pack.

Ransom had been clever, using my mother's magic to find and weaken me as I ran alone through the forest. But even though the playing field wasn't exactly level, I was glad of any shortcut that helped me fix Kira's problem now.

In other words, I was ready for our final showdown. So, rather than backpedaling away from the animal who was twice as large as I was, I pushed everything I had into one shift back to humanity. Then I sent my star ball fluttering toward my fingers to turn into a sword.

Only no weapon materialized. No magic remained to be called upon. Instead, the effort left me bent over and gasping for breath.

The wolf, meanwhile, strode steadily forward across the clearing. Wet leaves squished rather than crunched beneath his feet as he advanced. He raised his chin to inhale, then his jaws gaped open as if he couldn't wait to feel my skin sliding beneath his fangs.

What would happen if the Master bit into a kitsune? Would I become bound to Ransom like my mother was, forced to obey his every command?

Now I did backpedal, fingers trailing across the leaf litter as I crabwalked backwards away from the menacing shifter. *Ah, there.* A rock the size of a duck's egg. Rounded and hard, it fit in my palm and flew smooth and true toward my opponent, who was now no more than ten feet away.

I was already turning and running when a human voice erupted behind me. Didn't understand that the tone was high-pitched female, in fact, until I was already twenty feet into the sheltering trees.

"What's *wrong* with you?" Elle demanded. She'd caught up to me already, was slinging me around to face her while her left hand pressed against her streaming nostrils.

My wide eyes and raised brows must have said everything because my mentor's tone softened. "I thought you recognized me...."

"I thought so too," I murmured, adding up two and two and getting twenty-nine and a half. Of course Elle's wolf looked a lot like Ransom's. Because if her twin was the brothers' double cousin then Elle shared the same genetics...and the same likelihood of her wolf possessing red fur and white brows.

"Look, I'm sorry," I continued, struggling to keep my legs from folding as adrenaline left me. That last shift had been a doozy and I suddenly wasn't sure I could do anything until I rested and ate.

"It's okay." Elle brushed off my apology almost curtly, unworried about both the blood slowly dripping from her nostrils and my lack of further explanation. Clearly she had something else on her mind.

"Mai," the other female started, and I swallowed, not wanting to hear the rest of her sentence. "Your sister didn't wake up this morning. Gunner sent me to find you. He wants to give her blood."

Chapter 27

The forest was so much harder to walk through two-legged, with neither shoes nor clothes to protect sensitive human body parts. Still, it wasn't pain that raised my blood pressure. Instead, the infuriating part was my mentor, who turned out to have been keeping secrets from me all along.

"So you knew I could use werewolf blood just like you could use kitsune blood," I stated, pausing for only a second to pry a minuscule thorn out of the pad of my big toe before pressing onward after my companion. "How could you not mention that when Kira got sicker and sicker? Didn't you think it might help?"

"I wouldn't say 'help' exactly," Elle countered, leaping over a fallen tree as agilely as if she was still in wolf form. I didn't realize how much I was dragging until I tried to follow...and had to sit down on my butt then swing my legs across rather than risk falling flat on my face.

"Ignore the semantics," I ordered, hating the fact that exertion made my voice uneven. "Why didn't you tell me there was an easy way to tap into the powers you were supposedly teaching me to harness?"

I was breathing heavily now, and not just from the effort of bushwhacking. No wonder Elle glanced back over one shoulder, her lips pursing the way mine had done when Kira slicked up her hair into a mohawk ten minutes before we were due to leave for school one day last year.

"Because there are implications," my companion told me after one moment of loaded consideration. "I showed you how dangerous it is for your blood to fall into the hands of a werewolf. When blood flows the other way, between a werewolf and a kitsune, bonds are formed that might not be productive. Which is why I told Gunner to wait before doing anything rash with Kira."

Her words made sense...but they didn't entirely salve my disappointment. Because I'd thought pack mates trusted each other, and Elle had treated me with a distinct lack of trust.

Still, her knowledge was all I had to go on at the moment. And Kira had to be in bad shape for Gunner to send Elle out to track me down in the middle of the Solstice Hunt....

"We're almost there," the female in question promised, as if sensing my worry. Sure enough, the sound of a raging waterfall had overcome the residual dripping of rain off tree leaves. "Can you feel them through the pack bond?" she continued. "That's how I found you...."

And I *could* feel something. A warmth from in front of me, a vague indication of direction. So that's how Elle had managed to appear just as the Master's trap snapped shut. I supposed pack was good for something after all, even if it didn't provide the unconditional support I'd initially supposed.

"I'm actually surprised the rest of them haven't shown up already," Elle rambled, filling the uncomfortable silence that had fallen between us with a steady flow of words. "We went looking for you at dawn, but it was pretty obvious where you were once you tapped into the pack network...."

"The rest of them?" I interrupted, a shiver running up my spine as I realized my sister wasn't encircled by the handful of watchful werewolves I'd imagined. "Aren't Tank and Crow and Allen protecting Kira?"

Elle didn't turn back to face me this time, but I still sensed the reproof in her voice when she replied. "*Gunner* is protecting Kira. Everyone else went out to find you. And...here we are."

Here we were indeed. At the top of the same steep path Liam and I had traversed the night before, the rocks looking even more treacherous wet than they had in the dim light yesterday afternoon.

But the slick stones weren't what provoked a gasp from my companion. No, it was the sight of the alpha werewolf beneath us, blood dripping from his mouth as he hovered over the supine body of my sister. Matters, it appeared, had advanced in a direction neither Elle nor I had anticipated while we were gone.

Chapter 28

Elle realized what was happening before I did. "No!" we shouted in tandem, tumbling down the path so quickly I barely felt the stones slicing into my left foot's instep.

At the bottom, I hurled myself atop my sister to protect her while Elle hung upon Gunner's non-dominant hand as if preventing him from throwing a grenade. Only when I saw the blood welling up between her fingers did I realize what was going on.

Gunner wasn't trying to harm Kira. He was trying to help her. And his cousin was intent upon preventing the alpha from carrying out his humanitarian task.

"Mai?" Kira's reedy voice was nearly inaudible. And yet, the evidence that she'd regained consciousness still stopped the scuffle in its tracks.

"How are you feeling?" I demanded, rising so I could press my wrist against her forehead. The guys had rigged a canopy out of tent canvas and arching sticks, so the rain shouldn't have soaked her the way it had me. And yet, Kira's skin was cold and clammy, as if she'd run hard in the winter cold then chilled down without bothering to towel off.

"I'm..." Whatever lie Kira had intended to tell me was cut short as she began to cough. Deep, racking quakes shook her body for so long I could hardly bear it. And when she finally spluttered into silence, Elle released her cousin's hand.

"I still think it's a bad idea," my mentor whispered, as if we weren't all shifters and able to hear her as easily as if she'd spoken at full volume.

Only, we weren't all shifters. Or at least, Kira didn't appear to have caught the murmur. Instead, my sister nestled into my side the way she had as a toddler, wrapping both of her arms around my naked waist. "I don't feel so good, Mai," she murmured. Then her eyes closed as she drifted back into sleep.

I stroked her hair gently, even though, to all appearances, Kira was no longer conscious enough to feel the soothing gesture. And as I petted her, I couldn't help wondering when the strands in question had stopped being smooth and glossy. Had Kira been fading for months without me noticing, or was the Master only now sucking out her magic the way he had mine when I stumbled into that illusory tree?

Feeling the brittleness of my sister's body, I was more than willing to accept Gunner's offered strength no matter what the consequences. Elle, on the other hand, continued to harbor second thoughts.

"If you do this, there's a good chance whoever has the other star ball will be able to manipulate you," Elle argued in a hushed whisper. "And you know you're the shepherd of this clan."

"I'm not the pack leader. My brother is." Gunner spoke the words not as if he really meant them, but as if he'd said them so many times before that they came out by rote. And yet, the whole time, his gaze never left mine. The decision, he was telling me, was in no one's hands but my own.

I swallowed, weighing two bad outcomes. I'd sworn to uphold the Atwood pack...but my deeper allegiance lay with my sister. And even though desperation never led to smart choices, no other solution came to mind.

Meanwhile, Kira turned fitfully, her breath catching in a moan that jabbed at my stomach. Her vitality was slipping away so quickly, I wasn't sure there'd be anything left if I went off to hunt the Master a second time. No, we needed to solve this now...or at least delay Kira's deepening malaise.

So, even though I knew I'd regret it later, I met Gunner's gaze directly. Then I dipped my chin into a nod.

ELLE DIDN'T STAY TO watch the bloodletting. Instead, she muttered something about gathering up our pack mates then picked her way back up the slope nearly as quickly as she'd run down.

Which left me and Gunner to get blood out of his wrist into my unconscious sister, a task that wasn't nearly as easy as it had initially appeared. In the end, I was forced to suck up the liquid and dribble it between Kira's lips mouthful by mouthful, Gunner holding the child's lax body upright and rubbed at her throat to prompt her swallow reflex.

But the transfer, though slow and messy, worked admirably. A pink flush returned to Kira's cheeks within seconds. And as a bonus, the bits of blood that seeped into my own system rekindling my magic as well.

I only realized how pale Kira had grown, in fact, once her lips were no longer purple. And this time she curled into my lap like a sleeping child rather than like an invalid ready to collapse for good.

Gunner's blood wasn't a permanent solution, but at least we'd bought a pocket of breathing room. And I used a few of those precious moments to share information—and suppositions—with the alpha who had so willingly risked himself to give my sister a new lease on life.

"I don't want the culprit to be Ransom," I concluded at the end of a rough rundown of the morning's happenings. "But I think he really might be it."

Because Gunner's brother was a slimeball. Mama's hints led me directly to the male time after time. And, not only that, the elder brother had a supreme motive to delve into kitsune blood magic—he needed a dominance boost if he hoped to truly rule the Atwood pack.

Beside me, Gunner sighed and let his neck bend until his forehead rested on one upraised kneecap. "I don't want it to be Ransom either," he said after a moment. "But I wouldn't be entirely surprised."

And then, finally, he told me the story of Ransom's mistake.

Chapter 29

Ransom and Gunner were inseparable as children. Their father was a traditional pack leader—strong, gruff, and apparently incapable of softer sentiments. Their mother died when they were young, after which they largely raised themselves.

Ransom was the more dominant sibling. After all, one year makes a huge difference when you're five and six, respectively. The older brother coaxed Gunner into crazy adventures that became crazier as the pair grew older. Somehow, though, they always managed to get the aftermath cleaned up before their father found out.

"Until I turned eleven, that is," Gunner told me. Without me noticing, he'd scooted in closer so Kira draped across both of our laps, my stroking hand slipping off my sister's hair to tease the fabric covering Gunner's thighs. He didn't seem to notice, but I might as well have stuck my finger in an electric socket for the way the near-touch sent tremors racing up and down my spine.

"What happened when you turned eleven?" I asked. The rain had stopped, but the day was still far too cool for summer. I tried to tell myself the urge to lean into Gunner's side was just exhaustion combined with the appeal of his furnace-like body heat. But even in my head the argument sounded an awful lot like a lie.

"When I turned eleven, Liam and Elle came to visit," the werewolf beside me rumbled. And, as if it was nothing, he reached over to tuck my head into the hollow beneath his shoulder. I think I lost a sentence or two as I melted into his body, but then the story caught hold of my interest once again.

Gunner hadn't known about this particular set of cousins, so the two strangers invading clan central came as both a surprise and a delight to him.

The twins were almost exactly his age and were even more like-minded than his sibling. He spent hours showing them every secret he and his brother had ferreted out.

"If I'd been a little older, I would have understood that Ransom felt slighted by my changing loyalties. I would have included him in our adventures even when he told me he was busy with twelve-year-old things."

I shivered, suddenly not wanting to hear where this story was going. But Elle was now Ransom's favorite cousin. How badly could the childhood misunderstanding have played itself out?

Plenty badly, as I soon discovered.

One morning very much like this one, Gunner woke before dawn to find his brother's face looming over his in the dark. The older brother's eyes were wide, his body soaked as if he'd just stepped out of the shower. "Let's go hunting," Ransom whispered.

Gunner—young, innocent, glad of his brother's attention—willingly agreed.

It was afternoon before the rest of the pack found them. A hot, sweltering humidity had pushed the two siblings to shed their fur after sating themselves on the fawn they'd chased down and eaten two hours earlier. So when wolves raced out of the forest toward them, they just assumed the crossing of paths was coincidence.

But the adults didn't pass by and go on about their business. Nor did they shift back to two legs and speak. Instead, neighbors and relatives acted like strangers, herding Gunner and Ransom back toward clan central in a forced march that lasted the better part of an hour.

There, Gunner was shunted off to the kitchen where his twin cousins picked at cookies and pretended not to worry. "What's going on?" he whispered once the pack second had retreated a few steps to guard the open doorway.

Liam shrugged. Elle's lip quivered. But their throats remained mute.

Time stretched out after that the way it does when you're a child. Gunner wasn't sure if he and his cousins waited for ten minutes or ten hours. All he remembered was straining to hear the raised voices coming from the pack leader's study, being unable to make out words but catching the angry tone well enough.

Eventually, the meeting disbanded. Peering around the legs of the pack second, Gunner caught a glimpse of his brother slinking out of the office on two legs. The twelve-year-old's body was covered in scratches, his eye black and his nose dripping blood. He looked like he'd fought in wolf form and lost, but his spine was straight and his raised chin was proud.

Then Gunner's father was the one emerging. The pack leader marched into the kitchen and dismissed his second with a jerky nod that sent all three youngsters cowering backwards. Despite being Gunner's father, the alpha wasn't the sort of relative you could confide in. At that moment Gunner wished very much that he'd been raised by the aunt and uncle who were spending the summer in clan central along with their kids.

This time, though, Gunner's father managed to look almost approachable. He crouched down until he was several inches lower than the seated children's head level—a very un-alpha-like thing to do. Then he placed one large hand on each twin's knee and looked directly into their eyes.

"I'm sorry, children. You may not have known this, but your mother was very sick. She passed away during the night."

Elle inhaled the tiniest gulp of air as if someone had punched her in the stomach. Liam remained stoic as an Atwood male was expected to be.

"Where's Uncle Lucas?" Gunner demanded, suddenly feeling the need to protect his cousins. He straightened and glowered as if he had a chance in hell of staring his father down.

"He went home. He's mourning. You two will stay with us until he's better."

And that, apparently, was the end of the matter. The pack leader left. The twins collapsed into a heap of sobbing. And for the first time Gunner felt like a third wheel in the face of their obvious need for each other and equally obvious disregard for anybody else.

The children had been locked into the kitchen this time, the pack second having stepped outside and closed the door in the face of the children's audible grief. But Gunner knew every secret passage in the sprawling mansion—or, rather, he knew every servant's passageway left over from when the property had been owned by humans rather than by wolves.

So he padded over to the pantry and closed himself into the darkness. Then, feeling his way past huge chest freezers and shelves of non-perishables, he yanked open the small door at the other end and slipped up the stairs without bothering to turn on a light.

The visitors were staying in a suite on the third story, one room for the twins, a bathroom, then another for their parents to share. Gunner had intended to invade their territory and find something that would soothe his cousins' anguish. Maybe a stuffed animal, if Elle still slept with one. Or the locket his aunt had always worn on a gold chain around her neck.

But the suite smelled strange when he entered. As if someone had gone hunting then nestled into their sheets without bothering to wash away the blood. Curious, he crept past the twins' bunk beds and hesitated outside the door to the bathroom.

Only to hear voices from the hallway. "Clean it up," the pack leader growled. Not wanting to be caught where he didn't belong, Gunner opened the bathroom door and slipped inside...

...where he faced his aunt's body splayed across the tile, her skin torn as if a wolf had lit into her in a rage. Congealed blood splattered every surface, the rusty red stark against the bathroom's white tiles. This was no slow slipping into death as his father had suggested. This was clear evidence of foul play.

And premeditated action in addition. Because what were the chances of the horror happening in the bathroom if someone hadn't been concerned with the eventual cleanup?

Not wanting to look, Gunner had nonetheless leaned over to see into the shower. There should have been blood specks on the interior just as there were on the toilet and mirror.

But the white ceramic surface was as pristine as ever. Clean, slick...and slightly damp.

Chapter 30

"Ransom killed her?" I didn't even realize I was speaking until my words broke through the horrifying picture my companion had painted.

Gunner nodded, opened his mouth to elaborate...then our secluded niche by the waterfall erupted into a maelstrom of wolves.

They were *our* wolves, though. I could feel it even without trying to pick out individual aromas. Tank, Crow, and Allen being herded along by Elle in her Atwood-marked fur body. All of them shifted upwards in synchrony just as they came level with me, Kira, and Gunner. And at that moment, my sister finally woke up.

"Ew, gross!" The teenager pushed away with so much force that my torso slammed backwards, only Gunner's fast movement preventing my head from cracking open upon the rocks. "Clothes, dudes! How many times do I have to tell you we're not all werewolves? Put on some *clothes*!"

And *that* was the Kira I was used to. Bossy, annoying, and totally uninterested in the reality of situations beyond our ability to control.

Only, apparently, the guys had come prepared for Kira's sensitivities. Because Allen merely laughed, turning around to dig through a waterproof bag I hadn't noticed tucked up against the cliff face. "We've got clothes...."

Predictably, Kira wasn't satisfied by this hopping-to. Instead, she placed her hands on her hips rather than covering her privates, looking as wolf-like as any of the males when she barked out: "I don't want to see your ugly butt! Point that thing the other way!"

Whatever further insults the teen planned to fling in Allen's direction, however, were cut short when a lump of awful, puce-covered fabric slapped her in the face. A flurry of similar soft missiles slammed into the rest of us one after another. And when I glanced down at my own wad of fabric, I saw that Allen had come prepared with one-size-fits-all jogging pants and t-shirts, the latter with unique sayings lettered across the front.

"I love Goofy?" I asked, unable to prevent myself from reading my shirt aloud.

"Cute and cuddly," Gunner noted, eyes on his own pink shirt that boasted a white kitten with brilliant blue eyes beside the three curlicue-laden words.

"They were cheap," Allen countered...then ruined the assertion when the corners of his mouth started twitching. "Or, at least, I thought of you when I saw them...."

If our shirts were the buildup, I had a feeling Kira's was the punchline. So I turned back toward my sister, then paled as I caught a glimpse of Tank's torso seconds before "Lawyers have feelings too...allegedly" covered up the majority of his bare skin.

The joke was borderline funny, but the scratches covering his chest and shoulders were far too familiar. Scratches so much like the ones I'd seen beneath our shared fingers while harvesting blood for the Master with my mother. Scratches like the ones Lucinda's little sister must have left to end up with blood beneath her nails.

I would have liked to think Tank had gotten stuck in a briar thicket to end up with so many skin abrasions. Unfortunately, the evidence pointed elsewhere. Our loyal pack mate was loyal no longer, not after suffering a run-in with my mom.

"STEP BACK!" I DEMANDED, pushing myself between the source of danger and my snickering sister. Unfortunately, Kira failed to hear me as she pranced forward to engulf Allen in a full-body hug.

"I love it! It's perfect!" she emoted, twirling around to show off her t-shirt...which I didn't bother looking at since the girl's motion also sent her closer and closer to the scratched-up werewolf that the Master could now manipulate on a whim.

I wasn't fast enough to prevent their paths from crossing however. And Tank was oblivious to the danger he represented. His face crinkled up into a smile as Kira sprang from one werewolf to the other. Then the girl reached out to smack Tank in the chest...

Only, seconds before her fingers touched, the male's eyes reddened, his muscles tightened. His hand reached out even as my sword materialized one moment too late....

"Tank, *move away from the child!*" Gunner's words snapped over us harsh and sudden as a horse whip. And I felt my sword drifting downwards even as Tank scrambled backwards as if he'd been slapped.

So maybe the Master didn't have as much control over the wolves Mama harvested blood from as I'd imagined? Or perhaps those scratches really had been made by thorns and I'd just imagined the redness of Tank's eyes?

I wasn't yet up to speaking in full sentences, unfortunately. Instead, I finally succeeded in angling myself into the gap between Kira and Tank that I'd been going for from the beginning. Then I leveled my sword against the latter's shoulder, holding him away from my sister while letting Gunner do the talking for us both.

Luckily, the alpha understood my reasoning as easily as if he possessed telepathy. "What's with the scratches?" Gunner asked, his voice rougher than usual as he joined me in a solid wall separating Tank from the rest of our pack mates.

For his part, Tank's brows furrowed, his voice tentative as he angled his neck down so as not to provoke further attack...or perhaps to make 100% sure my sword wasn't pressing in through his flesh. "The story isn't really appropriate to tell around ladies..." he whispered, the husky words nearly as loud as a shout to my hypersensitive eardrums.

"Tell us anyway," Gunner countered.

So Tank did, offering a tale pretty much like I'd expected. One of the pack princesses—no he didn't remember her name—had come on to him this morning. She was cute, willing. "A vixen," he started. Then, his eyes flitted toward me as he realized what he'd said.

I would have laughed at the kitsune faux pas if the stakes hadn't been so serious. Instead, I told Gunner: "We can't trust him around Kira." Then, with my eyes, I added an extra message: *If Ransom is trying to turn your most loyal werewolves against us, you can't keep supporting him the way you have in the past.*

In response, Gunner closed his eyes as if he'd heard my unspoken addendum. Then he nodded, twisting his shoulders so he was speaking to the entire pack.

"Elle, Crow, and Allen—I need you to move camp and sugarcoat our situation for the social worker. Tank, you and I have a bear to kill."

Chapter 31

"**A** bear?"

I wasn't sure if Gunner had turned metaphorical on me, or if he really was planning to shunt off his responsibilities and join in the Solstice Hunt after all. But I had no time to pin him down on the subject. Because the alpha was spearing his pack mates with a gaze that sent them tumbling to their knees one after the other.

"Trust *no one* who isn't here beside you at this moment. Protect Kira to your last breath. Feed her blood if she weakens. Keep Mai and the social worker safe also. Swear it."

Gunner's demands came out in a staccato that peppered his underlings like bullets. They were so cowed, in fact, that no one managed to speak until their alpha provided a verbal nudge.

"Allen?"

"I swear, alpha."

"Crow."

"I promise."

"Elle?"

"I will, Gunner. You know I will."

"Mai?"

I didn't realize Gunner had planned to include me in the oath-taking until his dark eyes turned to grab my own. And, for the first time in living memory, I felt fully caught by an alpha werewolf's stare.

"Mai?" he repeated when words failed me, this second speaking of my name somehow releasing my muscles so I could turn and take in the werewolves gathered on either side of us.

Allen, Elle, and Crow were encircling my sister now, enfolding her within their pack as easily as if she was a pup and they were warriors. Tank, in contrast, waited five paces distant, his head averted as if he was afraid to even glance at the youngster he threatened due to the scratches on his back.

Gunner was taking all of the danger with him and leaving Kira with twice the protection she truly needed. Which meant there was only one way to respond to the question in his sienna eyes.

"Kira will be fine without me," I noted as easily as if naysaying an alpha werewolf didn't make my throat tighten and my muscles quiver. "I'm going with you to hunt this bear."

TO MY SURPRISE, GUNNER shrugged then nodded before turning to face Allen as if I hadn't just disagreed with him when he was in full-on Scary Alpha mode. "Any bears that need killing?"

"Actually, there is one." A cell phone tumbled end over end as it flew between us, Gunner's large palm snatching the device out of the air then tilting it so I could take in the screen.

"Bear eats toddler. Authorities left scrambling," read the headline. Below that was a grainy image that might or might not have been a wild animal.

"Are...?" I started, still not understanding why it was worth tracking down dangerous wildlife today rather than tomorrow.

But Gunner shrugged off my half-question. "Can you carry this in your magical pouch thingy?" he demanded, the words sounding strangely official in his deep, gravelly growl.

"Sure," I agreed, twisting my sword into a fanny pack even as the phone was handed off to me. Then, with no time wasted on farewells, Tank and Gunner were lupine and running, my fox form having to sprint to keep up.

Just like before, branches lashed me in the face while wet mud slipped dangerously beneath my paw pads, leaving me little energy to worry about my sister or wonder about bears. Instead, I just ran. Behind Tank, before Gunner. My speed slowing the pack who likely could have covered ground twice as quickly if I hadn't been in their midst.

Despite my shorter legs, however, we were all panting equally by the time we stepped out of the trees at the edge of what had to be the Atwood clan home. It looked like a settlement in suburbia, all rocking chairs and flowers. But the air smelled of ozone and wolves.

And no wonder, because a pup no larger than a house cat slid out an open doorway seconds after we stepped onto the pavement. I didn't know werewolves came in sizes that minuscule. But, oblivious to its puny status, the youngster yipped in excitement...then ran straight for Tank.

I shifted and lunged, half expecting the Master to somehow sense the opportunity to wreak havoc upon wolves his brother cared about. But Gunner was there and grabbing the puppy before I could insert myself between them. The alpha opened his jaws wide enough to fit the youngster's head inside, lowered his eyebrows, roared...

...And the puppy laughed in counterpoint. Or it barked out what passed for laughter in a young werewolf, wriggling its plump body and wagged its tail uncontrollably.

Only then did it leap out of Gunner's grip and into the arms of a female I hadn't even noticed approaching. "Is the hunt over?" she asked, her eyes hooded with worry even though she barely spared a second glance for the pup. "Is Marcus alright?"

"Your mate is in perfect condition," Gunner answered. "But we're hunting bear...."

The female, apparently, understood the implications of that sentence where I didn't. "Then you don't want to walk through town and be bombarded with questions. Here, let me grab my keys."

Clutching the puppy closer, she speed walked back up to her residence. Took, apparently, one moment longer than necessary because Tank shifted to join us two-legged, reached out to grip his alpha's bicep. "You trust her not to send someone to warn your brother?"

"Becky is my third cousin. She won't break."

Of course, Becky had to be *Ransom's* third cousin also. And what did bears and brothers have in common anyway?

Then the female in question was back, pup absent but keys dangling from outstretched fingers. "Marcus's SUV has four-wheel drive. It'll get you wherever you need to go. There's emergency gear and clothes behind the back seat..."

"Thank you," Gunner answered, cutting into her refrain. Still, he wasted one moment stepping forward and bending his head down to kiss her on the forehead. In a millisecond, Becky's stringent scent sweetened as worry slid off her shoulders, proving that the tall, broad Atwood before me was 100% pack-leader material.

He might be pack-leader material, but his role wasn't yet official. And that, I gathered, was why we leapt into the vehicle and drove off in search of a bear.

Chapter 32

"Alpha, may I speak?"

I'd never before seen Gunner's inner circle so tentative around him. But I wasn't entirely surprised by Tank's behavior either, not after Gunner had nearly bitten off his head when the lawyer made the egregious mistake of...offering me the passenger seat. Tank probably had no idea why the scratches on his shoulders meant he was no longer trusted to sit or stand behind me. Sometime soon, I'd have to pull him aside and clue him in.

Not right now though. Because Gunner was growling permission for further conversation even as he steered us off clan central's small gravel driveway and onto a paved, two-lane road. Pressing hard on the gas pedal, he zipped up to and past the speed limit in a matter of seconds. Then, when Tank still hesitated, he bit out: "Speak."

"Yes, alpha." Tank's eyes were firmly focused on the cell phone I'd handed over after we all shifted, and not due to his usual internet addiction either. Instead, I got the distinct impression that the male was submitting in the only way possible before a stronger werewolf whose behavior was even more terrifying for apparently lacking cause.

Without thinking, I reached forward and placed four fingertips against the lawyer's neck by way of consolation. And, wolf-like, Tank relaxed on an instant, flashing me a grateful half-smile before finally spitting out what he had to say.

"It's your prerogative to change your mind, alpha. And I'm not saying it's a bad idea to go after the bear. But last week, you told us you had no plan to challenge your brother. So we don't actually know where this animal is located. Perhaps it would be simpler to skip ahead to the sword fight...."

"No." Gunner's negation pushed me and Tank back in our seats as admirably as if he'd accelerated the vehicle. Noting our reaction, he smoothed out his tone as he explained: "Ransom deserves the chance to step down gracefully. Proving prowess at a hunt worked at deciding dominance between our father and our uncle, and it will work for me and Ransom as well. We'll find the bear."

The highway we were on reached a T then, and Gunner turned left without bothering to pause at the stop sign. There were no other vehicles around to make the traffic violation dangerous. And yet, the motion sent a spear of agony cutting through my head.

Pressing my fingers against my temples, I murmured, "Wait...."

My words were too quiet to impinge upon the loaded conversation taking place in the front seat. But as the SUV began accelerating, leaving my stomach behind at the crossroads, I realized what my body was trying to express.

We're going the wrong way. Yes, that was the problem. So, forcing a little volume into my voice, I added: "Turn around."

I didn't expect them to listen. Not when the pair's current conversation was loaded with implications, weighed down by Tank's scratches and whatever difficult brotherly decisions were flowing through Gunner's head.

But the alpha heard me anyway. Slammed on the brakes. Then made a U-turn that depended rather strongly upon Becky's promised four-wheel-drive feature as the passenger-side wheels ended up in—then out of—the ditch.

I barely felt the bumping beneath me, however. Instead, my breath was coming faster as I reached forward to tap Tank on the shoulder. "The phone..." I started.

Then the device was in my hand, the news article I'd only glanced at previously filling the screen. The image was somehow clearer than it had been previously, as if I was present there in that secluded residence by the photographer's side. There was blood on the animal's hind leg, I noted. Had it cut itself breaking in?

And suddenly I was consumed by the bear's body. Was stomping through leaf litter, heavy pads and thick claws scraping against rough rock.

Slinging my weight around, I didn't spare a thought for predators. Instead, when I smelled the stink of a weasel, I merely laughed....

Then I was back in my human body, my head so light and dizzy I felt like I hadn't eaten in three days. "He's to the west," I noted. Then, rolling down the window, I vomited up my guts.

"NO," GUNNER GROWLED.

"Yes," I answered.

"Save me from lovers' squabbles," Tank muttered. "If you two keep arguing, we won't get back before dark."

I sighed and tried to get a stronger hold on my temper. On the plus side, my first merging with the bear's consciousness had been enough to guide us toward a dead-end road at the edge of a vast wilderness area. But my magic was too weak to allow for a repeat of the endeavor. And Gunner stubbornly refused to allow me to boost the signal by consuming Tank's blood.

"You'll drink mine," the Atwood leader repeated through gritted teeth that appeared to be sharpening. But I'd drunk from Gunner multiple times over the last twenty-four hours. And, from what I'd read between the lines recently, he planned to kill a bear singlehandedly, drag it back to the meeting hill, then possibly fight his brother—to the death?—in an effort to wrench control of the Atwood pack out of Ransom's hands. I didn't particularly want to weaken him with a third bloodletting if there was another willing werewolf on hand.

I didn't say any of that, however. After all, I'd been around werewolves long enough to understand the alpha's well-deserved pride.

Instead, I started spinning half truths. "If I drink from Tank, there's a good chance it'll break whatever hold the Master has over him," I guessed, hoped. "It might..."

Gunner stepped forward so abruptly my subsequent words lapsed into breathlessness. "You want this?"

"Yes." I barely had breath enough to reply.

"And you're willing?" This to Tank.

"Of course, alpha."

"Then do it." Only, Gunner didn't stand aside and let Tank slip in between us. Instead, he crooked his finger, waited for his underling to approach, then reached down to encircle the latter's broad wrist in his even larger hand.

Gunner's fangs bit into Tank's skin so quickly I wasn't the only one left gasping. But the lawyer stifled his inhale, closed his eyes, and made no complaint as Gunner lifted the open wound up to my lips.

The gesture felt strangely intimate. And at the same time exactly as it should have been. Me, Gunner, and Tank united within our own small pack.

But the blood on my tongue was bitter, so acrid I almost spat it back out rather than swallowing. This experience was nothing like drinking from Gunner. Instead, it took all I had not to push Tank's wrist away.

Nonetheless, the rich blood strengthened me. I could feel it infusing my star ball with a burst of power, hooking me back into the mind of the bear....

"*Come,*" I whispered around Tank's bleeding body. Only, it wasn't me speaking. For half a second, I felt Mama's fingers on my shoulders. Warning, warming.

Then the blood slowed, sweetened. And I knew that the bear was much closer than I'd initially thought.

"Watch out!" I yelled, not minding the way words came out along with a spray of bloody spittle this time. Because the killer bear was right behind Gunner. Had gotten its wires crossed and decided werewolves were just as easy prey as the average pint-sized toddler.

Meanwhile, my warning had turned Gunner's attention toward me rather than toward the massive animal. So I could do nothing but watch as it reared up to slash at his back.

Chapter 33

Gunner shifted and twisted as the bear fell forward on top of him. Which didn't mean he came away unscathed, of course. But at least the bear's tremendous claws merely swiped a gash from furry shoulder to billowing ribcage rather than ripping the wolf's belly all the way out.

No wonder the bear roared out frustration at losing such an easy kill, its breath wafting over me in a vile wave that overwhelmed my senses despite the distance between us both. The stench resembled fly-covered carrion and sleepless nights spent ruminating, telling told me even better than the newspaper article had that this bear was the animal version of a serial killer, less interested in eating than it was in the kill.

I noted all this in the time it took to call my sword into existence. Even magical steel seemed too soft to pierce a bear's thick hide, actually. But I had to at least try to tilt the battle in our favor....

Except, Tank's hand swung down out of nowhere, pinching my fingers so abruptly that I reverted to mistakes of a beginner, dropping my blade as if my fingers had become coated in grease. The weapon flashed into pure magic as it left me, slipping around my ankles and melding back into my skin for later utilization. So I hadn't lost the potential for swordsmanship. And yet....

"What the...?" I demanded, whirling and peering into Tank's face. I expected the flash of red promising the Master had taken control of his senses. But, instead, the lawyer's eyes were as blue and clear as water reflecting the sky.

"No weapons," he explained tersely, his hand still clenched down on mine as if to ensure I listened. He spoke as quickly as if the judge had offered him a mere ten seconds for his summation. "That would be cheating. They'll check the hide for signs of gun or knife wounds. Which isn't to say Gunner can't have help in fur form from a second and a mate...."

Mate. The word left me speechless long enough that Tank had already shifted and dove into the fight before I came back to my senses. Now would have been a good time to retreat to the vehicle. But, instead, the pair flanked the bear from opposite directions, lunging forward so quickly the behemoth was hard-pressed to keep up.

That was our opponent's weakness, I gathered. Size meant it lacked both speed and agility. Still, the wolves were making little progress, their teeth sliding through fur without leaving blood trails behind.

And they were already wounded, both of them. Gunner now suffered slashes on his muzzle and hindquarters matching the one the bear had swiped across his side at the beginning. Meanwhile, Tank looked little better, with a wound on his temple that had barely missed taking out one eye.

Eyes. Of course. The bear's skin was impenetrable to the efforts of a wolf pack. But a fox might be able to run up its back and strike the animal blind....

Moving as quickly as the thought occurred to me, I was four-legged and fleet-footed in the time it took for Gunner and Tank to choreograph yet another attack against our shared enemy. The bear had previously seemed bamboozled by similar joint efforts. But this time, it ignored Gunner and swung at his companion, flinging the lawyer against a nearby tree so hard that he didn't even manage to yelp.

Move, Tank! I screamed silently, hoping the lawyer would manage to regain his footing before the bear lumbered into a charge. Unfortunately, Tank lay still and silent...and then I lost sight of him entirely as I clawed straight up the bear's body, clinging to its matted fur.

The beast shivered like a cow shaking a fly off its hindquarters, but otherwise seemed rather uninterested in me as I clambered up. Cresting its spine with little effort, I came to rest on top of its broad head just as the beast rose two-legged above Tank's comatose body....

Meanwhile, Gunner was nipping wildly at the bear's hind legs beneath us, attempting and failing to reach the softer skin of the animal's belly. Not that even a bite there would have halted the upcoming carnage. Because the bear's fur was even thicker on its underside, hanging down in long, tangled sheets.

And then it was time to put my plan into action, despite the stench so foul it nearly made me lose my grip. I braced my hind legs and leaned down to go after one beady eyeball, each orb as brown and liquidy as the next.

At that moment, however, Tank whimpered, coming awake just in time to see death looming above him. It wouldn't be *his* death, though. Not if I could help it....

I strained with all my might to reach the bear's eye without losing my footing. Then, just as I slashed, the pupil flashed bright red.

Chapter 34

So Mama summoned the bear after all, I noted even as the possessed animal beneath me twisted faster than a bear really should have been capable of. It flung me off its forehead and toward Tank, and all I could think was: *I failed my pack.*

Air pressed my fur against the skin underneath it, and I braced myself for impact with the surrounding brush. But it was human hands not hard wood that hit my body, human hands that grabbed my feet and boosted me back aloft.

Because my pack had felt me coming. And somehow Tank had understood my game plan well enough to fling me back into the exact right place.

I hit the bear's neck faster than I'd left it, scrambled upward even as Gunner nipped wildly at our enemy's flesh. Predictably, the bear lashed out at him, dinner-plate-sized paw extended...and this time Gunner didn't even try to dodge our shared enemy. Instead, he latched down on the soft skin between already bloodied claws, giving me time to complete my attack.

It was too late to gamble on a paw stroke, not when Gunner was already deeply entwined with the bear's claws. Instead, I dove at our opponent's eyeball, biting hard just as Gunner was doing down below.

The orb popped like a grape, but I had no time to be disgusted. Just scooted sideways to take out the other eye even as the bear raised both front legs to paw at its streaming face. Then I leapt free, barely making it off the toppling bear before being crushed beneath its descending body....

Because wolf teeth apparently *are* sufficient to tear out bear bellies. Or at least they are if the bear in question is blind and unable to fight back. Tank and Gunner were soaked in blood and half-digested intestinal contents before they finished. But all I felt was sublime relief.

Relief that even though Mama had obeyed the Master and drawn this bear here as ordered, she seemed to have been looking out for my best interests after all. Because now we had the means necessary to win Gunner's ascendancy to the head of clan Atwood. As long as we arrived back at the meeting hill before dark, that is.

Unfortunately, the sun was falling quickly toward the tree line, the hard work of rolling the bear carcass into the back of the SUV taking all the strength we had left. Wordlessly, we tumbled into the vehicle, Tank in the front and me and Gunner in the rear cargo area. The alpha pulled the scariest-looking hunting knife I'd ever seen out of the bag that had yielded up our clothes earlier, hacking into the animal's hide as he explained: "We'll bring the head to prove our kill...."

Despite the grisly spectacle, I felt safe beside my pack mates. And I must have fallen asleep for a few minutes after that. Because when I next looked up, we were turning back onto the gravel driveway that led to clan central. Daylight was fading, the sky burning with oranges and pinks as we rolled toward the street where we'd initially picked up this borrowed vehicle.

We'd need to run to get to the meeting spot by the deadline. A tough sell while carrying our macabre—and heavy—load....

Only, time wasn't the only factor working against us. Because Tank swore from the front seat, prompting me to half rise so I could peer out the windshield.

And what I saw there had my hand falling down to clamp upon Gunner's shoulder in search of reassurance. The quiet cul-de-sac we'd left a few hours earlier was no longer empty. Instead, Becky must have tattled on us. Because the tarmac was covered with what looked like an army of none-too-pleasant werewolves.

Chapter 35

Fox instincts can sometimes kick in at the most inopportune of moments. Like now, when the SUV screeched to a halt and a shifter I'd never before set eyes on stepped forward to pull the hatchback aloft. He and his comrades pressed inward, their scent of fur and electricity invading the vehicle quite thoroughly despite their two-legged stature. And all I could do was struggle against the imperative to shift into fox form, wriggle through the merest sliver of elbow room, and make my escape.

Because I was trapped. Stuck in an unyielding metal box while surrounded by werewolves. I knew it was a bad idea to don my fur and show how different I was from the others, but somehow that knowledge felt distant and vague....

Then Gunner's arm settled across my shoulders, his mere presence thawing the chill in my blood and settling my mind. "Edward," he greeted the closest werewolf.

Gunner's tone was cordial but his muscles were rope-like with tension as he angled me behind him. And even though the posturing of a dominant werewolf goes a long way, I wasn't so certain even Gunner could overcome all fifty of these werwolves while cornered in the back of the blood-stained vehicle....

Tank must have jumped to the same conclusion I had. Because I heard the creak of his door opening behind my left shoulder, then I smelled the lawyer's aroma drifting closer as he padded around to stand at the other werewolves' backs.

So we were three against fifty rather than two against fifty. Somehow that knowledge wasn't enough to soothe my racing heartbeat. Still, I held onto my human skin with an effort, not wanting to make matters worse by giving in to fox terror and skin.

For thirty long seconds, we stayed there, lost in some silent werewolf battle of willpower. Then, finally, Edward answered Gunner's greeting. "Alpha," the former started, dropped to one knee outside the vehicle, his gaze falling so rapidly that his chin thunked against his chest. "Pack leader. We've come to help you carry your kill."

Oh. My breath wheezed out far too loudly, but no one paid me any attention. Instead, the wave of kneeling swept out on both sides from its epicenter around Edward, until the sensation of pack surged up to surround us in a solid wave.

We had backup. I hadn't realized how little I relished the notion of Gunner standing alone against his brother until what seemed like two-thirds of the Atwood clan transferred their loyalties without even being asked to do so.

But Gunner didn't accept the offer as easily as I would have done. Instead, he hopped down out of the vehicle, resting his hand upon Edward's shoulder. And he waited for nearly a minute until the older male lost his fascination with the pavement and finally glanced back up.

"It's dangerous to take sides at this moment," the alpha warned his supporter. "If Ransom wins, you lose quite severely."

"It's more dangerous to be governed by the wrong pack leader," Edward answered just as carefully. And I could read between the lines that he had much more to say.

But there was no time to discuss repercussions and loyalties. Because the sun was dipping below the tree line. Time was running out even as a dozen hands pressed me sideways so they could reach the bear carcass in the back of the vehicle.

Being werewolves, they had no respect for my personal space. Nonetheless, I only had eyes for one werewolf: Gunner.

The younger brother looked so much like an alpha at that moment that it was hard to believe he'd allowed Ransom a shot at being pack leader. And if he was finally going to meet his destiny, I couldn't let my kitsune nature hold him back.

So: "Go. I'll follow," I told him, an unspoken understanding flowing between us.

Then, with a nod at two werewolf strangers who were clearly expected to stay two-legged alongside me, Gunner and his pack mates were running with the bear body between them away into the descending night.

THEIR PATH WAS EASY to follow, the mass of wolves and two-leggers having broken branches and matted down tangles as they arrowed directly toward the meeting hill. But I couldn't shift in front of strangers. So, two-legged, our journey turned into a slow and frustrating slog.

Night had nearly fallen by this point, which was maddening since each flashing lightning bug not only reminded me that Gunner and Ransom would already be meeting...it also made me shiver at the memory of my dream. Blood on the hilltop, me facing the Master directly. If that was to be the culmination of this evening, I wished we could fast forward ahead directly to the end.

But my human feet could only walk so swiftly. And as I opened my mouth to see whether the werewolves beside me might consider shifting and going ahead without me...someone stepped toward us out of the trees.

I didn't realize who it was for ten long seconds, my star ball gathering invisibly between my clenched fingers as I peered into the shadows beneath the pine trees. Was it worth revealing my kitsune nature to fight off this newcomer? I couldn't be sure, but I was ready to do whatever was necessary to ensure I made it to Gunner's side intact.

Only, before more than the hilt of my sword had materialized, Liam stepped out into the open. His eyes were wild as he ran both hands through already ruffled hair, and he barely gasped out "Kira needs you" before stopping to catch his breath.

"How did...?" I started then shook my head at the irrelevancy of asking how Liam had managed to track me down in the vast expanse of forest. He'd likely used the pack bond just like his sister had. And if Kira needed me...then I'd just have to send these two strangers to help Gunner in my place.

"Go," I told them, wishing I could remember the names they'd offered when they'd introduced themselves. But Gunner's furry tail had been receding into the treeline, and their names had gone in one ear and out the other as I stared at their alpha's back.

Now, the pair stood with furrowed brows and cocked heads, unwilling to either obey or gainsay me. We were losing time to their uncertainty, so I reached out and gestured at Liam. Surely the alpha's cousin was a more than acceptable bodyguard....

And, after one glance shared among themselves, the taller shifter shrugged, the shorter one nodded. Then they were dropping into wolf form, sprinting into the darkness, leaving me and Liam entirely alone.

Well, alone save my imaginings of what might have sent Liam running to find me when a succession battle was also taking place in the forest. "Where is she? What happened?" I demanded.

"This way," Liam answered, leading me beneath the glowering bulk of the pine tree from which he'd emerged and away from our fellow shifters who were likely already out of earshot as well as sight. It was pitch dark beneath the needled behemoths, hard for even shifter eyes to capture enough light to walk through. So I wasn't surprised when the male beside me stumbled, his toe seeming to catch on an upraised root.

I grabbed Liam's arm to keep him upright, felt his weight cave in on me as he barely managed not to fall. Yesterday, I would have been daunted by the sensation of a werewolf impinging upon my personal space. But, today, I understood what it meant to be part of a pack. So I gave Liam my strength willingly, accepting his hand as it searched blindly for my own in the dark.

"Ah, there we go," Liam murmured. And he no longer sounded breathless and weakened. Instead, the words were strangely smug even as pain shot through my index finger.

I tried to look down to see what had pierced my skin, but the forest was fading away around me. For an endless second, I floated in darkness...then I was seeing through someone else's eyes on an all-too-familiar hilltop that was already saturated with blood.

Chapter 36

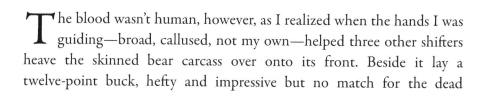

The blood wasn't human, however, as I realized when the hands I was guiding—broad, callused, not my own—helped three other shifters heave the skinned bear carcass over onto its front. Beside it lay a twelve-point buck, hefty and impressive but no match for the dead predator Gunner had brought back.

So this was what the brothers had been doing while I was trailing along behind them at a snail's pace—butchering recently slaughtered animals to make sure there'd been no foul play. Inside me, hope kindled. I wasn't too late to help the younger brother after all....

Meanwhile, my mouth spat out words both deep and masculine. "No sign of weapons," I growled.

On my left side, Edward dipped his head in a wordless nod of agreement. Immediately, three other shifters followed suit, an impartial jury facing the Atwood brothers and preventing further bloodshed from coming to pass.

Or, at least, that appeared to be our role. Liam was having none of it.

"But the bear's head is separated," Liam continued, pushing the words into the lungs of the male whose body I possessed no matter how hard I tried to bite my tongue against the admission. "Anything could have happened in the neck area. Stab wounds. Gunshots. It's impossible to be certain. This isn't a definitive wolf kill."

Behind my back, I could feel the quiver of dozens—hundreds?—of werewolves reacting to my assertion. Some smelled interested, like spectators at a ball game. Others exuded hunger, the bear and deer apparently having become more appetizing now that they had been thoroughly skinned.

Most, though, were tense and worried. An occasional murmur broke through the constant shuffle of human and lupine bodies, suggesting that the majority of the crowd didn't want this showdown to turn into a physical fight.

Liam on the other hand, was itching for bloodshed. I could feel his excitement quivering beside my real body, could feel his smug pleasure as he guided me up on the meeting hill. More blood meant more power for him. And wasn't the oft-overlooked cousin, even more than the legitimate pack leader, likely to benefit from an upheaval within the hierarchy of the Atwood clan?

I didn't think Liam was actually controlling his cousin, but Ransom was quick to jump into the presented gap. "You think that's all you have to do, eh, brother?" he growled. "Kill a bear, throw it at my feet, steal away the clan I've been raised to lead since birth." Then Ransom's tone smoothed as he recalled his ace in the hole. "Well, I won't let you. Gunner, *I remind you of your oath.*"

I held my breath, expecting that to be the end of it. But the compulsion had no effect on the younger sibling. Instead, Gunner merely shook his head before speaking. "My strongest oath is to this pack, Ransom. Again, I ask you to step down."

So Gunner's obedience in the past *had* all been stagecraft, even down to kneeling in front of his supposed pack leader in Wildacres' mud. Which should have meant the wolf I was backing had the advantage. Unfortunately, his younger brother's lack of obedience only enraged the weaker of the two contestants.

"You won't accept that I lead this pack by birthright?" Ransom ground out, only to be interrupted by a succinct history lesson.

"Our father was the younger brother," Gunner countered, "but the better shepherd of this pack."

"Or so we've been led to believe." Ransom spat, the gob of spittle barely missing his brother's bare toes before joining the bear blood puddling atop the soil. And behind me, the werewolves on the eastern side of the knoll erupted into grumbles that seemed fated to turn into snarls.

So that was where Gunner's supporters had gathered. I wished I was able to turn the neck of this borrowed body to make a count of how many shifters were for and how many against the younger brother....

But I could feel Liam's hand around mine back beneath the pine trees. Could feel his fingers squeezing, pressing blood out of the pinprick while I made no motion to get away.

Not for want of trying; that part goes without saying. But I could do nothing about either my own body or the one here on the hilltop. Instead, without my permission, the latter's feet were already beginning to move.

"Quiet," Gunner chided his followers even as my host body slipped back behind the first row of shifters, using their bulk to shield me/him from view as we padded silently around to the right. I didn't know where Liam was sending us, but I had a feeling it wasn't anywhere good....

Meanwhile, Ransom seemed to have decided he was a comic-book villain. Because rather than resting upon his laurels, he continued to speak.

"Our uncle was a pushover and a cuckold," the older brother proclaimed, the crowd quieting as the family's dirty laundry was aired in public view. "Why do you think his wife was murdered?"

"You mean why she *died*," Gunner interjected, reaching forward to grab his brother's shoulder so hard the latter's flesh turned red, then white. Why would Ransom want to tell this story when he was the villain? Gunner apparently felt the way I did, but the older brother was unwilling to be shut up.

"No, I mean our aunt was *killed* in cold blood," Ransom countered, shrugging off his sibling's hand and stepping forward in a werewolf display of dominance. "Our father slept with his brother's woman. And our half-brother was the one who snuffed out her traitorous life."

Chapter 37

"**H**alf-brother?" Gunner asked, his voice confused and faltering. *Half-brother*, I echoed inside my own mind. No wonder the bitter jealousy had built up within Liam so profoundly that it brought us all to this point.

Meanwhile, beneath the pine trees, Liam quivered at the revelation of his history. And for half a second, I thought I might be able to rip myself free of his grasp.

But then something warm and moist covered my bleeding finger. Pressure came, a mouth sucked.

I nearly vomited at the knowledge that Liam had taken my digit into his mouth and was even now lapping up my magic. And at the same moment, Ransom clarified his earlier words.

"Liam killed his mother in a fit of jealous anger," the pack leader elaborated. "Did you really think our father and aunt did the dirty in our mother's home only once?"

As that particular bombshell hit, I lost control of the body I was sitting in entirely. Became a passive bystander as borrowed male feet carried me the rest of the way around behind the brothers until we stood only eighteen inches from the pair's backsides.

Then I turned my head—or, rather, Liam turned it for me—noting that the few shifters here on the wrong side of the hill could see little with the moon still hidden beneath the curve of the earth's horizon.

Even as the secrecy of our position sank in, my sword materialized in dark silence. Its hilt fit between the possessed male's fingers as if he was as good a swordsman as I was. Meanwhile, his body shivered as I realized what Liam had brought me here to accomplish.

Gunner! I yelled...or tried to. But the body I possessed just stood stoically silent while everyone around us leaned forward, taken in by the telling of the previous generation's tale.

"...clan or a reality TV show?" "...don't blame him." "...should have known better..." The whispers rose up on every side, and Ransom waited out the reaction. Perhaps the older brother had the makings of a pack leader after all.

Because it was the younger brother who spoke quietly but intently, impinging upon the whispers and adding fuel to the fire. "But you were there. The shower. The hunt. The fight with our father," Gunner protested.

"I came to speak to Elle, found something horrible, and stayed to protect her," Ransom growled. "Our *sister* would have shattered if she knew what Liam was capable of. I thought you understood that. What did you think? Did you think it was...me?"

This was their final chance for reconciliation. Before me, I could smell Gunner rewriting the past and hoisting his brother back up onto a pedestal. And Ransom—even that power-hungry shifter softened. The straight line of his shoulders slumped slightly and his aroma sweetened as the duo hovered on the brink of brotherhood once again.

But that wasn't what Liam had brought us all together for. Instead, back beneath the pine trees, my body turned colder as the Master literally sucked up another healthy dose of my magic. Then, on the hilltop, the softness around the older brother dissipated. The chance for reconciliation fled.

"I see what you think of me," Ransom growled, mind changing in an instant. There were scratches on his shoulders, I now noted. Many of them, both healed and unhealed. As if Liam had wanted to be entirely sure his hold on the older sibling was freshly consolidated.

"Brother," Gunner started, only to be interrupted.

"There's no point in talking."

"The bear," Gunner countered. "Tradition...."

"Are you really so weak that you're afraid of a true contest?"

Even then, Gunner tried to argue. But before he could force out another sentence, I felt my own arm rising. Saw Ransom's body mimic the action. Felt the sword leave my fingers and turn one complete revolution before it thudded into his hand.

For his part, Gunner's head turned not toward the threatening werewolf beside him but to look over his left shoulder. To see the source of the weapon that was now beginning to glow.

Just like the possessed male's eyes would now be glowing. Just like my own eyes might be glowing back in that pine grove.

Because I wasn't just a passive bystander, I gathered. Instead, I felt my training and magic merging together to guide Ransom's fingers even as his brother mouthed my name soundlessly into the air.

"Mai..."

His disappointment was palpable. But there was no time to wallow in the alpha's regret over my actions, because Ransom was already surging forward into an attack.

Chapter 38

The brothers were better matched than I would have expected...especially with my training coming along for the ride on Ransom's sword. In fact, we might have ended the contest prematurely had Tank not stepped forward out of the darkness to hand the younger brother an entirely corporeal weapon that otherwise closely matched my own.

"First blood," Gunner suggested as he hefted the weapon as easily as if it was an extension of his body. And the first clang of blades sent a jolt of electricity up my spine.

This was *wrong*, having my magic diverted from my body. Even worse, though, was fighting against a werewolf I'd come to accept as a member of my pack.

I had no say in the matter, however. Instead, when Ransom started falling for a feint that would have left him wide open, I felt my sword obey my thoughts rather than his muscles, slipping sideways until it once again met Gunner's blade.

The clang was deafening. Gunner's disappointment in me almost as audible. And, as the last sliver of sunlight slipped beneath the horizon, Ransom finally deigned to speak.

"I told you this was no game, brother. We'll fight until there is only one leader left to rule this pack."

Rustles and murmurs from the crowd faded into stillness. I could now see nothing, my sword having muted its glow in the interest of stealth.

"Our father taught us..." Gunner countered. But then he gave in to the inevitable as his opponent pushed forward in a flurry of blows that left no time for further talk.

It was too dark to make out every thrust and parry, but I could feel the first time Ransom's blade cut into his brother's skin. Because the blood surged through me like a sugar rush, making Liam laugh back in the pine grove while my borrowed body on the hilltop gleefully tapped its feet.

Ransom wasn't the only one making contact, however. The air was now redolent with freshly spilled fluids, and the rich tang of immediacy promised most of the scent came from shifters rather than deer and bear. Every second, the metallic aroma grew stronger...and that wasn't the only danger Gunner faced.

Because I smelled the audience pressing in closer as loyal werewolves considered diving into battle in support of their respective alphas. The pack would be physically decimated if they fought each other—I knew this. Worse would be the lack of unity that would ripple outwards to take over the entirety of the clan.

"*I, Mai Fairchild, swear to protect and uphold the Atwood pack to the best of my ability....*" My oath reverberated in my ears, chattering the possessed male's teeth together painfully. But there was nothing I could do to stop the carnage. Nothing except stand there in the darkness and wait out a battle I couldn't even see.

Then, before me, a pained shriek and a thud as one of the contestants fell earthward. I strained against the bonds that held me stuck in this immobile body, needing to know who had been vanquished and what I could do to help.

"*Eh, eh, eh,*" Liam warned back in the pine grove. He was watching as avidly as I was, I gathered. Was waiting to see how the battle would turn out.

Meanwhile, around my borrowed body, the audience fell silent. It was almost as if only two shifters stood there rather than two hundred or more.

"It's no loss of face to surrender, brother." The victor's voice rose through the air so quietly I wouldn't have heard him if I'd been one row deeper amidst the avid watchers. But I was inches from the combatants, and I almost collapsed in relief at the gentleness of Gunner's tone.

The battle was over and the proper brother had been triumphant. I had one millisecond to relax before Ransom refused to submit.

"Never," the older male started. Then, louder: "*To me! Kill the imposter! Attack!*"

His words were terrifying in both their strength and their purpose, the alpha compulsion crackling outward across the crowd. Feet shuffled as shifters fought against an obviously inappropriate order. But werewolves were hardwired to obey their alphas, and soon I felt shifters pressing against me upon three sides.

The first was already pushing around my unmoving body in an effort to follow Ransom's order when Gunner finally opened his mouth and spoke. *"Stand down,"* he said both calmly and sadly, the two words enough to freeze the entire crowd mid-stride. Then, in explanation: "Atwoods don't fight amongst themselves. Not now, not ever." Never mind that he and his brother had just engaged in an ill-fated battle of their own.

Immediately, the scent of embarrassed submission rose along with a burst of flashing lightning bugs, the insects so bright that for one split second they illuminated the scene. In the light, I saw Ransom kneeling, held in place by the sword poised against his jugular. Meanwhile, Gunner stood above his vanquished older brother, my magically created weapon dangling laxly from his left hand.

And as dark descended around us a second time, the audience reacted to the scene as much as to Gunner's command. "Alpha," some murmured. "Pack leader," whispered others, a growl of agreement rising from those who hadn't spoken yet.

They were pack-oriented and that should have been the last of it. The brothers had fought and the proper alpha had won.

Only Liam wasn't ready for the battle to be over. *"Now,"* he murmured back in the pine grove. And, all around me, shifters lunged toward Gunner en masse.

Chapter 39

The pack was splintering as I stoody by and watched it happen. Then I wasn't watching but was instead joining in the fight...on the side that was not my own.

Because Liam had been around star balls long enough to know that I could draw the blade containing my magic back to me using pure willpower. And as the hilt snugged into the palm of the body I borrowed, my feet carried me across the intervening space and toward the male who had recently held my sword.

I felt rather than saw Ransom roll away between us. Smelled rather than saw Gunner ready himself for my attack.

Back in the pine grove, my stomach roiled with horror. I was about to strike the werewolf who had been nothing but kind to me. I was able to eviscerate my pack mate....

There on the hilltop, however, my hand remained steady. Even in darkness, I could gauge the distance between us through memory of recent sight.

I whirled to come at Gunner from an unexpected direction. Raised my star-ball sword then slashed downward where his neck ought to have been...

...Only to be halted by a flicker of starlight.

No, that was Gunner's blade, parrying. My sword screeched like claws on a chalkboard as it ran up my opponent's. But, at the hilt, it was forced to stop.

Relief flooded me...but not for long. Because my borrowed body was already disengaging and regrouping, making my real body pant in horror as my limbs turned weak. I'd nearly broken something precious in the previous moment. And no matter how much I tensed my real muscles, the ones Liam controlled geared up to do it all over again.

"Kill him," Liam whispered in my ear back in the pine grove.

Meanwhile: "Mai," Gunner breathed toward me out of the dark.

Beside my real body, the Master snickered, a low harsh sound that felt like sandpaper running over my skin. The darkness was Gunner's only real advantage...that plus the fact that he had no reason to do anything other than run away from me. But the alpha didn't retreat. Instead, he as good as painted a target on his chest as he continued speaking.

"You don't want to do this." The words weren't a question. Instead, they were warm and sweet as chamomile tea.

But, heartening or not, Gunner's speech served to locate him in the darkness. And once again my magical sword thrust forward, this time angling to slide through my opponent's ribcage and into his heart.

Somehow, though, Gunner managed to turn at the last instant so my blade cut through nothing. The lack of contact knocked me off balance so I faltered, misstepped, almost fell.

"Our *pack*." The alpha's whisper caught me as ably as physical hands might have. Set me back on my feet even as they filled my brain with an idea. Was he suggesting...?

"A pack is only as strong as its weakest member," Liam interjected, speaking through me. Our shared voice was cold now. Angry. Intent upon Gunner's death.

And just like that, my sword began glowing like a beacon. Claws scratched on hard earth behind me. A bark morphed into a growl. The magical light was attracting Gunner's enemies. It would only be a matter of seconds before I'd feel the hot breath of werewolf hunger flowing across my skin.

"If you can't do this, I will," the Master warned. *"You'll like my solution even less."*

Without me willing it, my head turned back to glance behind me. A dozen red-tinged eyes materialized behind my back. These wolves would tear Gunner apart in seconds, would skin him alive and laugh as he screamed.

Gunner must have sensed the danger as well as I did, but he barely acknowledged the newcomers' approach. Instead, he dropped his sword to the ground and grabbed my head in both of his hands. "Mai, you *owe* me," he growled.

And my debt slapped me in the face like a bucket of ice water. My voice—jerked free of the Master's grip for one split second—spouted powerful words.

"I, Mai Fairchild, swear to protect and uphold the Atwood pack to the best of my ability...."

Then the hold on my spirit that had been shaken by Gunner's debt was shattered. Blood flooded my mouth as I bit down as hard as possible on the inside of the male I possessed's cheek.

And as power rushed through me, wolves streamed past me. Gunner grunted as he fell beneath their assault.

"No!" I yelled...or thought...or murmured.

Then I slipped out of the body I'd been inhabiting and floated away into the void.

Chapter 40

When Liam pushed me out of my skin previously, I'd hovered disembodied for only a split second. This time, however, the darkness surrounded me for so long I thought I'd misgauged the ability of shared blood to pull me to my sister's side.

At least I wasn't back in my own body to be pushed around by the Master. At least I wasn't on that battlefield being forced to fight a werewolf I wanted instead to help.

Still, it was agonizing to wait there in nothingness. But then words flowed out of the darkness, proving that Kira—and I by proxy—was merely sitting quietly in the forest without a light.

"Don't you think it would be more fun to hang out by the campfire?"

"Not really," I felt and heard myself—my sister—answer the social worker. "Bigfoot isn't going to come near a campfire. Surely even you know that?"

As Kira spoke, she raised one hand to scratch her nose...and the effort, I sensed, was nearly enough to topple our shared body to the earth. Wherever we were, however we'd gotten here, my sister was *not* the chirpy, carefree teenager I'd left behind.

No wonder I felt so at home in her body. Because my spirit felt as weak as my sister's when I imagined Gunner falling on that hilltop beneath a wave of bloodthirsty wolves.

Stephanie, of course, was oblivious to all subtext. So she had nothing to react to other than the snarkiness in my sister's voice. "Kira," the social worker admonished.

And even though the pending adoption seemed like a vague storm cloud on a distant horizon at the present moment, loyal pack mates quickly jumped in to smooth down my sister's rough edges. "What she means..."

Crow started, before petering out as he failed to think of a way to make Kira's insubordination palatable.

Luckily, Allen was ready to fill in gaps with a profusion of information that effectively muddied the trail. "...is that cryptozoology is a common hobby. Bigfoot, the Loch Ness monster, and more minor species such as the adjule and bunyip are fun to research and hunt for even though we know they don't exist in the wild. It's no different from practicing stage magic. Knowing what's real and what's myth doesn't make the latter any less entertaining as a hobby to cultivate."

"Simon *did* say something strange was going on in your family...." Stephanie's cagy tone suggested she was reacting to more than Kira's ill-badly chosen comment. Or perhaps the social worker was merely taken aback by Allen's dissertation on cryptozoology. Either way, it was enough to take my thoughts away from Gunner for a few brief seconds. And to make me wish I could see the human woman's face.

Just like that, my fingers—Kira's fingers—flicked the switch on the flashlight that had been sitting in our lap. The glow was painfully bright after so long in darkness, but not so blinding that I couldn't see a flash of motion off to our right....

Elle. Of course. How had I forgotten who else would be present on this supposed camping trip? How could I have not wondered whether the Master's sister was in league with her twin's plans?

Only Elle gave me no reason—beyond her genetics—for me to doubt her motives. Instead, she bent her neck toward me, averted her eyes in submission. Then, filling her voice with hidden meaning, she said, "I think I need to pee. Kira, care to tag along?"

I WASN'T QUITE SURE what I'd done to give away my presence, but Elle definitely knew who was hiding behind my sister's eyeballs. Kira, on the other hand, just as definitely did not.

Because the child went with the flow until she and Elle were far enough from the others so human ears couldn't overhear our conversation. Then she dropped the flashlight she'd used to guide us, her hand shaking as if touching the plastic had stung.

"I didn't turn on that light!"

My sister's panic surged through me, her body quivering just like her voice had done. She was weak as a newborn kitten. Perhaps because the Master was draining Mama's star ball back at the gathering, turning Kira wan and pale by proxy?

"I know," Elle started, less interested in Kira's physical weakness than in her emotional distress. "I think...."

But Kira was past the point of listening to reason. "Then get it out of me!" she demanded, slapping her cheeks so hard the sting brought tears to our eyes.

And, for one instant, I returned to the hilltop. I could almost hear the growling and tearing as the carnage I'd already witnessed flashed before of my eyes.

Or...maybe I really could hear the battle. Was that why my sister had been sitting in the darkness away from any campsite? Had she talked the guys into creeping as close as they could safely come to the meeting hill?

If so, there was a sliver of a chance that these few shifters could turn the tide in Gunner's favor. But only if I could get my sister to stop batting at her face and let me speak with her tongue.

"Out, out, out!" my sister was wailing. And I hoped that Stephanie's hearing was worse than that of the average middle-aged human. Otherwise, we'd have a lot of explaining to do once we returned from this supposed bathroom break.

Elle must have had the same thought. Because she grabbed our slender wrists with firm fingers. Held our hands away from our eyes. "You know it's your sister inside you, Kira."

"I don't!" the child started, speaking in gasps and bursts of emotion. "It could be anybody! It could be the *bad guy!*"

And even though I didn't want to scare my sister further, I seized her vocal cords and spoke through both of us. "Don't be a doofus, bedhead. This is really me."

For a moment, the forest fell silent around us. Then, our shared voice asked plaintively, "Mai?"

There was no time to soothe her, so I spit out facts short and not-so-sweetly. "Gunner is in trouble. Liam is the Master. He controls half of the shifters at the meeting hill. They're trying to mow the others down at this moment...."

"Then we'd better help Gunner." Kira was as resilient and decisive as ever, never mind the fact that her knees wobbled as she stooped to grab the flashlight off the ground. I wanted to tell her that *she* wasn't going anywhere, that *she* was going back to camp and crawling into a sleeping bag until everything was over.

But the abrupt increase in illumination brightened our surroundings enough so we could see what the preceding drama had made us all miss. Stephanie had apparently decided to join the girls' pee party. And now she stared wide-eyed at Kira, who to all appearances was carrying on a conversation with herself.

"Simon was right. You *are* so much more troubled than any of us thought possible...."

"No," Elle started. "You don't understand."

Then, to my horror, Kira dove toward the other shifter and bit down hard on my mentor's wrist.

Chapter 41

I tasted the faintest hint of blood, then I was reeling from a slap to my cheek that should rightfully have knocked me earthward. Only, someone was holding onto my shoulders. Or, not holding—that was the icy hug of possession as Mama spoke through my lips.

"Yes, Master," she and I said together. And I shivered as I realized all of my efforts to escape the battlefield had been for naught. I was back under the control of a crazy, power-hungry shifter, and this time Mama was the one making my body move.

In desperation, I tried to lock my knees but instead found myself pacing the Master step for step as we neared the sounds of werewolves fighting. Vaguely, I noted that Liam and I must have been walking for most of the time I'd been absent from my body. Because we were back at the edge of the gathering hill, all signs of ceremonial hunt long since eradicated.

Geography was the least of my concerns, however, since a rising moon now revealed a sea of furry bodies, lunging, biting, tearing...dying. I couldn't see a single two-legger, nor anyone who appeared to be in touch with their rational senses. Gunner was similarly invisible, either lost in the melee or lost entirely beneath an avalanche of teeth and claws.

And I knew, in that moment, that whoever was winning, the unity of the Atwood pack had already been irrevocably broken.

Only...perhaps I'd been too hasty in my assessment. Because even as I took in a full breath of Atwood-flavored ozone, the fury of battle eased. And, beside me, Liam swore as he fumbled in his pocket before removing a vial and popping a cork out of the bottle's neck with his teeth.

The rich scent of blood rose between us, the cork returning to Liam's pocket unneeded. Then my captor was tilting the vial over his head to decant the contents, the boost of power Mama had worked so hard to harvest inches from his lips.

I couldn't let Liam top up his magic and hasten the battle before him...but I couldn't stop him either. Because my body was frozen just as he'd left it, inattention insufficient to break through the spell.

On the other hand, the bottle was nearly empty. And old blood doesn't flow like water, the last drop instead oozing down the glass wall so slowly that Liam was forced to tap the bottom violently in an effort to knock it loose.

"Lazy harlot," he growled, blaming my mother for...what? For failing to possess additional pack princesses and use sexual favors to lull shifter males into parting with their life fluids?

The insult was rude...and powerful. Because a kitsune honors her debts, but she doesn't have to obey a disparaging master.

And Mama must have been waiting for exactly that moment. Because invisible, icy fingers brushed over my hand momentarily...then I was abruptly freed from external control.

For half a second, I hesitated, gauging my path forward. If I killed Liam now, would Elle ever forgive me? Surely there was a less-than-fatal way to bring this struggle to an end....

Then the drop worked its way out of the bottle and onto the tongue beneath it. And, beside me, Liam began to laugh.

Which is when I realized we were in the midst of the dreamscape I so strongly remembered. Blood, moonlight, forest...and the Master before me smiling as he morphed Mama's star ball into a whip.

THE LASH OF MAGIC BIT through my clothes and into the skin beneath it, burning and freezing at the exact same time. Liam wasn't wearing a cloak and I wasn't wearing a kimono. Still, I felt myself being dragged forward just like in the dream as he murmured, "Come."

Mama was no longer possessing me, so I didn't have to obey this order. Still, the whip was unyielding as I dug in my heels and tried to wriggle my arms free of the magical noose. My star ball turned into a wedge and slid between the loops of the binding...only to begin dissolving as my captor's whip drained energy from me through it.

Shocked, I sucked in my remaining magic just as Liam grabbed onto my wrist, putting me back in the same predicament I'd started in. "You'll regret it if you disobey me," my captor growled, physically pulling me through the battling shifters on his way up the hillside. He was moving so quickly that the wolves around us didn't look up from their opponents long enough to decide we were worth a second glance. Still...impinging upon my personal space was my captor's first mistake.

Because I'd learned fighting long before possessing a star ball. Even with my arms bound around me, I wasn't defenseless, nor was I weak.

I bided my time, though, until we achieved the hilltop, the ground bloody but the area strangely vacant since the majority of the battle had drifted off to the western side. And as we crested the peak, the Atwood wolves were momentarily occluded by the steepness of the slope between us. Instead, all that met my eyes was dark canopies barely illuminated by the crescent moon...exactly the view I remembered from my dream.

When all of this is over, I need to ask Elle about kitsune foresight, I thought randomly. And then, without even warning myself that an attack was coming...I struck.

One leg hooked itself around Liam's left calf muscle. Meanwhile, the heel of my other foot pounded into his knee. I had no way of keeping myself upright, but at least my opponent plummeted also....

We fell to the earth in a tangle, Liam grunting—a disappointment since I'd been going for a kneecap-shattered howl. For a moment, either one of us might have come out triumphant. But I only had my legs to work with while he had use of both free hands.

Sure enough, tight fingers settled around my neck less than half a minute later. The Master's breath hissed as he whispered in my ear.

"Don't think you're irreplaceable. I already own another kitsune," Liam warned me. "Now watch...and learn."

Then one of his hands drifted a little higher until its fingers pinched my chin and twisted my head ninety degrees sideways. For a moment, I thought this was just another werewolf domination ritual. But then I noted a wolf standing eerily still in the middle of the battlefield....

"An eye for an eye," the Master continued. Then, releasing my chin, he snapped his fingers...and the wolf we'd been watching flipped its head back into an entirely unnatural posture before crumpling to the earth.

Chapter 42

"Here's how we're going to play this," Liam continued, rising off me and not bothering to offer a hand as I lay prone at his feet. Instead, he dusted off his clothing, reminding me that he was the only werewolf present who hadn't needed to shift in order to make his mark.

"You're going to pierce your own finger and give me some blood to start with," he explained, cadence overly patient as if speaking to a child. "Then you're going to squeeze out enough to fill this vial for snack time later on."

Demand and insult imparted with equal facility, the glass container dropped out of his fingers and grazed my forehead. The pain was immediate, but I was more interested in analyzing the contents as the bottle rolled off into the grass.

It was empty, meaning that Liam's borrowed magic was fading. If I delayed just a little longer, would the werewolves below us regain their senses and stop tearing into their kin?

"Look at me when I speak to you." Liam's words were backed up by a squeeze of the magical noose that bound me, and I struggled onto my knees in an effort to prevent another cautionary tale.

Because the Master's magic was still effective at this moment—I could hear the results behind my back. How much heel-dragging would Liam accept before he provided another example of his power? Would Tank be the wolf he chose to murder next?

As if following my thought processes, Liam smiled widely, reaching toward me with a needle in his hand. I wanted to snipe at him verbally, to tell him he was an idiot for binding my arms then expecting me to reach forward with appendages that were currently glued on either side of my torso. But all I could think about was Tank's earnest efforts to talk the judge around to giving me custody of Kira. So I struggled against the magical coils, attempting to obey the Master's wordless command.

And the effort was apparently acceptable. Because Liam laughed a deep, throaty chortle that was pure amusement at my terror and chagrin. "Ah, yes. How silly of me," he murmured. And as easily as that, the magical cord around me loosened, slipping back to its master like a retreating snake.

I was free of the physical binding but Liam smiled and rubbed his thumb absently across his four fingers, as if itching for the opportunity to teach me another lesson by taking an innocent's life. So, rather than attacking, I rose slowly and accepted the needle with my right hand.

The sliver of metal beneath my skin was a mere pin prick, nothing compared to the agony I'd feel once Liam used my blood to amp up the battle below. As if to prove that point, a howl rose from behind me. Higher pitched than the others, more of a yipping yelp morphing into a scream....

Meanwhile, before me, Liam reminded me of my duty. "Now hold out your finger," he demanded, his voice smooth again now that I'd started obeying him.

Something about the recent howl made me want to turn and peer across the battlefield. But our current detente was precarious, and I didn't dare to make any obvious move. Instead, I tried to get Liam talking. "I don't understand why you need to use Ransom as a puppet," I prodded, hating the fact that my voice quavered. "Surely you're strong enough to rule this pack by yourself....?"

Unfortunately, my captor didn't feel the need to explain himself the way he had earlier. Instead, he merely crooked one finger and raised both brows.

I could think of no solution save obeying him. So, hating every instant, I lifted my arm and offered up the bubble of blood pooling atop my skin.

This was it. The moment my weakness finished breaking my pack mates....

But Liam didn't accept the offering. Instead, he winced and turned sideways. His hand rose to his face. And when he removed the protective fingers and peered at them, even I could see the dark coating of blood.

Blood? Who could possibly have injured Liam from such a distance?

It made no sense because the hilltop was empty save for me and Liam. And Mama—but she was back beneath the Master's thumb. So what....?

Almost afraid to take my eyes off the Master, I nonetheless turned to peer back at the battlefield. And as I did so, I understood at once what had turned the tide.

Because there was a two-legger standing at the edge of the forest. Stephanie—the human social worker—had her mouth wide open as if she was shrieking words not quite loudly enough to reach me over the din between us.

Meanwhile, leaping from wolf to wolf like a child on a trampoline, a red-furred fox was nipping animal after animal on the nose.

KIRA WASN'T MERELY nipping. She was also licking. And as she swiped her long, pink tongue across yet another bamboozled werewolf's nostrils, the veneer of culture Liam had formerly dragged atop his rotten core wafted entirely away.

"You little bitch," the Master growled. But while his words were heated, they weren't steady. Instead, each scratch and lick clearly weakened him. I could see the effects as easily as if Liam had a magical meter pasted to the center of his forehead.

He swayed, cringed, barely managing to remain erect. Still, he wasn't so far gone that he couldn't fight against the damage. Thrusting his hand forward, he cast an inaudible order over the crowd.

A neck didn't snap this time; teeth did. Werewolf teeth one millimeter away from Kira's toes. Previously, the fighting had been dispersed and erratic. But now, at least half the shifters beneath us converged upon my sister as she spun sideways, pushed off balance by the unexpectedly united front.

Vaguely, I noted that Stephanie was forcing her way among the wolves in search of Kira. A flash of movement to one side was likely Crow or Allen in lupine form doing a better job beating a path toward their shared goal.

But they didn't have time to reach her. Not when Liam could see across the field with no obstructions and still had dozens of werewolves obeying his beck and call.

He'd forgotten me though. Had forgotten that the blood welling up out of my finger hadn't yet bound us back together. Had forgotten that his nosebleed continued unabated and he was currently flinging life fluids hither and yon.

All it took was a twist of my head to capture the first particle. All it took was one droplet landing on my tongue to break me free entirely.

And this time I didn't worry about Elle's hurt feelings. I didn't consider the possibility of Liam stealing my magic and using it to worsen his current depredations.

Instead, I thought only of the pack splintering around us. Then, pulling my star ball into sword form, I swung toward my opponent's jugular and mowed the Master down.

Chapter 43

My sword hit spine and lodged there. But lack of forward momentum was irrelevant, because Liam was already dead.

And as he crumpled to the ground beside me, Mama's magic oozed out of his body right alongside spurting blood. At first, the spray of bodily fluids was so intense I didn't even know what was happening. But then, somehow, my mother gathered enough energy to speak.

"Mai. I'm going. I'm almost gone. Kira...."

I immediately understood what my mother was telling me, but I couldn't seem to breathe sufficiently to do anything about it. Because Mama was right—she was already fading around the edges. The glowing star ball at her center was dimming as her fingers wisped away into the night.

Clods of dirt raining down upon a closed coffin. My father's tall body beside my own. My newborn sister relentlessly crying....

Mama had willingly ceded her body thirteen years earlier for the sake of my sister. Despite my current pain, I couldn't be the one responsible for turning that sacrifice into Kira's untimely death.

So I tore my gaze away from my mother's spirit. Screamed my sister's name across the field...

...Or, rather, croaked it. Because my face was wet, I realized, tears streaming down my cheeks and throat choked up too tight to speak normally.

Forcing air into my lungs, I tried one more time. *"Kira.* I need you up here *immediately."*

The tone that emerged was the same one I used to halt homework procrastination. Luckily, this time it had a better than usual effect.

Because the battle below was ending. Without Liam to pull the strings, wolves were pausing, shaking their heads in bemusement, then beginning to shift to their more rational form. Meanwhile, Stephanie had taken advantage of the confusion to pick her way between former combatants, and Crow had already reached my sister's side.

The latter met my eyes with steady willingness. Then, without even glancing to his alpha for permission, he grabbed Kira's fox body up like a football and swung her with all his might toward the top of the hill.

Kira must have drunk pints of blood in the preceding moments in order to manage a shift after being drained so thoroughly. But the exhilarating power coursing through her didn't make her laugh and play the way she usually would have. Instead, her brows furrowed and her eyes widened as she plummeted toward me. My sister had matured in the hours we'd been apart.

She'd matured, but she still possessed the needle-sharp claws bound to tear into me when she landed. I braced myself for the scratches...only Kira didn't scratch me because she didn't reach me. Instead, she flew through what remained of Mama's star ball, and the magic grabbed hold and refused to let loose.

Light embraced the fox that was my sister. For half a second, incorporeal fingers smoothed fur away from wide, dark eyeballs.

Then, Kira regained her humanity, a vibrant glow of health blushing cheeks that had been white and sickly just an hour earlier. And, just like that, Mama was entirely gone.

WE'D LOST AND WON ALL in the same moment. And all I wanted was to enfold my only surviving family member into my arms.

Kira, on the other hand, had other thoughts about the matter. "This is so cool!" she hooted, her earlier quietness erupting into joy as she opened her hand to reveal a star ball subtly different from the borrowed one that used to follow her around our apartment. That magical orb had stuck to Kira's heels but had never obeyed her transformation orders. This one, in contrast, molded in the blink of an eye into the form of a tremendous, curving blade.

"Woo hoo!" she started, then her hoot transitioned into a gurgling "Ergh!".

Because even though we were a sword-wielding family, neither of us had any idea what to do with a scimitar. So it was no surprise that the ax-like widening at the tip of the materialized magic overbalanced my sister. The newly created weapon swung downwards as she fumbled...and nearly lopped off a couple of my fingers as it dropped.

"Oopsie," Kira finished unapologetically before swiping the weapon sideways and adding serrations to the blade that caused a strangle whistling noise. But I'd already lost track of her enthusiasm, the prickling of hairs on the back of my neck proving that a magic-happy teenager was the least of my concern.

"Kira," I warned. And without another glance at her glowing weapon, I took a long step forward in front of her. My body, I hoped, would be enough to shield my sibling from danger...which came in the form of dozens of shifters now clambering up the side of the hill.

Most were two-legged, which should have been a relief after the animalistic battle that had recently ended. But there was something worse about knowing the rapidly approaching werewolves were in their right minds...and still intent upon a kill.

"*They* did this to us. Kitsunes."

Their leader wasn't an Atwood, but he *was* someone I recognized. Edward, the older male who had gathered forces from the village to assist Gunner's strike.

Which meant he was on our side...or should have been. But Edward's eyes focused on the glowing scimitar in Kira's hand for one split second before boring into my forehead. "Both of you are kitsunes," he decided, having apparently understood more of the preceding moments than I would have expected. "You turned brother against brother within our pack."

It was hard to tell through the grime and wounds of battle, but it appeared that several of Edward's compatriots had recently fought on the opposite side. Healing scratches marked Liam's lackeys—no wonder they were ready to tear into me and Kira to prevent similar possession from ever happening again.

"Kira, go," I ordered, my own star ball taking longer than I would have liked but eventually materializing into my tried and true weapon. It wasn't a flashy scimitar, but it would get the job done.

Only Kira didn't move...and no wonder with the scent of ozone popping up behind both of my shoulders. I didn't even have to look to know two brothers now flanked me—Gunner on the right side, Ransom on the left.

The only surprising part was who spoke first—the older sibling's voice loud enough to carry easily to the back of the approaching force. His words, however, were about what I expected. "See, little brother. *This* is why you are unsuited to rule."

Chapter 44

A week ago, pack had been something foisted upon me. Despite Gunner's best efforts, I'd flitted around the outside of his crew's unity, uncertain how I felt about them folding Kira closer and closer into their midst.

Now, though, I understood what it meant to literally stand between two brothers. The ties of blood and pack binding the duo together were palpable...and I could almost see that connection radiating out across all of the shifters currently joining us atop the hill.

Because every shifter who could walk or limp was climbing up behind Edward now. There were far too many crumpled bodies left lying, but no one stayed to assist allies or enemies they picked their way past. Instead, as one being, werewolves were drawn to the heart of the pack's power...and to the disagreement that had nearly succeeded at cracking that heart in twain.

Nearly, but not quite. Or so I hoped, based on the fact that Ransom was still needling his brother verbally rather than finishing the job he'd recently started. Both brothers were still standing, which meant the role of clan leader was still in doubt.

"Is that how you see it?" Gunner murmured before diving directly to the core of what his brother had insinuated. "You consider loyal kitsunes a weakness rather than a strength?"

"Loyal?" Ransom laughed shortly then peered across the crowd. "Who here thinks these vixens are *loyal* to anything other than their own best interests? Who here would sleep a wink knowing kitsunes lived in the house next door?"

For a moment, all shifters remained silent. Then Tank's voice spoke up from somewhere to the left of center. "I slept very well one floor below kitsunes," he asserted.

"As did I," Allen called from way down at the bottom of the hill.

In contrast, the angry murmurs closer up were daunting. And despite my best intentions to keep a low profile and try not to make matters worse for Gunner, I took a step backwards and grabbed my sister's arm.

Because when it came right down to it, I would do whatever it took to protect Kira. Gunner, I knew, would eventually understand.

I didn't immediately drag my sister to safety, however, planting my feet and waiting for Gunner's reaction instead. He'd sidestepped this issue so gracefully and often over the course of the spring and early summer that I fully expected him to repeat the maneuver now that it really mattered. He'd assist me and Kira in making our escape then glue the clan back together. After all, pack meant everything to an alpha werewolf.

Or so I thought until Gunner willingly broke families apart all around us.

"Then we have nothing in common after all," Gunner answered, his voice carrying easily to every listening shifter. "Those who feel as my brother does are free to follow him. Pack up your houses, your families, take anything that's yours by tomorrow lunchtime and go.

"But if you're smart," the younger Atwood brother continued, his voice sad but no quieter, "you'll think it over. Talk to your parents, your mate, your children and decide whether it's really so bad to live check-to-jowl with kitsunes."

He paused, the air around us seeming to suck into his body as every audience member held their breath, waiting. Then, finally, Gunner finished his thought.

"Because if you leave now, it's a forever decision. The Atwood clan will not welcome traitors back."

I HALF EXPECTED RANSOM to fight against his brother's edict. After all, the elder brother had wanted the full Atwood power, not whatever portion of it came with carving a new territory from outpack land.

But when I took my eyes off my sister long enough to look at Ransom head-on for the first time since the battle ended, I saw that the older brother literally had no leg to stand on. There was blood streaming down his temple and gashes all over his body. Meanwhile, Ransom's left calf bent at an unnatural angle, only the efforts of two other shifters holding him erect.

There would be no more fighting between the brothers. Not tonight. Not when Ransom couldn't walk without help.

But that didn't prevent the elder brother from following up on Gunner's ultimatum. "If you're *smart*," he told the crowd at large, "you'll leave now with me rather than bedding down with *foxes*."

Then, without a single glance at his younger brother, Ransom fell forward onto three legs. The fourth tucked up beneath him, and he hop-stepped forward through the crowd as regally as any alpha wolf.

So, yes, Ransom had the wounded-warrior thing going for him. But one day earlier, Gunner possessed the full loyalty of every other shifter in this territory. One day earlier, if the younger brother had stood up and declared himself pack leader, no one except his brother would have batted an eyelash before bowing to their new lord.

But now, hands drifted down to touch the vanquished brother's fur as he pressed past his pack mates. And far too many glanced once at me and Kira before turning to follow Ransom away from the life they'd cherished up until now.

The pain of the pack dissolving hit me like a blow to the solar plexus. But it was my little sister who made the demand I itched to dish out. "Gunner, *do* something. Mai and I can..."

Her voice petered out then, not just because there was no real solution but also because Gunner had taken the child into his arms and pressed his lips to her forehead. "It's not your fault," he murmured one inch from her skin, speaking almost too softly for me to hear him. "It's done. You're worth it. Now hush."

The gesture had been meant to comfort my sister, but it also consolidated the truth of Gunner's alliance with kitsunes. No wonder a sigh washed over the remaining shifters, the visible proof of their alpha's loyalties provoking yet more members of the audience to break away.

And still Gunner did nothing. Not even when a figure began moving toward us out of the dwindling gathering, materializing into Elle as she stopped directly in front of her half-brother's nose.

"I have to go with Ransom..." Gunner's cousin—half-sister—started. And for the first time I smelled a crack in the new pack leader's armor.

"Because I wasn't a brother to you." The alpha paused, swallowed. "I'm sorry for my part in your mother's loss."

"Don't be an idiot. It wasn't your fault." For half a second, Elle reached up to trail her hand across Gunner's cheek. Then she sighed and took one long step back. "But Ransom needs me more than you do...."

And Gunner was an alpha hardwired to protect his underlings. So he nodded, jerked his head into the half-darkness toward someone I couldn't make out in the distance. "Crow, go with your woman."

Then, just like that, half the werewolves I trusted were no longer part of our pack.

Chapter 45

"So this is what you were hiding."

Most of the nearby shifters had either followed Ransom or gone to tend to the injured by the time Stephanie made it to the top of the rise to join us. Which was probably a good thing, since the human had no concept of how to act around riled-up werewolves. Her flashlight slid across our faces, blinding me briefly and provoking the scent of fur from my companions. Then the beam settled resolutely at my sister's feet.

"Mrs. B..." Kira started. But the social worker talked right over the teenager, taking yet another step forward so she could wave a finger under Gunner's nose.

"Have you people never heard of pedophilia? Child endangerment? You really let a thirteen-year-old wander around with no clothes on where anyone can see?"

Clothes? After watching a pitched battle and shifters transforming from wolf to human, *this* was what Stephanie was most concerned about?

Luckily, Allen had us covered...quite literally. Unlike his pack mates, he hadn't shifted into animal form during the preceding battle. Which meant he was wearing human-appropriate clothing and possessed a backpack full of much-needed spare shirts.

"Big, bad wolf," read the one he tossed to Kira. Gunner shielded the child as she shrugged into the tent-like t-shirt, the large male's body seeming to shrink in on itself at the same time as he submitted in an entirely un-alpha-like manner to the social worker's wrath.

"I know what you saw today was upsetting," Gunner started....only to be silenced by Stephanie's "Eh, eh, eh."

"No, I don't want your explanations," the middle-aged matron rebutted. "The time for that would have been last week or last month.

Around the time you invited me to that first cookout." Then, dismissing the alpha werewolf entirely, Stephanie pushed him aside so she could offer my sister much softer words. "The fact that you're a fox girl..."

"Kitsune," my sister countered quietly. Despite the clarifying interruption, her tone suggested even she was cowed by the official's disappointment and barely restrained rage.

"Kitsune," Stephanie repeated, sounding out the word slowly to make sure she said it correctly. "Whatever your heritage, child, you're my responsibility. And I think you should come with me right now...."

Abruptly, there were growling two-leggers all around us. Gunner, Tank, even Allen sounded like they were inches away from donning fur.

Which meant I was currently the sole rational party present. So, leaving Kira where she was, I stepped between the werewolves and Stephanie, trying to tell the social worker with my eyes that now was, perhaps, not the best time for making demands. "We can hash this out tomorrow," I offered. Because the idea of Stephanie spilling our secrets in human court was daunting...but it was better than watching her get ripped apart by my pack mates right now.

"You'll be there?" Stephanie's eyebrows rose while her mouth pursed pensively. I could see her point—fleeing might be wiser than continuing to fight for custody.

Yet, despite everything, I found myself nodding. "Yes. Please. Let Allen walk you to your car now and I *promise* that Kira and I will be there tomorrow in court." Immediately, this new oath tugged at my belly lighter but no less virulent than the one that used to tie me to the alpha behind my back.

And after one long moment, Stephanie bent her neck in regal approval. Human or not, she knew when to accept an oath as fact.

The social worker wasn't quite done with us, however. "You, Allen—you're a wolf also?" she asked over my shoulder. Then, without waiting for an answer, she shook her head and glared at the least offensive werewolf present. "It doesn't matter. I need a guide, so you will stay human until I'm safely in my car."

"Yes, ma'am," Allen promised, dropping the backpack but otherwise acting for all the world like a submissive werewolf obeying his alpha as he brushed past the rest of us. Then he was leading Kira's social worker toward the encircling forest...although not quickly enough to prevent her from tossing back one last jab at those she left behind.

"I will see you all in court," the decider of Kira's future promised. Then Stephanie was gone, a problem for another day.

"SO," GUNNER STARTED. And I didn't realize we were alone and naked until I heard Kira's receding giggle as she and Tank rooted through Allen's backpack in search of additional clothing.

"So," I answered, breathing in the alpha's enticing scent. There was more granite in his aroma than I was used to, his voice rough around the edges from the difficulties of the preceding hours.

But he was here and I was here. We'd both survived the battle...and there was one thing left undone.

"You need to pull your pack together," I told him. "Go back to clan central and talk to your people so they don't do anything stupid."

"Once you and Kira are settled," Gunner started. But I reached up and placed one finger atop his lips.

The skin there was soft but prickly around the edges where the barest beginning of a beard was starting to grow in. I wanted to lean in closer and see if his taste was as good as his aroma. But instead, I merely shook my head.

"Gunner, you're the pack leader. Kira and I can't be your top priority. A lot of your clan members don't have the first idea what to do around kitsunes. They'll leave with Ransom if we return with you right now."

"They'll stay if I tell them to," Gunner growled. But he didn't look into my eyes as he said it. He knew I was right.

"They might, but they'll resent it," I countered. "Wasn't that the whole point of letting Ransom take so many shifters with him just now?"

My voice wanted to break, but I instead took a deep breath and treated this like any other adulting situation. If I could force Kira to brush her teeth when she was sleep deprived, then I could make an alpha werewolf do his job.

"Kira and I will make ourselves scarce for a while," I started.

"And then...."

"And then we'll cross that bridge when we come to it," I finished before Gunner started making promises he couldn't keep.

Because this was goodbye. Somewhere deep in my heart I knew it. So, without worrying about repercussions, I ensured there would be nothing for me to regret later. Grabbing onto Gunner's shoulders to steady myself, I eased onto tiptoes then I kissed those enticing lips.

Chapter 46

This kiss wasn't a distraction to keep Gunner from noticing my magic. Nor was it a claiming on his part. Instead, it was a sharing, an acknowledgement that we were more than mere pack mates.

And, in response, an explosion of stars flared behind my eyelids. The air filled with so much electricity I almost expected a lightning strike. This, right here, was as natural as breathing. I couldn't imagine why I'd fled from it for so long.

Then Gunner was pushing away from me, calling Tank toward him. "Take them back to the city. Protect them. Don't let either Mai or Kira out of your sight."

"Yes, pack leader." Tank's tone was so respectful he might as well have prostrated himself atop the bloody grass between us. And any thought I'd had of arguing that Gunner needed his faithful second as backup faded in the face of an alpha laying down the law.

Then we three were tramping back through the trees the way Kira and I had come two days earlier. It turned out that an easily traversable path paralleled our earlier bushwhacking, which—combined with Kira's newfound vigor—meant the journey went by far too fast.

Fast but not easy. Because every step yanked at my belly. Every step increased the spear of agony throbbing beneath my forehead. *I shouldn't be leaving my pack mates. I shouldn't be leaving Gunner.* So this is what it felt like to tie myself to werewolves...then to let those same wolves go.

Sure enough, the pain worsened as we drove back toward the city, miles separating me from the place where the majority of my pack now resided. Gunner's mansion, when we reached it, was musty even though we'd been gone for less than seventy-two hours. And while the sun had long since risen and begun fading into afternoon, the residence struck me as painfully dark.

"The death count was minimal," Tank offered half an hour later as he came up behind me in the third-floor hallway. I was standing outside the closed door of the bathroom, listening to Kira brush her teeth and twitching every time the teenager went quiet for more than a second at a time. Because as much as it had hurt to leave Gunner, letting Kira out of my sight stung even worse....

"Minimal doesn't mean zero," I answered without bothering to turn and greet my minder. I knew Tank was trying to cheer me. But his words instead triggered a replay of Liam's object lesson, the one I'd been incapable of halting in time.

Snapping fingers, snapping neck. Me allowing wolves to tear into each other to prevent another from being unceremoniously murdered....

I shivered, pushing the memory into some dark corner of my mind to be chewed over later. Only then did I finish my thought. "And what percentage of the pack left with Ransom? What will happen to the clan now that it's been split in half?"

Tank didn't answer verbally. Instead, his fingers touched the nape of my neck momentarily, the fleeting contact a werewolf show of support.

Then Kira was pushing out of the bathroom in pajama bottoms and that same *Big, bad wolf* t-shirt she'd been wearing for hours. "Nap with me," she demanded, seemingly untouched both by the recent past and by the fact that her custody hearing began in just a few short hours.

And how could I deny her? Nodding once at Tank, I followed my sibling down the hall to her not-so-tastefully decorated bedroom. Fell into the princess-canopied bed and pulled the curtains around us before morphing into a fox.

Kira was already vulpine. Red fox tail covered her nose as she fell asleep instantly. And I curled around her slightly smaller body, completing our fluffy lump.

I didn't sleep though. Just lay there staring at the stick-on stars on the ceiling and wondering whether Kira and I were better off now than we had been three months earlier. To find a pack then lose it—was that really better than never having belonged at all?

Only Kira and I weren't really alone, even here in the echoing mansion. Because, two hours later, Tank tapped on the closed door between us. "Wake up, ladies," his deep voice urged us.

It was time to go to court.

"AND YOU ARE HAPPY WITH this document, Ms. Fairchild?" The judge speared me with a gaze so piercing that it knocked my attention—for one split second—off the social workers whispering adamantly to each other two rows back.

"Yes, Your Honor," I agreed. "I think 'godbrother' is a perfect representation of Gunner Atwood's relationship to my sister, now and in the future. I'm very grateful for his offer and willingly accept."

My voice only quavered slightly as I made the statement Tank had drilled into me during the short drive over, and not from a fox's urge for self-determination either. Instead, my separation from said godbrother was still gnawing at my stomach, making it hard to keep a pleasant smile pasted on my lips.

Meanwhile, I caught a single word drifting forward from Simon that further chilled my body. "*Werewolf*," my former social worker hissed adamantly, the mumble before and after that scathing indictment impossible to decipher. Stephanie's response, unfortunately, was drowned beneath the judge's subsequent statement, which boomed out fill the entire chamber with his voice.

"If I could have your attention," he ordered, sounding for all the world like an alpha-leaning werewolf. There was no zing to the command, though. No electricity that ran up my spine like spiders. Still, I resolutely closed my ears to the discussion behind me and apologetically bowed my head.

"Well," the decider of Kira's fate continued more cordially after flipping through the pages before him the way he'd already done three times previously. "Gunner Atwood's addition to this guardianship hearing *does* relieve some of my concerns about Kira's future. *But...*"

He paused theatrically, and it was Kira who pinched me when I raised my head and narrowed my eyes into a glare. *Right.* Not getting into a fight with a human official...although if the judge ruled against us, all bets were off.

"...I understand the State has some reservations," the judge finished right about the time I'd decided strangling him wouldn't be so inappropriate. "Mrs. Baumgartner, would you like to speak next?"

"...of the *child*." Simon apparently didn't know how to whisper, because the tail end of his final admonition was clear to all of us. The social worker's harrumph after the judge silenced him with raised eyebrows was similarly audible, but by that point Stephanie had come forward to the witness stand.

"Yes, Your Honor," Stephanie said, glancing at Kira out of the corner of one eye before squaring her shoulders and facing the judge directly. I could smell the human's dilemma, could tell that she was still wavering from the slump of her spine and the cock of her head.

In my experience, time tended to make the shock of the supernatural less biting. Unfortunately, the robed male on the bench didn't give Stephanie so much as a minute to make up her mind about the matter at hand.

"Well, put us all out of our misery," the judge demanded. "What is your official standpoint on the adoption of Kira Fairchild?"

Chapter 47

"**I** think that Kira Fairchild is a strong-willed young woman with great potential, and I'm honored to have spent even a few months as part of her life," Stephanie said after one additional, harrowing pause. Kira grabbed my right hand while Tank grabbed my left hand, and I wasn't sure whether they were offering support or holding me down.

Then the social worker's scent cleared and she glanced back again, this time with a smile on her lips as she met my eyes and then my sister's. "But my advice is to remove her from my caseload," Stephanie finished. "Kira's best with her own family, and she deserves to have those relationships she's created legally affirmed."

Then it was all over except the pictures. Well, that plus the paperwork, which Tank told me would be ready the following week.

In the meantime, my pack of three filtered out to the steps of the courthouse, jostling and smiling as the sun beat down upon our faces. "I knew we'd get custody as soon as Allen gave me the t-shirt," Kira proclaimed blithely, twisting her body as if modeling the pink sequined monstrosity that covered her torso and back. *"Favorite pup,"* the rear stated. And, much smaller, where a front pocket would have been located, words that I was glad the judge hadn't noted from the bench....

"Well, Boss Bitch, where do you want your glamor shoot?" Tank asked, pulling out his ubiquitous cell phone and flipping it into photo mode.

"Over here!" my neck-risking sister answered, leaping onto a balustrade at the edge of the grand porch we'd gathered in, not appearing to notice that she now hovered above a thirty-foot drop to hard stone ground. And while a human guardian would have grabbed Kira's foot to steady her, I was just glad to see the pack-separated sadness wiped away by her short nap.

Plus, Stephanie was walking out the front door now. So I merely mouthed *"Be good"* at my sister before hurrying over to thank the social worker before she could rush out of our lives.

"I really appreciate..." I started.

But the middle-aged woman interrupted me. "It's my job to make sure foster kids end up in the best placement for the sake of the child. Kira may be surrounded by wolves and blood and scary things I'm probably not aware of. But anyone can see she thrives as part of a pack."

Then the same human who had recently taken in the horror of a pack battle slipped out of her suit jacket, revealing unexpected words on the underlying blouse. *"Honorary Werewolf,"* the shirt stated. And for a moment my throat clenched up as I realized Allen been come prepared for all eventualities...except the one where he wasn't actually present with us now.

Winning the adoption battle without the rest of our pack beside us hurt so much I had to close my eyes for one split second. And by the time I'd widened my lips back into a smile, Kira's gaze had settled upon the human who made this entire photo shoot possible.

"Mrs. B!" my sister exclaimed. She'd been spinning in a circle atop the railing, hands out to either side like a tightrope walker. But now, she motioned Stephanie over. "Come be in the picture!" And, like a magnet, the teenager's enthusiasm drew both me and the social worker back to the marble ground beneath our charge's feet.

"Say cheese," Tank told us from five feet distant. And I really would have...if the front door of the courthouse hadn't opened at that exact same moment, sending the furry scent of stalking werewolf wafting over us all like summer heat.

I DIDN'T TURN MY STAR ball into a sword, though. Nor did I yank Kira off the ledge and push her toward Tank to hustle out of harm's way. Instead, my fake smile morphed into a cheek-splitting grin as just the werewolves I'd been thinking off stepped out into the light.

Gunner and Allen wore lettered t-shirts just like Kira's, but I didn't bother trying to read the words this time around. Instead, I only had eyes for the pack leader as he snagged a random bystander with a panty-melting smile and roped her into taking over Tank's spot as photographer of the hour.

Then the werewolf I'd missed the most was there beside me, his arm settling over my shoulder and pulling me in even closer as we all smiled for the camera's sake. "Sorry I was late," he murmured, his breath tickling my earlobe.

"I'm just glad you're here now." Then, remembering the reason I'd left him in the first place. "But your pack needs you...."

"Yes you do. And here I am."

I punched his arm before blinking at my own physical show of affection. What...was I turning into a werewolf now?

And, as if he'd been privy to my internal monologue, Gunner's smile went from blinding to supernova, so warm it beat against my skin.

"Everyone who hasn't left with my brother will still be there tomorrow," he said, answering my real concern, albeit belatedly. "But Kira's adoption only happens once. I figured it was about time I learned to act like a fox and wiggle around the rules when necessary. Everyone who loves your sister should be here for her special day."

And everyone was...almost.

Because the spot where Crow and Elle should have stood remained empty. Meanwhile, the stress from leaving the Atwood pack unattended at such a critical moment was visible in Gunner's creased brow.

But all I saw when I looked at that photo days and weeks and years later was Kira's joyous kitsune nature as she leapt off the railing without warning and was caught quite easily by five pairs of waiting hands. All I heard in my memory was Gunner's voice whispering into my ear.

"A pack is only as weak as its strongest member."

I could only hope he was right.

Fox Blood

Chapter 1

"I think this is called the walk of shame," Kira suggested, her voice cutting through the foggy evening air like a sword through warm butter. I swiveled in unconscious reaction, peering through almost-raindrops hovering around us on every side.

Between the fog and the night, I couldn't see anything, unfortunately. Which didn't mean we were alone...just that visibility was painfully low. Unfriendly werewolves could be hovering just out of scent range, waiting for the perfect moment to pounce upon us. Good thing I wasn't as oblivious as my pampered younger sister to the danger we were currently walking through.

So—"Shh," I huffed out, hoisting a trio of cardboard containers a little higher in my arms while hoping the suddenly overwhelming aroma of stale beer wasn't emanating from one of them. Perhaps I should have sprung for new boxes rather than begging for used ones behind the neighborhood liquor store....

"Well, it is, isn't it?" Kira demanded, turning around to walk backwards down the gravel road leading up to our secluded cottage. "I mean, if we weren't ashamed, we would've taken Gunner up on his offer to rent a moving truck. We would have come when it was daylight out. And we wouldn't have parked twenty miles away so nobody would hear Old Red squeak her way up the drive."

"Old Red isn't so bad," I rebutted, defending the new-to-me car. I'd never wanted a vehicle until I began living over a hundred miles away from a boyfriend who only visited in the company of needy pack mates. Skype had kept us in contact, but I had needs that weren't being met via video chat.

Gunner had offered to throw money at the problem, but I wasn't ready for that level of entanglement just yet. So I'd found a new job, had saved my pennies, and had bought a twenty-year-old, off-brand vehicle the previous week.

Old Red made it feasible to move into a secluded, rural village without feeling like I was trapping myself and Kira next door to a bunch of werewolves. The car gave me an easy out if we needed to flee and allowed me to spend time with Gunner without having to become monetarily indebted to him. Now, however, I was having second thoughts about the cleverness of my ploy.

Because my skin prickled with warning of hidden werewolves in the vicinity. Turning in a tight circle, I barely managed to keep Kira's box of stage-magic paraphernalia from teetering off the top of the stack while I peered around the barrier. I *knew* they were out there. This was Atwood clan central after all. Even at the crack of dawn, there should have been patrollers out guarding the boundaries and early risers jogging down tree-lined paths.

Instead, the territory appeared empty even though it smelled far too strongly of wolf...plus impatient little sister. "And we didn't park twenty miles away," I continued, trying to get Kira off topic before I was forced to tell her what a walk of shame really was. "We parked a quarter of a mile away so Old Red's brakes wouldn't wake up the neighbors. It's the considerate thing to do. You need to learn to be polite now that we're denning with—"

"Whatever," Kira cut me off, darting away to dance up cobblestone steps toward our cottage. The first dead leaves of autumn lay on the stones between us, and in daylight I suspected they would have glowed beautifully orange or red.

In the evening fog, however, the discarded plant matter merely appeared gray, slippery, and dangerous...like everything else about this place.

"Kira, wait." I wasn't in fox form, so I couldn't be certain. But I got the distinct impression someone had marked his territory on the bottom step in the form of very lupine-smelling pee. Gunner had promised the pack was ready to welcome us into their midst, but urine wasn't generally considered a sign of open-armed acceptance. More worrisome, however, was the fact that the liquid had been deposited so recently that it still puddled atop the cobblestones in my path....

"*Kira.*" This time I snapped out her name as close as I could come to a werewolf compulsion. But, of course, we weren't wolves and my sister saw no reason to obey me.

Instead, she turned the knob of our new domicile without even glancing backwards. Pushed the door open into darkness...and walked straight through an overwhelming cascade of strangely sulfurous eau de wolf.

THE BOXES WERE ON THE ground and my sword was clasped in white-knuckled fingers before several sets of hands—at least they were furless—yanked my sister into the death trap. But I was four steps too slow to prevent them from enfolding her into their midst.

Enfolding her...and flipping on the light switch to reveal smiling faces and party banners. Apparently my attempt to move in after sunset hadn't been as secretive as I'd initially supposed.

"Surprise!" werewolves howled, only some of the voices human. Then a whoosh of displaced air warned me of Gunner's presence half a second before a large hand tucked itself into the small of my back. He guided me through the doorway, my sword reluctantly dissolving into the magical ether even as I did my best to paste a pleased smile onto my face.

"I take it surprise parties aren't your favorite," Gunner huffed into my ear while his free hand massaged tension out of my neck muscles. And even though I was bound and determined to give Gunner every opportunity to rebuild his splintered pack without our relationship derailing his efforts, I still found myself swiveling so his guiding arm turned into half of a hug.

"No, I'm not generally a fan of surprise parties," I agreed. "But I *am* glad to see you." After all, it had been nearly three weeks since we'd spent more than five minutes in close proximity. No wonder his fingers on my bare skin acted like balm. I melted into his arms, forgetting my worries as I tilted my head back in preparation for a kiss.

Only, no kiss was forthcoming. Instead, Gunner released me and pulled a small notebook out of one pocket.

"I'll be sure to remember that in case it comes up later," he said. And even though cold air where warm hands used to be explained the sudden rise of goosebumps along my exposed forearms, my shiver was out of proportion to the chilliness of the night.

Blinking slowly to tamp down my frustration, I stood up on tiptoes to peer at Gunner's notebook. And what he'd written returned the smile to my face. *"My place tonight once Kira's sleeping?"*

No wonder he hadn't wanted to even whisper the words in the midst of the pack where shifter ears were bound to overhear him. My cheeks heated even as my head snapped up to peruse the partygoers. Somehow I was positive every werewolf present had read Gunner's words right alongside me....

But the crowd looked just like it had previously. Werewolves partying. Werewolves laughing. Werewolves muttering in dark corners about the kitsunes in their midst.

"Maybe," I answered, trying to decide whether I trusted Atwood shifters enough to leave Kira alone in the cottage after night fell.

"Oh, that reminds me," Gunner interrupted, raising his voice until it was loud enough to be heard at the far end of the overcrowded living room. "New rule—all disputes must be settled with blades hereafter. Tournament rules, to first blood." Then, as someone near us complained that he knew nothing about blades, that swords were archaic. "If you need instruction, I recommend asking our new sword master for tips."

Gunner's hand settled against the small of my back, subtly pushing me forward. And once every eye was upon me—exactly what I'd hoped to avoid by taking the walk of shame with my sister—the pack leader added: "Don't forget to pay her. Old Red needs new brakes."

Then just like that, Gunner left me alone in a room full of werewolves with nowhere to hide and no choice but to follow him deeper in.

Chapter 2

"He's besotted with you."

The voice curling over my left shoulder sounded pleasant, but it wasn't. Instead, my instincts screamed *"Angry werewolf behind you. Careful!"* one second before I swiveled around with a fake smile pasted on my lips.

"Edward. Left your posse behind, did you? Braving the scary kitsune all on your lonesome?"

Because the middle-aged male who'd been Gunner's principal ally in the battle against Liam was apparently not my greatest supporter. Moments earlier, Edward had stood at the center of the huddle of unhappy shifters shooting angry glances in my direction. So the fact he'd come all the way across the room to engage me likely meant he had an ultimatum to drop on my head.

Meanwhile, the rotten-egg aroma that permeated my cottage was so strong now I could only conclude it emanated from this shifter. It couldn't have been his signature aroma, however, or someone would have warned me about the foul stench.

"Bad choice of cologne," I noted even as he grabbed my arm and drew me into the dimly lit hallway with a grasp so bruising I had to fight down a flinch.

"This pack is barely hanging together," Edward growled as soon as we were out of easy earshot of the rest of the partygoers, not bothering to comment on my snarkiness about his scent. "Liam was important to us and now he's gone. Ransom was an asshole, but the transition away from him is still difficult. We don't need you here making things more complicated. If you love Gunner, you'll leave him alone."

I wanted to snipe right back...but, unfortunately, Edward hadn't said anything I didn't already believe to be truthful. On the other hand—"Gunner asked me to come here. So I came."

As I spoke, I stared at the hand clenched around my arm until Edward realized what would happen if his pack leader saw the lines of parallel bruises welling up beneath his fingers. Reddening, he shrank back so rapidly I might as well have swiped at him with my sword.

"Shit," the male muttered under his breath. "If he smells me on you, he'll go berserk."

This, at least, I was prepared for. Reaching into my pocket, I pulled out an aerosol can of scent-reducing compound, spraying it liberally across my injured flesh.

"I'm not here to make your life difficult," I said as I worked, the chemical drifting up my nose in the process so I had to pause and stifle a sneeze before I could go on. But then I returned to the most important business—clarifying my place within the Atwood pack. "I'm here to support Gunner," I continued. "And if you care about the clan, you'll let me get on with my task."

Which was all very true even though the words sat between us like a lump of brussel sprouts on the plate of a picky toddler. If Edward wanted the Atwood clan to hang together, he'd make nice and pretend he didn't have a bone to pick with the pack leader's mate.

I could tell from his scent—no longer quite so harsh and astringent—that Edward had gotten the message. Unfortunately, werewolves have a hard time dropping a juicy bone. "What happened four months ago..."

"Was the fault of an Atwood werewolf," I interjected, not wanting to remember the awful battle of wolf against wolf fueled by the kitsune magic of my dead mother. "I would never do anything to damage this pack."

The vigor of belief added volume to what was meant to be a private conversation, and this time I really did wince as my words rang a little too loudly in the echoing hall. *Shit.* I'd intended to say my piece to Edward then let him propagate it through the pack at the speed of werewolf gossip. I hadn't intended to create a scene.

Ignoring the shifter beside me, I swiveled just as I'd done while walking up the path with Kira. Unfortunately, this time I wasn't lucky enough to find our surroundings devoid of life. Instead, a tall, broad-shouldered werewolf towered in the open doorway between hallway and living room, silhouetted against the light behind his back.

"Something the matter?" Gunner demanded, taking in our proximity, our stiff-legged anger, the strange floral overlay of the de-scenting compound.

"Of course not," I lied. "Edward was just giving me the recipe for his famous lasagna."

Grimacing in what was clearly meant to be a smile, the male in question played along. "The secret," he offered, "is in the sauce."

"Hmm," Gunner started, far from satisfied. Only he had no time to debrief us further, because the living room behind him erupted into howls, growls, and one long, quavering scream.

"KIRA." THE WORD EMERGED from both my and Gunner's lips in perfect synchrony, but we didn't have time to gaze meaningfully into each other's eyes. Instead, I sprinted down the hallway, sword materializing in my hand in a blaze of blue-tinted glory even as Gunner rounded the corner three steps faster and dove into the melee of angry wolves.

Because, despite their alpha's ultimatum moments earlier, two-thirds of the pack had donned their fur forms and turned their teeth into weapons the second they felt threatened. Those still human were more obedient but no less dangerous—they'd grabbed up cutlery, some of it as long as my forearm.

Meanwhile, the entire room smelled like a forgotten egg factory, the scent even worse here than it had been beside Edward in the hall. *How did everyone manage to go against a direct order from their pack leader? Did Gunner forget to imbue his words with alpha compulsion?* The questions hovered over me like a foul-smelling storm cloud. But I pushed premonitions aside, hunting for my sister instead.

There she was...then there she wasn't as she shivered down into the red fur of her fox. Ever since Kira had melded with our mother's star ball, she'd been unruly and snarky and prone to shifting at the drop of a hat. Which wasn't helpful in the current situation...but the chain of events also meant that her unusual fur form hadn't been what set the werewolves off.

So what...?

I waited only long enough to glimpse Tank—Gunner's trusted second—tackling my sister and enfolding her in a werewolf burrito of protection before I thrust my way deeper into the crowd away from them. Because the growling mob wasn't facing toward either me or Kira. Instead, they were pushing and shoving, trying to get into the kitchen, or perhaps through that to the dining room beyond.

Mindful of the fact that these were supposedly my pack mates, I used my elbows and knees rather than my weapon to open up a pathway. But it was slow going, teeth snapping and claws scraping as I pressed past. My favorite pair of jeans was going to be spaghetti by the time this was over...but on the plus side, Gunner would never know that Edward had been the one to leave a bruise on my upper arm.

With that heartening thought at the forefront, I thunked a werewolf on the nose with my sword hilt, taking advantage of the resulting pocket of space to press through the narrow doorway separating kitchen from living room. And my grin of triumph promptly faltered as I took in the scene on the other side.

Because there was a fox perched atop the stainless steel refrigerator. Its fur was puffed up like the pelt of a cornered cat while its body pressed back against the wall behind it. No wonder since a werewolf currently swiped toward it with human fingers, attempting to pull the stranger loose from its hiding place.

There were a dozen other werewolves in the room with a similar agenda. But I had interest only in the much smaller canine cowering above their heads. Because even though its fur was pitch black instead of blazing red like mine and my sister's, I knew the moment our eyes made contact that this wasn't any mere fox wandered in out of the forest who'd accidentally ended up in my new home.

No, this was a kitsune. A being the like of which I'd never met outside my own family. After all, what right-minded wild animal would willingly walk into a cottage full of wolves?

Chapter 3

Not such smart behavior for a kitsune either, I noted even as I continued elbowing my way closer to the refrigerator on which our uninvited visitor perched. Despite my snarky internal commentary, however, I was as in awe of this being as if it was a unicorn walking out of a rainbow and into my life.

Because I'd never met a kitsune who wasn't a direct relative. Could count the number of fox shifters I'd come in contact with on two fingers of one hand. If I'd thought about it, I would have realized that my mother had to emerge from somewhere. And yet, I'd somehow just assumed that Kira and I were the last of our kind.

"Who are you?" I murmured, knowing my words wouldn't carry over the yipping and snapping of the werewolves between us. But, somehow, the fox heard. Swiveled its ears. Gently inclined its head.

There was a spark in the center of the being's eyes that made me stretch forward to lean in closer. And my existence must have been equally attractive to the midnight-furred animal. Because it crept toward me in perfect synchrony, still crouching low enough to protect its belly even as it strove to capture a better view of me.

Not it—she. After all, we were the same in every way that mattered. Never mind that I was two-legged while she walked on four paws. Never mind that her fur was black while mine was red. This was someone who would understand my deepest yearnings. This was another kitsune just like myself.

The tiniest hint of a whine emerged from the black fox's muzzle, her eyes watery with trust and request. Could I help her escape these werewolves...?

And in that moment of inattention, the shifters between us struck. One minute they were pushing and shoving, trying to reach the fox on human tiptoes. The next, a two-legger had boosted a four-legger on top of the refrigerator, placing the kitsune's ability to nod at me ever again into doubt.

Luckily, fridges aren't made for werewolf perching; the tops are too small and slippery for claws to find traction of any sort. And while the wolf teetered, unable to snap up its prey while maintaining its own balance, I made a decision that I knew I'd later regret.

"Here!" I called to the black fox, letting my sword recede as I stretched out both arms toward her. "Jump! I'll protect you!"

Because I couldn't let an innocent being perish, even if the last thing this pack needed was two kitsunes facing off against a mob of angry werewolves.

And the fox trusted me. Leapt across the surging, seething shifters who separated us to settle into my arms as easily as Kira had done hundreds of times during our thirteen-year shared past. Only, unlike my little sister, the stranger tucked her paws inward to ensure she didn't scratch me. And her eyes, when they met mine, were full of gratitude rather than snark.

The lump in my throat came from instant bonding. My arms tightened, my shoulders hunching over to protect the black-furred critter I hugged into my chest. I inhaled the soft musk of fox fur...and in that moment of calm and quiet, the wolves forgot I was Gunner's and launched themselves at me en masse.

"*Get out!*"

Gunner's roar was so loud it rattled the windows. Or maybe that reverberation was due to the thunder of a hundred feet as werewolves fled in the face of their pack leader's wrath. Whatever the reason, I was no longer in danger of losing my throat to supposed pack mates and my nose was grateful for the abrupt cessation of sulfur. So I uncurled from around the black-furred kitsune and peered up at my rescuer...who held a very naked yet very human Kira against his chest.

The alpha's arm was steely without denting my sister's skin painfully. And at the same time he still managed to look so murderous he might have stopped his underlings' breath with a single command. In reaction, the black fox nestled closer into my body, clearly terrified of the aura of electricity emanating from the wolf blocking her ability to retreat.

The fox's fear I would deal with in a minute. For now, I rose while scanning Kira's exposed limbs. "Are you okay?" I asked.

"Not that you care," my sister answered, brows lowering. "I might have been dead. I might have been injured. And you ran off in the opposite direction without even bothering to check on me."

"I'm checking now." And I'd also seen both Tank and Gunner racing directly toward my sister, so I'd known she was better protected than anyone else in the house.

Still, the pout on Kira's face promised she wouldn't let me off the hook so easily. Meanwhile, my quick survey of her limbs proved that the werewolves in question had done their job quite well. So I sighed acceptance of the fact that I was currently incapable of pleasing my sister and returned my focus to the strange fox instead.

Was Gunner really willing to fold yet another kitsune into his faltering clan structure? And would the pack splinter further if I dared to ask?

"Gunner…" I started, not sure exactly how to explain the fact that I ached to help this black-furred kitsune. It wasn't so much a humanitarian mission as a compulsion and a *need* as imperative as hunger.

But apparently explanations were unimportant. Because the skin around his eyes crinkled ever so slightly as he jerked his chin upwards in a promise. As long as I didn't sneak off on my lonesome, this werewolf had my back.

So—"You can shift," I told the fox, prying her away from my neck and placing her on the kitchen table beside me, the separation hitting me in the gut for just a second before it eased. "Gunner won't hurt you. I promise. We'll protect you from whatever drove you here."

Of course, the kitsune didn't regain her human form immediately. Instead, her dark eyes flickered back and forth between me and Gunner. She was assessing, gauging, calculating her chances….

In response, the rest of us kept our bodies relaxed and our gazes averted. And even though our body language was more lupine than vulpine, the black fox still gave a tiny whine of acceptance before shimmering into the form of a naked, redheaded girl.

"I'm Oyo," she whispered, gaze trained on the floorboards as her legs beat against the side of the table she sat atop. She was younger than me but older than Kira. In human terms, I would have guessed she was just barely old enough to drink.

"My mate speaks for me," Gunner answered formally. "Just as she's promised, so do I promise. Tell us who's chasing you and we'll make sure they never find you again."

His words were protective, exactly what you'd expect from an alpha werewolf. But his tone was still gravelly with rage from the preceding battle, and his fur-form self was almost visible as he took one step toward the girl.

No wonder Oyo didn't realize his advance was an offer to guard rather than a threat of imminent danger. Squeaking in reaction to the vague menace, the redhead was a redhead no longer. Instead, she'd fallen back down into the skin of her fox.

Chapter 4

Oyo scurried for cover, disappearing behind the refrigerator. Gunner growled in frustration then pulled me in the opposite direction even as he barked orders at his most trusted underlings, who had braved his wrath by remaining in my disaster zone of a living room.

"Allen, I want to know why no one smelled or saw a stray kitsune walking into clan central under her own power. Tank, check the perimeter and figure out where she came in."

His gaze slid across me so fiercely that I found words tumbling out of my mouth before I could consider whether they helped or hurt matters. "Gunner, I didn't invite..." I started, his sudden burst of alpha highhandedness making me wish my fingers were wrapped around a sword hilt rather than stuck in his crushing handhold.

"Edward, the pack needs reassurance," Gunner continued as if I hadn't spoken. "Think of a solution *now*." Then, as the last few werewolves waiting in the living room scattered, he turned to face me at last. "Yes, Mai, I know you didn't invite her." The statement seemed to absolve me of all wrongdoing, but his harsh tone didn't quite match his words.

And even though I knew Gunner was on edge from the recent risk to me and Kira, annoyance nonetheless flared at being treated like a toddler's doll. Because every time the alpha turned one way, I was dragged along behind him. Then he'd swivel in the opposite direction and give me a severe case of whiplash.

"I'm not..." I started, not quite sure what I wasn't. But this time the high-handed alpha hushed me with a finger to my lips even as he yanked out his phone and tapped rapidly at the screen.

"Brother, what a surprise." The call went through after only one ring, Ransom's voice so saccharine that it made my teeth ache. Or maybe that was just my fox incisors pushing their way through human dentition and gums in an effort to get out.

Either way, I wished I could see the elder Atwood's face through the cell phone. Had he answered so quickly because he'd sent Oyo to disrupt clan central? Or had he simply been at loose ends and thought baiting his brother might be a good way to fill an otherwise quiet night?

If I'd been the one in charge, I would have danced around the matter in an effort to tempt Ransom into dropping private information. But Gunner wasn't human enough for small talk, at the moment. Instead, he merely demanded, "Who did you tell?"

The words were a mistake—all three of us understood that as soon as they were uttered. And the smugness in Ransom's silence spurred me to take matters into my own hands in an effort at damage control.

"Ransom, thank you for accepting our call," I interjected, pressing my face closer to the phone and half expecting Gunner to yank the device away from me even as I spoke. But he didn't. Instead, he closed his eyes then swiped one huge palm across his face as if to remove overwhelming frustration. And when his sienna eyes blinked back open, they were full of both apology and praise.

Taking that as my cue to continue, I offered Ransom a sliver of information, hoping he'd give us something back in exchange. "A strange fox shifter showed up here this evening, which has your brother understandably excited. What he meant to ask was—do you have any idea how a kitsune might have heard this would be a safe place to hide?"

That conundrum had been roiling through my head ever since Oyo appeared on top of my refrigerator. After all, Gunner had kept my and Kira's identity so closely under wraps that only our pack and Ransom's should have known there were any kitsunes still living. So how had a stray fox shifter known to sneak into my home?

But apparently Oyo wasn't the biggest issue for the pair of siblings. Instead, Ransom's reply was clearly aimed not at me but rather at his brother.

"Who did I tell about you harboring illegal kitsunes? Is that what you meant to ask me?" Then, without waiting for confirmation: "No one yet, brother. But just imagine what might happen if I did."

"I SHOULDN'T HAVE TOLD him about Oyo."

I was kicking myself for playing right into Ransom's hands. But—despite the cell phone shattered on the ground and the strong scent of fur hovering around us—Gunner was back in control of himself and didn't appear to blame me.

No, it was his brother who served as the focus of the pack leader's ire. "He was lying," Gunner grumbled as he paced back and forth through the living room, crunching shattered glass and crockery beneath his boots.

"Maybe not," I interjected from my spot perched atop the arm of a blue, plush sofa. "Maybe I just gave Ransom an opening to threaten you. I'd be more certain he was responsible if you hadn't been the one to call him first."

Unfortunately, rational cause and effect clearly weren't working yet inside my favorite alpha's noggin. Because he kept walking and talking as if he hadn't heard my words at all. "If Ransom is spreading the word that you and your sister are under my protection," he growled, "then everyone knows he and I are no longer an unbeatable alliance. Our pack didn't have to fend off vultures when our father died because Ransom and I were united in our defense of clan central. But with only me on the job...we should start expecting visits from neighboring packs."

"Visits?" That didn't sound horrible. But from Gunner's tone, I had a feeling these neighbors weren't the welcome-wagon sort of werewolves. Sure enough, he shook his head as he continued pacing. Then, abruptly, he pulled me to my feet and brushed one absurdly gentle hand across the top of my head.

"Please be a little more careful of your own skin," he murmured, warm breath brushing over my forehead. His voice was still gravelly, but the *please* made up for all of his former heavy-handedness, warming locations lower down than my heart.

"I will," I promised, leaning into his broad body. But before I made contact, before I could turn that opening into a moment of shared pleasure...Gunner had set me back down on my sofa arm and disappeared out the door.

Unfortunately, the larger problem didn't disappear along with him. Instead, once my libidinous haze lifted, I clearly heard Kira slamming around in the kitchen. Oyo was silent but presumably still hiding. And my phone beeped to herald the arrival of an incoming text.

Cringing at the appearance of a number I'd never seen before but that I suspected corresponded to Gunner's brother, I swiped a reluctant finger to open the message up.

"I grant you free passage to and from Kelleys Island if you'd like to come and talk about it."

And wasn't that just going to float Gunner's boat?

Chapter 5

While I was focusing on Ransom, Oyo must have found a better hiding place. Because she was no longer behind the refrigerator when Kira picked her way through a minefield of spilled cheese dip and broken crockery to reach my side.

"I'm starving," my sister noted.

"So eat," I replied, dismissing Oyo's absence—if I couldn't find the visiting kitsune, then likely the pack couldn't either—while turning Ransom's text over in my mind.

Was Gunner right in pointing the finger at his brother? Was Oyo's arrival merely bait intended to tempt neighboring packs into tearing Atwood clan central down?

"Maaaaiiiii. You don't care about me at aaaaaaallllllll." Kira's whine was an eleven on the one-to-ten whine-o-meter. And even though I didn't want to encourage that behavior, one glance at paw prints on counters and glass shards peppering every edible item gave me an idea on how to keep her busy and allow me to reward good behavior at the same time.

"Help me clean up the worst of this mess and we'll go find a restaurant."

"Pancakes?" Kira's eyes lit up even as she half-heartedly opened a closet door in search of a dustpan.

"Whatever you want," I answered, hoping I wasn't making a promise I couldn't make good on. After all, it was getting late even for dinner. I wasn't so sure an all-day-breakfast joint would miraculously materialize within an easy drive.

But Old Red was outside, ready and waiting. And the agreement was enough to spur my sister into action. Starting in the kitchen, we swept and scrubbed and cleaned intensively enough for us both to grow filthy and sweaty, for Kira to turn cranky, and for me to wonder what I was doing moving in with this pack.

Because our neighbors were werewolves. They walked into each others' houses without knocking, knew everything there was to know about everybody else's business...and yet not a single neighbor had returned to the scene of the crime to help us deal with this horrifying mess.

"How much longer do we have to...?" Kira started. But I didn't need her whine to spur me into action this time.

"We're going," I interjected, deciding that both clutter and Oyo would be okay on their own for a little while longer. If the black-furred kitsune was savvy enough to have made her way through pack territory without being sniffed out, she could continue hiding in the cottage until we got back.

"Just give me five minutes to shower," I started, intending to finish with: *And then we'll find pancakes.* But as Kira pushed ahead of me into the living room—a disaster zone we hadn't even started to deal with—I froze, smelling the scent of fur so strongly that I knew a werewolf was right outside the open door.

Only, I was wrong. Because, with a yip, the cutest wolf pup imaginable jumped out from under the couch and dove into a bowlful of beef jerky.

There weren't werewolves outside stalking us. There was one very curious youngster right inside our home.

Inside our home and getting ready to chow down on food that was likely full of glass shards. "Kira, grab it!" I commanded, knowing I wouldn't be able to sidestep my sister's body in time to stop the pup myself.

And, for once, my sister obeyed without argument. She launched herself at the young werewolf, snagging its rear foot and dragging it toward her even as it wriggled in protest at losing access to its chosen feast.

"Calm down," she chided as she grabbed for the pup's ruff and ended up encircling its neck instead. The grip was meant to be protective but looked an awful lot like attempted murder....

No wonder a roar of rage preceded the arrival of a much larger animal into our midst. The werewolf in question leapt through the open doorway with eyes blazing, then she landed stiff-legged right in the middle of a spray of broken glass.

WHETHER OR NOT THE adult wolf cut her paws, none of us noticed. Because she was far more dangerous than the glass beneath her feet. The wolf took one look at Kira's stranglehold on the wriggling puppy, then she skidded across carpet in her haste to tear my sister apart.

"Hey! Over here!" I waved the sword that had materialized in my hand, doing my best to look both imposing and dangerous. Not that I planned to slice open a mother protecting her child. But I also refused to let my own sister be injured due to an overprotective parent's wrath.

And the sword did the job I'd intended—it focused the adult wolf's attention quite firmly on me rather than on my sister. Swiveling, the female bared her teeth in momentary warning, then she lunged directly at me.

Dodging wasn't an option when my opponent was traveling so quickly. Meanwhile, behind my back, Kira emitted a terrified squeak. So I did the only thing I could think of. I softened my sword magic until it became immaterial, then I hardened it again into the form of a club.

Thwack! My edgeless weapon struck the wolf's shoulder so hard she tumbled forward into a summersault, but she was back on her feet before I'd regathered my own momentum and put up my guard. This time, her paws struck my shoulders and I was the one falling backward, something sharp slicing through the side of my left arm as I tried—and failed—to make my escape.

"No teeth!" Kira roared, her words sounding distant as the wolf's hot breath licked against my cheek, my chin, then lower. I struggled to turn my magic into a shield to protect my jugular, but I couldn't seem to regather either my powers or my wind.

I couldn't believe I'd lost to a mother wolf protecting her child. I couldn't believe....

Then we both shuddered in tandem as Kira slammed a fist into the wolf's belly. "Your *alpha*"—punch, pant—"said to fight with swords *only*"—kick, twist—"so what kind of pack wolf are you?"

Kira was magnificent above us, and she also brought up a very good question. Why was yet another Atwood shifter willing and able to disobey her pack leader's overt command? Perhaps I could chalk this up to maternal instinct, but after the melee surrounding Oyo I wasn't so sure.

The inconsistency felt important...but not quite as important as the claws digging into my skin. Then the pup was on top of me also, attracted by the blood of my oozing forearm. The youngster bared its teeth and started gnawing, and in reaction the female above me growled before shifting back into human form.

Becky. I remembered her name from our meeting last summer. Recalled the way she'd helped Gunner with transportation so he could hunt a bear and wrench the pack away from his brother without descending to the level of a physical fight.

Not that it had worked out as painlessly as we'd hoped after Becky tossed us those car keys. There'd been plenty of blood on the ground before the night was over, and Becky's mate had been one of the few who lost his life.

No wonder she'd been ready to tear me to pieces. But, to my surprise, the naked woman's face twisted apologetically as she scooped up the puppy, then she danced backwards rather than menacing me a second time.

"Curly, we do *not* gnaw on humans," she chastised, holding her offspring by his ruff and shaking him until he whimpered acknowledgement of the misunderstanding.

Then, turning back to me, Becky dropped her eyes to the floor even as that rotten-egg odor I was becoming unfortunately familiar with filled the room. "Alpha's mate. I was overwrought and out of line. I apologize for the misunderstanding. Please forgive me for the mistake."

Chapter 6

"Everything will be forgiven," I said simply, "if you tell me the fastest way to get pancakes into this starving teenager."

"The *fastest* way?" Becky's eyebrows rose and the sulfurous scent fled. "The fastest way is to go to the midnight breakfast Edward is organizing. But I'm not sure it's the smartest thing to...."

"Who cares about smart? I want pancakes," Kira interrupted, heading toward the door. "Midnight breakfast! I love being a wolf!"

And I *could* have stopped her forward motion. I probably should have too, given the way her usually sunny temperament seemed to be descending into demands and domineering at the drop of a hat. But, for once, Kira was smiling...and I was starting to get an idea of what caused the here-one-moment-gone-the-next scent of sulfur. So I didn't even interrupt my sister's chatterbox monologue as we strode along a secluded road and out into a well-lit picnic scene.

I was physically hungry, the salty tang of bacon dragging me toward the food being carried out in huge vats and on platters. And I was also hungry for companionship, glad to find the clan had forgotten us for a reason that didn't relate to the shape of our fur-form skins.

Still...Gunner must have known about this community mealtime and he hadn't dropped back by to invite me. Which suggested Becky was right and this wasn't the smartest place to feed my sister and my soul.

No wonder my eyes scanned our surroundings, looking out for signs of danger even as I noted the distinct lack of familiar faces in the werewolves' midst. Tank, Allen, and Gunner were all elsewhere, but at least there was no rotten-egg aroma filling the Green. Well, there wasn't until a gob of spittle struck the grass before us, a sulfur-scented werewolf I'd never met pressing her way into our personal space.

"Disgusting," the old woman growled, and I had my sword in hand to protect Kira before I realized the speaker wasn't interested in the two of us. Instead, Becky was the one scooping up her son, neck bent in submission. And Becky was the target of the old woman's jabbing finger as the crone continued with her tirade.

"If Old Chief Atwood was still alive, he never would have allowed such an abomination," the older woman said while spraying us all with spittle. "Liam knew better too. If he'd lived, he would have dealt with this rot before it went so deep."

She raised her cane as if to strike either Becky or Curly, which made me, in turn, prepare to tackle the foul-mouthed bitch. But clearly the call of pancakes was greater than the allure of ornery hatefulness. Or maybe the crone had finally noticed my aggressive stance. Either way, the old woman turned away with only a sniff of dismissal, taking her foul scent with her as she stepped into the longer of two lines forming up on either side of the expanse of grass.

I wanted to ask Becky what the deal was, but the female barely knew me and was unlikely to spill her guts in public. So, instead, I changed the subject. Heading toward the shorter line—the only one with bacon, were these werewolves crazy?—I offered, "Let's find ourselves something to eat."

"Not there." Becky's hand was on my arm then off again so quickly I barely registered the contact, and her gaze was still riveted on the ground as she spoke. But her voice was nonetheless loud enough for me to understand as she deciphered the bacon mystery for me. "That's the line for warriors. If you join it, you'll be asking for a fight."

Sure enough, a newly arrived family split up on the threshold. The father headed for the bacon, the mother and two children veered right toward pancakes and eggs. Rather than joining the end of the line, however, the male insinuated himself midway down it, setting the neighboring shifters bristling for a moment before they chose to subside. And, in reaction, the pancake line easily made room for the newcomer's family in the middle of the queue, right about where her mate would have stood had he chosen the longer line instead.

Seriously? Werewolves made even group meals into power struggles? Well, that answered the question about how to carve out a place for me and Kira within the Atwood community.

"I want scrambled eggs, pancakes, and a banana," I told my sister. Then, allowing my sword to form in its sheath along my backbone, I headed for the bacon line.

GIVEN THAT GUNNER AND his closest lieutenants were apparently occupied elsewhere, I shouldn't have been surprised by the square shoulders and closely shorn hair at the head of the line. But as Edward turned around to face me and immediately emitted enough sulfur to drown out the delicious bacon aroma, I grumbled internally. Of course my least favorite Atwood werewolf would be the one I was facing to get my fair share of pig fat.

For half a second, I hesitated, considered choosing a spot a few werewolves back instead. Did I—and Becky and Kira by proxy—really need to proclaim ourselves the most dominant shifters in the entire clan? Wouldn't second or third best suffice just as well?

"Lost?" Edward asked as I debated. His smile was so smug as he motioned to the head of the opposite line that I felt my teeth grinding together even as the decision made itself. "The alpha's mate eats over there."

His words were a minor concession and everyone knew it. An acknowledgement that if Gunner were here, the pack leader would win by default and I'd head up the non-bacon-enabled queue.

But I didn't intend to hang upon Gunner's coattails. He had enough on his plate without slapping down shifters who disrespected me. Instead, I was perfectly willing to fight this battle on my own.

Willing...and excited as I drew my sword out of its sheath with a musical ring of magic-imbued metal. I was sick and tired of backhanded put-downs. It was time for Edward to find a weapon and face me like a man.

Only, my chosen opponent had no intention of engaging in a sword fight. Instead, the male made room for me before him, somehow managing to turn a motion that should have been submissive into a slight instead. "By all means, if your only other option is to use a weapon none of us is familiar with. Stand in for Gunner. The rest of us will all move back."

There were grumbles from the queue behind me, high-pitched annoyance from the opposite side of the grass. Now I looked like a bully, unable to bend to Atwood customs and instead hiding behind Gunner's requirement that everyone in the pack settle their differences with swords.

That wasn't going to garner Becky the protection I was going for, nor would it smooth the path for my sister in the days ahead. So, opening my hands wide, I let my sword flare back into an immaterial star ball. Then, toeing out of my sneakers, I shifted into the form of my fox.

Chapter 7

"First blood, one-year moratorium on further fighting?"
The question came from behind me, the male second in line for bacon suggesting rules I understood to be the Atwood default in duels such as this. But Edward didn't answer, nor did he take the time to untie his shoelaces. Instead, he shifted in a burst of alpha aggression, shreds of fabric flying everywhere...including into the food trays we were all hoping to serve ourselves from.

Good thing I wasn't married to the idea of bacon, I noted even as I danced backward, assessing the shape of Edward's wolf. He was every bit as large as Gunner in fur form, his more advanced age far from obvious as he paced toward me on silent lupine feet.

Which would have been daunting eight months earlier. But I'd been sparring with the guys off and on all summer. I knew the relative strengths and weaknesses of fox form and was confident I could win first blood.

I was far less confident that I could vanquish my opponent if Edward declined to stop at a simple scratch and instead aimed for serious injury. But, in the skin of my animal, future worries quickly faded away. Instead, I yipped a playful taunt at the large canine facing me, then I slimmed down my body and scurried fast as an adder between his front legs.

Because male wolves were so blissfully predictable—get close to their reproductive organs and they transitioned from posturing warriors into terrified children in an instant. Edward was no exception. With a yelp, he plopped down on top of me, lying prostrate in an attempt to protect his family jewels from imminent attack.

Which solved the problem he was going for, but left his paw pads exposed, bare skin easy to scratch. Nipping hard with sharp fox teeth, I tasted salt exploding on my tongue.

First blood. Ten seconds after commencing our battle, I'd earned the right to stand at the head of the line.

Which should have been the end of the matter. Would have been if Edward had agreed to the other shifter's suggestion or if Gunner had been standing over us ready to growl the loser into defeat. As it was, however, my opponent wasn't thrilled at my not-quite-kosher victory. Or so I gathered as his snout darted toward me, teeth closing so hard around my ruff they nearly met in the middle despite the intervening fur and skin.

At least it was just a fold of pelt he was holding onto. He *could* have bitten straight through my neck and ended this entire game the easy way. But as I was slung back and forth so hard my eyeballs threatened to pop out of their sockets, I had a hard time feeling gratitude for anything at all.

Especially when Edward dropped me in front of another werewolf a few seconds later, this one in human form but with no less aggression in his grip as he used my ribs as a punching bag. I scratched as best I could, trying to escape or at least buy enough time to summon my star ball. But my magic was elusive and a fox was no match for a werewolf when the latter wasn't bound by the agreement of first blood.

And now I was being tossed to a third shifter. Then to another and another yet. As if no one wanted to hog the pleasure of proving the hard way that I didn't belong within their pack.

"Gunner won't answer his cell phone." Kira's voice sounded very far away as my head thudded against a shifter's foot this time. *Smart little sister to call for backup,* I thought vaguely even as I tried and failed to bring my magic to the fore once again. *Too bad she didn't realize Gunner crushed his phone underneath his boot.*

I was too confused to even attempt shifting to tell her that, though, and was starting to lose my ability to think. All I could muster was the knowledge that none of the preceding punches had cut through my skin or broken any bones. Which meant these shifters were, perhaps, hoping their alpha would never find out what had happened behind his back?

"The pack bond isn't working either." That was Becky. Or at least I thought it was Becky. I was starting to lose track of names...including my own.

Then my teeth contacted with the fist of yet another werewolf. And I *knew* the solution my addled brain hadn't been able to come up with before now.

I'd use kitsune magic to control these shifters. Would force them to release me. And, in the process, consolidate my place within the pack.

It was brilliant. Okay, maybe not so brilliant. But at least the strategy would ensure I made it out of this hazing alive.

I SHOULD HAVE POSSESSED a vast reservoir of available magic already since I'd bitten at least two of the werewolves in my efforts to escape from the beating. But my opponents had shaken that energy right out of me with their kicks and punches. Good thing I had more blood waiting to be swallowed...and with it access to the wills of every single shifter who had beaten me up until this point.

Because I'd fought back as best I was able while being manhandled. So little bits of werewolf matter were bound to be embedded beneath my claws. The only trick was reaching them, and doing so without biting off my own tongue in the process....

Even as I thought through a plan of action, my current manhandler tossed me skyward, probably intending to scare me but actually providing a much-needed reprieve. I almost scratched myself in the eye while attempting to lick the first toenail, but then dirty salt saturated my senses and hit me like a sugar rush right between the eyes.

Hold me over your head, I ordered the male who caught me as I descended. And I was pleased to find his two spread hands now formed a wide, raised platform rather than clenching back into menacing fists. Just what I needed—space and time to search for werewolf fluids while I was kept far out of other shifters' reach.

"Hey! What're you doing?"

"Come on! We weren't finished!"

The complaints grew louder and louder, but I ignored them as I licked and gnawed at my own nails. Then...

There. Heady energy flooded my senses, dulling the aches and pains that resulted from being pummeled so dramatically.

Now *I* was the powerful one. The one able to do whatever I wished with these werewolves. Time to see what my assailants thought of that.

Chapter 8

It was tempting to revenge myself upon the bullies. But now that my head was clearer, I understood that there was only one way to end this debacle. I had to rebuild the clan with me in the center rather than trying to fight my way inside.

Even as the thought coalesced into existence, visions emerged before my eyes. Glowing threads of connection slid hither and yon around me and I struggled to make sense of the images materializing beneath the magically obedient shifter's hands.

Could someone have kicked me in the head hard enough that I was hallucinating? I would have jumped to that conclusion quite willingly if the illuminated lines hadn't made far too much sense.

Because my own bonds were just what I would have expected. There was one connecting me with Kira, a slender thread leading to Becky, and several others flowing into the distance and out of sight.

The thickest led to Gunner. I somehow knew this without having to see the far terminus, knew this even though the scent of rose petals seemed to waft toward me down that particular bond.

What are you up to? I murmured, intrigued despite myself. And for half a second I looked out through the alpha's eyeballs. Felt my/his fingers setting a bottle of bath salts on the edge of a massive tub even as wax melted from flickering candles arrayed all around the edge.

Aw. Gunner was setting the scene for our date this evening. Which was unbelievably sweet...and at the same time reminded me of what would happen if I called him here to save my skin.

The overprotective alpha would take one look at my bruises and go ballistic, a problem when pack bonds were already stretched and strained. After all, I could see Becky tugging hard on a thread that should have connected her to Gunner but was instead severed and faded. No wonder the alpha hadn't answered. He had no idea what was happening since Becky's connection was rotten and stinking five feet away from her hand.

The female wasn't the only one with that problem either. No, from up here werewolves looked like they were caught in an aged and decaying spider web. Even as I watched, more bonds snarled and splintered, each break setting off another burst of sulfurous scent.

Was this what my arrival had done to the pack that meant so much to Gunner? I was already regretting using kitsune powers to free myself since similar actions were likely responsible for the tangle we were all caught within.

But, on the plus side, watching Becky had filled me in on how pack bonds operated. So, tilting my head until my own tethers wrapped around my muzzle, I gave one of my lesser connections a tug.

ALLEN—GUNNER'S NERDY and level-headed lieutenant—didn't show up until I'd already shifted and started solving the problem the hard way. No, not with swords or punches but with much-needed TLC.

"It's over," I informed the watching shifters, trying to look like I wasn't analyzing them for signs of further attack...while covertly analyzing them for signs of further attack.

Because I'd relinquished magical control over their actions as soon as my feet hit the ground and my sword was back in my fist. Which left me wide open to the mob mentality, but I hoped also gave my audience an incentive to listen rather than react.

They glared at me but didn't argue, the sight of my injured body enough to give most of my recent assailants pause. Now that they weren't in the midst of their instinct-fueled blood haze, I could tell they'd started wondering what Gunner would do to them once he heard about the evening's events.

In the interest of returning their attention to what really mattered, I let them off the hook on that matter at least. "I'm not going to tell Gunner who hit me," I informed my audience. "I'll take a shower so he can't smell you. And if you're smart, you'll all wrestle or go for a run or do whatever werewolves do to get scratched up."

"Yeah, go sniff each others' butts," Kira snarked, not as quietly as she should have. My sister was going to be the death of me...and I had no solution other than to mouth, *"Go home."*

Luckily, Allen had been the right pack mate to summon. Because he took in my sister's orneriness and my precarious hold over the werewolves' attention in one split second of eye-squinting assessment. Then, snagging a relatively clean piece of bacon and a plateful of pancakes, he lured Kira away...while leaving Becky behind.

Okay, so Allen wasn't a perfect mind reader. Or maybe he knew that Kira was enough to keep his hands entirely full. So the older female would have to be part of my object lesson. But, first, I had to reel these werewolves the rest of the way in.

"Each of you needs to get over your snits," I continued, watching the rotted pack bonds with half my attention even as I met each shifter's eyes in turn. "For example—Edward, whatever you have against that pup beside you, you need to let it go."

Because the older shifter's bond to the nearby teenager looked like it had been shredded and gnawed on. Sure enough, both males' faces reddened as I called them on their relationship, then a young woman slapped Edward on the arm.

"Daddy, are you still mad at Chester from years ago?"

"He broke your heart. He doesn't deserve to be your mate."

"Sir—" the male in question started. But Edward's daughter spoke over him, standing up on her tiptoes so she could stare her father directly in the eyes.

"He had a small lapse when we were *children*," the young woman countered, and I had to admire her spirit even though I was pretty sure by my standards she hadn't grown out of being a child quite yet. "But it's over and done with, Daddy. You need to let the past stay in the past."

Old grudges don't heal in an instant. But I was relieved to note new tendrils of connection forming before I turned my gaze the other way. "Which brings me to another matter," I continued. I knew I was on a roll from the way each werewolf focused intently upon me—or maybe they were staring at the bacon behind my back.

No, they were buying what I was selling. "She can see the pack bonds clearly," one male murmured. "She *is* the alpha's mate," someone else quietly agreed.

"Yes, I am the alpha's mate," I continued. "And as such, I want to know what in the world you have against Becky and her son Curly?"

And, immediately, the virtual sunlight that had illuminated the gathering squelched into gathering storm. Brows lowered, shifters growled, and someone in the back shouted out a reply.

"That so-called *son* was born a bloodling with fur and wolf claws. If the old chief was still around to do something about it, that particular abomination would already be dead."

Chapter 9

S o *that* was why I hadn't seen any other tiny pups scampering through clan central. I took another look at Curly and realized that the youngster was probably less than a year old, his life apparently saved by the change of leadership that had occurred after Gunner's father died.

"Don't you think...?" I started, not sure how I was going to sway someone so mired in the past that he failed to realize a shifter in wolf form was still very much human. But before I could get my thoughts together, a woman around Becky's age darted out of the crowd and began screaming at the male who'd recently spoken.

"Oh, you'd like that, wouldn't you? To return to the Dark Ages? Not that we aren't there already. Who says I have to find a mate before I can enjoy bacon? Who do you think cooked all of the bacon in the first place? The women, that's who! And if we want to serve ourselves from the left line, we'll do that..."

"Mind your place, woman." It wasn't just the bloodling hater who was against this particular female, I realized. Watching the pack bonds with half my attention while trying not to sneeze against the rising tide of sulfur, I noted that fully a third of the males—including the current speaker—had withdrawn emotional support from the outspoken female the instant she began her harangue.

And there was nothing I could do about it. Nothing I could do but watch all of my good intentions crash and burn around me.

Because the magic that had gotten the pack's attention earlier was already slipping. My ability to yank on immaterial connections was dissipating even as the illuminated threads faded out of sight.

Unless I took another sip of werewolf blood, I had no way to stop this shouting match. And if I didn't calm agitated tempers, someone—like Curly—was bound to get hurt.

I turned around, searching the crowd for the young bloodling. And in the process I nearly ran into Becky, whose hand slipped into mine in order to urge me away.

"Let's go." She had Curly tucked under her other arm, a piece of bacon clenched in the pup's needle-sharp incisors. At least *someone* had profited from my misguided attempt to shake up the Atwood status quo.

Still—"I can't just leave them like this," I countered, struggling to come up with a solution that wouldn't make things worse in the long term. Gunner wasn't going to be pleased that I'd riled up the masses and left them to duke it out amongst themselves...just as he wasn't going to be pleased when he took a look at the bruises welling up all over my torso, legs, and arms.

Welling up...and aching the way they hadn't when they'd first been inflicted. I only realized the protective adrenaline was fading out of my bloodstream when I stumbled, leaning against Becky's shoulder in order to keep myself upright.

"You're in no position to stop them," Becky said, stating the obvious. "And...maybe it'll help to air all of our dirty laundry in public. It's worth a shot."

It was worth a shot only because we had no alternative. But a smart warrior knows when to retreat so she can later rise up and return to the fight.

So—hating to give in without a resolution, but unable to think of a better alternative—I pulled Becky forward this time, leaving the werewolves behind us to do their worst.

"YOU LOOK AWFUL."

I'd accepted Becky's offer to shower at her house, not really intending her to see the wounds her pack mates had inflicted upon me. But apparently she was as soft-footed as a fox. So she'd managed to sneak up on me as

I stood in the bathroom, trying to decide whether my ripped and ruined clothing was worth putting anywhere other than in the trash.

"Here." She handed over an armful of clothing, apparently having thought of everything I hadn't. And even though I gladly slipped into the gifted underwear, I hesitated before pulling on the rest of her offerings.

Because my enemies hadn't just peppered me with bruises. In several places, my skin had split open, blood still oozing out and promising to ruin Becky's shirt and pants. Gunner wasn't just going to be disappointed. He was going to be furious. And what he did as a result would make my precarious position in the pack much, much worse.

I sank down onto the toilet lid, my knees suddenly refusing to hold me. In my mind's eye, I imagined the alpha waiting for me amid his bath salts and candles. He was trying so hard to make me welcome...and his efforts were tearing an already broken clan apart.

Kira and I should leave. The reality bit into my gut more painfully than any physical bruise or laceration. I needed to take myself away from this pack, but I didn't want to. Didn't want to lose not only my growing bond with Gunner but also the possibility of being part of something greater than I'd ever dreamed of involving myself in.

If I stayed, I'd no longer be a woman alone with her sister. I'd be a member of a pack.

But was it worth becoming part of a pack if that pack didn't want me? What if the pack in question was painfully misogynistic and actively dangerous to those I loved?

I knew the answer, much as I didn't want to. No wonder I barely registered Becky crouching down beside me and beginning to smear something green and gooey across my wounded skin.

"You know, Ransom's weaknesses and their father's ancient notions aren't the entirety of our pack's problem," she said tentatively, perhaps reading my mind or perhaps speaking from her own experience. "A werewolf leader needs to be mated. It sounds old-fashioned, but the female energy of an alpha's mate brings peacefulness to a clan."

"Yeah." I laughed despite myself. "I'm doing a really great job promoting peacefulness."

"You might be. In the long run. I at least appreciate what you've done for me." Her fingers were so skillful I didn't even realize I'd been plastered with bandaids until I looked down and saw a dozen pink stripes dotting my skin and hiding cuts and bruises. Tiny, rainbow-colored wolves danced and frolicked atop the plastic, and despite myself I barked out a curt but honest laugh.

I was cleaned up and bandaged...and somehow I'd decided not to flee into the night in the process. Or at least not into *this* night. I'd stick it out for one more day and see if there was a way to help rather than harm this pack.

But I couldn't deepen my bond to Gunner until I knew how long I was staying. So after hugging Becky in gratitude, I turned right instead of left out of my new friend's driveway.

After all, Kira needed someone to watch over her. Plus, I was exhausted and, apparently, cowardly. So rather than hunting down the alpha who had claimed me, I headed back to the cottage I had tentatively begun calling my own.

Chapter 10

Allen must have traded off with Tank sometime after dropping off my sister, because the latter nodded at me from his post beneath Kira's window as I headed back up the steps to the shadowed front door. So Kira would have been fine if I'd kept my word and gone to Gunner's as promised. Still...I wouldn't sleep until I was sure that both my charges hadn't been harmed while I was away.

So I padded through the living room and kitchen before giving in to the beckoning bedrooms. "Oyo?" I murmured into the darkness, rising on tiptoes to swipe a hand across the empty top of the refrigerator where the kitsune had first been found. The space was bare, unsurprisingly. After all, our guest was too smart to hole up anywhere so obvious. Still, various other nooks and crannies were equally unoccupied. So perhaps the missing female had gotten smart and snuggled up with Kira on her bed?

Retracing my footsteps through the living room, I turned right this time into the hallway that led to the two bedrooms beyond. And there I stopped as I caught sight of a lump on the floor in front of Kira's door. A body swaddled in blankets as if Oyo had been afraid to choose a bedroom and had instead made herself a pallet. It clenched my stomach to think of her sleeping on the floor.

"Oyo?" I whispered, not wanting to wake my sister but aware that a kitsune can be dangerous to startle in the darkness.

And the sleeper woke instantly, rising upwards while shedding blankets right and left. Only this wasn't Oyo. This was Gunner, shirtless and so handsome the vision stole my breath. "Our guest is hiding in the laundry room," he offered, making me frown for one split second as I considered the fact that I hadn't even realized my new home possessed a washer and dryer let alone a room to keep them in.

"Laundry nook," he corrected himself as he stood and took three long strides forward to meet me halfway down the hall. "Behind the folding doors off the kitchen."

Oh, right. I'd assumed that was a pantry and hadn't bothered to look inside it. Not a very comfortable spot to spend the night...but whatever made Oyo feel safe.

We were eye to eye now, and Gunner's proximity was sending messages to my battered body that I was hard-pressed to fight against. Leaning forward, I murmured, "Sorry I didn't show up for the bubble bath."

"I saw you had your hands full when you contacted me through the pack bond," Gunner answered, his own hands rising to rub firm circles of pleasure across shoulders that ached then soothed. "I figured I'd finish cleaning up your cottage since you were cleaning up my pack for me."

So he wasn't angry about the mob scene? I was glad...and also subtly disappointed. Maybe I'd gotten a little too used to an alpha werewolf's overprotective streak.

Perhaps that's why I didn't fill him in about the as-yet-unanswered text from his brother. Or perhaps it was the warm comfort of Gunner's fingers on my skin sidetracking me from that line of thinking. His hand slid beneath my shirt's collar, skimming lines of fire sideways across my upper chest while giving other parts of my body intriguing notions I was suddenly ready to act upon.

"Perhaps..." Gunner started.

Then his nail caught on a bandaid and his wolf emerged behind his eyes with a growl. "What exactly," the alpha demanded, forgetting to be quiet for the sake of my sleeping sister, "happened to you?"

"CALM DOWN."

Okay, so even I knew that was no way to start a conversation with an angry werewolf. Still, I was desperate to finish what we'd started. Desperate enough to tug Gunner back toward the pallet of blankets and muffle my own admonition by pressing lips against bare skin.

I kissed my way up his fingers, his arm, and onto his neck, the whole time trying to make myself believe that Gunner was still riding the same libidinous train I was. But his muscles were not only hard, they were unyielding. The discovery of my bandaids had thoroughly derailed us from the pleasure-seeking track.

Eventually, I settled back on my heels, accepting that Gunner's interest wasn't going to flick back on until we'd dealt with his outrage. And when he spoke, his voice was quieter but no less intense as he demanded the same information in a slightly different way.

"Who injured you?"

The hand I'd been kissing was still relaxed and open against my body. But his left fist, I noted, was so tightly clenched it was obvious that identifying my assailants would send Gunner rushing off to pound them into a pulp.

"You know it's inevitable that I'll get a little injured on occasion if I'm denning with werewolves," I started, forcing his fist back into the shape of a hand even as I let my dreams for the evening fade into the dark. My goal now was to keep Gunner from slaughtering his pack mates. Getting lucky would have to wait for another night.

"I'll kill them."

I was very glad now that I'd taken advantage of Becky's shower before running into Gunner. And also glad that, while hunting through the cottage for Oyo, I'd come up with a potential cure both for my contusions and for Gunner's over-protective rage.

So I reached over to tip his head down until our eyes met, then I offered a partial solution. "If you're willing, I think I can heal most of these wounds with a little turbocharge."

"Blood, you mean?" Gunner hesitated, his urge to annihilate my opponents battling with his ever-present need to keep me safe.

"If you're willing," I repeated. And I could see the moment his softer side won out over his bloodlust.

"We're not done talking about this," he told me. But then he used his mouth for something more useful, ripping a small cut at the crook of his elbow and offering up the wound so I could take a sip.

We hadn't shared blood in months, and the rightness of the experience was oddly arousing. My nipples tightened, my skin prickled, and I found myself smearing Gunner's fluids over his face as I moved my head upward to steal a kiss.

I thought he was right there with me, too, until a sting on my shoulder alerted me to the removal of one of my bandaids. Then Gunner drew away from my lips and pulled the collar of my shirt sideways so we could both peer underneath.

There was nothing to see but clear skin, unblemished and smooth as if I'd never been hit in the first place. Meanwhile, aching muscles soothed as if I was enjoying that promised bubble bath after all.

And even though I hadn't really done anything to make the healing happen, I could feel exhaustion cascading back over me. Which meant I was the one who shut down further shenanigans. I was the one who murmured a thank you even as I subsided back onto the blankets spread across the floor beneath us.

Still, I was awake enough to hear Gunner's answer. "Thank you for sacrificing yourself for the pack's problems," he rumbled. Then, intertwined in each other's arms, we fell deeply asleep.

Chapter 11

I woke to cold air, a solitary pallet, and my sister shrieking. "I've been stabbed!"

So Gunner had gone to deal with my assailants after all. And one of them must have snuck through our defenses to return the favor....

Those thoughts tumbled through my head as I wrenched the door open, only to find Kira standing on her bed in a tank top and undies, blood running down the insides of her thighs. She hadn't been stabbed. If I didn't miss my guess, she'd merely become a woman, starting her menstrual cycle for the very first time.

Which should have been my cue to commence mothering. But instead...I froze.

Froze and flashed back to my own first period. To hiding in the bathroom and clutching my belly while my father struggled to take care of an infant without letting us know he'd succumbed to grief at the death of his wife.

We'd been lost without my mother just as I was now lost calming Kira. Up until this point, I'd just mimicked Mama's parenting. But by the time I started my period, our own mother had been dead.

So I stood and Kira shrieked....and the window shattered behind her to disgorge a human-form werewolf. Tank had slivers of glass embedded in his skin from tumbling through the opening. But he did no more than brush free his hands before scooping my sister up off the bed.

"Who did it? Where are you injured?" He spun her around seeking a wound, and Kira let him manhandle her for a moment before looping her arms around his neck so she could sob into her protector's sweatshirt.

"It hurts," the teenager moaned. "And it's nasty." Meanwhile, Tank's search found the obvious source of the red fluid and the werewolf turned unaccountably pale.

Typical male reaction. I tried to laugh off Tank's weakness so I could step forward to take over care of my sister. But what was the right way to calm down a hysterical teenager whose fists were even now pounding a staccato rhythm on her protector's broad chest?

"What's wrong?" Dad had asked me twelve years earlier, after I slammed a plate onto the table so hard it shattered into sharp-edged shards.

"Nothing, nothing, nothing!" I'd howled, wanting to shift to fox form and bite him until he hurt as much as I did.

"Mai, honey. I know it's hard without your mother. But we're all in this together. You don't have to suffer alone."

His words hadn't actually helped me, but they *had* shamed me into silence. Which wasn't what I wanted—to squelch my sister's feelings. The trouble was, I couldn't recall what kind of reaction I'd actually been looking for when I was newly menstrual. I hadn't known then and I definitely didn't know now.

So once again I hesitated, frozen by difficult memories. And during that hiatus, someone pushed past me wrapped in a robe and smelling strongly of dryer sheets.

"Kira, stop it." Oyo gently tugged my sister away from the werewolf who actually *was* bleeding from various wounds still embedded with wicked glass shards. "It's just your period, honey," she continued, setting Kira down on the edge of the bed. "We'll clean you up and you'll be hunky dory again."

"You don't understand!" Kira countered, pounding her fists against Oyo's shoulder this time. If I didn't miss my guess, horror had turned the corner while we weren't looking and morphed into rage. "My body betrayed me! It's a disaster! I'll never be the same person I was yesterday."

"Get us some damp washcloths," Oyo told the hovering werewolf, giving Tank something helpful to do while he caught his breath. Then, drawing me forward with raised eyebrows, she grasped one hand from each of us, waiting until Kira and I had intertwined our other fingers and created a triangle of unity with my sister inside.

"You're right, Kira. You'll never be the same as you were yesterday," the formerly quiet kitsune continued. She no longer appeared small and scared, I noted. Instead, I leaned into the younger woman, trusting her implicitly. "You've joined the womanhood. It's sometimes painful, sometimes difficult. But it's always worth the blood."

And that was apparently the right thing to say after all. Because Kira raised our joined hands to swipe tears off her cheeks. "You promise?"

"I promise," Oyo answered.

"Mai?"

"It's worth it," I said honestly, remembering how shaken up I'd been by my first period but how glad I was to be a woman now.

Which wasn't at all what I would have told Kira if Oyo hadn't insinuated herself into the family drama. I likely would have gone all sex ed on her, providing a rundown on hygienic products along with a tart reminder that she could now become pregnant if she risked unprotected sex.

All of the hard data could wait for later, however. Instead, what Kira needed this morning was unconditional love and support.

So I squeezed two kitsunes' hands with warming fingers and growing gratitude. It was such a relief to take part in a ritual like Mama might have come up with. And right then and there, I decided that I'd find some way to keep everything. The pack, Gunner, and Oyo also.

Because even if the doing was painful and difficult, I had a feeling incorporating this stranger into my family would be well worth the blood.

Chapter 12

"Thank you," Oyo told me ten minutes later as I handed over a pair of jogging pants. She sounded so genuinely grateful for such a small gift that I paused in the act of rooting through my as-yet-to-be-unpacked boxes in search of a semi-matching shirt.

"Hey, I should be the one thanking you," I told her before delving deeper into the mess of fabric. "I had no idea what to tell Kira. You must have a big family to know exactly what to say."

"A big family?"

Right. Kitsunes didn't come from big families. Barring those who made a mistake with birth control and chose to sacrifice their own lives for the sake of a second child, we were a one-mother-one-daughter kind of race.

In an attempt to pull my foot out of my mouth, I pivoted verbally to the subject I'd lured Oyo into my room to talk about. "What I should have said is—your solution to Kira's problem was both thoughtful and clever. And, speaking of clever, I was curious how you knew Kira and I were living here with the Atwood pack?"

After all, werewolves and kitsunes weren't a predictable combination. And the two of us had been in wolf territory for only a few minutes before Oyo showed up.

"I'm not that clever," Oyo evaded, turning her back to slip out of her robe and into the borrowed clothing. "You're clever to convince werewolves to protect you. It's something I've never seen before."

"They'll protect you too." Her shoulders looked so slender, all hunched over with cold or fear as she faced away from me. But I squashed my immediate impulse to accept the change of subject and returned to my original point instead. "We'll all protect you. But it'll be easier if we know who might be following and what kind of trail you left behind. Did…"

421

Only I received no answer. Because Oyo was shifting, the air around her shimmering as she shrunk down into fox form right inside her borrowed clothing.

Then Allen's voice came through the closed door behind her—"Everybody decent? If so, the boss brought breakfast. Better get out here before Kira puts it all inside her hollow leg."

Whether or not Allen's approach had been what originally spooked her, Oyo was thoroughly terrified now. She scurried for cover under my bed, wisp of a fox tail tucking away into the darkness behind her. Then—if my ears served me right—she started clawing through drywall in search of an even safer hiding place.

So I wasn't getting any answers to my questions this morning. Well, I'd do my best to be patient. "Lead on," I told the waiting werewolf as I opened the door and greeted Allen with an almost-genuine smile on my face.

"LOOK, MAI, GOBS OF bacon!"

Someone must have fed my sister sugar, because she was bouncing off the walls...almost literally. Behind her, Gunner raised his eyebrows at me by way of greeting, and I couldn't quite tell if he'd been out righting wrongs or just hunting down food for the hyperactive teenager in our midst.

"I need to talk to you," Gunner mouthed, his expression not as welcoming as I would have hoped for. But Kira was hanging onto my shoulders now, trying to leap up so I'd carry her piggyback.

"Kira, you're strangling me!"

"Am not," my sister countered, but she did slide off long enough to stuff an entire piece of French toast into her mouth. Which, in turn, gave me the opportunity to slip past her without being drawn deeper into her sugar rush.

"I'm on Kira duty this morning," Allen promised as I walked toward his alpha. Then I was up close and personal with Gunner, whose face was still surprisingly grim. His fingers on my arm, however, were gentle as he guided me through the living room and out the front door.

"You know I want you and Kira here," he started without a formal greeting. And as much as I'd been looking forward to spending a moment alone together, I suddenly wished I could join Oyo in her hole in my bedroom wall.

Still, it was always better to rip off the proverbial bandaid quickly. So, sure Gunner was going no place I wanted to follow, I still prodded him to continue. "But?"

"No 'but.'" Gunner hesitated, then lowered himself down onto the top porch step, placing his head a good distance below mine. This wasn't the behavior of an alpha werewolf about to evict someone from his territory. And even though I appreciated his gesture, I still found myself sinking down right alongside him so I wouldn't end up towering above his head.

"Gunner, you're scaring me."

"There's no need to be scared." His huge hand landed on mine, furless and clawless and perfectly human. Still, I could *feel* the wolf vibrating inside him, itching to get out and hold this conversation in the two-legger's place. Given the fact that my fox form was a fraction the size of his animal, that realization wasn't a heartening feeling at all.

"I have a single request," he continued, unaware of my continued trepidation. "And you are free to ignore it if you feel it restricts your range of movement unduly..."

"Gunner." Now I finally smiled, understanding at last what he was so on edge about. He wasn't getting ready to evict me to ease the strain on his pack mates. Instead, he was trying not to send me fleeing with wolf demands couched as human requests.

Given my past problems with similar behavior, the alpha's caution was sweet...but we were well beyond that stage. "Talk," I told him. "I'm not leaving unless you kick me out."

"And I'm not kicking you out." At least *that* got his lips moving. "Everything you did last night was powerful," Gunner continued, diving into the heart of the matter at last. "The pack bonds actually look better this morning than they did yesterday. Still not good, but you solved as much in one evening as I have in four months."

It made me feel good to hear that. And yet...Gunner had looked undeniably sour when I stepped into the kitchen this morning. "What's your request?" I prodded him.

"Next time you walk into danger, please take me with you," he growled. He pulled out a brand new cell phone, texted me its number right there and then. And yet, despite the humanity of the gesture, I could see his inner wolf wild and angry behind sienna human eyes.

The two-legged pack leader was impressed by my lancing of the pack's metaphorical boils. But his four-legged counterpart was terrified I could have been even more badly hurt. And he was right to have sat us down for this conversation, because for one split second I was spitting mad.

How *dared* he distrust my ability to protect myself from danger? How *dared* he make a fox come begging for a wolf's help every time she felt like taking a piss?

The anger washed over me...and out of me. Then I was taking Gunner's hand in mine, glad to see my fingers were no more furry than his had been.

Because I wouldn't have asked any less of Gunner. I wouldn't have wanted him running off into battle on his lonesome. So—

"I promise," I told him. "I won't do anything dangerous without telling you. As long as you make the same promise in return."

Chapter 13

We sealed the deal with a kiss...or would have if a shiny steel blade hadn't sliced down between us just as our lips were a whisper away from meeting.

"Really?" the voice emerged from the other end of the blade even as the weapon twisted so it menaced only me. "You want us to be trained by someone who doesn't notice an armed swordswoman walking up beside her in a public space?"

I tried to see who was speaking, but I couldn't move without slicing my own jugular. So I used half of my attention to create a metal choker around my sensitive neck while responding to the opponent I still couldn't see.

"You want to be trained? It seems like you already know what you're doing." With my words as cover, I materialized the other half of my magic into a sword that clanked ever so slightly as it settled on the step below me.

Meanwhile, Gunner—darn him—merely chuckled as he stood and descended down the stairs away from the female with her sword at my neck. "Looks like you're busy," he noted. "How about we meet up for lunch later?"

"What happened to our promise?" I complained. "You watch my back, I watch your back?"

"You appear to have everything under control."

As we bantered, I used half my senses to guess how many werewolves had snuck up on us. Because I wasn't just facing the single female whose blade was now separated from me by a thin sheet of magical metal. No, from the scents and sounds, I'd guess there were half a dozen here at least.

Despite his dismissal, Gunner still hovered, ready to assist me. But this was clearly a problem I needed to solve myself. The trick was to make my escape not only effective but also flashy enough to prevent a repeat occurrence....

Stepping onto my sword hilt with one foot, I flicked it upward with the other. Then I twirled and caught my own weapon even as I used the metallic choker to knock my opponent's blade aside.

Edward's daughter. I wasn't sure whether to be pleased or daunted by the fact that my opponent was instantly recognizable. Ditto by the sheer number of females arrayed behind her back.

There were fifteen bystanders, most young but a few middle-aged or older. Becky wasn't among them, and even though a few faces looked vaguely familiar I didn't know anybody's name. Had they really come to me for lessons, or was this the female version of the welcoming committee that had left me black and blue yesterday when I failed to respect my place within the pack?

Whatever the sword wielder's purpose, I didn't slow my steps to debrief her nor did I bother to introduce myself. Instead, I slipped beneath my primary opponent's guard, gauging my angle carefully. She was clearly a clothes hog, her outfit perfectly coordinated and apparently tailored to her form.

So I hit her where it hurt the most. Turning my blade at an angle, I sliced off the lace collar lining the top half of her shirt. Her free hand rose to catch the descending fabric even as I slashed slices into her tight-fitting pants.

There was an art to ruining clothes without scratching the skin beneath it. Good thing I was a pro at that art.

Behind her, the other werewolves were wide-eyed, some gasping, a few giggling. Meanwhile, Edward's daughter seemed torn between anger...and was that amusement fighting for dominance on her face?

I'd almost forgotten Gunner was waiting until he spoke into the silence. "Yep, you definitely have this covered," Gunner noted. "Enjoy your girl time." And he strode away down the sidewalk, leaving me to teach swordsmanship to females who might or might not actually want to be taught.

"I'M ELIZABETH," EDWARD'S daughter told me as she shifted her sword to her left hand and stretched out the other so we could shake on it. "And you're impressive."

"Well, you're clearly not a beginner yourself," I countered, providing a bit of well-deserved praise to reduce the sting of her recent loss.

"Gunner gave us a DVD to practice with in August," the youngest girl interjected from behind the group's spokeswoman. "But it's hard to understand if you're not face to face with your teacher."

"So we'll practice face to face," I assured her. "Just give me a minute to gather some gear...." And I headed back up to the cottage in search of face masks and blade protectors, glad I'd packed all of my teaching equipment even though Gunner hadn't bothered to give me a heads-up about my soon-to-be place within his clan prior to my move.

I had this covered, though. So it was hard to blame Gunner for his omission as we started with the basics, giving me time to take stock of my students one by one. They were better than I would have expected after just two months of DVD lessons, but they *did* have shifter agility to call upon after all.

Still, there were inevitable blunders. "No, not like that," I corrected, stepping up to place my own hand over the hilt of the oldest woman's weapon. "You want to—"

"—Get back in the kitchen where you belong!"

We all turned to face the interrupter of our lesson, and I didn't need to see the pack bonds or smell the sulfur to know there was definite rot developing between this twenty-something bystander and the females armed with swords. What I couldn't decipher was the reason for the former's venom. Had he been spurned by one of the young ladies, or was he simply threatened by any shift to the status quo?

"If you'd like to join us," I told the male carefully while waving in the appropriate direction, "there are extra masks over on the porch."

"*Join* you?" The werewolf looked like he'd smelled something vile. And maybe he had with his head stuffed so high up his own butt. "I'd rather f—"

"*Move it.*"

Yet again, a werewolf had snuck up on me while I wasn't looking. But this time the arriving shifter was a friend. Tank's hand landed on the other male's shoulder so hard the latter stumbled and almost fell to the pavement. Nonetheless, the nameless male puffed up his chest and opened his mouth to spew out more invective...until, that is, his gaze and Tank's met.

I reached out my hand, wanting to warn Tank that fighting my battles wasn't going to help matters in the long run. But Gunner's lieutenant was too intent upon subduing his opponent with a single glance. Sure enough, our unwelcome audience member shriveled beneath Tank's stare-down, turning without another word and beating it out of sight.

"I guess that's our cue to get back to work," I noted, trying to keep frustration out of my voice. How was I supposed to do my job as the alpha's mate if well-meaning werewolves kept stepping in and doing that work for me?

But this time Tank's gaze met mine as he shook his head. "They'll have to finish up by themselves, chica. Because there's someone here to see you. She says she's your grandmother."

Chapter 14

Grand*mother*. It was almost as if my struggles with Kira and the resultant yearnings had created a family member where none previously existed. Not even realizing I was leaving Tank behind me, I padded down the road in the direction he must have come from, drawn forward by what I suspected was a pack-like bond but couldn't confirm without werewolf blood to energize my latent skills.

Only, it turned out I didn't need a turbocharge to solve the mystery. Because an old woman with a fox-like cant to her neck walked spryly out to meet me. "Granddaughter." She was tiny but not wizened. Clearly Japanese in a way my sister and I were not. The stranger-who-wasn't-a-stranger inclined her head ever so slightly, then frowned when I fumbled through a mirroring nod by way of reply.

And that show of disapproval was enough to knock loose my rose-tinted glasses. Family connection or no, it was time to remember that I was in charge of my own destiny. Step one: Figure out how and why kitsunes—because this was clearly another kitsune—kept showing up on our doorstep. Step two: Get rid of this particular kitsune before the pack blew its collective lid.

So, ignoring the fact that I was sorely in need of an older family member who had a clue how to raise a teenager, I forced my voice to turn hard as I demanded: "How did you find us?"

But the old woman was having none of it. "I'll answer all of your questions, granddaughter," she told me, "but not standing out here in the cold. Remember—patience is bitter..."

"...But its fruit is sweet." Despite myself, I mouthed the end of the proverb right alongside her, remembering the way Mama had admonished me with those exact same words when I childishly complained about inevitable daily delays.

And maybe that's why I didn't protest when this elderly stranger led me back down the street away from my cottage and toward an RV parked at the edge of the Green where breakfast had been served yesterday evening. Maybe that's why I didn't pull out my sword and threaten five of the most handsome males I'd ever seen—the old woman's entourage?—as they brushed past me to begin cranking out the vehicle's walls.

Even without benefit of the additions, the RV was the largest one I'd ever seen. "Wow." I didn't mean to, but the word emerged from my mouth as easily as if I was Kira and always spoke before I thought.

"One of many benefits of our heritage, granddaughter," the old woman told me, face mischievous as if she was letting me in on the first secret of many she'd been saving just for me. But rather than elaborating, she raised both eyebrows, slipped up the stairs someone had set out for her, then disappeared inside.

I itched to follow, but I didn't immediately. Instead, I turned and peered back toward the spot we'd recently left behind.

I'd only been gone for a moment, but already the female werewolves had dispersed, taking Tank along with them. Instead, Gunner had reappeared, broad shoulders sagging ever so slightly from the weight of his load. Meanwhile, the air between us smelled just a little bit foul with the same scent that hung around clan central every time something was gearing up to go wrong.

I was adding to that load—and perhaps to that scent?—by spending time with this supposed grandmother. And yet...I couldn't quite talk myself into telling this strange kitsune to leave without discovering whether she really was related to me first.

So, without meeting Gunner's eyes or requesting his permission, I clambered up the stairs and entered the unknown.

"YOU MAY CALL ME SOBO," the old woman informed me as I stepped into a space perfectly designed to fit everything one woman and five men might need in their living room. There were two couches, a recliner, heat blowing out of wall registers, a picture window opening onto forest, and even a large TV covering the opposite wall.

Despite the various seating areas, however, two of her companions—definitely human if my nose served me—knelt on either side of Sobo's easy chair. Both gazed up at her adoringly, and in response she patted their heads as if they were dogs.

That was...odd. But I was here for answers, not to pass judgment. So I walked deeper into the old woman's domain, feeling the door click shut behind me, presumably closed by yet another member of Sobo's silent entourage.

And that's enough of thinking about random humans, I reminded myself. Ignoring the males' strange behavior, I instead rolled the unfamiliar name around in my mouth like a new food I wasn't quite sure I liked the flavor of. "Sobo," I repeated aloud.

"My name is Sakurako," the old woman clarified. "But it is appropriate that my granddaughter call me Sobo instead. It means grandmother. Or, maybe...grandma?"

And even though I hated myself for being so simple, the idea that I was being offered a pet name melted the cold ache that had settled in my stomach ever since Kira started treating me like an enemy rather than a friend. It reminded me of the days when I hadn't been the matriarch of my own tiny family, when Mama had called me Mai-chan and hugged me close up against her waist before spinning me around the kitchen in our own made-up dance.

Blinking away that seductive memory, I forced myself to remember Oyo's fear and the problems facing Atwood clan central. Even if Sobo was my relative, that wasn't the most important point to consider now.

So I remained standing rather than taking a seat on the couch Sobo motioned to. And I repeated my own words from earlier, this time demanding a reply. "How did you find us?" I asked a second time, piercing the old woman with a gaze that refused to be sidetracked by proverbs, a luxurious residence, or even familial love.

"Direct, just like your mother." For the first time since I'd met her, Sobo seemed uncomfortable, shifting on the plush leather beneath her. And just like Mama when she was unhappy, Sobo's face remained smooth save her cheek, which twitched ever so slightly up by her left eye.

I opened my mouth, struck by the similarity. Before I could relent, however, Sobo answered my question.

"I felt the moment your sister merged with her star ball," Sobo told me. "I thought that was *your* coming of age, actually. What a...surprise...to discover my daughter chose undue fertility over long life."

I knew this wasn't the whole story. It wasn't lost upon me that—if her story was to be believed—our grandmother had felt Kira's presence four months earlier and in an entirely different spot from the one where she'd finally tracked us down.

Still, the tremor in the old woman's hands told the truth of her pain at the loss of a daughter. The sad bend of Sobo's neck was so much like Mama's during her darkest hours that I sank down onto the couch despite myself and cupped her papery fingers in both of my hands.

Whether or not this old woman was here under false pretenses, I believed she was my grandmother. And that meant she deserved my compassion and respect.

"Sobo, I'm sorry," I murmured. And I could feel the bonds of family clicking closed between us with my touch.

Chapter 15

"That must have come as a shock," I continued, trying to send warm healing energy into the older woman through both my words and my fingers. The two humans flanking us leaned in closer, like dogs offering comfort through their presence alone.

"It was a disappointment," the older woman countered. But rather than pulling away from my touch, she squeezed my fingers one second longer while offering me the fairy tale I'd spent a decade pretending I didn't crave with the yearning of an orphaned fox pup.

"*You*, however, were not a disappointment," my grandmother informed me. "I have long searched for a granddaughter. A firm, strong woman to train and to nurture. A brave kitsune to carry on the family name after I leave this plane."

As she spoke, she gazed at me with eyes so dark they might as well have been Mama's. There was a warmth to her smile now, a pride that seemed to stroke my cheeks while making my spine straighten.

And like a fish in a pond, I rose toward the bobber, opened my mouth to accept the offered nourishment. Of course, bait inevitably comes with a fish hook. But at that moment, I didn't even care that this was bound to end in pain....

Before I could speak, however, Sakurako continued, "I just need one small favor from you, granddaughter. Nothing major. No skin off your teeth."

"Yes, Sobo?" I nudged her when she turned silent.

Rather than answering, the old woman peered at me for one long moment, her pursed lips reminding me so much of Mama's that my breath caught in my throat. Then, finally, she told me the price of becoming part of her family.

"All I need from you," she finished, "is that black fox you and your sister are hiding. Oyo is difficult, dangerous. Too much for you to handle on your own without further training. Turn her over to me to take care of, then we can build up our family as it should be with the next generation at its heart."

"OF COURSE, SOBO."

I could feel the words lingering there on the tip of my tongue, ready to escape if I unclenched my teeth and let my mouth fall open. Which was absurd given that what Sakurako was asking was both dishonorable and patently unwise...while also going against my oath to the black-furred kitsune both Gunner and I had promised to protect.

Worse was the knowledge that the woman before me wasn't manipulating me via magic the way Liam had done four months earlier. No, this decision—chosen family versus blood family—would be mine to make and mine alone.

I couldn't say no and I wouldn't say yes, so I merely disentangled my hand from Sakurako's and stepped backwards. Meanwhile, the old woman's words flew after me like a thrusting sword.

"Next time I see you, granddaughter, I will expect your answer."

And I couldn't even shake my head as I stumbled out the door and shut it between us. My answer. I had no answer. Wouldn't bring even more conflict to this ailing pack, and at the same time couldn't talk myself into giving either Sakurako or Oyo away.

I have a grandmother. A manipulative grandmother who appeared to possess a heart of ice, but a grandmother nonetheless.

Striding blindly down the street, I imagined for one awestruck moment becoming part of a large, loving family. Possessing older, wiser family members able and willing to steer me away from bad decisions before the results slapped me in the face.

Why did even dreaming of such a rosy picture feel like a mistake?

I was so lost in the confusion of my roiling feelings that I nearly walked past the two werewolves half-hidden by the trunk of the oak tree that spread huge and magnificent across the pack's gathering space. But I couldn't miss the sulfurous stench that rose around me, cuing me to extend my senses just as Gunner murmured, "I understand that Edward."

"*You* understand? I don't think you do, *alpha*," Edward countered. And, through the brush, I could just barely see him shake off Gunner's physical show of support so violently that any other pack leader would have taken mortal offense at the slight. As it was, I could barely smell the faintest hint of electricity invading the sulfur as Gunner tamped his frustration down enough to reply.

"I understand you thought this pack was worth saving or you wouldn't have stayed when so many others left with my brother," Gunner answered, not a single growl in his tone even though his voice grew firmer as his statement progressed. "I ask that you remember our purpose here before..."

"Before you act like a spiteful child and tear up everything your father built? Before your kitsune concubine makes so many mistakes there's no pack to even attempt saving? You let her do this even though she's not really your mate?"

Edward was so red-faced, I was a little afraid he might succumb to a heart attack. A little afraid...and also very faintly hoping that the greatest rabble-rouser in Atwood territory would take himself out of the picture without either me or Gunner having to do the deed ourselves. *Concubine, my ass.*

"*Edward.*" Now Gunner did finally growl out a chastisement.

"Don't bark at me, Gunner." Edward stood taller as he spoke, a sure sign of a werewolf in search of a fur-form turf battle. "I remember when you were a toddler gnawing on your father's fingers. I never thought I'd see the day you forgot your duty over some fox in a skirt."

The last time I'd worn a skirt was during an ill-fated job interview. But I think we all got Edward's point, because this time Gunner's order was both more specific and more adamant. "*You will respect my mate.*"

"I'll respect those who deserve respect," Edward countered. "And if you don't wake up and do your duty to this pack before kitsunes invite in our neighbors, then I'll correct my own mistake and join your brother in exile. You know half the pack will follow me." He paused, then threw down the gauntlet. "And is it truly exile when no one but the weak are left behind?"

I only realized my fists were clenched and my sword visible when the tip of the latter caught in the hem of my trousers and nearly tripped me. *Okay, that's not helping matters,* I chided, imagining literally stumbling into Gunner and Edward's conversation before falling flat on my face.

Edward would be enraged. Gunner would be mortified. No, that definitely wouldn't help defuse the older male's anger...but what would?

My fingers slid across the face of my cell phone, Ransom's unanswered text rising up in my mind's eye. *"I grant you free passage to and from Kelleys Island if you'd like to come and talk about it."*

The message suddenly seemed less like a trap and more like much-needed breathing space given the drama I'd be leaving behind.

Chapter 16

Relieved of her load of boxes, Old Red rumbled down the highway with fewer complaints than she'd regaled me with previously. Unfortunately, that didn't make me feel any better about driving away from Atwood pack central at the exact moment when my sister and Oyo needed me most.

Beep!

Glancing sideways at the empty passenger seat, I couldn't help smiling at Kira's text. *"Stop worrying. I'm fine,"* she chided. Clearly, Oyo's pep talk—and the chocolate, potato chips, and hot-water bottle I'd left the teenager with—had rebooted her ailing mood.

I would have replied, too, but Old Red was far from a driverless vehicle. In fact, she was prone to drifting sideways, a problem that I knew would be remedied once I got the tires balanced and aligned.

But I'd stopped accepting Gunner's financial support the moment Kira was adopted, and my part-time summer gig teaching fencing at the Y hadn't paid very well. A wolf wouldn't have batted an eyelash at accepting pack largesse, but I was very much a fox shifter. So while my bank account slowly grew into an appreciable buffer, I kept my hands very firmly grasping the wheel.

A difficult matter when the chime of another incoming text drew my eyes to the phone a second time in a matter of moments. *"Nobody's eaten me or Oyo. Not even when we played fox tag on Allen and Tank's heads. That was really fun."*

Flicking on the turn signal in the direction of the ferry dock, Oyo's black fur dueled with the sienna tinge of Gunner's irises in my mind's eye. The pack seemed to be doing quite well without me present. So why did I feel so guilty about taking a fox-like stab at the heart of the problem on my own?

Guilty or guiltless, I was almost there and the decision was long since made. Old Red's brakes squealed as I pulled to a halt behind two other cars lined up at the ticket booth. And I took advantage of the lack of forward momentum to text Kira back. *"Remember you're a guest in Atwood clan central,"* I told her. *"Take care of Oyo but be smart about it."*

Then I turned away from the phone and tuned up my senses. Because I wasn't safely secluded in Atwood territory with Oyo and my sister. Instead, I'd spent the last few hours passing through outpack land where lawless werewolves did as they pleased...which likely included slaughtering vagrant kitsunes on sight.

As if my thoughts had called danger into existence, hairs rose along the back of my neck half a second before a knock shook the nearest window. Inhaling sharply, I turned to take in the visage of a werewolf...and not one I was familiar with either.

This male was just as tall and broad as Gunner. But his face was craggier, as if he'd been punched a dozen times then healed without courtesy of a doctor visit. Not a pack wolf then.

The question became—was my window rapper a curious stranger, or the outguard watching over Ransom's exiled lair?

"GET OUT."

His voice was soft, barely a whisper. But it carried through the window and stroked tendrils of ice up and down my spine. And while my impulse was to make a U-turn and head back up the highway, I instead rolled down the window a fraction of an inch, raised my chin, and sniffed.

Because I should have been able to tell if this male was Ransom's lackey by the presence or absence of that tongue-tingling ozone. And I also could have, perhaps, detected his loyalty by the presence or absence of a rotten-egg smell.

Unfortunately, all I could make out from inside my metal cocoon was the overwhelming stench of diesel, tar, and half-rotten fish emanating from the nearby lake.

"Why should I?" I asked, playing for time while I calculated other options. One car had already rolled past the ticket booth while the driver in the second vehicle was busy buying a pass for the ferry loading at the end of the road. If I waited until the coast was clear, perhaps I could gun it and apologize to the humans for not paying even as I left this werewolf behind on the mainland....

"Not gonna happen," the male said, clearly picking up on my plans via scent and body language. "Get out," he repeated. "Ransom wants me to take you across in our boat."

Get on a boat with an unknown werewolf? Even if this stranger knew I was here to meet Ransom, the answer was still nopety, nope, nope, nope.

The wind changed at that moment, pushing the werewolf's scent through the crack and into my nostrils. He smelled of wet gravel and newly mown lawn without a hint of ozone...which, unfortunately, could have meant anything at all. I didn't know enough about werewolves to understand whether their scents shifted when they evicted themselves from a pack as a unit. So I didn't really know if a loyal ally of Gunner's brother would still boast the distinctive Atwood scent.

"I'd prefer to stick to the original plan," I countered just as my phone trilled from the passenger seat. And even though, instinct demanded that I keep my attention tuned to the stranger, I still couldn't resist glancing down at the screen.

"Eric is mine," Ransom had texted, making me shiver and peer out across the nearly empty parking area to figure out how the alpha had known I was balking at the pickup. There was nothing to see, however. Just the ticket booth, the waiting ferry, and a couple of empty vehicles parked off to one side.

Which meant Ransom was guessing, playing cat and mouse with me. Too bad for him that I was a fox instead of a mouse.

A fox who noted what Ransom *hadn't* said as much as what he *had* said. The exiled alpha had been the one to invite me into his not-quite-territory in the first place, and he hadn't issued an ultimatum telling me to ride across with Eric or go home without the offered meeting either.

Which meant Ransom wanted this get-together as much as I did. Had as good as handed over leverage to use against this shifter guarding the virtual gate.

While I pondered, the unnamed werewolf had been padding around the vehicle like a stalking panther. And the fact that he wasn't hovering directly over me made it just a little easier to expose my neck as I leaned over to pop open the lock on the passenger-side door.

"I'm not getting on a boat alone with a strange werewolf," I said once I'd straightened. "But if you want to ride across with me on the public ferry, then I'm game."

Thirty minutes cooped up in Old Red alongside a simmering werewolf felt like three hours. But it was better than the alternative—jumping out of the parked vehicle and letting Eric wander around behind my back.

So I stuck it out, made the bare minimum pleasantries, and allowed the shifter to guide me to my destination after the ferry workers finally ushered us off the floating prison on the other side. "Left," Eric grunted as we turned onto the main street, rolling past huge houses with green, sweeping lawns and lakeside vistas. Ransom might have left Atwood pack central with nothing more than the clothes on his back, but he appeared to have landed quite solidly on his feet.

"Here," Eric said at last, as we passed an ice-cream parlor crowded with hungry tourists then a small but well-maintained city park. My guide barely waited for the car to slow before opening his door and hurrying down the sidewalk away from me. By the time I'd pulled the key from the ignition, he was already out of sight.

"Now what?" I murmured, sniffing the air surreptitiously. It would be hard to find Eric's scent in the midst of all of these tourists, people pressing past me as I blocked the flow of the human tide....

But I needn't have worried. Because as I turned in a slow circle, I caught sight of Ransom watching from behind a restaurant's plate-glass window. The elder Atwood brother was cupping a mug of coffee, his shoulders hunched ever so subtly. As if being a pack leader in exile was harder than he'd initially assumed.

Or maybe that was just my imagination. Because as our gazes snapped together, my breath caught in reaction. *This* wasn't the look of a beaten-down pack leader; it was the stare of a two-legged predator trying to decide whether I'd be better eaten with biscuits or toast.

Run, run, run, instinct told me. And I had to forcibly pry my fingers away from the car door to prevent myself from hopping back inside and gunning it out of there.

We were separated by thirty feet of air and a thick pane of glass, so Ransom couldn't smell my terror. Still, he must have noted the change in my demeanor anyway. Because his mouth spread into his characteristic smirking smile. Then, crooking a single finger, he raised his eyebrows and motioned for me to approach.

"SICK OF MY BROTHER already?" the elder Atwood sibling greeted me as the door whooshed shut behind my back. My muscles tensed in reaction, the reality of being stuck inside a nearly empty restaurant with an alpha werewolf who smelled of fur giving me the urge to turn on my heel and hurry back the way I'd come.

I was done retreating however. Instead, it was time to attack.

"This isn't about your brother," I countered as I padded forward on the balls of my feet, magic whirling invisibly around my fingers. "This is about loose lips and strangers suddenly knowing that clan Atwood has taken in two kitsunes. How did that information go mainstream, do you think?"

"Perhaps you should ask my brother," Ransom countered, bringing the conversation back where he clearly wanted it to stay. "But—wait—Gunner doesn't know you came to speak with me or you'd never be here unguarded. So what does that make *you* for sneaking out behind your alpha's back?"

A mate rather than a sycophant, I wanted to answer, never mind Edward's assessment of the matter. But, instead, I merely shrugged and murmured, "A fox."

Despite my best intentions to hold myself wolf-like and tall, I couldn't prevent my body from swiveling as I spoke, cringing at having my identity outed in a public space. Because I wasn't on Atwood turf any longer where pack-leader compulsion required that kitsunes be treated respectfully. Good thing the restaurant really was as empty as I'd initially supposed.

Ransom's laugh brought my head back around to face him. "A cagey fox," he agreed, pouring a packet of sugar into his coffee then stirring the liquid around with a plastic straw. "But you want something, now don't you? Which means you'll give me something in return."

Ah, here we go. Slipping into the booth across from him, I leaned forward despite the instinct that told me not to squeeze myself into an enclosed space with an alpha wolf. "Perhaps," I answered. And since werewolves were big fans of dominance rituals, I met and held his gaze for several long seconds after that.

Ransom had eyes exactly like his brother's. Deep and brown and not quite dark enough to appear black even in dimly lit corners. Also like his brother, Ransom smelled of Atwood ozone, the scent so sharp it made the hairs inside my nostrils itch.

Unlike Gunner, however, Ransom was always on the hunt for an overt show of submission. "I want your debt," he told me now, voice smooth as silk caressed by sunlight. "Like the debt you owed my brother, to be called in whenever I wish."

I shook my head, not so much in rejection as in denial of the situation. Because what Ransom apparently failed to realize was that, by coming to him for a favor, I'd already accepted that I'd owe a brand new debt to this exiled werewolf. Accepted that...along with the wedge I knew it would form between myself and his brother, the same brother who called himself my mate.

"No?" Ransom prodded.

"You're an idiot," I answered, my words unheated. "Yes, I will be in your debt to the degree you help me track down this kitsune's history."

As I spoke, I pulled out my cell phone, Oyo's picture already drawn up on its screen. I didn't have any image of my grandmother, but Kira had snapped this shot after our bonding ritual then had texted the image to me for use in my questioning.

I didn't explain any of that to Ransom, however. Instead, I angled the phone in his direction while bracing myself for smug recognition. After all, the feelers Gunner had put out this morning suggested the neighboring packs were, indeed, sending an unusual number of messages back and forth between the clans. Which pointed a finger at the brother who had means, motive, and opportunity to throw the original Atwood pack to the neighboring wolves.

But all I got from Ransom was cold intensity. "Name?" he demanded as he stared at my phone's screen.

"Oyo," I answered. I hadn't thought to request a surname while she was human so I had nothing else to provide other than a reiteration of my original request. "Do you have any idea who might know that foxes now live within Gunner's pack?"

"No," the exiled alpha answered, head shaking as his resemblance to Gunner deepened. Then, giving me the answer I wanted but for a reason I couldn't quite decipher: "But I certainly intend to find out."

Chapter 18

Despite my relatively benign conversation with Ransom, I was no more confident that werewolves would leave me alone when I emerged from the restaurant than I had been going into it. Sure enough, the air when I stepped out onto the sidewalk was redolent with fur, and I found my feet moving faster than I'd intended as I scurried back toward my car.

Inside, I flicked the locks, turned the key in the ignition…then noticed that the engine-temperature gauge wasn't as cold as I'd expected after a prolonged resting period. Biting my lip, I considered popping the hood and checking coolant levels. But I couldn't afford for Ransom to see inside the trunk if I went rooting around for the requisite tools….

Meanwhile, during those few seconds I pondered car repair, a mob of werewolves had already materialized, traveling rapidly toward me from opposite ends of the street. Sandwiched in the middle were dozens of human tourists, bound to spook at a shifter altercation that could attract the attention of non-shifter police.

So I'll deal with potential overheating on the ferry, I decided. After all, that shifter-free zone was only a few minutes' drive away.

Backing out of my parking spot, a werewolf snarled from inches behind my taillights. Slamming down my foot to pull forward away from him, I almost ran over the one familiar shifter standing two-legged in front of my car.

Elle. She was brown-eyed just like Gunner and Ransom, and now that I knew her heritage I could easily see the resemblance to both brothers in her face.

In human parlance, Elle was my sister-in-law. She was also my mentor and one of the most friendly werewolves I'd ever met. During stolen afternoons spread across the previous summer, we'd talked about everything from kitsune magic to girly gossip. And, in the process, we must have started building a pack bond because I now felt my body lean toward her as something immaterial tugged at my gut.

"Meet me at the ferry dock. I'll buy you a coffee," the other female mouthed, the words easy to pick out despite the smeared glass of my windshield. In that moment, it was hard to remember that we hadn't written or spoken since Elle and her mate left with Ransom rather than staying in Atwood clan central with the rest of us.

Our incipient friendship had been frozen by the stubbornness of two pack leaders, Gunner mandating that no exile could return even for a visit and Ransom retaliating with the order that no communication was allowed between the two clans at all. So Elle and I had lost the chance to talk, not only about shared interests but also about the fact that I was the one responsible for her twin brother's death.

I'd never been able to make that loss up to her, but Elle must have found it in her heart to forgive me anyway. Because her eyes now crinkled up into a smile, and I felt my own face opening happily in response.

This moment was our chance to thaw our relationship. To place it in the sun, water it, and watch it grow.

And yet...I couldn't do that. Not when Elle and I had made our respective decisions about pack affiliation months earlier. Not when I risked so much by parking Old Red on Kelleys Island a minute longer than I absolutely had to.

So shaking my head then averting my eyes from Elle's crestfallen expression, I drove away from her down the street.

I MADE IT APPROXIMATELY a quarter of the way back to clan central before a white cloud started gushing out from beneath the hood of my vehicle. *Oops.* I'd let the disappointment on Elle's face sidetrack me, and now Old Red was paying the price.

"Shh, quiet, you can do this," I crooned at my ancient sedan as I pulled her over to the side of the highway. Was that steam or smoke emerging through cracks in the metal? It suddenly looked more like the latter, with gray twisting up to spiral through the white.

"No! You can't do this!" I demanded, forcing myself not to pound on the steering wheel. "You know why you can't do this...." Even alone in the vehicle in outpack territory, I couldn't quite make myself mention the precious cargo still stashed in the trunk.

I *could* do something about the upcoming disaster however. Ignoring the wind of a passing tractor-trailer shaking the vehicle around me, I frantically pulled levers at my feet before thrusting open the door. A car honked in protest, swerving away but still coming far too close for comfort. Meanwhile, my attention flew straight to the gas tank and I swore loudly—I'd opened the wrong metal lid by mistake.

Hopping back into the driver's seat, I looked down this time as I hunted for plastic handles beside my feet. *There.* I wasn't quite breathing as I located the appropriate lever then emerged a second time.

Emerged into smoke that choked me even as I raced away from the front end of the vehicle. Had noxious gases gathered in the rear compartment that wasn't intended to carry passengers? Had...?

"Breathe." Gunner emerged from the trunk, his arms settled around me even as he drew me away from Old Red at a trot. Together, we fled as fleetly as two-legged shifters are able to. And despite the fact that he had spent hours hiding in the trunk to provide backup without spooking his brother, I was the one shaking as we raced backwards away from my car.

Gunner is fine, I reminded myself. *Get it together.* And, finally, the alpha's solid presence beside me was enough to provide breathing room in which to glance back over my shoulder at the smoking car we'd so recently left behind.

"It's not going to explode," my mate promised. Then, rightly understanding my body's twitch, he corrected himself. "*She.* She's not going to explode. But Old Red might not be quite the same after this."

And that was okay as long as Gunner was safely beside me rather than asphyxiating in the trunk of the still smoking vehicle. I squeezed his hand hard enough to be certain I wasn't dreaming...then I buried my face in his shoulder so I wouldn't have to watch the devastation of what had been my pride and joy the day before.

Old Red wasn't much, but she was my first stab at self-owned transportation. It was hard watching her erupt into a cloud of smoke.

"You probably want to know about Ransom," I murmured into the fabric of Gunner's sweatshirt, attempting to distract myself.

"I do. But first let me call a tow truck."

Which—capable werewolf—he managed to do without dislodging my limpet-like attachment to his body. The moment of letting him fix everything served as a balm to my soul.

Still, I wasn't used to being dependent on anyone else to solve my problems. So by the time Gunner hung up the phone, I was ready to take a peek at my car—no longer smoking quite so badly—then to answer the questions that had to be rolling through Gunner's head.

"He didn't know anything about Oyo, but he said he'd ask around for us." Then, taking a step backwards without separating our intertwined fingers, I relayed the part I would have been worried about in his place. "Your brother looked tired but healthy," I informed him. Ransom had also appeared predatory and wolfish. But the tiredness, I figured, was what Gunner most wanted to know about.

"Leading a pack is hard work," the alpha beside me rumbled, pulling me back up against his skin.

And now that I thought about it, Gunner boasted the same predatory stance his brother did, along with the same world-weary cant to his neck. So maybe Old Red imploding would lead to something good after all. Because Gunner sorely needed a break from his pack, craved a little time to forget how badly divided formerly close friends had become.

"What if we got a room and dealt with transportation in the morning?" I suggested before Gunner could place the call he'd queued up to his second-in-command. Sure, someone could come get us...but would it kill the pack for us to steal one evening for ourselves before that occurred?

I held my breath, expecting Gunner's responsibilities to take precedence over his own wishes. Only, this time I turned out to be mistaken.

"That's the best suggestion I've heard in hours," my mate rumbled. Then, preventing me from answering in the easiest way possible, he bent down to complete our far-too-often-interrupted kiss.

Chapter 19

Unfortunately, everything crumbled once we reached our rundown motel on the seedy side of town. The problem wasn't the accommodations, either. In fact, by the time we checked in, I had eyes for one thing only: the bed.

It was queen-sized, just right for two people who liked each other and hadn't been in the same zip code for an entire season. Plus, Gunner and I had shared a house with keen-eared shifters even when we cohabited, which added to my body's frustration by quite a lot.

So, toeing out of my shoes, I took his hand and tugged him in the appropriate direction before shedding layer after layer of clothing. "Mates shouldn't spend so much time away from each other," I murmured, reaching over to tug Gunner's head down so his lips were within reach.

But his neck didn't bend as predicted. Nor did his clothes magically fly in the opposite direction the way I willed them to. Instead, Gunner's hands landed on my shoulders...and, very gently, he pushed me away from him until I fell into a seated position on the edge of the bed.

"Gunner?" I started, then went quiet so I could hear what he was muttering.

"Allen was right, the bastard," he growled, his words clearly not intended for me.

Allen not Edward? I remembered Edward calling me a concubine—understandable given his antipathy toward fox shifters. But I'd thought Allen liked me. The geeky werewolf certainly seemed willing to come when I pulled on his pack bond.

I was about to request clarification when Gunner finally met my eyes and offered exactly what I was about to ask for. "We aren't mates," he said, his simple words hitting me like a bombshell. "Well, you're my mate, but I'm not yours."

THE DETONATION EXPLODED deep within my belly, and like any wounded fox I lashed out in an attempt at self-preservation. "What are you talking about? I moved in with you, didn't I? I let myself get beaten up by werewolves. What greater commitment do you need than that?"

"I didn't ask you to fight my battles."

I should have known better than to bring up the ill-fated bacon episode. Still, the growled dismissal in Gunner's voice rubbed me entirely the wrong way.

Because I felt like I gave and gave and gave to this werewolf. Now he was telling me my compromises weren't good enough?

Which might explain why months of smoothed-over slights bubbled to the surface with the force of a volcanic eruption. "You said you wanted me to be part of the pack," I started, "so how exactly does that make my battles yours to take over? And let's talk about you insisting I take you with me to talk to Ransom. As if I'm just a weak woman who couldn't be trusted to deal with your brother on my own."

I hadn't realized how angry I was until I started speaking. How hurt I felt by werewolf instincts that might have been intended as supportive but instead came across as an undermining of my own authority and free will.

Gunner's patience, apparently, had been similarly strained by dealing with my vulpine nature. Or so I gathered as he snapped out his reply.

"I don't trust you to watch out for yourself because you don't do it," he spat back. "Perhaps you didn't notice the fact you almost died on the highway this evening? I *told* you that rustbucket wasn't safe enough to drive down the block let alone across the state."

"So you want to make another decision for me, is that it? You want to take over yet another aspect of my life?"

I expected him to yell a rebuttal. Because, yes, I was yelling. Heat suffused my face while my hands shook with the urge to turn into fists.

Only, Gunner didn't speak. Instead, he stalked over to the closet. Silently, he pulled the spare blanket and pillow off a shelf before retreating to a padded chair as far as he could get from the waiting mattress.

For my part, I headed in the opposite direction, swishing my mouth out in the bathroom while wishing I had toothpaste to cover the foul flavor of my own mistakes. Because my words—while based on reality—had been intentionally hurtful. Yes, Gunner stepped on my toes from time to time and impinged upon my autonomy. But my arguments became small and petty when I realized his only return complaint was that I didn't take good enough care of my own skin.

Whether or not I was wrong, I wasn't about to apologize. Not when doing so would relinquish the last shred of independence I clutched so frantically to my chest. Instead, I slipped alone between scratchy sheets while straining my ears in hopes Gunner would be the one to relent first.

And he did speak even though he didn't apologize. Instead, he explained what Allen had guessed and what I hadn't previously known.

"I'm going to spell it out for you," Gunner growled, his voice tight with barely restrained anger. "If you want to be my mate, it's a simple matter, although breaking a mate bond isn't easy and it isn't fun. So, be sure before you do it. Then say you're mated and I'll become your mate."

That was it? I opened my mouth to release words that would have ended the battle between us by confirming that I loved the frustrating yet adorable alpha curled into a chair on the other side of the hotel room. I opened my mouth...then choked as something stilled my tongue.

No, not something—some*one*. Or make that several someones.

Because promising myself to Gunner meant promising I wouldn't take Kira and flee if living in the pack became too dangerous. Meanwhile, a bond as ironclad as Gunner was suggesting meant his own pack might suffer if they were unable to come to terms with a kitsune in their midst.

My breath caught as I realized I was caught on a ledge with yawning crevasses on both the right hand and the left hand, with only one small path leading to safety on the other side. I fully expected Gunner to push me toward that knife-edge trail, demanding a declaration I wasn't ready for. But instead, he let me off the hook.

"It's not a choice to be made hastily," he continued, his voice gravelly with repressed emotion. "Until you tell me to leave you, I'll still be here."

He *was* still there...and was just as heavy-handed about his urge to take over my life as ever. I hadn't missed the fact there was no promise to abide by my future decisions emanating from the opposite side of the room.

So I did what foxes do best—I slid out from under a difficult situation. Sighing, I closed my eyes and waited for sleep to descend. Tonight, I'd recover my equanimity. Tomorrow would be plenty soon enough to figure out the puzzle of becoming an alpha werewolf's mate.

Chapter 20

I woke to an Atwood male leaning over me...but not the one I'd gone to bed with. Instead, it was Ransom's eyes gleaming with approval as he took in my unclad state.

"My brother should learn to share," he murmured, lips twisting into a smirking smile. I didn't smell any actual arousal and had a feeling he was just being a jerk. But that didn't prevent me from closing my fingers around a sword that was abruptly under the bedclothes along with me, just in case.

Then I remembered what was missing from this picture. Where was Gunner and why wasn't he tearing out his brother's throat?

For half a second, I thought last night's argument had been more divisive than even I realized. Then the hotel-room door banged open and Gunner came in backwards, his hands full of a paper bag and a container of steaming coffee cups.

"I got you a..." he started. Then liquid splattered as he dropped my breakfast—or maybe, from the height of the sun outside the window, lunch—ruining the already stained carpet in front of the door.

Before Gunner could shift or roar or just strangle his brother, I leapt out of bed to prevent cold-blooded fratricide. But both brothers remained rooted where they'd been when they first saw each other, more expressions than I could identify flitting across nearly identical faces.

"So you didn't let her come alone after all," Ransom murmured after a moment, taking a single step toward his brother and giving me the space to slip into my clothes.

"She's my mate. I don't leave her," Gunner answered. "But I held true to the letter of our agreement. I didn't set foot on the soil of your land."

And in that moment, I learned what a werewolf bond looked like when it was shattered. Like two brothers who itched to hug each other but instead stood separated by far more than ten feet of musty air.

I shivered, realizing that the dull ache I felt from having to refuse Elle was nothing compared to Gunner and Ransom's agony. But they could still fix this. All it would take was the right gesture of reconciliation and I knew both brothers would embrace the other and put the previous four months firmly in the past.

So I held my breath and waited. Waited so long, in fact, that I not only started breathing again but inhaled the scent of donuts disintegrating in a pool of coffee on the floor. And when it became clear that neither brother was willing or able to speak about the real issue, I decided it was finally time to break the ice.

"You found something about Oyo?" I suggested, stepping into the no-man's-land of empty space between the brothers.

"What I found out is that everyone and their mother knows Atwood clan central is home to kitsunes," Ransom agreed, his eyes meeting mine with what actually looked like gratitude. "One of the outpack males we took in last month heard the story and apparently thought it was a good idea to spread it around outside our territory. He won't make that mistake again."

So Ransom's pack really was the source of the leak...and the problem was larger than either Gunner or I had supposed. I shivered, wondering if less friendly kitsunes—and werewolves—would be showing up at clan central by the time we got home.

But it wasn't cool to shoot the messenger. "You can ask for what I owe you," I reminded the older Atwood brother. "I'll be glad to fulfill my debt."

"Later. Maybe," Ransom answered. Then as abruptly as he'd appeared above me, he brushed past his brother and padded out the door.

"THE CAR IS TOAST."

An hour later, with a silent Gunner beside me, I stood on the other side of the counter in a well-lit automobile dealership and felt like I'd taken a misstep forward and stumbled off a cliff. "You mean it'll be expensive to repair her," I suggested. "How much are we talking? Five hundred dollars? Six hundred? More?"

The human glanced at me once with pity in his eyes, then returned his attention to Gunner. "For fifty bucks, we'll take it to the crusher. Or, if you're looking for a new set of wheels, Joe here can likely give you five percent off any new vehicle on the lot."

Joe nodded from a nearby counter, exuding the same smarmy pleasantry shared by salesmen everywhere. But that wasn't why my hackles rose. Instead, I tensed as Gunner hesitated, clearly wishing to replace my vehicle with something more reliable but at the same time well aware that I'd never let Old Red—and the freedom she represented—slip away without a fight.

Perhaps it was my flaring nostrils that won him over. Whatever the reason, after only a millisecond of internal debate, Gunner backed me up. "How much to repair the vehicle we brought in yesterday?"

"Two."

I wanted that to mean two hundred, but I knew from the way the mechanic twisted up his face that he meant a whole lot more. Two *thousand?* At the same time, my phone chimed and I glanced down, noting an incoming call.

From Kira. From a sister who usually texted, saying it was too time consuming to actually *talk* with me.

Reality was literally calling. So, caving to the inevitable, I told Gunner, "You deal with this." Then I stepped away to answer the phone.

Behind me, the werewolf dealt with the car situation in the exact way I didn't want him to. "You—make that discount ten percent and we'll take the best car on the lot."

"The *best* car?" I could see dollar signs rolling through the salesman's head as he considered a commission on what was bound to be the most expensive car he had available rather than the best. Meanwhile, I could feel my own debt piling back up like walls around me, just months after I'd last wiggled my way out from under its weight.

But Kira was speaking into my ear now, her words running together in a way that made hairs rise along the back of my neck. "Oyo wasn't here when

I woke up this morning," she said. "Tank and Allen aren't answering their cell phones. And there are scary noises coming from the direction of the Green. What do I do next?"

It looked like I had far greater problems than losing Old Red.

Chapter 21

"Maybe you should try calling Tank?" I offered three hours later as we sped along the final leg of our journey toward home. I was driving the shiny new sedan that was superior to Old Red in every way...at least from Gunner's point of view.

Not that we'd had time to argue about his vehicular decision. Instead, Gunner was trying to figure out what had happened at clan central during our absence, a task made significantly more difficult when everyone refused to answer their phones. Even Kira's texts had transitioned from vague to outright evasive as the afternoon faded closer and closer toward night.

Adding to our stress levels, there were werewolves who didn't belong scattered all along the drive home. First, the scent of fur had surrounded us at a service station well into Atwood territory where we'd stopped to fill my new car with gas. Old Red would have required refueling long before then, making me grudgingly admit that the new car's improved gas efficiency would save me money in the long run—money I wouldn't have to ask Gunner for.

Still, I refused to name our current ride, instead keeping my attention riveted on our surroundings. Sure enough, a flicker of movement out of the corner of my eye an hour later had resolved into a trio of unfamiliar wolves racing down the side of the interstate as if they owned the place.

"Not ours," Gunner had confirmed when I glanced in his direction. But we hadn't stopped to investigate. We couldn't afford to get sidetracked when the replies from Kira had stopped arriving by that point.

No wonder Gunner couldn't quite manage to come up with human words as he growled out a curt reply to my suggestion to call his most trusted lieutenant. *Of course*, he'd already tried Tank half a dozen times over the course of our travels. That went without saying. But it was better that

457

he beat his head against the cell phone than turn four-legged and feral as I drove.

Then we were there, the unmarked driveway disappearing into darkness beneath the glowering tree canopy. Gunner's hand—almost a paw—landed atop my arm as I prepared to flick on the headlights. "No," he ordered. "Park here."

Obediently, I pulled over and shut off the engine. Rolled down my window and listened to the night. It was quieter than it should have been, as if wildlife had fled in the face of a terrifying predator—like the wolf who now appeared by my side.

Gunner hadn't bothered to undress before shifting, and he wriggled out of his clothes as he stepped across my lap. The boxer shorts landing on my knee might have been intimate under other circumstances. As it was, I knew Gunner was merely angling for the window so he could make his escape.

"Wait," I told him...and he *did* wait just long enough for me to crack open the car door so we could disembark together. With a whisper of magic, my star ball materialized into my hand then solidified into the reassuring mass of a sword's hilt. At last, I was armed and ready to take off down the road at a run.

Only Gunner halted our forward motion a second time. Taking my left hand into his jaws as gently as if I was made of tissue paper, he pulled me off the road, through a hanging curtain of ivy...and onto a trail I hadn't known existed before today.

Which would have been no surprise if our move-in day had been my first introduction to Atwood territory. But Kira and I had come here at least half a dozen times over the last few months since Gunner had become the alpha in residence. I'd run nearby trails with Tank and Allen...and many times with Gunner himself. The fact I'd never been in this vegetation-shrouded tunnel suggested I'd been deliberately left out of the loop.

Is that how mates treat each other? Ignoring the twinge in my gut at the omission, I followed Gunner through the tunnel without protesting the past. There was no time to mull over hurt feelings when the setting sun made silence from my sister more ominous with every step.

After that, we traveled for several minutes in silence before Gunner stopped so abruptly that I almost stepped on his feet. I reached forward to catch my balance, steadying myself on his furry rump...

...Then my fingers clenched into fists as I heard what had stopped him. Outside our tunnel, the air rang with the clanging of swords.

NOW WE WERE RUNNING as best we could within the confined tunnel. And as the trail split in two before us, Gunner, to my distress, turned away from rather than toward the much louder battle sounds.

"But..." I started, then decided to trust him. And was glad I had when, barely a minute later, we emerged from the trees just behind the roiling melee.

This was the same spot of the ill-fated bacon breakfast. The same spot where Edward and I made our differences worse rather than better as we fought. So I wasn't entirely surprised to come out of the tunnel into fighting...I was merely shocked at the extent of the pitched battle made up of angry wolves.

It appeared as if the entire pack was present, the haze of sulfur so strong it nearly made me choke. All of them were human, too, as they sliced at their friends with wicked metal blades.

As I watched, Tank—the level-headed lawyer who used words as his weapon—slashed twin knives at a female I couldn't remember the name of but who'd attended my spur-of-the-moment swordsmanship class the day before. No milquetoast, his opponent grinned ferociously and fought back with a sword that looked remarkably like one of the advanced-level training blades I'd packed into a duffel. The only problem was, she'd removed the protective foam intended to shield the tip.

The female lunged forward with more grace than I remembered her being capable of. And, sure enough, her sword raised a streak of blood along Tank's forearm before the latter managed to knock the blow aside.

Now that I saw them together, in fact, I was relatively sure this same female had been flirting with Tank just a few weeks earlier. Which would have been fine if they'd only been sparring rather than, apparently, battling to the death.

Something was seriously wrong here. But all I could think was—*Kira, Kira, where is Kira?* Spinning, I ignored battling pack mates in search of the teenager I knew would be somewhere in their midst.

And there she was, on a picnic blanket in the center of the disaster, bouncing with excitement as Sakurako held her in place with one gnarled hand.

This was so wrong I didn't know where to begin chipping away at the problem. "Gunner," I started, speaking to the wolf vibrating with anger beside me.

Unfortunately, at that moment the battling shifters took note of my presence. And rather than offering the real or feigned respect they usually showed me, one in particular shed his facade of pleasantry and leapt away from his current opponent so he could threaten me instead.

Edward's face contorted with rage as he raised a massive ax over his head with both hands while roaring like a berserker. And all I thought was, *Gunner will have no doubt of Edward's allegiances now.*

Chapter 22

My sword was useless against an ax. But, luckily, my weaponry was magical. So instead of stabbing the attacking werewolf, I flattened my star ball out into a shield as the tremendous wedge fell toward me from above.

The weight, when the ax struck, was excruciating, the star ball's magical-yet-material gripping straps reverberating painfully within my hands. But my energy-infused armor held. And I breathed more deeply as it became apparent that Edward's attack would do no more than bruise my skin.

Gunner, on the other hand, was enraged by his underling's disloyalty. His ominous growl was nearly too quiet to hear above my own panting, but the alpha's scent promised that Edward might not live to see the light of another day.

I wasn't particularly thrilled with Edward either. But we'd all regret it if Gunner tore out Edward's throat in a fit of rage without first understanding what had happened to the rest of the pack.

So my next parry involved diving between the two shifters, clunking the alpha's chin with my knee as a mild hint that now might be a good time to take a calming breath. Gunner growled then whimpered, clearly getting the message. But Edward was the one who dropped his ax and stood dazed and blinking between us, his brow furrowed and mouth gaping as he strained to come up with words.

It was almost as if a kitsune had stolen his blood and used it to force him into the prior fighting...then had lost interest and left the male cold and confused. "What...?" Edward started, oblivious to the fact that yet another pack mate was rushing toward us with edged metal glinting. Or, rather, was rushing toward Edward, never mind that I was pretty sure the younger shifter was his sister's son.

In reaction, my star ball shrunk, stretched, glistened into swordishness. Edward might be annoying, but he was an Atwood pack mate and I was bound to protect his life. So I pivoted, retreated, then lunged toward the new attacker. And now Edward was picking up his ax to join me...even as the blond werewolf fumbled and cut himself on his own blade.

Cut himself while trying for one of the easiest sword-fighting maneuvers imaginable. What was the male doing wielding a weapon if he didn't know how to fight with one?

It was an easy matter to swipe my own sword sideways and send the younger male's weapon skittering off into the dark. Harder was managing not to injure the shifter's unshielded body as he came at me with bare hands.

Then someone shouted from behind me. The hairs on my neck prickled, and I whirled away from a werewolf who I suspected wouldn't manage to do more than scratch me with human nails.

Because something had shifted. Something was different....

There. Not where the shout had come from, but in the opposite direction where the cluster of werewolves was more densely packed together. An arm rose above the crowd. A long dark shape arched back then flew directly toward us.

The tip glinted—a knife point affixed to a wooden handle creating a homemade javelin. And, unaware that he stood at the terminus of its trajectory, Gunner raised his muzzle in preparation for howling his pack back into line.

THERE WAS NO TIME FOR warning, for magic, for anything. I was too far away from Gunner, having become separated while preventing him from tearing out the throat of his own pack mate.

But Edward was close enough to save him. Edward, who hated me but whose gaze latched onto mine at just the perfect moment. Whose eyes flicked toward the falling javelin in an attempt to understand the horror on my face.

Edward didn't hesitate before throwing himself between his alpha and the descending danger. The thunk of knife hitting flesh was sickening. The wheeze of air erupting from a lung, not through a trachea but out between ribcage and punctured skin, made my own breath seize up in response.

While I stood frozen, the blond nephew dropped to his knees beside Edward, already keening out his sorrow. "No! Uncle! *No!*"

Even dying, Edward somehow found the energy to pat his nephew's hand consolingly. Meanwhile, his gaze once again latched onto mine. *"Protect our pack,"* he ordered, the words soundless yet the motion of his lips visible in the near darkness.

Then Gunner was shifting to replace the grief-stricken nephew, the battlefield growing silent as the pack leader's hands pressed hard against the gaping wound on the older male's chest. The javelin had gone straight through and out the other side cleanly—and who would have been able to do that from a hundred feet distant without practicing day and night?

Whoever had done it, however they'd done it, Edward wasn't getting back up from this injury. And Gunner accepted that fact with the grace of a clan leader thinking of his larger responsibilities rather than about only one member of his pack.

"You have my gratitude," the alpha started. Electricity from shifting werewolves filled the air even as an undulating howl rose up from dozens of shifters who had, one moment earlier, been battling against their family and friends. "Go in peace into the afterlife."

"Promise." Edward's gaze met mine rather than responding to his alpha, his eyes already starting to glaze over with death. He wasn't even looking at me, I realized. Was instead peering over my left shoulder, as if he'd lost track of his surroundings and was only hanging on long enough to hear my response.

Gunner glanced backwards in reaction, raising his eyebrows when he saw I was on the receiving end of Edward's mouthed admonition. Then he scooted sideways, making room for me by the dying werewolf's side.

"I promise," I murmured to both of them, not certain what, exactly, I was agreeing to. I had no time to press Edward for further information however. Because, with one last wheeze from the hole in his chest cavity, my clearest enemy within the clan subsided into death.

Chapter 23

"I'll take care of this," Gunner told me, his voice curt as he strode away to trail his hands across the heads of panting shifters. They were clearly in need of a pack leader's attention, so I didn't complain about the tone of his voice. Not when I had a pressing problem of my own to attend to—Kira standing hand-in-hand with our grandmother, both fully surrounded by a ring of men wielding swords.

These were the humans our grandmother had treated like puppies yesterday, but they didn't appear particularly gentle at the moment. Instead, they held their weapons in exactly the proper manner. Loosely en garde and ready to slice into anyone who looked at their charges with the wrong gleam in their eye.

Despite their clear training, however, I approached without hesitation, stopping just far enough away from the closest male so my sword could meet his advance should he decide to attack. But that was all the attention I gave to the humans. Instead, I peered over the guard's shoulder at the old woman in their midst.

She was still small and still wrinkled. But—if I guessed right—she was also the impetus of the recent battle that had caused at least one werewolf's death. And Sakurako made no effort to explain her actions. Instead, the elderly kitsune greeted me with a single word.

"Granddaughter."

Well, if she wasn't going to explain herself, then I'd deal with the only thing she held that I still cared about. "Kira, come here," I demanded, knowing it wouldn't be so easy to get my sister safely out from behind the ring of swords.

I expected the males to stop her from passing between them. Or, perhaps, for my grandmother to finally show her true colors and use kitsune magic to hold Kira in place. Instead, it was Kira herself who planted her feet and refused me. "Mai, chill," she answered with yet another teenagerly roll of the eyes.

So I'd have to cut my way through the swordsmen to reach her. A matter made slightly more realistic when two wolves bumped their shoulders into my hips. Tank and Allen—I could smell them without looking downward. Unlike the rest of Gunner's pack mates, I would trust these two with my—or rather, with my sister's—life.

So I didn't pause as I strode forward, ignoring the way five swords swung toward me in tandem as they prepared to hinder my approach. The bodyguards were almost too pretty to be fighters, their perfect faces so similar I couldn't help thinking they'd been chosen not for skill but rather for looks.

I couldn't count on that, however. Couldn't count on anything except the star-ball sword that was now raised between me and danger, plus the two wolves standing firmly at my back. Three against five wasn't terrible...but the battle would be dicey with Kira unprotected and open to enemy attack.

As if hearing those thoughts, my sister snorted, wrenched her hand free of our grandmother's, then slipped between the guards as easily as if they were trees planted in a grassy meadow. "Mai, I *told* you, they're protecting *me*."

She hadn't actually said that, but I was the one failing to listen now. Because I held my breath as Kira padded forward, waiting for someone to restrain the departing child.

Except...all five guards plus my wily kitsune grandmother did nothing. No, that wasn't quite true. One guard scooted sideways to give Kira space to pass unhindered. Another bowed ever so subtly while, behind them, our grandmother merely smiled as if this had been her intention all along.

"Thanks for the help, guys," Kira called back over one shoulder. Then she was beside me while Allen shifted upwards to grab onto her before she could slip away from us.

"Ow!" Kira complained, attempting to shrug free of the protective grip of the werewolf. And this time the armed humans hardened, took a step forward...then halted at the subtlest clearing of my grandmother's throat.

It really did appear that these swordsmen had been charged with protecting Kira rather than with menacing her. Still, "Take her home," I murmured. And Tank and Allen obeyed me, drawing Kira away from the danger, the latter two-legged and the former still in the shape of his wolf.

As for myself, I firmed up my stance between the strangers and my retreating sister, fully expecting complaint from the swordsmen or from the woman who had told me to call her by a pet name the day before. Instead, the old woman cackled, pressing through her guard just as Kira had done moments earlier. She didn't stop when she'd breached her guards, however. Instead Sakurako just kept coming until she could reach up and cup my face with crinkly fingers that felt unbearably cold against my over-heated skin.

"Now that you've called off your dogs, granddaughter," she told me, "perhaps we can finally finish our little talk."

"YOU WANT TO TALK?" I barely restrained myself from physically shaking sense back into the woman who swore she was my grandmother but acted like someone intent upon tearing everything I cared about apart. "We have nothing left to talk about. You asked if I was willing to give up Oyo and...."

"Stop." Sakurako held a hand palm-out between us, and I wasn't quite rude enough to talk over her. After all, she was old and was one of only two surviving relatives. So I obeyed the gesture and gave her space in which to speak.

Only the old woman didn't. Instead, she nodded at her guards, sending all except one striding away from us into the darkness. Then, once her final lackey started folding the picnic blanket, she slipped her fingers around my elbow and led us away from the carnage of the battlefield.

"I misunderstood your affection for these werewolves," she said after a moment, and I could tell she rarely admitted to having been wrong. "This is not my work, but I could have stopped it if I'd made an effort. Next time, I'll think more deeply about what you might have wished."

It wasn't quite an apology and I definitely didn't believe in her supposed lack of involvement. Still, I didn't tear my arm out of her grasp and storm away into the night. "What do you want?" I asked instead, my tone not quite cordial but not so antagonistic that the male now trotting behind us dropped Sakurako's picnic paraphernalia and drew his sword.

"I want a chance to explain to you about the larger world you are a part of," my grandmother answered quickly. "Oyo—yes, I want Oyo also. But I was premature to set a deadline on that decision. I know you well enough by now to see that once you understand the repercussions, you will make the proper choice."

She thought I was wrapped around her little finger just like her guards and—apparently—Kira were. She assumed that acting like a doddering old woman would win my affection and garner my regard.

But I wasn't stupid enough to be fooled a second time. So I merely shook my head. "My decision is made, Sakurako. I don't trust you around my friends or around Kira. You know my answer. I want you out of clan central before..."

"What if I made a promise?" Once again, my grandmother had spoken over me. And, once again, I closed my mouth and allowed her to speak. "I swear to protect, not harm, everyone you care about for the next twenty-four hours. Is that good enough to buy one more day to change your mind?"

It wouldn't have been if she'd been a werewolf or a human. But I could feel Sakurako's kitsune oath binding us together and placing her in my debt as she spoke.

Plus, I remembered how carefully she'd guarded Kira. How easily she'd released my sister back into my care once I demanded the youngster be returned to me.

And yet.... *"Now that you've called off your dogs, granddaughter."* The words rolled through my mind in belated warning. Sakurako was protecting my "dogs" only because she wanted something from me, not because she thought they deserved protection for their own sake.

Still, I trusted the kitsune oath to keep the pack together for twenty-four hours. And I was also getting the distinct impression that my familial stubbornness may have seen its source in Sakurako's veins.

So I accepted defeat gracefully. Bowing my head, I caved to her offer. "Tomorrow we will speak again, Sobo. Tonight, I need to help my pack lick their wounds."

Chapter 24

Only, the pack didn't need me. Or so I gathered when I reached the far end of the Green and saw the way wolves encircled Gunner in a tight cluster. They were just standing there, over a hundred furry bodies all touching their neighbors with chins, necks, and noses. And, even though I couldn't feel it, I could imagine the rebuilding of shattered bonds taking place before me, the magic of pack recreating what had recently been lost.

This was the sort of thing a fox shouldn't stick her nose into. Just watching them made me feel small, cold, and sad. So I backtracked to the scene of the battle, intent upon doing at least a little good before falling into my bed and calling it a night.

Because if Sakurako was to be believed and the recent fight hadn't been instigated by a kitsune, that meant a member of that cluster of shifters had murderously thrown a homemade javelin at his or her alpha. But who would do that to Gunner? Edward was the one who'd shared the most overt disapproval of the alpha's governing processes...and yet Edward had also been the one who'd leapt to Gunner's defense without regard for the safety of his own skin.

I winced, remembering the way the javelin had struck with so much force it slid all the way through the deceased male's body. No wonder the weapon was now lying abandoned on the ground even though Edward had been carried away in preparation for some sort of werewolf farewell to the dead.

"Haven't you done enough already?"

My hand skittered away from the bloody broomstick that made up the weapon's handle, the ball of my hand nicking itself on the knife lashed to the end as haste flubbed my retreat. But, despite the pain, I remained crouched on the grass beside the weapon. After all, Elizabeth's father had died less than an hour earlier. She deserved the courtesy of the upper hand.

Plus, Gunner was close enough that he could be here almost immediately if my awkward posture left me open to attack by this werewolf. So I let Elizabeth's words hang between us for several seconds, then I answered the question she hadn't asked.

"I'm trying to figure out who killed your father," I told her, leaning down further until my nose nearly touched the spot where a hand would have clutched the broomstick while throwing it. Unfortunately, it was impossible to pick out identifying aromas through the coating of blood smeared across the handle, so I soon settled back on my heels in regret.

"You won't find any scent there," Elizabeth told me. And for half a second I thought she was admitting to having been involved in her own father's murder. But then something long and heavy landed on the ground beside me. A throwing stick with a protrusion just big enough for the hollowed out end of the broomstick to fit over—no wonder the javelin had flown so forcefully. And when I leaned down to sniff this second item, I found no scent at all along its length.

A plastic grocery bag half wrapped around the end answered the question of why Elizabeth's odor hadn't rubbed off on the wooden handle while she carried it across the field. But shouldn't even gloved fingers have left some scent, whether leather or plastic? I was pretty sure they should have, which meant the killer had used a trick like the scent-reducing compound I'd sprayed on my own flesh two nights earlier to prevent Gunner from smelling the fact that I'd been manhandled by another wolf.

"You promised my father that you would protect the Atwoods," Elizabeth continued. And for the first time I heard something other than anger in her voice. She'd lost a parent this evening. Of course she was traumatized. I wanted to stand up and hug her, but I knew she'd resist the embrace.

"I did," I said simply.

"Then do what you promised." For half a second, the young woman reeked of fur and electricity. She needed to shift, needed to accept the unity Gunner was offering the rest of the pack.

Instead, she kicked the throwing stick lightly with one blood-stained sneaker. "Find out who killed my father and prevent it from happening again. Or solve the problem the easy way and get out of our pack."

I WAS HALFWAY BACK to my cottage, intent upon calling it a night, when a voice in the darkness stopped me. "Mai-san." Whirling, my hand was on my sword hilt even before I made out the shape of one of the five human swordsmen who'd recently dogged my grandmother's footsteps.

Just a few minutes earlier, this human had appeared ominous and forbidding as he trapped my sister within a ring of swords. Now, though, his body language was entirely the opposite as he deferred to me not only in posture but also with the honorific tacked onto the end of my name.

The Atwood pack wasn't interested in including me in their rituals this evening, but my grandmother's lackey had clearly taken the time to search me out. And as I noted his obvious Japanese heritage, I wondered if the reason might be shared blood.

"I came to explain, to speak with you," he said when curiosity held me in place. Then he proved himself clever by getting straight to the point. "Sakurako-sama has had a difficult life, so she builds up walls to protect herself. It takes some getting used to."

"Yeah, like eating raw fish." The words flowed out of me before I could stop them. But, to my surprise, the human laughed rather than taking offense.

"I'm Yuki," he said, offering a bow but no comment about my assessment of his employer. "Would it be too forward of me to ask if you plan to accept Sakurako-sama's invitation tomorrow? I hope you will choose to come."

"Invitation?" I'd gotten the impression my grandmother merely wanted to speak with me. But Yuki made this sound like an event rather than a simple conversation.

"She didn't explain." Yuki laughed quietly, the chuckle warming me due to its similarity to my mother's laughter when I was very young.

"Sakurako-sama believes everything is on a need-to-know basis. But this, I think, you need to know."

We were walking as we talked, back toward my cottage. And I hesitated ten feet from my door, intrigued by this possible family member...but not enough that I wanted to invite him inside.

"I'm all ears," I offered. Then, as Yuki cocked his head in confusion, I realized that his stilted speech probably meant English was his second language. So—"I'm listening," I offered instead.

"The mistress wants to show you your heritage," Yuki told me, accepting my explanation gracefully. And when I didn't interject a comment, he elaborated as best he could. "It's not my place to tell you where she wishes to take you or what she plans to show you there. But I'll be coming tomorrow and would be honored if you traveled by my side."

Traveled. This wasn't a decision I could make tonight while exhausted and lonely. "I'll see you tomorrow," I answered noncommittally. Then, bowing a farewell to Yuki, I entered my cottage alone.

Chapter 25

Or I thought I was alone until a voice rang out from deeper within the darkened living room. "So you're the kitsune." Clearly, lack of lights meant very little when denning with wolves.

I tensed, prepared for another ultimatum like the one I'd recently had dumped on me by Elizabeth. Only...this was no Atwood. I was pretty sure everyone in Gunner's pack was either being soothed by their alpha or was protecting my sister. Meanwhile, the air within my cottage was redolent with the unfamiliar scent of bitter almond, suggesting my questioner was someone I'd never met before.

Someone I'd never met but who just happened to know my identity. Ignoring my racing heart, I flicked on the light switch as if my world wasn't crumbling down around me.

"What's a kit sunny?" I asked, purposefully mispronouncing the name of my own kind while assessing my uninvited visitor out of the corner of one eye.

Despite being in another shifter's territory, the broad, menacing stranger lounged on my plush sofa as if he owned the place, legs splayed and arms spread so he took up enough room for three people or more. I didn't smell any fur or electricity to go along with the power pose, but something told me not to turn my back on this werewolf.

I did so anyway. Walked past him without waiting for an answer then padded down the hall in search of the sister who should have been asleep in her bed. The air didn't smell like Tank, Allen, or Kira, however, suggesting the trio had made a pitstop before obeying my order. Oyo on the other hand could pop out at any moment directly into the jaws of the strange, bitter-almond-scented wolf....

In an effort to prevent that eventuality, I crouched down to peer into the darkness beneath my bedstead, stretching my fingers into the hole in the wall. When Kira had called to tell me the redheaded kitsune was missing, I'd assumed Oyo had heard about my grandmother's arrival then dug herself in deeper. But the gap in the drywall was both empty and cold.

"I'm speaking to you, fox."

Head under the bed, I'd missed the stranger sneaking up behind me. But I couldn't miss the way he dragged me out of the darkness by my hips. Hard hands on my shoulders slammed me up against the wall before I could make a comment on being manhandled, and I silently berated myself for turning my back on someone much larger and stronger than myself.

Aloud, though, I disavowed all understanding of the situation. "What's wrong with you?" I blustered. "And what do you mean by calling me a fox?"

The shifter silenced me the easy way, backhanding me so hard my head slammed into the drywall. Darkness tried to claim me as his hot breath flowed across my stinging cheek. And I tried without success to think of a way out of the situation that didn't involve creating a magical dagger to thrust into my opponent's gut.

I can't show what I am unless I'm ready to kill him. The knowledge chilled me even as it narrowed my options to...well, none.

Meanwhile, the male who held me began speaking, his voice so cold I shivered despite every effort to appear impervious. "Let me spell it out for you, kitsune," he murmured. "I'm an enforcer." At my blank look, he sighed and elaborated. "I decide on life or death for werewolves...and all who come in contact with them."

"No, Gunner is the pack leader. His word is law." This part wasn't bluster. I thoroughly believed that fact or I never would have brought Kira to live in Atwood clan central.

"A *werewolf* would know that is true only of problems that don't threaten the neighbors." My opponent dropped me so abruptly I slid down onto my butt rather than regaining my footing. "But enough about me. I want to hear about you."

This wasn't a threat—this was a warning. So I did the only thing I could think of. I raised my hand to my mouth as if in terror. And, surreptitiously, I licked up a stray droplet of Edward's blood.

THE PACK BONDS FLARED to life so quickly that I almost thought they'd always been there. This was no time for analyzing magic, however. Instead, as the enforcer dragged me upright, I ignored his muttered demands and tugged as hard as I could on the solid rope that led from me to my not-quite-mate.

"Gunner!"

"Isn't here to help you, kitsune." A fist slammed into my stomach and I lost my ability to verbalize. Instead, I strove to send the pack leader an image of what he'd be walking into if he raced here to help me. I needed his assistance, but it was too dangerous for him to walk into this ambush blind.

And Gunner must have heard me. Both heard and understood me. Because images now flowed back the other way in answer. Images of a gathering of alpha-leaning werewolves, the mass of them telling this stranger what to do.

So, an enforcer was some kind of regional sheriff? I wasn't entirely sure I understood what Gunner was trying to tell me. Rather than providing time for questions, however, he managed to send through two words loud and clear.

"Get away."

Good idea. I both wanted to laugh at the obviousness of Gunner's suggestion and to vomit from the sharp agony spiking through my gut where the enforcer had driven his fist. Instead of doing either, I let my legs crumple a second time...then I dove between the enforcer's knees as he allowed me to drop.

Only my opponent was fast and smart and ready for me. His foot came down on my spine as I slid past him. Then I was supine on the floor while once again struggling to regain my breath.

"These are simple questions, kitsune." His words seemed to come from the other end of a long tunnel, and I couldn't have answered even if I'd wanted to with carpet fibers embedded in my mouth. "Which werewolves do you manipulate?" he demanded, sending my mind off on a tangent of guesswork.

Did kitsunes have a pattern of behavior, insinuating themselves into werewolf clan centrals and tearing down not only that pack but the neighbors also? Was that why Sakurako had come here, what had riled up non-Atwood wolves enough to send this enforcer to find me? Was that fate what Oyo was hiding from?

"This is your last chance," the enforcer growled as he flipped me over. There was a knife in his hand now, I noted. A knife that hovered so close above my left eyeball that I couldn't focus on the tip poised to impale me.

It was finally time to shift, I decided. I had nothing left to lose and everything to gain....

Only Gunner leapt through the door in a whirlwind of cold air and enraged werewolf before I could get my magic together. He was mostly human—kinda human. Human enough to bellow instructions in my direction before diving onto the enforcer in the full skin of his wolf.

"Kira is on her way to your grandmother's. Join her and flee as far and as fast as you're able."

And even though the enforcer laughed, frost spreading out from the stranger's feet as if he was as magical as I was, I did what Gunner suggested. I turned tail and fled from the battleground that had recently been a welcoming home.

Chapter 26

Kira had to be my top priority. I knew this even as the pack bond informed me that Gunner was fighting...and losing.

Meanwhile, shifters streamed past in the opposite direction, rushing to assist their alpha as the pack bond alerted them to Gunner's fate. But they piled up in the doorway, frozen by the enforcer's dominance and unable to set a single step inside.

Gunner, for his part, was being shredded and battered. Blood stung his/my eyeball as I experienced the pain right alongside him, and he limped to avoid putting pressure on his front left foot.

Still, Gunner fought with all the abandon of a werewolf protecting his partner even though I'd never overtly chosen him. *"Hurry,"* he suggested, the word warm in my belly. And I blinked back tears that blocked my vision, using my second-strongest tether as a guide leading me toward family and escape.

"The neighbors are gathering." Tank appeared out of nowhere with Kira wide-eyed and panting behind him. "We have to get you out of here before they block the exits. Did the enforcer see you shift?"

"No." That much, at least, I'd done correctly. But—"I can't find Oyo. If she shows up in fox form, what will happen to Gunner then?"

Tank didn't speak, but his grim silence was its own sort of answer. Then we were in front of my grandmother's camper, the massive bulk of it menacing in the dark.

And for the first time since leaving my cottage, I hesitated. I'd parted from these near strangers with no real conclusion earlier, didn't trust any of them despite my grandmother's recent oath.

Kira, on the other hand, had no such reservations. "Sobo!" Her voice—and her pounding fists—broke the silence. Lights flared on inside the RV a millisecond before Yuki answered the door.

It's going to be alright. Despite the pain I felt every time Gunner accepted a blow that was meant for my ribcage, Yuki's appearance gave me hope. Sure enough, the human took only one look at our faces before ushering us inside the vehicle. Meanwhile, the rest of Sakurako's entourage flowed out around us, began working in seamless synchrony to crank in the RV's popped-out sides.

"The best route away is east," Tank informed me from beyond the still-open doorway. He wasn't coming with us. None of these werewolves would leave clan central while their alpha was engaged in a deadly battle.

Or maybe I'd misgauged the loyalty of Gunner's pack mates. Because a dark shape pushed past Gunner's most loyal underling, materializing into Becky with her bloodling pup cradled in both arms.

Cradled...then extended towards me. "Take him. Please," she begged, ignoring everyone else as she ran halfway up the stairs and attempted to thrust the sleeping pup into my arms. The female was terrified, hesitated only long enough to glance back over one shoulder before descending into a litany of promises I knew she couldn't keep.

"I'll do anything for you if you'll protect him. And he'll help you. Werewolf blood is powerful. Curly, tell them you want them to take your blood if they need it. That you won't fight against a cut."

The puppy hadn't been sleeping, I realized. He'd been doing the only thing he could to help—keeping himself silent and still.

Now, as his body slid away from his mother's and up against my sweatshirt, he didn't attempt to reverse the flow of his own motion. Instead, he peered up at me with dark eyes full of understanding, then he nodded his lupine head.

But, of course, despite his cuteness, Curly wasn't a puppy. He was a young werewolf, well aware of what would happen if the Atwood pack was overrun. I wasn't exactly sure what that awfulness would consist of. And yet, given the slights Becky had faced from supposedly friendly shifters, I was able to take a wild guess.

"You come too," I demanded, pulling Becky up beside me. But she resisted and I had to release my hold so Curly wouldn't fall to the ground.

"No, I can't leave my pack," the other female murmured. For a millisecond, her hand extended as if to pet—or regain—Curly. But then the gesture aborted. And without a word of farewell to her only offspring, she turned on her heel and sprinted back toward the cottage where Gunner fought.

TANK FOLLOWED HIS PACK mate, leaving me alone with two kitsunes, a bloodling pup, and five male humans. To my surprise, Sakurako slipped into the driver's seat, taking the curves far faster than I would have been able to without risking a spill.

Beside me, Kira cradled Curly, the pup so silent I thought at first that he was soundly sleeping. But, no, Curly was merely feeling what I was feeling—that brittle breaking in his middle as he was spirited away from every other member of the Atwood pack.

Because my own connection to Gunner had begun to falter as the distance increased between us. I could no longer see what the enforcer was doing back in our cottage, only felt fists and teeth cutting into my mate as a dull, distant ache.

Then even that bodily contact faded. And I gasped, unable to breathe around the thought that Gunner might have faded right along with it. I'd made the wrong decision, choosing Kira over my partner....

Yuki was the one who noted my silent anguish, who knelt before me and clutched five of my frozen fingers in ten of his own. "We'll make it out of here," he promised...even as Sakurako slammed on the brakes and abruptly shut off both engine and headlights.

Pay attention, I told myself, shutting Gunner's fate away in a tiny box shrouded in black ribbons. I'd chosen my family over our romantic partnership; it was time to ensure neither Kira nor Sakurako was caught in the undertow now.

To that end, I scooted around Yuki and peered out the windshield into darkness. There were snowflakes in the air despite the fact that it was only early October. Snowflakes that settled on the glass and might soon stick to the soil.

How easy would it be to follow our trail with a blanket of snow on the ground to turn tracks into billboards? Our enemies wouldn't even need a predator's nose.

"They're ahead. A quarter of a mile," the old woman said tersely. She glanced in my direction, raised one brow. "Your werewolf didn't know what he was talking about. I hope you have another way out of these woods."

And, as I peered at the brand new yet abandoned vehicle Gunner and I had arrived in not long ago, I realized that I did. It seemed disloyal to reveal Gunner's tunnel to strangers. Still, would it even matter that Sakurako knew about the secret passageway if the Atwood pack leader might already be dead?

"Mai?" Kira's voice was so small I barely heard her, but it slammed me back into the present and out of the abyss of loss. I'd resolved to protect my sister above all others. So I'd lead us to safety...then, later, I could fall apart.

"This way," I told them, descending from the vehicle so I could lead two kitsunes and five humans away into the forest. Curly I clutched to my chest as much to soothe me as to warm him. Meanwhile, behind us, one of the males sprayed an aerosol of de-scenting compound across the ground to eliminate our trail.

Chapter 27

I was so shaken by thoughts of Gunner that it took a solid minute for the implications of that spray can to sink into my conscious thought processes. But then I flinched as the male in question slipped past my arm and into the tunnel I'd just pointed out, his possible identity making me want nothing more than to turn tail and run.

Was this the male who'd tried to kill Gunner? Who'd thrown a javelin without imbuing it with his aroma? If so, I'd been looking at this issue from all the wrong angles...or, rather, I'd thrown in my lot with the enemy when I'd opted to include Sakurako and her lackeys in my escape.

"It's standard issue." Yuki was the only one who noticed my hesitation, the only one who didn't slip beneath the overhanging greenery and follow our companions inside. "Werewolves are our greatest e—" He paused, glanced at Curly still clutched in my arms, then chose a different word. "Danger. So we carry these spray cans to cover our footsteps, to protect ourselves from attack."

Sure enough, a similar canister appeared between his fingers...which didn't make me particularly inclined to trust him more than his friend. But my grandmother reemerged from behind the veil of plants at that moment, grabbed my shirtsleeve, and yanked me inside.

"Shift," she demanded, her word lacking alpha compulsion but nonetheless spurring everyone around her into action. Kira's clothes dropped into a pile along with the males' cell phones, then my sister shimmered into fox form even as two different humans sprayed the pile of discarded possessions to make it harder for werewolves to find us using either biology or technology.

So maybe Yuki was right. Maybe there were dozens of people out there carrying similar sprays meant to confuse werewolf nostrils. I'd stay alert, but my choice of allies had already been set in stone when I abandoned my mate.

Still, I didn't obey Sakurako, merely stood my ground and stated my case for remaining human. "I'm not leaving Curly." I couldn't carry the pup in fox form, and he'd last about three minutes under his own volition at a sprint.

Sakurako shook her head in answer then turned her back to slither out of her nightgown. Like Kira, the old woman glowed as she shifted, but her transition was more of a supernova than the twinkle of a distant star. I rubbed my eyes, trying to make sense of the vision. Sakurako's luminous white fur gleamed in the near darkness. And was night playing tricks on me or did she really boast multiple tails?

I only had a second to stare at the strange kitsune, however, before tires on gravel heralded the arrival of enemy werewolves. We'd left the RV blocking the roadway, so it was inevitable our enemies would begin searching momentarily. We had to be out of earshot before that happened. Was I really ready to endanger our entire party for the sake of one bloodling wolf?

Curly whined, peering up at me. Then Yuki was at my shoulder, arms outstretched. "I'll carry him." He glanced toward the white fox, already receding into the darkness, then told me: "I'll put his life before mine, I promise."

And Yuki must have had kitsune blood somewhere inside him, because his words came out oath-like and binding. That was exactly the confirmation I was waiting for. So even as the first car door creaked open, I relinquished my burden and fell down into the form of my fox.

WE RAN FOR EONS. OUTSIDE the tunnel, snow fell harder and faster, the fraction that filtered down through interwoven trees and shrubs not quite sufficient to slow our footsteps. I'd never thought kitsunes could control the weather, but it seemed like a strange coincidence that such a dramatic snowstorm had blown in out of nowhere at the exact moment we started fleeing from hunting wolves.

Because I'd been wrong—the snow helped rather than hindered us. It muffled our scent and covered our tracks even as we fled through the network of tunnels some long-dead werewolf had created out of bushes and trees.

Our enemies didn't give up the chase, however, even though passage through the forest had to be much more difficult outside our vegetative pathway. Instead, their howls were terrifyingly close at first, then only a little more distant when trees laden with both leaves and snow began thundering to the ground and further blocking our pursuers' paths.

One huge trunk in particular smashed into the tunnel behind us, making Kira squeak and Curly whimper inside the shirt-turned-knapsack twined across Yuki's shoulders. But Sakurako didn't hesitate as she chose turn after turn in a winding, twisting labyrinth that led us who knew where.

Then the cold air outside descended into eerie silence, nothing but our own pants of exertion evident as moment after moment flowed past without any additional werewolf howls. We'd lost them, had shed our followers like winter fur wafted away by a breeze in springtime. And in that elation of survival, my pack bond momentarily flickered back to life....

Gunner, living. His lungs billowing and his muscles aching so drastically I stumbled over my next footstep.

Pain was acceptable, however. Pain and the knowledge that even though Gunner was losing the battle, I could now tell him that he'd won the war.

"We're safe," I attempted to shout down the pack bond. *"Stop fighting. Save yourself!"*

But my presence just spurred Gunner to work harder, leaping at his enemy until they went down together in a pile of fur and claws. Something broke in one of his extremities, something tore above his ribcage....

Then I was knocked backwards into my own body by brilliant lights above us combined with wind roaring so loudly it couldn't have been a natural part of the storm.

Sakurako squeezed out through a gap in the shrubbery, led us into a whirlwind of snow and ice. Above our heads, a helicopter hovered. Somehow, my grandmother had called upon human technology to complete our escape.

As I stared, a rope ladder fell from the open access hatch. The first of Sakurako's guards was already climbing up while the second reached down to grasp Kira's fox body in his arms.

This was it—the moment of decision. I could trust my grandmother to protect those I cared about and run back to assist my partner. Or I could follow her into the chopper and leave Gunner behind.

A mate wouldn't have hesitated, but I stood so long in the snow that ice formed pellets between my vulpine foot pads. Meanwhile, the fifth male knelt beside me, offering his arms as an easy route up.

This was the same male who'd sprayed our footprints as we entered the tunnel, the same one who might have tried to kill Gunner and actually killed Edward. Could I really leave him alone with my sister and a defenseless bloodling puppy? Could I trust any of these strangers to do the job I'd accepted as my own?

I couldn't and I didn't. But I did accept the male's offer of assistance, leaping into his arms and closing my eyes against the pain in my temples as he clambered upward into the aircraft above our heads.

Then we weren't hovering but rather flying. And my connection to Gunner abruptly winked all the way out.

Chapter 28

The pilot and I were the only ones awake by the time we landed, swooping in on a helipad on the roof of a mansion that made Gunner's city abode look like a run-down row house by comparison. Snow gusted away from the raised surface as we descended, but it was only a dusting. As if the vast blanket that had hindered our footsteps during our rush away from clan central had avoided this location...or as if Sakurako had another dozen minions on call just to sweep her roof clear.

The latter appeared to be the truth of the matter, because two additional specimens of perfect manhood came out to greet us as the helicopter rotors slowed from a roaring storm into a gentle breeze. The pair didn't even glance in my direction as they assisted Sakurako in descending, the robe that had been waiting for her in the chopper sweeping out behind them all like a bride's train.

Kira followed, eyes wide as she took in the lighted facade of the building, heated fountains flowing through zones of red and blue amid the snow below. "Wow," she breathed, spinning a circle so her own robe floated around her like a princess's, a few final snowflakes landing jewel-like in her hair.

Which meant I was the only one estimating the width of the windows while stiffly unfolding myself from the position in which I'd waited out the journey. How deep was the snow? How far away was the road? Would the wrought-iron fence surrounding this residence keep enemy werewolves at bay?

"Three miles." Yuki's voice drew me out of the helicopter before Kira could follow our grandmother inside the mansion. His hand was strong as he helped me down onto the helipad, and I appreciated the support after a day that still stretched before me with no obvious conclusion in sight.

"Three miles?" I repeated, trying to make sense of the observation as I released his hand a little more quickly than I'd intended to. The memory of Gunner's pain made it difficult to touch another man.

"Three miles to the nearest roadway, and even that is gated and completely covered with snow at the moment. We're safe here, Mai-san. But you can bunk with me if it will help you sleep soundly tonight."

I glanced backwards at Yuki rather than taking in the opulence as we passed through the doorway, me leading and him hovering not far behind. If he was insinuating what I thought he was insinuating, perhaps Soba's attendants weren't my cousins after all....

We trailed the rest of the party down a circular staircase in the center of a tremendous, four-story atrium. There was more to look at here than there had been outside the residence, chandeliers and vast, shiny tables and vases large enough I could have stepped inside. Still, my attention was riveted on Yuki, trying to figure out how to reject his offer without coming across as irredeemably rude.

"Prepare our guests a chamber." My grandmother was the one who saved me from answering, sending Yuki away on an errand that even I knew had already been completed. He didn't complain, though. Merely bowed and left us even as Sakurako pulled me into a corner where I could keep an eye on Kira without worrying that anyone might overhear our words.

"Sobo, thank you for your hospitality," I started. But the high-handed kitsune shushed me in her usual manner, speaking over me without waiting for a lull.

"It's best not to play favorites, granddaughter. At least in the beginning. Later, once they all have a chance of being the father, it's easier to keep them at heel."

A chance of being the *father*? I must have twitched because Sakurako sighed, and for the first time looked the tiniest bit tired. "Sleep with Kira tonight if you're cold. That's all I ask from you."

That suggestion, at least, I could comply with. Well, except for the sleeping part. Because after Kira and Curly snuggled up together on the tremendous, canopied bed in their fur forms, I used the last gasp of my energy to materialize my star ball into its familiar sword shape. Then I sank down to the floor to listen for intruders while staring at Curly's side as it rose and fell with his breath.

He was just as cute as ever, but all I saw was a potential source of blood. Because the last of Edward's fluids had been lost on snowy leaf litter, so this tiny werewolf was my only remaining avenue to discover whether my partner had survived his ill-matched fight.

But I wasn't about to steal energy from a toddler, no matter whether both he and his mother had given overt approval of that course of action. So, laying my sword across my lap, I settled in to wait.

I MUST HAVE ENDED UP sleeping after all. Because when I woke, it was to Sakurako's crinkled fingers shaking me back to life.

"Granddaughter, walk with me."

Sunlight streamed through the windows so brilliantly I was pretty sure it was once again closer to lunch than to breakfast. And I considered waking Kira and Curly so I wouldn't have to let them out of my sight.

But Sakurako raised one eyebrow, reminding me of her promise. And I reluctantly admitted that her kitsune nature would force her to stick to her word.

So I nodded, following Sakurako past two males guarding the outside of my doorway. Then we traveled at a pace that should have been beyond such an elderly lady as we strode rapidly down the hall.

At first, I thought this was going to be another information-gathering session where my grandmother's stubbornness exceeded my ability to batter through it. But she only waited until we were beyond the range of Kira's hearing before she began filling me in.

"This is one of several properties our lineage manages," Sakurako told me, waving her hand at the expanse of snow-covered forest we could see through the long line of windows we were currently walking past. "There are four lineages left, ten kitsunes in the entire world that we know of." She paused, corrected herself. "No. With you and your sister, that total comes to twelve."

So few. The weight in my stomach was nothing compared to what settled there when I thought of Gunner—of Gunner who *had* to have survived the previous night. Still, it was significant that Kira and I each made up eight percent of the total world kitsune population. And it also explained the males who fawned over Sakurako...and the one who had already started fawning over me.

"That's why you wanted us to join you," I suggested. "To carry on that lineage. With, what, a harem of males to ensure we reproduce in a timely manner?"

"We call them an honor guard. They are chosen as much for their skills as for their genetics. But, yes, your statement is correct factually. The important point, however...."

I wasn't fated to learn what the important point was, unfortunately. Because Sakurako stepped closer to the glass expanse rather than finishing her explanation. And when I leaned sideways to see around her, my attention was captivated just as hers had been.

Outside, the snow was waist high with no plowed pathway to enable a vehicle to drive through it. According to Yuki, the road lay three miles distant with a gate blocking the way. And yet, a gray animal bounded through the drifts toward us, tail and ears iced over but the beast most definitely a wolf.

Chapter 29

"That's Elle." My first burst of fear was replaced by breathless anticipation as I discerned the werewolf's identity. Maybe my former mentor knew what had happened to Gunner. Maybe she'd come to inform me that her half-brother was safe.

But Sakurako was no longer close enough to hear my explanation. Instead, she'd pushed open the nearest window...and was now striding down a staircase of snow that I was 99% positive hadn't existed one moment before.

Meanwhile, wind created a mini spiral of white with my grandmother at its center. Her feet slid rather than stepped forward, skimming across the tops of drifts as if she was surfing. So this is what a kitsune could do at the height of her power. The snowstorm hadn't been a coincidence...and I hadn't even seen my grandmother charge herself up with werewolf blood.

I shivered in place for one split second, then I pushed through heavy snow in Sakurako's wake. Unlike my grandmother, I wasn't able to levitate so I had no chance of closing the distance between us. Still, Sakurako was slowed by the wrought-iron fence encircling her residence, and I nearly caught up as she melted drifted snow away from the gate.

I wasn't close enough to interrupt, however, as my grandmother spoke without a single glance in my direction. "You dare to invade my home without permission, werewolf?" Sakurako's words didn't soften even as Elle struggled to regain her human form.

"I...used...the pack bond...to find...Mai...so I could deliver...a message. I came..." Gunner's half-sister looked pitiful, naked in the snow. Meanwhile, cold made her teeth chatter so rapidly she barely managed to spit out her words.

But I understood what she was saying. Understood that my connection to Elle was still strong enough to be used to locate me...which made the absence of a tether between myself and Gunner more ominous yet.

"Is...?" I started, not able to voice the possibility. In answer, Elle raised one hand to a strange, bulky choker encircling her neck.

And maybe my grandmother thought the choker was a weapon. Or maybe she was simply annoyed by the fact that Elle wasn't lying prostrate, groveling in the snow. Whatever the reason, a flash of light leapt between them, Elle flinched, then a long line of blood rose along the outside of my friend's arm.

"Sobo!" I yelled, as I attempted to push my way between them. "Elle is my friend! She isn't an invader! Leave her alone!"

Rather than answering, Sakurako reached toward the naked werewolf with bony, cronish fingers. Scooping up a streak of red, she brought it to her mouth. "Now she'll be obedient," the old woman agreed, turning at last to face me with the tiniest smear of blood clinging to one corner of her mouth.

This was last summer all over again. A kitsune stealing werewolf power to force those I cared about to obey someone else's will. And regardless of the fact that I was a guest in Sakurako's mansion, that wasn't a fate I could allow to befall someone I called my friend.

So, without another word, I pushed myself between the two females. And this time it was me who stole a long lick from Elle's blood-streaked forearm, claiming Gunner's half-sister as my own.

I EXPECTED ANGER, BUT Sakurako only smiled and turned her back on us both to lead the way toward a wide-open door on the ground-floor level. The old woman should have been angry that I'd contradicted her, but I got the distinct impression this was, instead, the first time I'd ever made her proud.

Ignoring the fleeting thought that I'd played directly into the old woman's hands, I wrapped my arms around Elle to warm her while explaining what I'd done. "I had to break her hold over you, but I won't coerce you," I promised...feeling like a hypocrite as I latched onto the burst of werewolf power flooding my body in an attempt to connect with my not-quite-mate.

Gunner, where are you? I pushed outwards with all my might, attempting to rebuild the connection I'd lost yesterday. But either the few drops of blood I'd consumed were too minuscule to overcome such a vast distance or the alpha wasn't alive to answer. Either way, no pack bond flared to life between us, and an uncontrollable shiver racked my body from head to toe.

Although she had just as much reason to lose herself to the darkness as I did, Elle was the one who brought me back to reality. She planted her bare feet and tugged at the choker rather than continuing to follow me toward the door.

Only it wasn't a choker. It was a hollow collar that clicked open to reveal a slightly damp sheet of paper. "From Ransom," Elle managed between chattering teeth.

Ransom, not Gunner. Shoulders slumping, I accepted the letter only because Elle was so adamant about it, then I did my best to usher the naked female a little faster through the snow. She was so cold now that her lips were blue and she'd actually stopped shivering. Even I knew that couldn't be good.

But Sakurako's underlings were prepared for every eventuality. Two ran out to meet us wielding a big, woolly blanket, and I wrapped Elle up even as I snapped out orders at the others waiting just inside the door.

"We need a hot bath and someone who knows how to treat hypothermia," I demanded, ignoring the fact that my grandmother had chosen these men to be part of my honor guard. Giving them commands felt like a first step down a slippery slope that ended in me owning their bodies and souls. Like stealing blood from Elle, the notion made me subtly sick.

But my friend needed medical attention and she needed it immediately. So, ignoring the frisson of discomfort in my stomach, I accepted the bows of Sakurako's attendants and the way they sprinted off to do as I'd asked.

Then both Elle and I were inside, walking down a hallway into a room that was blissfully warm and decked out like a small-scale clinic. "I have medic training," Yuki offered as he sorted through a doctor's bag on the table beside him. "If you'll ask the patient to sit, I'll see what I can do."

He was clearly wary of touching a wounded, unpredictable werewolf. And, for her part, Elle was becoming more agitated rather than less so as we walked through the clinic door.

At first, I thought the issue was being surrounded by a kitsune's loyal retainers. But then the female grabbed my arm with surprisingly strong fingers before bringing the nearly forgotten paper up from where it dangled at my side.

"Read this," she managed between teeth chattering so badly they nicked her tongue.

"If you'll sit down, I'll read it," I soothed her. And, thankfully, my friend finally accepted the chair one of Sakurako's honor guard had pulled out for her use.

Her gaze remained focused on me, however, and she ignored Yuki's questions and promptings to bend and wiggle various body parts. So, finally, I gave in, unfolded the paper, and began to read as a way of getting this medical exam back on track.

"I'm ready to call in my debt."

I hunched over in surprise at the pain in my middle. Because a tether had been created just like the one I'd been trying to resurrect moments earlier. Too bad this bond led to the elder Atwood brother rather than to the one I wanted to connect with the most.

Ransom was west of me, not north on his island the way he should have been. And the rest of the message confirmed that point by listing an address only a few miles from where I'd left Gunner to be pounded up by another wolf.

The note ended with no explanation, just further orders: *"Come as soon as you are able. I'll be waiting for you."*

Chapter 30

"**G**randdaughter, if you have a moment...."

I froze in the darkness, fingers on the tank of the snowmobile I'd found along with five others in the basement. The debt had spurred me into immediate action, and I'd rightly guessed that my grandmother wouldn't bury her mansion under three feet of snow if she didn't have ground transportation at the ready. What I hadn't guessed was that she'd be able to find me so quickly when I slipped my leash and began exploring the residence on my own.

"Yes, Sobo?" I backed away from the vehicle and into the light of the hallway, mind buzzing through possible explanations for lurking down here in the darkness. What could I possibly say I'd been looking for other than an easy way out of her clutches? Usually adept at making up stories, I was currently drawing a blank.

"There are things you need to know, granddaughter." Sakurako's eyes flicked behind me once, but she spoke as if my location wasn't suspiciously telling. Still, I sensed her restraint in the hum of kitsune power seething beneath her skin. The old woman was currently stronger than I'd ever seen her. As if summoning snowstorms revved her up rather than wearing her down.

And maybe Sakurako's skills included mind reading, because she went on to confirm my analysis of her strength. "You've been dabbling in the barest edges of kitsune power, granddaughter. Blood magic is minor and fleeting. I can show you how to harvest energy from the adoration of your honor guard and even from the sky."

There it was, out in the open. For days she'd been dancing around this subject and I was suddenly sick of fending off advances without knowing for sure what we were talking about.

So I stepped in a little closer, accepting the direct path. "Stop beating around the bush, Sakurako. What exactly do you want from me?"

My grandmother was small and alone there in the basement, with the brittle bones and sagging skin of old age. But her words were powerful as she told me: "I want you to live here, be my apprentice, accept your honor guard, and take over this lineage after I'm gone."

For the last few days, some rainbows-and-kittens part of me had insisted I'd be able to maintain a relationship with my grandmother without falling into her world completely. But there was too much at stake now to dream of impossibilities. So I countered: "If I won't?"

"If you won't, then I'll be forced to select another heiress."

Well, that didn't sound so bad. Money and properties were irrelevant. For the first time all day, my shoulders relaxed away from my ears...too soon, as I discovered when my grandmother continued to speak.

"I've been the epitome of patience, granddaughter. But the time has come for you to make a choice. Do you want to be my apprentice, or would you rather I trained your sister instead?"

"WHAT HAVE YOU DONE with Kira?" Despite the fact that weapons were of little use against magic, my sword was at the old woman's throat as soon as she'd spoken.

Unfortunately, Sakurako reacted just as quickly. She twitched her fingers ever so slightly...then my sword began dissolving into pure magic that seeped like lotion into her skin.

Yelping, I yanked back all that remained to me, hiding my star ball inside my body where it couldn't be stolen. But I'd lost a third of my energy already, the absence making my legs shake so badly they threatened to drop me onto my face.

Sakurako wasn't just powerful...she was unbeatable. A supervillain laughing at the weakness of mere mortals as she soared above us with cape streaming in the wind.

Still, I stood up to the old woman, measuring the distance between us carefully. She was, when it came right down to it, small and relatively feeble. It was possible I could overpower her with my bare hands alone....

"Kira is perfectly safe," Sakurako answered before I'd decided whether it was worth trying to strangle one of my two remaining relatives in order to save the other one. "And she will remain safe, along with your pet werewolves, while you prove your worth and goodwill. Now come."

Without waiting for an answer, she turned her back on me and began striding toward the staircase that led back to the living area above us. And I had no choice but to trot after her, realizing as I did so that yesterday's twenty-four-hour oath must have recently lapsed.

That explained why the kid gloves had come off my grandmother. But it also gave me an inkling of a solution....

Unfortunately, Ransom's debt still tugged at my stomach, making it difficult to ascend behind Sakurako rather than returning to the basement and leaving this mansion behind me. Only the fact that I didn't actually know how to drive a snowmobile prevented the Atwood werewolf's demand from determining my immediate future.

So...maybe if I could pin my grandmother down to a similar promise, I could ensure my friends didn't suffer for my mistakes. Of course, I'd have to give something to get something. Good thing I had a bargaining chip on hand.

"Oyo." The name of the black-furred fox Sakurako had demanded I hand over made the old woman pause. She turned to face me from two steps higher, leaving us standing eye to eye.

"You say her name as if you know her." So my grandmother had only been guessing earlier when she'd asked for the black fox who'd showed up terrified at my party. Well, I was only guessing now as I pieced together information that would allow me to break my oath to someone I'd promised to protect.

"She was your original heir, wasn't she?" I ascended one step until I was even closer to my grandmother, looking down now in order to meet her eyes. "You trained her to use affection to harvest magic. Then, what, you heard about me and Kira and you tossed her aside?"

"I didn't *toss* anyone. The ungrateful wench left me."

"Left you and followed the breadcrumbs you'd uncovered to Atwood clan central. No wonder my pack started to crumble as soon as she arrived."

Because Gunner was an excellent alpha. He would never have let so many resentments smolder beneath the surface, just waiting to flare up into fur-form fights.

No, it was Oyo's presence that had been the instigating factor. Her presence...and maybe magic she'd used on the sly?

Either way, I could feel my promise to the black-furred kitsune sloughing off as I prepared to make Sakurako an offer I hoped she couldn't refuse. I'd need proof that my guesses held water, but if Oyo was the one responsible for killing Edward....

"I'll bring you Oyo. You can breed her to your harem, end up with two young kitsunes to raise as you wish." The offer was horrendous—I was signing Oyo's death warrant and setting up her children for a lifetime of servitude...the same sort of servitude I would also be forced to accept.

"Along with Oyo, I'll obey you, do whatever you ask of me...." I swallowed, hating the fact that my voice cracked as I sealed my fate.

"And in exchange, granddaughter?"

"In exchange, you'll relinquish Kira, Elle, and Curly. You'll return them to their home and never contact them or any other werewolves ever again."

Chapter 31

With Sakurako as an ally, transport to Ransom's proposed meeting location was simple and expedient. I boarded the helicopter beside Yuki, Elle, and Curly, reluctantly leaving my sister behind after a brief bear hug.

"Be strong. I'll come back for you tomorrow," I whispered into the top of her head...which was now closer to my nose than to my chin. In the midst of all the drama, my sister was growing. And her answer proved that point.

"*You* be strong," countered my little sister. "Don't worry about me. I'll be fine."

Which left me with only one final family member to speak with before I climbed into the aircraft slated to carry me away for a very short while. "You promised another twenty-four hours of leeway," I hissed at my grandmother. "I expect you to leave Kira alone while you wait."

We'd already hashed this out an hour earlier and I *thought* I'd trapped the wily old kitsune into a binding oath. Well, I *hoped* I'd trapped her. But it still felt like driving on the left side of the road to leave my sister behind for even a single day.

"You do your job and I'll do my job," Sakurako answered, which wasn't as heartening as she might have supposed.

Or maybe she knew her words weren't heartening. Perhaps this was just another test to determine whether I was worth cultivating in Kira's place.

So I stiffened my spine and stooped to rush under the blades of the helicopter, which were already spinning their way up to gale-force speed. I'd neutralize Oyo, relieve my debt to Ransom, then return to take my place by my grandmother's side.

And Gunner? I squashed the thought as soon as it rose within me. This was why we'd never fully mated. Because my own wishes had to play second fiddle to the safety of those I cared about.

Elle raised her brows as I joined her, widened her eyes yet further when Yuki reached over to pull me onto his lap. The helicopter wasn't so small we needed to share seating, but I knew the hard decision Yuki would soon be faced with and didn't argue. Instead, I fingered the cold shard of magic in my pocket and watched Elle pet Curly, wondering whether I'd made the right choice by bringing the werewolf pup along.

Unfortunately, there was no safe place for a bloodling at present. Not when the youngster was too useful to Sakurako to leave behind and too distasteful to hidebound alphas to be integrated into Ransom's pack. Elle, however, I could depend upon to protect a bloodling puppy. Now that she'd regained her color and her energy, I trusted my not-quite-sister-in-law as much as I trusted Gunner to keep an eye out for the weak.

Gunner. Again, I pushed his face out of my mind. Refused to consider the fact that my partner might be dead already. Couldn't fathom the thought of leaving him forever if he still lived.

So, instead, I watched the sunset as we flew westward, darkness descending over the half-melted snow beneath us. Was it only three nights since Kira and I had surreptitiously moved into our werewolf-scented cottage? Only seventy-two hours since I'd been hopeful about life as the mate of a werewolf pack leader with no notion of what my heritage meant for those caught in the crossfire?

Then the helicopter was hovering over an open field, a car waiting to carry us to the spot Ransom had designated for our meeting. I'd borrowed a cell phone and called ahead with our itinerary, but I still expected to be made to wait on the other end of our travels.

Only I wasn't. The instant we pulled up in front of the fast-food joint, Ransom rushed out to meet us. Despite tinted windows, he somehow chose the door closest to me and opened it with a hard yank. Then he drew me out of the vehicle so roughly I had to struggle against instinct, barely managing to keep my star ball under wraps.

Patience, I warned myself, crossing my arms to prevent my fists from striking my accoster. If I had any hope of convincing Ransom to save his brother rather than using me to depose Gunner, I had to keep my head.

Ransom, on the other hand, had descended into that werewolf ball of fury where he was physically human but emotionally a wolf. "I require you to fulfill your debt," he demanded, eyes blazing as he towered above me. And I knew I'd lost the gamble because I hadn't even been granted a single second in which to state my case.

"I'm ready." The words were yanked out of me by magic, my head bending down in submission despite every impulse to keep the angry werewolf in my sights. Had I misread the elder brother's character? Now, finally, was the moment of truth.

Or it would have been if Ransom hadn't started pacing a circle around me without speaking. Would have been if he hadn't waited until my knees were trembling and my breath gasping before he put me out of my misery at last.

"You will go into Atwood clan central, and you will save my brother from whatever danger he faces. *That* is what I require in exchange for your debt."

"SO HE'S ALIVE?" I GRABBED Ransom's arm as much to keep myself upright as to stop the relentless, circular pacing that was making my head whirl uncomfortably. In response, his brow furrowed exactly the way Gunner's did when he wasn't following the conversation, the similarity sucking away the remainder of my breath.

Unfortunately, Ransom's answer didn't help jumpstart my breathing. "I don't know. I expected you to know. Mate woo-woo and all that." He waved his hands around to indicate tether magic, and I suddenly wondered whether this so-called alpha had ever managed to see the connections within his own clan during the years he'd spent leading a pack.

So Ransom knew no more than I did. Gunner might be dead already. I closed my eyes for one split second then took a deep breath and returned to my original plan. Ransom had feet on the ground and a wish to help his brother. It was better to use him than to go off half-cocked without any information at all.

I opened my mouth to ask questions...just as Curly leapt through the open limousine door and into Ransom's arms. Despite myself, I laughed at the incongruous picture. This was exactly the way the puppy greeted Gunner. Too bad the elder Atwood brother was less amenable to the invasion of his space.

"You brought a *pet* to a war council?" I don't think he intended to punch Curly, but the hand intended to ward off the youngster's approach turned into a blow anyway. Yelping, Curly retreated beneath the vehicle, prompting Elle and Yuki to disembark and pull him out.

"And what is *that*?" Ransom continued, staring at the human while making the hair on the back of my neck stand on end with his use of "what" instead of "who." Dehumanizing much?

"That's an ally," I said simply. "Now tell me what you know about clan central."

And he did, finally, after Curly was stuffed back inside the limousine and Yuki was similarly out of sight beside Elle. It took the alpha half an hour to tell me, but what it boiled down to could be summed up in just a few key points.

The alphas and selected warriors from three neighboring packs had sealed the borders of Atwood clan central sometime late yesterday. Ransom had managed to send in multiple scouts, but none had reemerged.

What *had* come out was a message promising to cleanse the Atwood pack of dangerous kitsunes. "When they're done, they plan to divide the territory," Ransom finished, his feet once again carrying him in circles which I was now almost agitated enough to join him in.

"They plan to divide the territory," I repeated, not wanting to state the obvious—that if Atwood territory was about to be divvied up, that meant no alpha remained to head up Gunner's friends and family.

"Which is where you come in." Whatever his feelings about bloodlings, Ransom and I were of one mind when it came to Gunner. "They want a kitsune, we'll give them a kitsune. Then they'll let my brother free."

Chapter 32

The snow had turned crusty by the time Yuki and I strode into Atwood clan central an hour later. Ransom's intel suggested the village should have been full of all the werewolves I'd left behind plus a strong contingent of invading neighbors. But the streets were empty, porch lights were extinguished, and the entire area was as silent as the grave.

It reeked of sulfur, however. The rotten-egg aroma nipped at my nostrils from the first moment I stepped out of the limousine and it grew stronger and stronger as I followed pack bonds illuminated by Elle's freely offered blood.

Both sulfur stench and pack bonds led me in the same direction. The community hall. It rose before us, tall and looming...and loud with raised voices apparently engaged in extended debate.

"...has not yet been decided!" This was a stranger, no one I recognized. But from the timbre of his voice, I suspected he might be Gunner's counterpart from one of the neighboring territories.

"Isn't it obvious, Russell? This pack has fallen under the sway of a kitsune. Without further information, the safest course of action is to slay them all."

The words should have been chilling. But, instead, it was all I could do not to dance and sing right there on the sidewalk. Because I was close enough now to disentangle the ropes of light arrowing away from my midriff, and one in particular let me breathe fully for the first time in what felt like days.

Stroking the wide tether with one cautious finger, I could hardly believe this bond sprang out straight and true from my person. I couldn't still be connected to a dead werewolf, could I? If not...then this thick rope of light meant Gunner hadn't perished when I left him behind to be overwhelmed by a stronger wolf.

Whether Gunner's life continued after today, however, was apparently up to the neighboring alphas. So I was relieved when a third voice spoke up, calm and measured and apparently on my side.

"Easy for you to say when your clan has been at odds with the Atwoods for generations." So we had at least one supporter on this council. It was good to know...and that fact made it easier for me to walk on past the community hall's main entrance, nodding at Yuki to separate our paths as I continued following the evidence of my nose.

Because the sulfurous reek was strong around the front of the community hall...but it emanated from above rather than from within. Without the need for words, Yuki padded silently along a fire escape leading up the west face of the building while I mirrored his movements on the opposite side.

The climb was simple, even in human form. Near the top, however, I hesitated, letting Yuki draw ahead of me.

Because he was my ace in the hole and the solution to the dueling compulsions in my belly. So I hung back as my human bait stepped toward Oyo, giving him time to prepare the path so I could turn my former charge over to a fate worse than death.

THE WAIT WAS AGONIZING. So I occupied myself peering through a dirty clerestory window into the meeting space below me.

Gunner. He was the first thing I saw, and for long seconds the only thing I had eyes for. My never-to-be mate was bound and gagged atop a raised dais, naked save for the ropes that encircled both body and chair in a complicated arrangement I assumed was meant to contain him even if he attempted to shift.

Gunner's attention, however, wasn't on me, or even on the alpha werewolves arguing beside him. Instead, his gaze was trained upon Atwood pack members huddled together in the main section of the hall.

Or, rather, upon the males and children huddling while females stood around them with weapons at the ready. The guards included Elizabeth, Becky, plus several other shifters I'd met in passing. They weren't protecting their clan mates, however. Instead, the females were preventing rebellion as ably as Gunner's ropes and gag currently restrained him.

Had the Atwood females gotten so angry with the pack's misogyny that they'd risen up against their mates, fathers, and brothers? Or was this just another indication that Oyo's powers were far greater than I'd originally supposed?

"Oyo-chan."

Yuki's murmured endearment drew my attention away from the odd disloyalty of the Atwood females...but not before I saw them react to a word they shouldn't have been able to hear. Elizabeth, in particular, nearly swiped her sword across a neighbor's belly as she raised one arm as if to soothe an aching forehead. Beside her, Becky—who I'd never seen wield a sword before—winced and sliced apart the top of her boot.

So Oyo *was* manipulating my pack mates just as I'd suspected. Was manipulating them...and had almost lost her hold in surprise at being discovered by the male she'd once considered more than a pawn.

This was evidence enough for me...but apparently not sufficient to relieve my magically fueled debt to Oyo. Because my feet still refused to move as I fingered the shard of magic Sakurako had provided. Instead, I waited as the other kitsune spoke.

"You came for me," the female whispered. And from the rustle of movement on the rooftop, I suspected she and Yuki were engaging in a hasty embrace of greeting.

"I will always come for you, Oyo-chan," he assured her. "But I knew you were clever enough to hold your own."

"Clever." Her laugh was a fox's bark, short and almost painful. "Was it clever to kill that werewolf? Edmund? Edward? Whatever. I thought he was Mai's enemy, but his death only made matters worse. And now look what's happening...."

There. That was the admission I'd been waiting for, the confirmation that Oyo had been poaching on my pack bonds, using my debt to manipulate those who cared about me.

And yet...I remained crouched on the snowy fire escape with head bowed, trying to think of another solution. Trying to think of a way out that didn't involve turning Oyo over to Sakurako to mate herself to death.

Because, yes, the black-furred fox was both a manipulator and a murderer. But she'd also been raised as the pawn of my grandmother, trained to fixate the attention of a harem of human males in an effort to steal their power. In her shoes would I have been any more ethical? Would I have been any less desperate to escape?

But there was no other solution available to me. My hard-earned protection for Kira was ticking away by the second. Meanwhile, beneath us, the neighboring alphas converged upon Gunner, the same enforcer who had beaten my partner now slicing through his gag carelessly enough to leave a line of red running down Gunner's cheek.

"Explain again why you believe this pack is salvageable." This was the voice of the Atwood-friendly alpha, but from above I could see how tired even our supposed ally was growing of the debate.

"My mate is a kitsune." Gunner's voice was hoarse and scratchy, as if he'd said the same thing half a dozen times previously. "She is not responsible for this problem. If you'll let her return, she'll stop the problem in its tracks."

"Or cover it up." This was the alpha most obviously against us, and beside him the third pack leader nodded his head in agreement. No, I couldn't trust these werewolves to come to the appropriate decision and save Gunner.

So, without allowing myself to think about what I was doing, I hopped onto the rooftop, strode fox-silent up behind Oyo, and slapped the frigid shard of magic into Yuki's waiting hand.

Chapter 33

Oyo was deeply entwined in the arms of her lover, but my grandmother had been right—she sensed the shard of magic the instant it touched him. Struggling to free herself, her eyes met mine for a split second...just as Yuki thrust the magical dagger directly into his beloved's breast.

I'd thought I was prepared for this eventuality. After all, Sakurako had assured me this was only a magical neutering, not a death blow. But I still flinched at the horror on Oyo's face as she realized that the man she loved had conspired with the woman she'd trusted in order to take her down.

Light flared around her body as fox ears sprouted from the top of a still-human forehead. The sulfurous stench deepened as Oyo cringed down over her belly, moaning as she was caught in the worst sort of shift.

"I thought you loved me," she cried...or at least I guessed that was what she was saying. Because vulpine teeth were now sprouting past lips that had been plump and human a moment earlier. Her words were almost irreparably slurred.

Then Oyo could speak no longer. The flare of light shrouded her, shrunk her...and settled into a golden collar encircling the throat of a black-furred fox. At the same time, the rotten-egg aroma was abruptly and entirely gone.

Beneath us, the meeting erupted into shouting followed by the unmistakable metallic clangs of swordplay. Oyo's hold over my pack mates had faded the instant she was separated from her powers and I *needed* to get below as quickly as possible to make sure neighbor werewolves didn't do anything terrible in their haste to regain the upper hand.

But, instead, I stood frozen by the tableau before me. Watched and listened as Yuki proved that Oyo wasn't the only one who had been broken by my grandmother's heavy-handed control.

"I love the mistress," Yuki answered coldly. "And I loved you when I thought you might one day be the new mistress. Unfortunately, it looks like that will no longer be the case."

Then he turned away as if Oyo was nothing, never mind the fact that the fox he ignored was scratching so frantically at her collar that it spun around and around her throat without stopping. In half an hour, she'd be raw and bleeding. But Sakurako had assured me Oyo would never get the restraining circlet off.

And, given the certainty of his job's completion, Yuki simply didn't care about the agony he had left behind. Didn't even reach out to calm Oyo's scratching to prevent future pain to the shifter he supposedly cared for. Instead, he strode over to the fire escape, preparing to guard my pathway to the ground.

This was the pack I was willingly walking into. This was the pack I'd chosen as my own.

For Kira's sake, I reminded myself. Then ignoring my own squeamishness, I snapped a lead onto Oyo's collar. "Let's go," I told her as I followed the male down.

BY THE TIME WE REACHED the door at the front of the community hall, the interior had become a battleground with no clear evidence of who might win. Atwoods outnumbered the invaders by a wide margin, but only the sword-bearing females seemed willing to do more than protect themselves.

Instead, it was as if the command Gunner uttered three days earlier—fight only with swords—had gone into effect with a belated vengeance. Which gave our enemies an extreme advantage as they pressed in against the ring of females now intent upon safeguarding rather than containing their family and friends.

"Where to?" Yuki asked, his sword angling across to guard me rather than his own body. Together, we watched wolves in their prime lunge at Atwood grannies while Gunner's best warriors snapped, feinted...then failed to fight back.

This was going to be a slaughter if we didn't shut it down quickly. So despite Yuki's not-so-subtle wish for us to return to Sakurako's secluded hideout, I told him the obvious: "I'm going to cut off the head of the serpent." In other words, I intended to make the invading alphas call off their underlings by hook or by crook.

And, to my surprise, Yuki didn't even attempt to argue. "Sounds like fun," he admitted. Then, glancing at Oyo and raising his eyebrows, he added: "May I?"

It seemed cruel to place the collared fox into the arms of her former lover. But I wasn't used to fighting with a living being tucked under one arm and I *needed* to reach Gunner ASAP. So I nodded...then lost track of Yuki entirely as I took a running leap onto the top of a banister that encircled one side of the room.

From my elevated perch, I could see the invaders much better.....and, unfortunately, could be seen by them as well. So I wasn't surprised to be met by a wall of weapons at the far end of my raised pathway, proving that the Atwood tradition of swordcraft extended to the neighboring packs.

"I don't suppose you guys would like to let me through to talk to your alphas?" I called downward...then dove forward without waiting for a reply. Because at any minute the enemy alphas would realize they only had to threaten Gunner in order to make his entire pack—including me—submit to the boot poised atop our neck.

Which would leave us in a worse bind than we currently suffered from. So I slashed and parried and noted that the five males I faced were good enough to overcome a lone swordswoman of any caliber if given enough time. Which meant I couldn't risk disarming them gradually. I'd have to dole out more punishing blows and hope the injuries didn't scuttle future reconciliation with neighboring packs.

Or that would have been the case if two warm bodies hadn't materialized at my shoulders. Elizabeth on one side, the male who'd snarled during our sword practice on the other. Neither one had a reason to help me, and Elizabeth had a very good reason to push me in front of a bus.

After all, even though I hadn't wanted anything to happen to her father, I had indeed turned out to be the reason for his death. But perhaps Elizabeth hadn't yet come to that conclusion. Or perhaps pack was simply more important to her than personal grudges. Whatever the reason, she met my gaze evenly before she and her companion both dove into the battle so furiously I was able to slip around my opponents and ascend the stairs onto the stage.

"You came back."

The enforcer who'd beaten Gunner stood before me, and I barely managed not to skewer him in retaliation for the pain he'd doled out. But this battle wouldn't be won with a weapon. Instead, I let my sword trickle back into my skin while I peered over the enforcer's shoulder and met the eyes of three neighboring alphas one by one.

The males were glancing back and forth between me and Yuki, who held Oyo in his arms in a very visible spot at the other end of the hall. The visual aid was appreciated, so I used it. "I've collared the rogue kitsune," I told the alphas, having to raise my voice almost into a shout to be heard above the battle. "Her power has been neutralized and she will be punished...."

I'd intended to continue explaining then to move on to threats if necessary, stopping only when the neighboring alphas released their hold over all Atwood wolves. But to my surprise, Gunner was the one who answered, his voice rough, urgent, yet entirely clear.

"No, Mai, you can't do that. Oyo is under my protection. I refuse to allow you to trade her life for mine."

Chapter 34

"Gunner, you have to trust me."

This wasn't the time to explain the full extent of Oyo's awfulness. I couldn't mention my grandmother's magic in front of the assembled alphas either, not if the goal was to assure our opponents that the Atwood pack was no longer under a kitsune's sway.

Especially since I could already see the three strange alphas turning against me. "This is your mate?" asked the fence-sitter, his face not giving away a single clue about whether my sword-wielding appearance had swayed him over to the other side of the fence.

"Yes." Gunner was firm, but his brow remained furrowed. Meanwhile, he neglected to back up my assertion that Oyo had been the one responsible for manipulating his clan.

"And you believe she's truly partnering with you rather than controlling you?" This was the neighbor whose apparent goal was to behead Gunner and take over at least a portion of his territory. "Then you should have regained control of your pack by now. Tell them to stop fighting..."

"...And you'll do the same for your wolves?" Gunner wasn't an idiot so he didn't trust the greedy alpha as far as he could throw him. Still, his attention remained riveted on me rather than on his opponent, sienna eyes searching my face.

Gunner was buying time while coming to a decision, I realized. So I pushed as hard as I could to send information down our tether the way he'd once shared his own vision. If Gunner heard Oyo's admission in my memory, then he'd stop looking for another solution that didn't involve the redhead being punished for her past actions....

But the tether—still obvious and visible with Elle's blood empowering me—remained inert beneath my hand. And, finally, Gunner came to a decision without any additional information. "I'll..." he started, only to be interrupted by a change in the sounds of battle echoing up to us from the floor of the hall.

At first, I thought that the conflict between Atwoods and invaders had been settled. Why else would a lull be rolling across the crowd? Then I noted that the Atwood sword-wielders were still fighting frantically. It was their opponents who turned in a wave to face the doorway that I had recently come through.

And no wonder when that dark rectangle was no longer empty and open to the snowy night beyond it. Instead, Ransom stood bold and tall in its center, innumerable well-armed shifters at his flank.

Backup had arrived. Backup...or a deposed alpha ready to take his rightful place at the head of the clan he'd been ejected from. I shivered, hesitated. Gunner, in contrast, trusted his sibling implicitly.

"*Stand down,*" he commanded his underlings. And as the wave of discarded weapons fell from the hands of my students, Ransom's pack mates raised their own blades to take over the fight.

Gunner had proven his control without giving our enemies the advantage. And Ransom had been the ally who made that parry work.

"I'LL BE WATCHING YOU."

The least friendly neighboring alpha stepped past us as I slipped my sword through Gunner's bonds to free him. And even though he should have been stiff and sore after hours without moving, Gunner rose as lithely as he'd leapt from the trunk of Old Red two days before.

"The feeling is mutual," my partner growled as I stepped around the pair of them to deal with my own problems. Where was she? In the midst of the Atwood reunion and enemy outflux, it took a long moment to find the black-furred fox within the crowd.

But there was Yuki holding tightly onto Oyo. I'd been half fearful that Kira's ticket to safety would have escaped while my attention was elsewhere, or that Yuki would have changed his mind again, taken his lover, and run. But the duo instead waited just past the edges of the fighting...beneath a clock that promised I had only nineteen hours left before my sister's safety ran thin.

Nineteen hours and a ten-hour drive to fit into that window. Because the helicopter had departed immediately after dropping us off. Which left me so little time to spend with my never-to-be partner before leaving his pack behind for good....

I turned back around just as the third and final alpha spoke to Gunner. "Our agreement still stands?" This was the pro-Atwood neighbor nailing down details of yet another alliance. Gunner clearly wasn't done saying farewell to his uninvited house guests, so this time I turned my attention to Elle instead.

"Can you watch them for me?" I mouthed, silently tugging on our tether to get her attention before cutting my eyes to Yuki and Oyo. I didn't expect my friend to hear me, but comprehension dawned on her face more easily than it should have. Was this what it would have been like to be part of a pack?

Sure enough, Elle was already pushing through the crowd toward Yuki and Oyo even though her mouth was now pinched into a straight line. She disagreed with my intention to turn myself back over to Sakurako. But apparently she was willing to assist me in the matter nonetheless.

Then the community hall was emptying, enemy shifters leaving as quickly as they'd come. Meanwhile, wolves from both Atwood packs intermingled, spending a few precious minutes with one-time neighbors they hadn't seen for several months due to the actions of their alphas.

Which left Gunner and Ransom alone on the dais...well, alone except for me.

"Brother." Gunner held out one hand to his sibling, waiting a beat longer than I would have for reciprocation that clearly wasn't forthcoming before allowing the appendage in question to drop back down to his side. Still, he continued attempting to build bridges. "I'm glad you've come home. It's high time we learned to rule together."

Together. It was a tremendous admission...but apparently not quite tremendous enough to mollify the older brother. Because Ransom remained dour as he eyed Gunner consideringly. Then, slowly, he shook his head.

"I will be your ally if you support my bid for the northern territory," Ransom growled. "But don't think I'm going to retreat with my tail between my legs to accept your scraps. You cast us out and we've made new lives for ourselves. Lives that don't involve bloodlings and kitsunes and losing ground our grandfather bought."

Beneath us, the members of both Atwood packs let their conversations falter into silence, shifter ears catching every word from up above. This wasn't the reconciliation Gunner had been hoping for...but at least it wasn't the coup I'd feared.

"Take what Ransom offers," I begged Gunner silently, wishing once again that he could hear my words.

And maybe he did. Because my never-mate's eyes slipped toward me momentarily, then he nodded graciously. "Of course I'll support your territory, brother. I hope the lines of communication will remain open between our packs."

At long last, Ransom was gone, Gunner's underlings had settled in for the night, and I was alone with my never-to-be mate. Without Kira present to necessitate the keeping up of appearances, he drew me not toward my cottage but toward his own residence...a home that was considerably larger than it had been the last time I'd walked through its doors.

"This is Kira's room," I guessed, turning an awestruck circle within the addition that Gunner had created on the far side of his living room. There were fox ledges on the walls for playing in fur form, a glass-fronted cabinet full of yearned-for magic-trick paraphernalia, a full-size desk for schoolwork, and of course the mandatory canopied princess bed.

"Mm hm," Gunner answered, hovering so close to my body I could feel his heat without our skin ever touching. The alpha's restraint was doing crazy things to my thermal-regulation system...and his subsequent words were like a bucket of cold water poured over my head. "Where is my favorite teenager anyway?"

This was the beginning of the questions I couldn't answer...well, that I couldn't answer without losing the few hours I'd hoped to spend in Gunner's arms. So, rather than lying to a wolf who could detect prevarication through pure instinct, I curled my finger through his belt loop and drew him away from the teenager's paradise and toward the adult bedroom at the other end of his home.

"Come to bed," I murmured, plucking at his sleeve as he hesitated in the doorway then recoiling as my finger slipped across an open wound and came away bloody. His current pain was my fault...and I'd just made it even worse.

To my surprise, Gunner didn't wince at being poked in the middle of a red and angry laceration. Instead, he chuckled, grabbing my hand and replacing it around his wrist.

"I'm not so broken I can't welcome you home properly," he told me, using one hand to fumble at buttons that nonetheless obeyed his command with alacrity.

It was finally happening, the moment I'd been craving for weeks. So why did my heart hurt when Gunner paused before continuing, speaking a sentiment we hadn't yet shared aloud?

"I love you."

Three words. Three arrows piercing lungs and stomach and head as certainly as if they'd been made of wood and steel and murderous intention. I froze, unable to answer as the reality of my choice became thoroughly clear.

Because this was what I'd be losing when I returned to my grandmother tomorrow. Sure, Sakurako was an old woman. Eventually, she'd die and leave me to make my own choices. But even though becoming her apprentice wasn't a life sentence, I'd never again be someone Gunner looked at so warmly. Not after being molded by my grandmother's iron will.

I couldn't bear the thought of the alpha's disappointment upon seeing what I was fated to turn into. And I couldn't risk harming pack mates who had already lost so much at a kitsune's hand.

So once I left this home, I'd never again see Atwood clan central. Instead, I'd trust the alpha who might have been my mate to raise my sister. And I'd treat his memory as a spark of fire to warm an increasingly frigid heart.

Eventually, I'd be just like my grandmother. Eventually I'd stop caring. If I was lucky, I might even begin to forget.

My face must have broadcast this tumult of emotions because Gunner's caresses turned platonic and soothing, his huge hand cupping my chin. "I don't expect an answer," he told me, incorrectly interpreting my lack of a reply as a continuation of my ongoing independence battle. "I'm just happy to have you beside me. I'm so grateful that you're here."

And I *was* here. For an hour or two—the most I could spare from Sakurako's timeline. I shivered as the full force of the future brushed up against me. And Gunner, always attuned to my emotions, provided yet another opening for me to get weighty secrets off my chest.

"Do you want to talk about it?"

Gunner was willing to ignore the demands of our flesh and hash out the argument that still simmered unresolved between us. But I wasn't. Not when any explanation would leave me without the single memory I ached to carry with me back into the snow.

"Tomorrow," I answered, brushing my lips against Gunner's. But those final words were a lie, because in the morning I intended to be gone.

I WOKE IN GUNNER'S arms an uncountable number of hours later, my heart pounding with fear that I'd overslept. I hadn't meant to close my eyes at all, actually. Had intended to wait out Gunner's exhaustion then leave once he was deeply asleep.

Only, I'd been the one to wear myself out and descend into slumber. I'd been the one to snuggle into his safe harbor and forget about the impending storm.

Now, as I gently disentangled myself from the werewolf I'd once thought would be my life partner, I powered up my cell phone and sent Elle the long-awaited text. *"Bring Yuki and Oyo. We're going."*

"Are you sure?" she countered immediately, clearly wide awake and waiting for me.

"Be ready in five minutes," was my only answer. Of course I wasn't sure...but I'd do whatever had to be done.

It wasn't as late as I'd thought, however. So I slipped into the kitchen, found a pen and pad of paper, and sat down to explain myself to the mate I was leaving behind.

Because it wasn't fair to leave Gunner dangling. Wasn't fair to make him think I was rejecting our mating through anything other than a desperate bid to save my sister's last few years of childhood. The only way to even the scales a smidgeon was to tell the truth so he could find another female to fill the hole in his pack and his heart.

"*I need to explain,*" I started. Scratched that out and tried another opening: "*It isn't because of you that I'm doing this....*"

Okay, that was so trite as to be depressing. Gunner deserved to understand how I really felt. And this time when I pushed my pen's point into the paper, the words finally began to flow.

"*I have to leave for the sake of my sister,*" I started. "*But in my heart, you will always be my mate....*"

Only, rather than finishing my explanation, the pen streaked a crazy line across the paper. Then it fell out of nerveless fingers as our mate bond clicked into place with the force of a tractor trailer hitting a pedestrian on a crosswalk.

For an instant, my vision dimmed, my ears rang, and I lost all track of reality. "You implied I had to *say* the words," I moaned in protest.

Wait, had I sent that emoting down the mate bond? Had Gunner felt the contact even though he slept?

I gasped, trying to regain enough breath to rush out of the house without looking backwards. I couldn't afford to be bogged down in explanations with Kira's future on the line. Plus, if Gunner understood what I was planning, he'd never let me go....

But my legs crumpled beneath me and I ended up leaning against the counter instead of sprinting away out the door. All I could do was beg silently: "*Stay where you are. Stay safe,*" as wooden legs gradually carried me through the kitchen at the speed of a beer-soaked garden snail. One step after the other, from counter to counter to cabinet to door.

There. I was walking almost normally again even though the pain in my stomach was so intense I would have thrown up if I'd bothered eating before I slept. This I could handle. Being mated then leaving my mate forever wasn't so horrible....

And as if the thought had called agony back into existence, I doubled up over a spear of pain as intense as a sword slicing into my gut.

Gut wounds are usually fatal, I thought vaguely. Then, more clearly—*Ten hours is all I have left.*

I refused to leave Kira to our grandmother's mercy. So I straightened, looked down at a stomach I'd thought would be bleeding but wasn't.

Finding no wound evident, I opened the door and walked out into the night.

Chapter 36

"This is a terrible idea," Elle informed me. "You can't even drive."

I leaned back against the heated, leather seat on the passenger side of the vehicle, trying to ignore how disloyal I felt taking the car Gunner had bought me while making my escape. Glancing back over my shoulder, I assured myself that Yuki and Oyo were sleeping. Then I countered, "I *can* drive. You just wouldn't let me behind the wheel."

"Because you look like death. You do realize Gunner will feel exactly like you do when he wakes up and finds you missing?"

No, I hadn't realized that. Somehow, I'd assumed the pain of mating then leaving would all be mine to bear. The knowledge that Gunner would deal with the same sort of agony started my head pounding as if Kira were using my skull as her own personal drum.

"Can I protect him by breaking the mate bond?" I didn't even manage to finish the question since the last word stuck in my throat like the fifth cracker swallowed without a sip of water in between.

Rather than answering immediately, Elle glanced at me sideways, the dark, empty highway giving her leeway to divide her attention as she drove. "Do you want to?"

Yes, of course I did. I didn't want to spend the rest of my life getting used to this pain, nor did I want to subject Gunner to the same agony.

And yet, the word that came out of my mouth—this time crackerless and adamant—was: "No."

"There's your answer."

For another half hour, the car rolled down the highway in silence, road noise dulled by the cocoon of comfort Gunner had paid top dollar for. Eventually, the warmth of the leather started feeling like Gunner's body spooning me. And I was halfway asleep when his half-sister spoke once again.

"Maybe we can come up with a compromise before we get there. You and Kira dividing your time between your grandmother's estate and Atwood clan central. Or we could find something else the old woman covets...."

"Elle, stop it." She meant well, but every time I was reminded of my situation another wave of pain racked my body. And now I was starting to wonder whether my friend would betray my location after she returned with Kira, giving Gunner a roadmap to walk straight into a powerful kitsune's lair.

That couldn't happen. I could leave him—just barely. But I couldn't be responsible for further injury or death. "You have to promise not to tell your brother—either brother—where I'm going," I demanded, my voice so harsh Yuki turned over on the back seat.

"What if...?" Elle started.

But I shushed her in the werewolf way, with a hand laid gently on her forearm. "Elle, *promise*."

And, after one long moment of silence, my friend agreed.

WE WERE FIVE MINUTES tardy when the gate opened up before us despite there being no human operator visible. Snow had melted off the road, so the approach to Sakurako's mansion was easy to navigate. Within moments, Elle had pulled up beside the multi-colored fountain, then she and I glanced at each other in a sudden unity of thought.

We did not want to get out of that car.

Yuki, on the other hand, was glad to return to his mistress. He opened the back door with alacrity...and before any of us knew what was happening, Oyo had slipped between his legs and escaped.

"Grab her!" I yelled, scrambling to follow my own order. Without the fox, I had nothing to trade for Kira. And despite Oyo's leash spinning out behind her, we three resembled a circus act as we futilely tumbled over each other in the haste of our pursuit.

Only our clownishness was irrelevant because...

"Going somewhere?"

The elderly kitsune appeared out of nowhere inches in front of Oyo's nose. How had I ever thought of Sakurako as a little old lady? Now she towered above her former apprentice, magic buzzing like insects as Oyo's feet literally froze to the ground.

The four-legger yelped as she tried—and failed—to free them. But Sakurako's attention had already moved on to spear me as I pulled myself up out of the slush pile that seemed to have been placed there for the sole purpose of soaking my clothes.

"And *you*," she continued. "*You* are late."

"Where's Kira?" With an effort, I ignored the electricity seeping out of the pores of the other kitsune and headed toward the open front door instead. I hadn't missed the deadline by enough minutes that Kira should have suffered for it. But her absence was telling, to say the least.

Only my sister wasn't being punished for my lapses. Because even as I brushed past Sakurako, Kira was stepping out into the sunlight with a big smile on her face. "Mai! I've been waiting for you. I want to show you the library and..."

And no one had told the thirteen-year-old about the swap. Now it was my turn to glare at Sakurako, and I thought she might have actually wilted slightly beneath the force of my rage.

"Kira, walk with me," I interjected, taking my sister's hand for what was likely to be the last time in decades or at least years. The ache of my mate bond had dulled with distance, but now the pounding in my head leapt back to life with a jolt.

In response, my feet tried to stumble, but I pushed aside physical ailments and made my sister the entirety of my world for one brief moment. Still, she noticed my trembling, glanced back over one shoulder, asked me, "What's wrong?"

Rather than answering, I picked up the pace, surprised to find no complaint from my sister as she trotted right alongside me. Only when we were far enough away from our audience so shifter ears couldn't pick up on our conversation did we turn and face each other, neither of us initiating the movement but our toe tips meeting at the exact same time.

This was what we were losing. Sisterhood. Bonds of blood that ran deeper than mere genetics. I would never watch Kira blossom into womanhood, would never teach her to fight with a sharp-edged sword.

"You're going and I'm staying," I started. Then, as bargains and complaints rose in my sister's eyes, I shut her down abruptly. "I can't change this, Kira. Please don't ask me to."

Given the way she liked to gripe about everything from breakfast to homework, I thought she'd argue or at least rail against the fates and the world. Instead, my little sister stood as tall and straight as I did, asked a single question: "Until when?"

"I don't know," I told her truthfully. But, as Kira slipped cold fingers around my waist and hugged me tight enough to last a lifetime, I had a sinking suspicion our separation would last for a long, long time.

Chapter 37

Without Kira and Curly to guard from danger, I slept in the bed. Assuming, that is, the hours of tossing and turning could really be called sleep. Eventually, though, the sun rose and I groggily sat up to greet the daylight...only to be met by an agonizing burning where the mate tether intersected with my gut.

"Stay away. Stay safe," I whispered, barely able to speak over the spears of pain piercing my center. I knew I was too distant for my words to be captured by their intended recipient, but I *had* to try to keep Gunner in clan central. All it would take was one wave of Sakurako's fingers and he'd turn into a blood donor fueling who knew what kitsune atrocities at her whim.

And perhaps my request made it through after all. More likely, my body simply couldn't sustain that level of pain indefinitely. Whatever the reason, the throbbing receded to a dull ache after only a few seconds, and I sank back down into the soft mattress, pulling the comforter up over my head.

I lay there for minutes or hours, stroking the tendril of magic that connected me to my absent mate. The tether curled like a kitten around my fingers, warmed when I touched it...then surged back into piercing torment as the covers were ripped off from over my head.

"You've wallowed enough."

My grandmother stood above me, fully dressed and redolent with magic. When had I started smelling and seeing the influx of power as it gently seeped into her wrinkled skin? Whatever the reason behind my newfound abilities, the old woman now appeared spider-like, the only difference being that she consumed rather than spun her own web.

"Are you sick of tormenting Oyo already?" I muttered, turning over and trying to bury my face in one of the half dozen pillows arrayed across the bed between us. Then that soft cushion was yanked out from under me and I found myself tumbling over to land on my butt on the cold, hard floor.

"Oyo is immaterial," Sakurako answered. Then, raising one eyebrow, she offered information I hadn't asked for. "A golden collar isn't temporary, granddaughter. Oyo will remain a fox forever. I've sent her out into the forest to live as she wills."

Harsh. But perhaps kinder than the fate I'd thought the redheaded kitsune would be faced with. How would Sakurako punish my sister if I similarly failed to obey her commands?

The reminder of why I was here had me on my feet before Sakurako could prod me further. "What did you have in mind for today?" I asked even though I didn't really care how my apprenticeship started.

But Sakurako took my words at face value. "We are twenty years behind in your training, granddaughter," the old woman answered. "Today we will begin to remedy that mistake."

WE RECONVENED IN MY grandmother's study, a room decorated with reds and yellows and further warmed by a raging fireplace. Despite the moderate temperatures, however, I couldn't stop shivering as I huddled beneath a vast lap robe.

"Lighting a candle is the simplest example of pure magic," Sakurako explained, creating flame on all ten wicks simultaneously without expending any apparent effort at all. The candles flickered out, then she turned to face me. "Now you try."

I didn't want to, but this was what I'd signed up for. Learning to harness my kitsune nature and becoming my grandmother's mini-me. Ignoring the stab of complaint where my mate tether circled around my belly, I pulled up my star ball...then drew a blank.

Because—beyond blood magic, which was currently unavailable to me—the only thing I knew how to do was to physically toss my star ball at the candles and hope it sparked one of them on fire. But even I knew that was a terrible idea when loss of my magic made me droop and my hands were already shaking with a combination of exhaustion and cold.

Then Sakurako's fingers covered mine, her flesh warmer than expected as she pushed the star ball back inside my skin. "Not like that, granddaughter. You can't waste your own energy so flagrantly. You need to send out magic you've sucked in."

My head was pounding so hard it was difficult to focus. But I squinted against the pain and forced myself to pay attention as my grandmother lit the candles a second time. Ah, now I saw what she was doing. Saw the surge of power flowing from elsewhere—from her honor guard?—into her chest then back out through her fingers, igniting into flame.

Yuck. My grandmother was an energy vampire. And Sakurako must have understood my thought processes because she narrowed her eyes as she spoke.

"This is your heritage, granddaughter. A kitsune mistress gains the admiration of her honor guard then she uses that freely given power to protect them in exchange. It's an equal trade of energy, not so much different from what happens within a werewolf pack."

It was different. It was a whole-nother-ballpark different. Even as I assured myself of that fact, I stroked the tiny mating tendril still twined around my waist.

"Don't waste the werewolf for practice." I hadn't spoken a word since entering her study, but Sakurako carried on a conversation as if oblivious to that fact. "That bond is your most powerful source of energy. Save it for a rainy day."

"I won't use Gunner's affection. Rainy day or any day." My voice cracked as I spoke but I was no less adamant for the show of weakness.

"Then you'd better get to work on that honor guard, hadn't you?" Sakurako countered. "The most expedient path is getting hot and sweaty together. Just remember what I told you about showing favoritism at such an early date."

Chapter 38

The members of Sakurako's honor guard lived in their own wing on the first story of the mansion, behind a long line of doors with no identifying features to hint at who slept within. Given no way of guessing who was in residence at the moment, I banged on the first six doors one after another, then stood back as sleepy males stumbled out in pajamas, boxers, or in one case entirely nude.

"Um." I looked them over, noted that my grandmother had *definitely* included physique in her requirements for service. Then my gaze caught on Yuki at the end of the line.

Oyo's former lover appeared delighted to see me, despite the fact that he must have been on the night shift like the others. And yet, his presence sent a queasy rumbling through my gut.

"Yuki, go back to bed." Turning away so I wouldn't have to see the light in his eyes fade into disappointment, I addressed the other five men with more warmth in my tone. "I'd like to get to know you all better." Then I dropped my hand down to the sword belted at my hip, raised my eyebrows, and waited for them to catch on.

Then waited. And waited. For warriors, they were remarkably slow to get the message. Perhaps binding yourself to a kitsune mistress had a dulling effect on the mind?

Whatever the reason, all five of them just stood there awaiting further instructions. So, at last, I sighed then elaborated. "Get dressed and show me where you keep your swords. We're going to spar."

And *that* got them moving like I'd kicked over a hornet's nest.

I'D EXPECTED THERE to be a practice hall inside the mansion. But, instead, my five chosen warriors led me out the back and into a courtyard where flowering vines dripped and rotted off the rock walls and onto the ground. This was the result of kitsune magic, brilliant autumnal foliage killed before its proper hour by an unseasonal snow. Ignoring the shiver that passed through me at the realization, I split us up into three duos then proceeded to fight.

We were practicing rather than engaging in true battle, but we still used real weapons rather than padded blades. "I'm Koki," offered my opponent even as he dipped beneath my guard and nearly sliced through my jugular, the sun glinting brilliantly off his sword.

Rather than answering audibly, my blade deflected his and twisted sideways to slice at his exposed fingers as a retaliatory measure. He grinned as he danced backwards, sword flying so rapidly it turned into a blur before my eyes.

It was a pleasure to spar with a well-matched partner, even when he lunged nearly horizontally and managed to slice a thin nick in the only pair of jeans I now had to my name. I took advantage of the resistance of the fabric, however, and managed to cut the thinnest scratch across his forearm even as I told him, "I'm Mai."

Instantly, my opponent was bowing, speaking acknowledgement of my success directly to the ground. "I know who you are, Mai-sama. It is a great honor to lose to you."

I smiled...and that's when it happened. A streak of magic arced like lightning away from his groin and into my center. It was lewd and unpleasant...and infused me with so much energy I thought I might have been able to levitate into open air.

"SWITCH PARTNERS!" MY voice came out high and breathy, an almost orgasmic pleasure suffusing my core. I'd thought I was so clever choosing swordplay rather than bedplay...and yet it appeared the results were largely the same.

But I grimaced and bore it. Learned names and fighting habits of four other devotees then gritted my teeth as, one after another, magical connections formed between me and the humans I crossed swords with. Only when the fifth tether threatened to dislodge my older connection to Gunner did I bend over gasping, drawing the concerned attention of the rest of the honor guard.

"What did you do to her?" Koki demanded. "We allow the mistress to win always!"

They hadn't even been fighting to the full extent of their prowess? Grabbing Gunner's tether in one fist so it couldn't escape me, I didn't bother to dismiss them. Just stormed out of the training yard and back into the mansion from which we'd come.

Up the stairs, down a hallway, into the study where Sakurako had recently prodded me with beginner magic. My nemesis sat behind her desk with a book open before her, not bothering to glance up when I pushed my way inside the room.

"Done already?" she asked after a moment of silence. Or not silence, but the harsh sound of me panting as I strained to cling to a slippery mate bond that kept trying to slide out of my grasp.

Later, I'd wonder why I didn't release the connection. Why I didn't break the bond between me and Gunner and put us both out of our misery. In the moment, however, I merely demanded, "Put my mate bond back."

"*I* didn't dislodge it. And *I* can't replace it." Despite the quietness of her words, Sakurako deigned to place one finger on the page to hold her place before looking up from her book. Her eyes had all the warmth of hard nubs of coal stuck in a snowman's head.

"So how do *I* fix it?" I growled, sounding an awful lot like a werewolf. And I was somehow unsurprised when the old woman raised her left hand and gestured at the candelabra I'd failed to light earlier in the day.

Yes, that was right. I felt like I'd eaten too much, like the last bite of dessert was hovering halfway down my throat wanting to come back up as vomit. The obvious answer was to bleed off some of the excess magic and hope my connection to Gunner would snap back into place once given sufficient room.

So I focused all of my anger on those unlit wicks, expecting the process to be time-consuming and difficult. But, instead, I merely opened my mouth and breathed toward the candles...then watched wax puddle on the tabletop as the entire candelabra went up in a massive blaze.

"Control will be next on our agenda," Sakurako noted dryly, dropping her head back down to the book she'd been reading. But I caught a faint hint of a smile ghosting across her features and her eyes didn't slide back and forth across the page.

My grandmother was proud of my first attempt at pure kitsune magic. A week ago, such familial pride would have warmed the sodden lump in my stomach and threatened to create a full-on thaw.

Now, though, I had interest in nothing other than the way Gunner's mate bond wove itself amidst the honor guard's tethers as it was cemented back into my stomach. *That* connection was now solid and immovable, exactly what I'd been aiming for.

So why did I feel profoundly disloyal as I turned my back on my grandmother and took my leave?

Chapter 39

"*Stay away. Stay safe.*" I spoke before I'd fully woken, a dream of Sakurako stealing my tether and using Gunner as a blood slave sending me fumbling for the light. Only after I stared down at my stomach and easily picked out my mate bond did I relax my muscles. Two of the human males' tethers had sloughed off during the intervening hours, but Gunner's had burrowed deeper down into my flesh and stuck.

Being able to physically see a connection that pulsed beneath the skin of my belly should have been disconcerting. But, instead, I stroked the tether gently while straining—and failing—to feel the werewolf on the other end of the line.

Nothing.

Closing my eyes, I reminded myself that Gunner was there even if I couldn't communicate with him. Still, he was also at risk due to my proximity to Sakurako. I pursed my lips, fully aware that the smart solution involved breaking our mate bond immediately. But, instead, I resolved to find a way to maintain our connection without risking my werewolf partner to Sakurako's wrath.

A seemingly impossible task...so I'd better get right on it. Even though it wasn't yet dawn, I pulled on clothes and padded out into the hallway. *The library.* Kira had emoted over that room before I'd told her she was leaving, and it seemed like the obvious place to start.

Light was beginning to filter in various windows by the time I'd peeked into ballrooms and kitchens and guest rooms before finally arrowing in on my goal. But then I stood gaping in the doorway rather than getting right to work.

There were so many books. Hundreds of them, thousands of them, spines spanning every inch from vaulted ceiling to tiled floor. This collection bore no resemblance to the few, handwritten journal entries Elle had found during the summer we spent sussing out my abilities. Instead, as I slipped book after book from the shelves, flipping through pages full of fox shifters and magic, I knew I'd struck the mother lode.

The question was—how to find a needle in this tremendous haystack? The only solution appeared to be to read. Which is exactly how Sakurako found me three hours later, my nose in the tenth or perhaps twentieth musty old book.

"Looking for something?"

I jumped at her question, slammed the cover shut so quickly I nearly took off my own hand. Then the book was being yanked out of my possession by impatient fingers, the same pages fluttering open as my hostess pored over the title page.

"*Kitsune History for Beginners.*" Sakurako raised one eyebrow. "Very basic information, granddaughter."

"In case you weren't aware, that's the level I'm currently at."

We watched each other in silence for one long moment before a hint of softness rose behind the old woman's eyes. "Your mother was equally willing to admit to weakness. It's a surprisingly useful trait."

She graced me with that same smile of a proud teacher I'd seen on her features earlier. And to my disgust, a cloud of confused acceptance promptly roiled through my gut.

WE SETTLED INTO A PREDICTABLE rhythm thereafter. Mornings were for reading and practicing. Afternoons were for building bonds with my honor guard. Every day, I woke with a plea on my lips—*"Stay away. Stay safe."* And every night, I fell into an exhausted slumber, alone in my solitary bed.

"When will it be my turn to spar again?" Koki asked me a week—nine days?—later when we passed each other in the hall. He must have rotated off night shift because it was just after lunchtime, yet he appeared unusually bright-eyed and bushy-tailed.

"You cheat. It's no fun to fight a cheater." I tried to glower at the human, but he was too perkily cheerful to serve as the focus of my ire. The last time we'd sparred together, I'd been sure he was actually struggling flat out against me...until I'd slipped on a patch of mud and still managed to come out ahead.

"Mai-sama, losing to you is such supreme pleasure. Why would I want to win?" As he spoke, the human raised my hand to his lips, eyes not flickering away from mine for even a second. And, in response, the surge of energy along our shared tether transitioned from a trickle into a flood.

"I haven't sparred with everyone yet," I protested. "It's not fair to fight against you a third time until everyone else has had a shot." As I spoke, I removed my hand from his and averted my own gaze while butterflies danced in my belly. It was painfully difficult in that moment to remember the shape of Gunner's face.

"Not true," Koki countered and began spouting off semi-familiar names. I counted on my fingers as he listed his compatriots, then I nodded definitively when he came to the end.

"That's seventeen," I agreed. "But there are eighteen doors in the honor-guard hallway."

And, for the first time in our acquaintance, Koki turned evasive. "Mai-sama, perhaps now is not the time to..."

"The eighteenth door is locked. I tried it yesterday. I want to know what—or who—is inside."

"Mai-chan." The endearment wasn't entirely unexpected, but it nonetheless raised a knot in my throat I couldn't quite decipher. "Please believe me. You don't want this."

"I do want this. Do you have the key or should I ask my grandmother?"

Our standoff lasted for nearly thirty seconds before Koki caved beneath my stubbornness. He was the unofficial leader of the honor guard and we both knew it. Of course he possessed the requested key.

So, silently, we descended to the ground-floor level. Koki reluctantly trailed me down the hallway before slipping a thin chain off over his head once we reached the end. The silver key waited there between us, Koki's mouth compressing with the effort to restrain the warning on the tip of his tongue.

I accepted the key but not the warning, noted how the metal was hot against my fingers while the doorknob was cold against my skin. I was suddenly unsure whether I did want to uncover this secret. And Koki confirmed that fact as his fingers drifted reassuringly across the back of my neck.

"What you have to understand, Mai-sama, is that any of us would willingly sacrifice ourselves for the sake of the mistress. Kaito volunteered to help Sakurako-sama punish the wrongdoer and was chosen above all of us for his strength and loyalty. I also requested the honor, many of us requested the honor, and Kaito would do it all over again."

The door swung open as I struggled—and failed—to come up with an answer to that expression of extreme fidelity. And what I saw inside wasn't as terrible as I'd been led to expect.

In the room, IVs trailed from a strange male's body as he lay unmoving on a hospital bed. His chest rose and fell with regularity, but I didn't see so much as an eyelash-flicker of voluntary movement in response to our presence or to Koki's voice.

This wasn't a monster, but simply a man in a coma. The monster lay elsewhere in the mansion, far above this formerly locked room.

Chapter 40

"You're going to *fix* this."

I slammed into Sakurako's study in a high temper. And when the old woman tried to hide behind her book this time, I ripped the object out of her hands and flung it across the room. Elle would have been horrified at the way the book landed spine up, pages crumpling beneath the cover. But I was grimly satisfied to have broken something that didn't live and breathe.

"So you found Kaito."

"Is that your only answer? About a man who can't even feed himself, who just lies there staring at the ceiling with no life force left for you to harvest?"

I wasn't actually asking, but Sakurako answered anyway. "Yes. It was a shame, but necessary. And, no, it cannot be fixed."

Necessary. Sakurako's cold acceptance of her underling's vegetative state forced the air out of my lungs and I found myself sinking into the nearest armchair. My own rage was abruptly extinguished, the future yawning out before me like a dark tunnel with no end.

This is what I'd signed on for when I traded my future for Kira's. I had no grounds for complaint when I'd offered myself up as Sakurako's apprentice without requiring a single reassurance on her part.

And Sakurako must have smelled the regret I drowned in because her voice gentled when she spoke to me. "Granddaughter," the old woman said quietly. Then, when I failed to respond, her voice sharpened. "You will *not* be as weak as your mother. If you can't handle the truth, then I will train your sister instead."

"We had a deal." Now the fire was back in my veins and I had to cling to my temper to prevent myself from leaping across the desk and strangling the old woman.

"We did. And if you don't hold up your end of the bargain then I see no reason to hold up mine."

My magic was a mere pinprick compared to my grandmother's, but for one split second I considered blasting her with everything I had and hoping it would wipe her off the face of the earth. But the likelihood of failure rose before me along with the specter of Kira's lost innocence. So I forced my voice to harden as I returned to business instead.

"I'm here, aren't I? And I understand that Oyo needed to be prevented from continuing what she was doing. But couldn't you have harvested a little bit of energy from each member of your honor guard rather than draining Kaito dry? Can't you push power back into him from his friends?"

Now I was just grasping at straws, but Sakurako provided me more leeway than I'd expected. She sighed, and for a second I thought she might regret her own actions. "That's not how big magic works," she started. Then her subsequent words turned that supposed empathy into a lie. "Kaito's life is a small price to pay for keeping the werewolf packs from restarting their vendetta against all kitsunes. The sacrifice was necessary and I'd do it again tomorrow. When the time comes, so will you."

No. Just—*no*. I refused to accept that the ends justified the means when it came to stealing the life of an innocent. I refused to think that Sakurako would expect me to take part in similar atrocities as my own magic grew.

All I managed to say aloud, however, was: "That's inhuman."

"Yes, it is, granddaughter. Because we aren't humans; neither one of us is. Instead, we are kitsunes. And expedience is what we do best."

I TORE THE LIBRARY apart in search of another solution. There had to be a way to embrace my heritage that didn't involve vampiric energy harvests and questionable moral choices.

But there were so many books and they were all so disorganized. It seemed highly unlikely I'd find the answer in a single night.

Still, I gritted my teeth and dipped into histories of kitsune lineages, lesson plans for advanced magical techniques, and picture books clearly intended for soon-to-be foxes. All the while, Gunner's tether twisted and tugged at my stomach, like a bloodling puppy who didn't understand why he was being ignored.

"There has to be a compromise," I murmured, laughing grimly as I realized how closely my words mirrored Elle's sentiments when I chose to leave Gunner behind. She'd been wrong then and I was wrong now...and yet I still had to try.

So I read and skimmed and climbed tall ladders searching through books on the upper levels. And sometime long after midnight I must have fallen asleep in the midst of my research because gnarled fingers once again shook me awake.

"Stay..." I started my morning mantra, only to be interrupted by Sakurako's belated explanation for Kaito's fate and my own apprenticeship.

"My child, I do this to protect you." Her voice was scratchy, reluctant, as if she expected to be rebuffed before she finished what she'd come here to say. "I wish I'd done the same for your mother. It's my own fault that she's dead."

And something about the older woman's admission made me want to wrap her up in a blanket and hug her to my chest. This was, after all, the mother of my mother. My own flesh and blood.

"Sobo," I murmured, using the pet name I hadn't even thought since being blackmailed into trading places with my sister.

"Granddaughter," she answered, her bones creaking as she lowered herself down onto the ottoman on which my feet rested. "This is a difficult situation for both of us. But please know how glad I am to have you here beside me. It's a lonely life, being a kitsune. Less lonely since you arrived to make my house into a home."

I was still half asleep, but in that moment I could imagine Sakurako as a young woman. Could guess how her own mother or grandmother had indoctrinated her into their beliefs, how she'd had no more choice coming to terms with her heritage than I did with mine.

If I stayed on my current road, someday I'd do the same thing to my own daughter or granddaughter. Someday I'd rip the rug out from under my offspring's feet and watch innocence fade from her dark-irised eyes.

Then this hypothetical descendant would repeat the maneuver for the sake of her own daughter or granddaughter. And on and on the wheel would turn until it was sad-eyed foxes all the way down.

Which is why I did it. Used the information discovered in the hundredth book but rejected as too awful to contemplate.

Scrabbled at my waist without looking downward and yanked at the first tether my fingers came in contact with.

Materialized a shard of pure magic...then thrust that disloyal dagger directly into my grandmother's heaving breast.

Chapter 41

D*id I steal the life force from Gunner?*
I was wide awake the moment the thought struck me. Ignoring the brilliant flare of magic surrounding my grandmother, I instead frantically felt at my stomach in search of my mate bond.

Surely I would have known if the magic beneath my fingers belonged to a werewolf instead of to a human. The odds were seventeen to one against, and yet....

Gunner's tether was the one I stroked when I felt lonely. Gunner's tether was the one that rose to my fingers like an affectionate cat. Would his tether also be the one that responded to my frantic need unbidden? Would he throw himself into the void with the same loyalty as a member of Sakurako's honor guard?

Unfortunately, stolen magic flared and buzzed all around me. I couldn't for the life of me tell whether the missing tether belonged to an alpha werewolf.

Meanwhile, Sakurako was slowing her own transition even as magic twined into a collar around her neck just as it had done around Oyo's. "I'm proud of you," she whispered, fighting the magic...and failing to escape just as the book had said she would.

Because, although powerful, this magic was seductively simple. Or so the book had promised. I couldn't have gotten it wrong when the recipe included only three parts.

Use every ounce of magic embodied by a loyal underling. Strike in a moment of trust and shared understanding. Watch your loved one turn into a fox with no possibility of ever coming back.

The book hadn't mentioned how my eyes would fill with water, tears making it impossible to figure out whose tether I'd stolen even as my grandmother was forced out of her human skin forever. "Sobo," I murmured. "I'm sorry."

"Never apologize for the necessary, granddaughter."

And then she was my grandmother no longer. Instead, sharp, dark eyes met mine from within the face of a fox.

Only this was a subtly different fox than the one I'd fled beside when racing away from Atwood clan central. Sakurako then had been snow-white and nine-tailed. Now, her fur was speckled with gray and she possessed only one tail.

In other words, she looked like a wild animal, not a fox-form kitsune. Still, she maintained the same lithe fluidity as she leapt from chair to floor to window ledge. Her collar gleamed golden, then she was outside in the early morning. Was sprinting for distant trees as a herd of bare feet heralded her honor guard racing into the library to lend their mistress aid.

Or, rather, to lend their *new* mistress aid. "Mai-sama. I knew you would be triumphant." This was Koki, kneeling at my feet, his hand on my knee even as his tether refilled the empty reservoir of magic inside me. The surge of power was heady and riveting...and gave me a nearly uncontrollable urge to throw up.

But then my gorge calmed as I noted my mate bond springing back into existence at the same moment. I hadn't turned the vibrant alpha into a vegetable after all. And for at least a minute, I didn't care whose life I'd ruined in his place.

"HE WILL BE TAKEN CARE of Mai-sama."

We stood around the bed of the male whose life I'd stolen for the sake of my own freedom. And I hated the fact that I couldn't remember his name, couldn't recall the sleeper's signature fencing move nor bring to mind a single identifying feature that set him apart from all of the other humans squeezed into the small space that made up his sickroom.

But that wasn't the point. The point—after the better part of a day spent poring over Sakurako's finances—was dealing with responsibilities that were now my own. As my grandmother's sole heir, I would inherit her extravagant wealth and numerous properties. I planned to use both to ensure these males who had sacrificed so much for the sake of a kitsune mistress could now live simple human lives.

The first step in achieving that goal was breaking the bonds that bound them so they could figure out their own paths into the future. So I raised my voice and spoke to the assemblage. "I appreciate your service. But you are now dismissed."

Magic bit into my waist as one tether snapped and sprang away from me, then someone in the back turned and left the sickroom. Yuki. Gone to seek out his fox-form lover? Everyone else, however, stood their ground and stared at me as if I was speaking Portuguese.

"You can go out into the world. Take whatever you want from the mansion. Use Sakurako's money to live on. But make your own lives. Be free." As I spoke, I tried to push past the nearest humans to follow Yuki, but I found myself blocked at every turn.

"We don't want to be free, Mai-sama." This was Koki, speaking for the remaining fifteen humans. "You are the new mistress. We will stay here beside you. Or go anywhere you wish to wander. We are your honor guard."

"No, you're not." My face was hot, and I suddenly felt trapped in the midst of the assembled humans. Would I be forced to fight my way free due to my own manipulations? Sakurako would be laughing up her sleeve if she hadn't fled so preemptively into the cold.

"It's all we know, Mai-sama," Koki said.

"Yes, it is our honor and our duty to serve you," offered another voice. Then the same sentiment in multiple different incarnations rose to fill the room.

So I did the only thing I could think of—I chose my own selfishness over extended explanations. Donning the form of my fox, I grabbed tethers in my teeth one after another and gnawed through every one of them until I was one bond away from entirely free.

Because these men might think they wanted to be my honor guard. But they couldn't think, not really, not with my kitsune nature skimming off the cream of their energy.

In time, I suspected they'd come to their senses. But, for now, there was only one place I wanted to be...and it certainly wasn't here.

So I gnawed until magic flung itself away from me like broken rubber bands, knocking male after male down into a tumble of bellows and elbows. And I was as heartless as my grandmother because I didn't care about their pain or confusion. All I cared about was the single tether remaining. The one thick rope of glowing magic leading me out of the mansion toward the west.

I'd been separated from my mate for far too long already. With a mental promise to reassess my responsibilities in the near future, I took to my heels and I ran.

Chapter 42

Returning to fox form after days spent entirely human should have come as a relief, even more so when I was finally traveling toward my absent mate. But the tethers of my honor guards snapped back into place before I'd gone half a mile, and I ended up slogging slowly through a sodden landscape rather than dancing fleet-footed toward the west.

Still, I was single-mindedly adamant about pushing onward. Even after rational sense reasserted itself and told me that I'd get to Gunner faster if I retreated to the mansion, used Sakurako's telephone, and called a cab.

Instead, I fought against the magical headwind, pausing only when I reached a vast pool of water that cut me off from running straight toward Gunner. Right or left? Either direction made my stomach equally queasy. And as I racked my brain, trying to remember which route Elle had used to drive here, my attention caught on the reflection in the lake that blocked my path.

I was as familiar with my fox form as I was with my human one. Red fur, white-tipped tail, black nose and paws. But that wasn't the sight that greeted me in the water. Instead, my pelt had turned so white I might as well have been albino, although my eyes still gleamed black on either side of my head.

I spun in a circle, trying to catch sight of the other obvious visual difference between myself and my grandmother. As best I could tell, I still had only one tail....

And even though the change in coloration—and the change in self it likely represented—was disconcerting, the spinning action managed to unstick my latent sense of direction. *Left.* I was somehow positive that was the direction closest to Gunner. So I shook off the surprise of being bleached white in an instant and followed the lakeshore south even as the sun sank down toward the west.

I'd be spending the night outside in fur form if I didn't achieve civilization quickly, which would be annoying given the muddy soil and the lack of dry leaves to nest within. Still it was impatience rather than discomfort that hastened my footsteps. I *needed* to see Gunner so badly the wish had turned into a physical ache.

Tethers still streamed behind me like anchors. But they were weaker than they had been earlier, less likely to make me stumble and fall. So I picked up the pace and was running headlong when I felt my nails clicking against pavement after topping a short rise.

A road. And this time my tether informed me to turn right instead of left.

Only...there were headlights approaching from that direction. Headlights that materialized into a strangely familiar vehicle—Old Red screeching to a halt.

I leapt upward into humanity as Gunner emerged and raced toward me. I grabbed my mate and clung tightly even as he lifted me off my feet and spun me in a circle as if he was searching for my human tail.

"I love you." I laughed into the wind of our passing before adding: "But you know that already. Because you came for me."

His answer made me laugh harder despite the growly undertones. "I would have been here a week earlier if you hadn't kept telling me to stay away."

His mouth covered mine for one long, hard moment. Then he separated us long enough to demand precisely what I longed to give him. "I won't push you to change and you won't keep me out of your life any longer."

"Of course not," I told my forever mate.

OUR ROAD TRIP HOME was slow and meandering, but not because of Old Red's infirmities. While I was gone, Gunner had not only reclaimed my beloved vehicle, he'd also totally replaced everything underneath the hood.

"So, really, she's not Old Red any longer," I teased as we got back into the car after stopping for ice cream only a few miles out from clan central. There had been various other treats during the intervening twenty-four hours, the ones in our hotel room largely responsible for the huge grin currently plastered across my face.

"I didn't replace the car's body or the interior," Gunner countered, his hands intertwining with mine atop the center console as if the sixty seconds we'd been separated to get into our respective seats had lasted far too long. My favorite alpha was physically healed but still had a hard time letting a moment pass without touching me. Luckily, that wasn't a problem since I felt the exact same way.

"We could call her Not-so-old Red," I suggested. "Or Cinnamon Rocket." There was some serious horsepower now when I punched down on the gas pedal.

"Or Safer Rustbucket," Gunner countered even as we turned onto the driveway for clan central and rolled toward the main street.

After that, we fell silent as I remembered that I wouldn't be sneaking into a cottage on the periphery of the werewolf settlement this time. Kira had made that decision while I was absent, informing me over the phone that Gunner's addition "is way too cool to leave while you get your panties out of their twist and accept the good thing knocking on your door."

Despite her mixed metaphors, I decided my sister was surprisingly wise, at least in this instance. As a result, I'd be moving in as the pack leader's mate today the way I should have done from the beginning. Smiling, I gave Gunner's hand a squeeze.

Intention was powerful among werewolves, so I wasn't surprised that bonds zapped toward me out of nowhere as I maneuvered Old Red down the narrow street that bisected clan central. Still, I flinched when the first returning tether struck my stomach, then I held my breath and waited for the strangely orgasmic reaction that had resulted from building connections with Sakurako's honor guard.

Instead, only a faint hint of warmth infused my belly. And shifter neighbors nodded easy greetings without seeming unduly affected by our presence as we rolled past.

Okay, now I was curious. Given our speed of under ten miles per hour combined with an arrow-straight trajectory, I didn't hesitate to take my hand off the wheel and tug at one of the stronger bonds connecting me to Gunner's pack mates. Were Atwood shifters feeding me magic the way Sakurako's honor guard had, or did the power flow the other way?

"Stop!"

Gunner's hand spun the wheel sideways even as I slammed on the brakes. And it was a good thing he'd replaced the pads and rotors or I would have struck the bloodling puppy who'd responded to my summoning by launching himself directly into our path.

"Curly!" I threw the car into park and leapt out of the vehicle, knowing I hadn't hit the youngster but still worried he'd somehow gotten hurt in the process. And as I did so, I could feel my own energy streaming down the tether, perking up Curly's ears and making him prance with delight.

So this was what a werewolf connection looked like. Energy flowing freely in both directions, from the stronger shifter to wherever it was needed most. This was as different from a kitsune's tether as day was from night.

And for the first time in over a week, my shoulders relaxed fully. Because, yes, I'd made terrible mistakes getting here. I hadn't been fast enough or smart enough to save Edward. I'd stolen the humanity from Oyo and from my own grandmother. And I'd thoroughly shaken up the Atwood pack.

But, despite literally changing my skin while denning with my grandmother, Curly recognized me as the same person who had left here a little over a week before. Plus, what I lacked in kitsune power, I now made up for with the wealth of a werewolf pack.

And, apparently, the shifters around me were glad to have me present. Because tethers arrowed in one after another, weaving themselves together like a blanket enfolding my body until it seemed not a single additional tether would fit.

Only there was room for one more after all, as I discovered when the werewolf gossip tree propagated further. There was always room for one more.

Curly, bored by self realization, reared up on his hind legs to claw at my kneecaps, and I answered by hoisting him into my arms. Then I leaned into Gunner—who, predictably, was right there behind me when I needed him. And I stated the obvious.

"It's good to be home."

Epilogue

"No! Not the serrated knife!" As I watched, Becky yanked the utensil in question out of the hand of an inept male werewolf. "Use *this* one to slice carrots."

I couldn't help smiling at the formerly quiet werewolf's bossiness, and even more so at the way her student obeyed immediately with no biting commentary about the bloodling puppy frolicking at their feet. Six weeks after my return, the pack was almost unrecognizable. Which wasn't to say the male werewolves had entirely come around.

For example, they'd nearly universally chosen the afternoon shift when presented with Thanksgiving-cooking choices. And I'd been dumb enough to let Gunner join the early-bird females while leaving the untrained werewolf males to me.

As a result of my lack of foresight, I'd been responsible for bandaging up the first chef wannabe who injured himself through improper use of kitchen equipment. And when a second male had accidentally-on-purpose sliced into the pad of his hand instead of into the potatoes he was supposedly peeling, I'd slapped rubber gloves over the shifter's bandage and started him on the huge pile of dishes in the sink rather than sending him home as he clearly wished.

Since then, the only injuries had been accidents. Which didn't mean there hadn't been dozens of them. Perhaps that explained the shiver of premonition that kept fluttering up my spine?

"Something wrong?" Elle diverted Curly before the pup could land in the vat of mashed potatoes, my friend's mere presence relaxing my shoulders down away from my ears. I'd sent a formal Thanksgiving invitation over to Ransom's territory two weeks earlier, but Elle was the only one who'd bothered showing up.

"I wish your brother was here," I told her honestly. "Your other brother, I mean."

"If Gunner had invited him, Ransom would have come," Elle answered carefully.

"I know." And I did.

Because—as much as I loved Gunner—I could admit that both brothers were equally bull-headed in their stubbornness. It was a wonder, really that they'd found a way to work together from a distance in the weeks since clan central had been invaded by neighboring wolves. On the plus side, the siblings' alliance meant the sentries patrolling our boundary were bored out of their skulls after weeks of searching without sighting a single intruder. I was apparently the only one who felt an empty space in the web of pack bonds where Ransom should have slotted in.

"Hey, this might make you feel better." Elle was a master at changing the subject so she didn't get caught in the middle between hard-headed half-brothers who still stubbornly refused to talk to each other. And her choice of topic sucked me in just as she'd known it would. "Koki left Sakurako's compound last week, and Haru checked out on Monday. Which only leaves five guys still there, plus the bedridden."

That *was* good news. And I was even more grateful to Elle for making weekly trips to work on my grandmother's library while also taking the slowly dwindling honor guard under her wing. I kept hoping she would find a way to break through whatever magic kept two of the males in a coma. But even if my grandmother was right and that damage turned out to be permanent, at least sixteen lives would have been saved from the vagaries of a kitsune's whim.

"Thank you," I started, smiling as I watched Curly dance up to a male who would have kicked the pup aside three months earlier. This time, the youngster ended up ensconced on the shifter's broad lap instead. Atwood pack bonds grew smoother and stronger every time I looked at them. What could be better than that?

Then the flutter of premonition that had been bothering me for hours turned into a spear of ice striking between my shoulder blades. I whirled, eyes scanning the assemblage even as the chatter of voices around us slowed then entirely faded away.

Because Elizabeth was standing in the doorway naked, one hand pressed into her side as if she'd run so fast she'd injured herself. "There are enemies at the border," she gasped out after a terrifying second.

Only, she was wrong, because I could hear wolves racing closer in the newfound silence. There weren't enemies at the border. There were enemies outside our door.

I REACHED DOWN AND yanked at the tethers twining around my waist as one unit, felt absent pack mates respond at once to the wordless summons I'd sent out. Meanwhile, I barked orders to the shifters present in the kitchen. "Get the elderly and children into attics." Wolves were bad at ladders and I had a feeling our invaders would stick, at least for a while, to fur and claws.

Then I was sprinting out the door to greet the enemy, my sword glowing and whistling through the air as I ran. Who would invade clan central on Thanksgiving? Unfortunately, only one alpha was aware of our plans down to the hour...and I'd been the stupid traitor who clued him in.

Sure enough, I recognized Ransom at the head of the wolves streaming toward me. There were dozens of them, more than had followed Ransom into exile, more than I'd seen on Kelleys Island, and definitely more than I had at my own back.

Meanwhile, their leader's scent was nothing like the Atwood ozone it had been when I first met him. Instead, Ransom now smelled like a thumbnail run across the skin of an unripe orange—bitter and sour and biting all at once.

"Find Gunner and..." I started. But then strong hands were pushing me sideways. My mate was before me even as he dropped down into the form of his wolf.

So Gunner wasn't even going to try words first. I swallowed and forced myself not to gainsay him. This was what it meant to be the mate of an alpha—backing my partner up even when I thought he was wrong.

I expected Ransom's entire pack to surge forward and for the males behind me to shift and retaliate. But, instead, only the two alphas crashed together, the rest of us an avid audience to their heated attack.

"Should we...?" a male behind me started. But I held up one hand even though blood sprayed across the pavement, the pair of wolves moving too quickly for me to tell which one had gotten hurt.

Blood wasn't good...but it was still better than a full-clan pitched battle. So I clamped my hands down on the pack bonds that spiraled out away from me, forcing angry shifters to hold their tempers and stand their ground.

Whether Ransom would be able to do the same while tearing into his brother was another matter. But even as I eyed our opponents, the fighting wolves were wolves no longer. Instead, the brothers were human and naked, rolling across the pavement with Gunner's arm around Ransom's neck while Ransom's fist pounded into Gunner's gut.

"You're late," Gunner growled, releasing Ransom and surging upward, then reaching down to help his brother to his feet.

"I heard you were making everybody help with the cooking. So the way I see it, I'm right on time."

Wait. So this wasn't an invasion...it was guests arriving for Thanksgiving dinner?

As if he'd heard my question, Gunner glanced sideways, an eye that was already starting to swell and purple closing into the tiniest, subtlest wink. An alpha really did know everything that happened in his pack apparently...including his mate's illicit attempt to bring the prodigal brother back into the fold.

"Well, there's always dishwashing afterwards," Gunner said companionably. And as one unit, both Atwood alphas and every shifter they ruled over interwove seamlessly as they raced for the nearly completed Thanksgiving feast.

"Can you move any faster? I'm starving!" This was Kira, mini drama queen who had wisely joined Gunner for the earlier shift in the kitchen. Her tone was snarky, but I was beginning to speak teenager. This particular example meant, *Thanks for finding such awesome werewolves to den with. And, by the way, let's eat.*

Behind her, Tank and Allen winked at me, then headed toward the long series of food-laden tables with Becky safely sandwiched in their midst. There were males and females, children and warriors all intermingled without regard for status within a single line.

And as I surveyed the crowd, I realized I had everything I'd ever wanted spread out before me. Mate, family, and a pack.

Well, almost everything I'd ever wanted. Because my sister had a point, as usual. Given the ferocity of werewolf appetites, I'd better hurry if I wanted to grab some pumpkin pie and stuffing before the best parts of the feast were gone.

From the Author

I hope you enjoyed Mai's adventures! If so, you won't want to miss my next series, full of prehistory, pack, and peril. Archaeologist Olivia Hart has spent her entire life medicating away her inner monster. But she's about to learn monsters are real in *Wolf Dreams*.

Before you snag your copy, though, why not join my email list at www.aimeeeasterling.com? Newsletter subscribers are always the first to hear about new releases and will enjoy lots of free short stories and bonus materials. To sweeten the pot, I'll throw in two additional werewolf novels so you don't have to come up for air for days.

Thanks for reading! You are why I write.

Made in the USA
Coppell, TX
04 July 2021

58565134R00326